By Invitation Only

By Invitation Only

Jodi Della Femina

and

Sheri McInnis

ST. MARTIN'S PRESS ✹ NEW YORK

For John and Mark

BY INVITATION ONLY. Copyright © 2009 by Jodi Della Femina and Sheri McInnis. All rights reserved. Printed in the United States of America. For information, address St. Martin's Press, 175 Fifth Avenue, New York, N.Y. 10010.

www.stmartins.com

Design by Sarah Maya Gubkin

Library of Congress Cataloging-in-Publication Data

Della Femina, Jodi.
  By invitation only / Jodi Della Femina and Sheri McInnis. — 1st ed.
      p. cm.
  ISBN-13: 978-0-312-38475-3
  ISBN-10: 0-312-38475-0
  1. Restaurateurs—Fiction.   2. Caterers and catering—Fiction.   3. Weddings—Fiction.   4. East Hampton (N.Y.)—Fiction.   5. Chik lit.   I. McInnis, Sheri.   II. Title.
  PS3604.E4443B9 2009
  813'.6—dc22

                                                                              2009007277

First Edition: June 2009

10   9   8   7   6   5   4   3   2   1

Acknowledgments

We'd like to give huge thanks to our agent, Heather Schroder, for bringing us together to work on this book. Thanks also to the "real" Tabitha Shick at ICM. Big thanks to our editor, Jennifer Weis, and to Hilary Rubin Teeman, Anne Bensson, and everyone at St. Martin's Press.

For their help and expertise, thank you to Sgt. David Griffiths and the East Hampton Village Police; Kate Pratt at East Hampton Gourmet Foods; the lifeguards at Main Beach; the staff at Della Femina; and Kitty Merrill of *The Independent*.

Much love and thanks to Jerry Della Femina, Judy Licht, and John Kim for his business advice. Although the characters are fictional, we have to say a special thanks to Lara and Lela for being such great inspiration. Thank you to all our friends and families for their support, especially John and Mark. And big love to Annabel, Charlie, and Maggie for being such great kids, and for still napping long enough so we could actually get this book done.

Chapter 1

"Have you finished packing?"

"All done. Last night." *Everything boxed, taped, stacked in a U-Haul, and ready to go.* "But what if I have trouble sleeping out there? It's so quiet. Maybe I'll need a prescription or something."

"You haven't had insomnia for a while."

"No, but I'm not going to be in my bed anymore. I mean, I will—but I won't. It's all going to be different. Or the same? I mean"—she takes a deep breath—"I'm going *home.*"

A word that was supposed to evoke happy memories. Christmas. Reunions. Birthdays.

Home.

But today it just makes her feel desperate.

"Lots of people move back home, Toni."

She notices he said *back* home. Back in time. Back on the path of her life.

"But my father roams around all hours of the night. He makes a pot of espresso at midnight and then wonders why he can't sleep. He'll probably keep me up too."

"Let's worry about that when it happens, okay?"

She sighs and goes back to staring at the framed poster on the far wall, an explosion of black and gray drips.

Dr. Weinberg picks up a chocolate-chip cookie from a plate on his desk. She brought him a dozen this morning wrapped in blue-checked tissue paper, stacked together and tied with white ribbons like a New Year's Eve firecracker. He tells her again how delicious they are.

"Thanks," she says. "Salt. That's the secret. You always add a dash of salt, but I use extra. It enhances the sweetness. Really opens up the flavors." She starts to expound on the virtues of adding just the right amount of salt to recipes, how many different kinds of salt there are—rock, sea, kosher, *fleur de sel*—and how her grandmother's salt and pepper shaker collection inspired her love of vintage dishes. She's so lost in her reverie that when the doctor's watch makes a little *ping* at the end of the hour, it actually surprises her.

Outside on the sidewalk, she buttons up her jean jacket and catches a glimpse of her reflection in the glass door. Chocolate brown eyes, wide mouth, long dark hair looking like it could've used a blow-dry this morning.

Why didn't she dress up? Put on some makeup, at least.

Because the cookies were more important, that's why.

She sees people hurrying down the sidewalk, hugging themselves against the late April chill. She smiles to herself. New Yorkers are always so eager for the winter to be over, they toss their scarves and gloves at the first sign of spring—then freeze for a month.

She's the same way.

She takes a spiral-ringed notebook out of her bag and flips to today's To Do List. She strokes off *Cookies for Dr. W.* and heads toward the drugstore on the corner.

Inside the entrance, she stops and savors fluorescent lighting for the first time in her life. She looks at the long lines of people waiting at the counter. She is filled with nostalgia. She must be the only person in New York who's actually going to miss the ubiquitous Duane Reade.

Someone bumps her from behind. "Sorry," she says.

But the man keeps walking, barely noticing her. He has dark trendy hair, an expensive pin-striped suit. "God, I hate my life," he's saying into his Black-Berry. "I was up half the night singing Bee Gees songs. Remind me never to . . ." He seems lost, checking the signs above each aisle, before disappearing into First Aid.

Toni grabs a shopping basket and wanders through the store, picking up more things than she'd planned. Conditioner. Hand sanitizer. Sunblock. In Stationery she sees them, her favorite spiral-ringed notebooks for her To Do Lists. She grabs a handful and heads for the cashier.

On line, she's the only person not tapping a foot or looking at a watch.

"God, my head . . ."

She turns to see the man in the pin-striped suit approach a woman standing on line behind her. The woman is in her late twenties, her black coat open to reveal a cashmere sweater. She holds a bottle of Advil and some sodas.

Toni turns forward again.

"What time did you get in?" the woman asks.

"Who knows? But if I have to go to one more karaoke bar with a bunch of guys who can't—" The violent clatter of tablets. "What is *wrong* with this thing?"

"It's childproof." The crack of the plastic seal.

"You don't have anything stronger—like bullets?" he says. "What the hell's taking so long? Is it National Trainee Day or something?"

Toni just rolls her eyes.

At the counter, a cashier walks up and unlocks another register, motioning to Toni. "May I help who's next, please."

Toni goes to step forward, but the man butts in front of her, tossing his Advil on the counter. While he digs for his wallet, his cell phone rings. "Yeah? . . . No, no, he defaults on the debt if"—he seems frustrated, motioning for the woman in the black coat to pay—"if it's more than *six* times the cash flow . . . Yeah, that's what we . . ." He walks out of the store still on his phone. The woman in the black coat smiles and motions for Toni to go ahead.

Out on the street, Toni walks slowly toward the subway, taking in every sight she can. The Starbucks where she used to get green-tea lemonade before her sessions. The diner where she had breakfast with Kevin that time.

She bristles when she sees the man in the suit, pacing the sidewalk outside a black town car. He's now yelling into his phone.

"That is total bullshit! Then he's the only goddamn person in the history of"—his voice drops as he notices her; he has that dead look in his eyes Kevin sometimes got when he was on his phone—"in the history of Delaware corporate law to get out of a binding contract!"

Figures, she thinks. Her stroll down memory lane ruined by a self-important Master of the . . .

She stops in her tracks.

Her heart squeezes in her chest when she sees a little girl turn the corner with her mother. The girl has two balloons on different lengths of string, one red, one blue, as she skips along holding her mother's hand. Toni watches the balloons as they pass. A song is suddenly going through her head.

"Row, row, row your boat . . ."

She feels a deep twist in her stomach.

"Gently down the . . ."

The next thing she is aware of is a swing of sky and tree branches, everything not where it's supposed to be.

After that, she is drifting. Everything is dark. She tastes copper and salt, like potato chips in her mouth, and if she were a little older she would know that this taste is blood. But she is only three.

Chapter 2

Then there is air and coolness and the cliff of buildings on West 92nd Street. She feels herself sit up, only she's not sitting up on her own, someone is holding her. There's a dull ache in her head.

"Are you okay?"

A man has stopped to help, his arm supporting her back. "I . . . I think so," she says. She tries to remember what happened.

The little girl. The balloons.

She looks down the sidewalk, but the girl is gone.

People are turning to stare as they walk past. God, she feels stupid, splayed out on her butt in the middle of 92nd Street like this. She tries to stand up but feels unsteady on her feet. The man catches her weight again.

"I'm not sure you should move," he says.

"No, no, I'm fine . . . really." His hands are like an iron fence as she uses them to stand. He walks her to the stoop of a walk-up with a red door. She sits down, touching her sore head. "Did I bang my head on the sidewalk?"

"No, that." He points to a plastic recycling bin set out in front of a nearby building.

Saved by a recycler, Toni thinks. *Perfect.*

The girl in the black coat comes running out of the store. "What happened?"

"She fainted or something," says the man.

That's when Toni sees the pinstripes. She didn't even recognize him. His BlackBerry is on the sidewalk, a staticky voice audible from the little speaker.

"Maybe we should call an ambulance," the girl says.

"No, no, I'll be okay. I'm just . . ." She's staring into the eyes of the stranger. *She misjudged him, obviously.* "Gluco-sensitive, that's all."

"Gluco-what?" the girl asks.

"I'm just sensitive to swings in my blood sugar."

"Marcy, hand me a Coke."

The woman digs in the Duane Reade bag.

"No, I had enough sugar last night. I baked—"

"It's for the bump," he says. "Where'd you hit yourself?"

Toni shows him the wedge-shaped bump above her left ear; his fingers are gentle as they run through her curls and he rests the Coke can against it. She meets his dark, almond-shaped eyes. His sharp jaw is cleanly shaven. His lips are full. There's a softness in his face she can't reconcile with the man in the store.

Then, "Shit!" He backs away from her, looking around for his BlackBerry.

"You sure you're gonna be okay?" Marcy asks, leaning over her.

"Absolutely. This just happens to me sometimes. It's not that serious, not like diabetes or . . ."

"Damnit!" The man now looks as if he's about to punch his phone. "Marcy, he's gone! I lost him and it won't let me redial. Why the hell won't—"

The girl sighs. "Let me do it," she says, taking the phone.

He starts pacing again. "Who the hell meets up here, anyway? It's above the tree line for chrissake." He bunches his fists and looks at the sky. "Damnit! This is the worst day of my life!"

"It's not Christmas for me either," Toni says, as she hobbles around, picking up the notebooks and bottles that spilled from her bag. He doesn't help her, standing next to Marcy waiting for the call to go through. Toni looks around for her purse and sees it on the sidewalk at his feet, the heel of his expensive shoe resting on the strap. She gives it a tug, but he doesn't move. A harder tug and he lifts his foot.

"Thank you," she says. As she hoists the heavy bag onto her shoulder he stares at it as if it's something that might explode any second. It's an old red-canvas schoolbag with a mountain-climbing carabiner attached to the strap.

"This really works," she says about the Coke can. "Where'd you learn it? Boy Scouts?"

"No. Boxing."

"I was kidding," she mumbles.

"Got him!" Marcy hands him the BlackBerry. "We're going downtown. Can we give you a ride somewhere?"

The man groans. "Are you joking? We're carpooling now? She said she was fine." He looks at Toni. "You're fine, right?"

Toni grits her teeth. "Fine."

"See? She's fine. We're all fine. C'mon. I'm late." He gets into the car.

Marcy turns to Toni. "You sure you're okay?"

"Absolutely."

"I have to apologize for him," she says. "He's not usually this bad. It's just been a really rough week." She hurries into the car and slams the door.

Toni dusts herself off. As she watches the limousine disappear into traffic, she actually feels relieved. He reminded her of the one thing she's not going to miss about New York.

Chapter 3

Didi Blackhart Flagstone prowls the Oscar de la Renta section of Bergdorf's like a lioness on the hunt. Steps slow and deliberate. Nostrils flared in concentration. If not for her standing Botox appointment, she might even be frowning, but she hasn't been able to do that for five years.

Her personal shopper walks over with a down payment of Italian silk in his arms. He holds up a flowered shirtdress for her.

She shakes her head.

A striped lounger.

She shrugs.

A black shift.

Please. She hates black in the Hamptons.

He turns on his heel, his blond head disappearing back into the racks.

She continues her hunt. She sees a Pucci cocktail dress in colors that remind her so much of her youth she actually has to stop and touch it. The seventies. Dewy skin and lip gloss. When smiling was something she did without thinking. Now she's so terrified of deepening the fine lines around her eyes and mouth that smiling is a moral dilemma.

Didi catches her reflection in a mirror and is struck by a dart of displeasure. It's not her frame. She carries herself well, always has, tall and slim with long legs. But her neck looks stringy. Her dark bob could use coloring. And her large brown eyes look saggy and a little sad, as if they miss the company of eyebrows that can actually move around.

Ah, but the bag. A custom-made Hermès Birkin in matte gray croc. She hasn't seen one like it anywhere—not yet, anyway. In a world where purses are a competitive sport, Didi Blackhart Flagstone is top-seeded. That's important to her. She turned fifty-six in January, and it feels as if nobody has looked at her, or would look at any woman over forty-five, if not for her expensive handbags.

She turns away from the mirror, trying to think happier thoughts. She still needs a gown for the Southampton Hospital gala, something for the Parrish Art Museum benefit. Several more dresses. Tennis whites. Cover-ups. And hats, of course.

Lots of hats.

Her cell phone rings and she debates answering it. With all the buckles and straps, opening her purse is like disarming a dirty bomb. Her spirits lift when she sees Hudson's name.

"Hi, Ma," he says, sounding flustered.

Ma, she hates that. Since high school, *Ma*.

"Darling? What's wrong?"

He's at the bank. He didn't know he needed her. Her or Dad. Dad's busy—of course. Gran came but she's not a co-agent. Stupid really. Twenty-eight years old and he needs a co-agent to open his own safety deposit box. Where is she? Bergdorf's? Could she come?

She can tell by his voice that he needs her. Knowing Hudson needed her—for anything—is what has grounded her most of her adult life. Her one undeniable accomplishment.

A son. And heir.

"Anything, darling. You know that. But why on earth do you have to get into your safety deposit box?"

As he answers, she flicks her fingernail and watches her reflection in the mirror. The sinewy neck. The hollow cheeks. The sunken eyes. But then . . . ahhh . . . the perfection of a really good handbag.

Chapter 4

"Was he married?" Layla asks.

"Are you kidding?" Toni's on her cell, walking down Ninth Avenue, her black Lab terrier mix tugging on his leash ahead of her. "I did *not* look for a ring."

"You should always look for a ring, Toni. Just get in the habit of it. You act as if you like being alone or something."

"I *do* like being alone."

"Is that why you were up all night baking cookies for your shrink?"

"It wasn't just for him. It was for my super too. And the dog walker. And the lady who runs the Korean market down the street."

"That's what I mean," Layla says.

"Who cares, anyway? He was one of the rudest guys I ever met." A beat passes. "Why do you stink so much?"

"What?" Layla sounds offended.

"Not you. Tucker. F-R-E-D must have peed on him again."

"F-R-E-who?"

"His best friend from the dog walker. German shepherd. Total basket case. Pees on Tucker all the time. I don't want Tucker to hear his name. I don't want him to know he's never going to see his best friend again." Toni checks Tucker for any indication he understands the severity of his situation, but he's preoccupied with sniffing a bike rack.

"I think you give that dog too much credit," she says. "Are we still on for Saturday?"

"Of course we're still on. Noon sharp."

"Can we make it one instead? Hudson says he wants to take me out for a nice dinner and I don't want to get up too early."

"One it is," Toni says, already planning for one thirty. It was a cosmic balance between them—for every minute Toni had been early in her life, Layla had been late.

"I gotta run," Layla says. "I'm working tonight, and I've got to get my legs waxed."

"The way you say that, it makes you sound like a hooker."

"Beats waiting on tables," she says.

Toni stops in her tracks. "I'm *not* going to be waiting on tables. I told you that."

"Baby, I didn't mean you."

At the corner of West 23rd Street, Toni looks up at her apartment building. A block long, beige brick; it fills her with awe, like staring at Notre Dame Cathedral. She was on the waiting list for a year before she got in. Couldn't wait to live in Chelsea. Fantasized about all the art galleries she'd go to. But she hadn't been to a single one in years.

And now?

She refuses to acknowledge the term "boomerang kid."

When she steps off the elevator she's shocked to see something in the hallway that's not supposed to be there.

Her oven.

The old white Westinghouse with the missing knob for the back right burner. She finds it strange she would recognize her oven in the middle of the hallway when she's only ever seen it in the kitchen before. Sort of like bumping into a barista at a club or bookstore, she thought she wouldn't be able to place the face. But she recognizes that Westinghouse like an old friend.

Her super shoves it back and forth, trying to get it on a dolly, talking to his assistant, a skinny boy with straggly blond hair. "Okay, when I lift, you push."

Tucker tugs on his leash and she lets him run through her open door. "Hi, Mr. Thurman."

"Hey, Toni." There's sweat on his forehead, dandruff in his gray hair.

"What are you doing?"

He glances at her as if to say, *What does it look like I'm doing?*

She gives a hurt laugh. "But I've been telling you that burner's been broken for a year. And *now* you're changing it?"

"Yeah, before the new tenant moves in."

New tenant? She suddenly feels so ordinary, as if her entire life in this apartment had vanished with the expired lease.

She sighs and runs her hand along the cold element of the oven. Flicks the metal prong where the top right burner knob used to be. "Just tell me—is the new oven gas?"

Mr. Thurman starts to answer.

"No, no. Never mind. I don't want to know." She feels tears start to come and she digs in her bag for Kleenex. "Don't mind me. I'm just a little depressed, that's all."

Mr. Thurman says, "Imagine, moving out to the Hamptons and being depressed about it."

"Wow," the partner says. "Wish I could afford to live out there."

Toni just smiles, dabbing her eyes. Everyone was always so damn impressed with the Hamptons. "It's not what you think," she says.

In the kitchen there's a hole where the oven used to be about the same size as the one in her heart. She hates the idea of never seeing this place again. She hates the idea of the last time of anything. She wishes she'd kept a small bottle of champagne. She'd pour a glass and stare at her empty walls and remember all the happy times she had here.

Building shelves for her cookbooks.

Bringing Tucker home from the pound.

Making Kevin watch *Say Anything* whenever it came on.

The bad times too: like seeing the smoke from the World Trade towers from her window and feeling the need to run.

Tucker comes in and sniffs around the empty corners of the room, the carabiner attached to his leash clattering on the floor. Maybe he knows they're leaving too. They say dogs can sense these things.

"Come on, Tuck," she says. She looks around the apartment. "See you . . ." Her eyes fill with tears as she locks up and slides the key under the door for the last time.

East Hampton

April in Paradise

Chapter 5

Nestled along the shores of the Atlantic Ocean, roughly one hundred miles east of Manhattan, the village of East Hampton has long been touted as one of the most beautiful in America. Founded in 1648 by fishermen and farmers, it wasn't until the late 1800s that wealthy New Yorkers began building summer homes along the thin strip of land known as the South Fork. For a hundred years East Hampton continued to be a quiet beach community for the well-heeled—until clever real estate investors saw the potential of the village's bucolic charm.

—*The Guru's Guide to the Hamptons,* © eighth edition

Bill Mitchell had been alone in the main office of the *East Hampton Sun* waiting for inspiration to strike on a town hall article when his mind began to drift. The old white mansion creaked around him in the spring breeze. He leaned back in his chair and saw it tucked in with the dictionaries and style guides, a paperback book about an inch thick, the green spine cracked from use.

The Guru's Guide to the Hamptons.

Constructive procrastination, Bill thought. A journalist's best friend.

But the moment he was able to settle down into the musty pages, there was a bang on the left side of the room.

"Sorry, hi," says Toni, leaning in the door, out of breath. "Do you allow dogs in here anymore?"

"Uh, dog or dogs?"

"Dog. Singular."

"I don't see why not."

"Thanks. Be right back!" She leaves the room yelling, "Tucker!" only it sounds like something more obscene to Bill.

The door bangs open again and a blockheaded black dog comes in, straining on his leash, dragging the woman behind him. She's loaded down with a picnic basket, a faded red bag, and a small white cake box.

"Tucker, stay." Toni drops the leash. But Tucker doesn't stay. He begins sniffing around the legs of the empty waiting room chairs. "So long in New York, you give him a few days out here and he goes all Baskerville on you." The dog is now gnawing at the nozzle of the water cooler. "Tucker, *no*. Is Mrs. Latham in?"

"She's working from home today," says Bill, approaching the counter.

"Ahh. Right. It's window box time again," Toni says with a smile.

"Can I help you with something?"

"I have to take out a classified ad. How much is that?"

He tells her it's a dollar a word for the first insertion, eighty cents after that.

"Used to be seventy."

"Used to be?"

"I worked here for a summer. Ages ago. Used to sit right over"—she points to a desk in the corner—"there."

"That's a coincidence," he says.

"Not really. I worked everywhere." She grabs a form from the rack on the counter and begins filling it out. "What if I want to take out an ad? Not a classified, but a display ad."

"We need camera-ready artwork. Or a disk. JPEG. Qbit. Anything with three hundred dpi."

She blinks at him a few times. "That means absolutely nothing to me."

He laughs. "I could help you if you want. I'm pretty good at it." One of the reasons Margaret Latham hired him last year was because he could update their design software.

"Really? That would be so great of you." For the first time Toni really notices him: tall, wavy light brown hair, a small mouth, blue eyes. *Did he look a little like John Cusack?* She digs in her tote and finds a rumpled matchbook, the little drawing of the trattoria shaded by chestnut trees. "Can you use this?"

"I could work with it."

"It's gonna be Fratelli's Restaurant *and* Catering, though. Not just restaurant. Got it?"

"Got it."

"How much do I owe you?"

He looks at the form.

Help Wanted: Catering Staff. Exp. Req'd.

"Ten dollars."

"Oh, *man.* Where's my wallet?" She begins unloading her tote bag on the counter. Food magazines emerge first. *Gourmet. Food & Wine. Saveur.* A flowery makeup kit. Kleenex. A dented can of Coke. A vintage pressing iron.

An iron?

But it's the Coke can that seems to preoccupy her; she glares at it for a moment.

Bill looks down at the matchbook. "Fratelli's," he says. "I love it there. Go all the time. The pizza's the best."

"Thanks. I'll tell my dad. You should try the ceviche sometime. I came up with the recipe when I was, like, twelve. I worked there too, obviously. A *lot.*" She finally finds her wallet, slaps a ten-dollar bill on the counter, and begins refilling her bag. "I'm sorry to be so . . . you know, frazzled. I'm just in a rush, that's all."

"No problem." But something tells Bill that Toni Fratelli spends a lot more time "frazzled" than she lets on.

"Will you make sure Mrs. Latham gets that?" She points to the cake box.

"Sure."

"And could you do something with this?" She shoves the Coke can across the counter. "I wouldn't recommend drinking it. It might explode on you."

"Sure . . ."

"Thanks. You've been great. Tucker, *come.*" But Tucker does not come. He chews the leg of a chair. "I'll be in touch. If you ever need a caterer, you know who to call!" She gives Bill one last wave and drags the dog out the door.

Bill picks up the mysterious white box. He lifts it to his nose and smells cherries, lemon, and vanilla. It makes his mouth water. He sets it on the corner of Margaret's desk and decides to have the ceviche for lunch.

Whatever that is.

Chapter 6

Rararrararararararararrah!

"Tucker, *no!*" Toni circles the old VW van behind Hook Pond to avoid the red light. She hates wasting even a minute on her way to the beach.

Tucker whines a bit and does his best to sit still, but then he's up on his hind legs again, barking out the window at East Hampton's Royal Couple: the swans of Hook Pond.

Toni sees them as she drives by, the big one sitting on the bank preening, the other drifting on the water with four tiny cygnets following behind like a string of fuzzy gray tennis balls. She can't count how many hours she and Layla sat cross-legged on the grass watching them. Laughing at the tourists who made the mistake of trying to feed them. The swans were a lot like the rich women who strolled the streets in the summertime—they were beautiful, but they could be bitchy as hell.

"Do you know swans mate for life?" Toni used to say.

"For, like, evurrr?"

"That's what my dad told me."

"How do they know that?" Layla would ask. "Who sits around watching swans all day?"

"No kidding," Toni said. But she thought there were worse things to do with your life.

Hook Pond has always been one of the ways Toni gauged the changing seasons out here. Not just watching the cygnets grow, but the trees too. They were the first to bloom in the spring and the first to change color and lose their leaves in the fall. Right now they're covered in a mist of green buds. It makes her smile.

Summer hasn't even started yet. . . .

In her rearview mirror, the pond, the churches, the white clapboard shops of Main Street disappear, replaced by the shingled houses and residential streets of the town proper. She turns left on Ocean Avenue.

The houses become bigger.

Right on Lily Pond Lane.

Bigger still.

In the summer, the privet hedges were so lush and dense they hid the mansions from view. But this time of year Toni sees straight through bare branches to knots of activity on vast grounds. Gardening vans and painting trucks and window cleaners. Or FOR SALE signs as speculators flipped—or ditched—their dream homes. It always baffled her, thirty-, forty-, fifty-million-dollar mansions, empty for most of the year. Like her dad said, wealth is wasted on the rich.

She remembers he used to take her driving around these roads when she was a little girl. "Bob Dylan wrote a song about this place," he'd say. "Some day we're going to live here. Which house do you want?" And she'd believe him, pointing—that one, or, no, that one!—with no idea that almost twenty-five years later he'd still be living in the same modest house on Church Street.

And so would she.

She turns the corner and sees the endless blue-gray slate of the Atlantic Ocean.

"Tucker, look! We're here!" She leans her head out the window and takes a big breath of air. No matter how many "marine-scented" candles and soaps she'd bought over the years, nothing even came close.

Loaded down with her picnic basket, an umbrella, a blanket, and her tote bag, Toni looks like a bellhop trudging across the empty parking lot to the beach. But as soon as her feet hit the sand, she feels her blood pressure drop. The waves are rhythmic and loud. The cusp between sea and sky is a muted blue on blue. The wind is fresh and warm.

It's a perfect day for their first picnic of the year.

She adjusts her load and starts heading west, Tucker running on ahead, kicking up sand and barking at seagulls.

She loves the beach in April. So quiet and empty, the odd jogger here and there. The mansions along the grassy dunes sit empty like great ships anchored at sea, a few FOR SALE signs out front.

She's reminded of the optical illusion she feels when she walks the beaches in the Hamptons. She can pick out a landmark in the distance—a mansion, a lifeguard tower, a jetty—and walk for half an hour without feeling as if she's getting anywhere.

Kind of like her life lately.

The sand begins to fill her running shoes and she stops to take them off. She always loves finding sand in a shoe or the cuff of an old pair of jeans in the winter. It's the most exciting thing in the world for her, to be reminded of the summer. As she gets up and starts walking again, barefoot this time, she wonders if she'll still love finding sand in her shoes this year.

Chapter 7

One hundred miles to the west, on the fourth floor of a brown-brick warehouse in the Meatpacking District, a god and a goddess sleep. The god on his side, facing the windows. The goddess on her stomach, head buried in her pillow. A coil of white Frette linens lies across their tan and naked bodies. The large windows, covered in custom-made blackout blinds, let in a crack of New York sunlight, like a silver lining around a square cloud. Then somewhere in the dim gray light, a note.

Getting louder.

It's the ring tone for "Dancing Queen."

The god stirs slightly. But the goddess doesn't even shift her blond head on the pillow. After a few more refrains from ABBA, Layla's cell phone goes to voice mail and there is silence again.

On Georgica Beach, Toni is on the phone, pacing. Beside her, on a coral picnic blanket and beneath a striped umbrella, is an arrangement of gourmet dishes and vintage Fiesta ware that looks more like a four-star dinner than a picnic on the beach.

"Hey, it's me. Just wondering where you are. Hope you're not stuck in traffic or—Tucker, *no!*—anything. Anyway, gimme a call when you get a chance."

She hangs up the phone, grabs Tucker's green ball, and tosses it down the beach. He runs after it, barking. Behind her on the grassy dune is a sprawling dove gray mansion that has marked her favorite spot on the beach for fifteen years. Toni still calls it Calvin Klein's place even though he moved to Southampton years ago.

She looks around.

Now what?

She straightens the fringe on the blanket and surveys the picnic:

Chicken salad with dried apricot.

Homemade pretzel bread.

Heirloom tomatoes with fresh herbs.

Cherry citrus lemonade.

And, of course, her triple-chocolate-chip cookies with a little extra salt.

She sits back and opens *Gourmet* magazine. It's a summer theme this month and the featured food is duck. Grilled duck. Asian duck salad. She used to love eating duck—especially the duck with elderberry sauce at Shezen on North Main Street. Her dad would make quacking sounds every time she ordered it. But she's seen so many ducks swimming around the ponds out here that she can't eat them anymore, let alone skin or cook them. She remembers the caveat in Thomas Keller's *French Laundry Cookbook*: if you can't kill, skin, and bone something you're about to cook, then you can't call yourself a real chef. It used to give her a complex.

A low grumble breaks into the imaginary kitchen in Toni's head. She looks up to see a white flatbed truck drive across the sand toward her, the Town of East Hampton logo on the door. She smells diesel as it rumbles toward the sloping dune grasses, sand spinning away from the tires. It stops and two people get out, a woman with a long braid and a man with a straggly beard, both wearing coveralls. They walk around the back and drag out a coil of chicken wire and some signs.

She hears a voice. "Toni?"

She shades her eyes and looks over.

"Toni, it's me! Jan Walters. Look, Fish—it's Toni!"

"Jan?" Toni's voice is excited. She gets up and meets them halfway; hugs are disbursed all around.

"Wow, you look great, Toni!" says Rick Pyke—"Fish" since high school, not just because of his name but because of his obsession with protecting local wildlife. "We heard you were coming back."

"Yeah," says Jan. "Welcome back."

"Thanks," she says, but she wishes they'd stop saying "back."

"That looks so pretty," Jan says, pointing to the picnic. "Too bad we have to ask you to move."

"What?"

Fish turns over a white sign under his arm. There's a sketch of a plump little white bird with a black stripe on its forehead.

PIPING PLOVER NESTING AREA

These birds are protected under New York State and Federal Law. Persons may be arrested and fined for killing, harassing, or in any way disturbing birds nesting in the area. This area is pursuant to section 11-0303 and 11-0321 of the Fish and Wildlife Law. New York State of Environmental Conservation.

"You're kidding?" Toni says.

"Sorry. Right over there." Jan points to the dune. "Reported a nest."

"But I just . . ." She sighs. "Never mind. I'll move."

"Awesome! So great seeing you, Toni."

"Yeah, Toni. Good to have you back."

They step carefully into the dune with their chicken wire and signs.

Toni grabs the edge of her picnic blanket and eases it along the sand. Vintage silver tinkles out of place. Tucker dashes over, thinking it's a game, tugging on the fringe.

"Tucker, no!" She lunges at him, but he slips out of her grasp. Her cell phone starts ringing and she checks caller ID. "Mom?"

"Hello, honey! How's picnic day?"

"She's late."

"Go figure." A laugh. "What about you? How's everything going out there?"

"Okay, I guess. Everything's the same. Different. I can't tell yet. I'm sort of fixated on my ballerina lamp. I need to get rid of it."

"Oh, honey. He wasn't the one for you. That's all. Don't worry about it. The right one will come along. What about your father? How're things going with him?"

"Well, we're both still alive, so—" Beep. "Mom, that's her. I should go."

"All right, honey. Say hi for me. Love you!"

"Love you too." Toni switches lines. "Hey."

"Oops."

"Oops what?"

"Oops, I slept in."

"How *oops-you-slept-in*? Like—oops, you're on twenty-seven slept in or—"

"More like oops, I'm still in bed."

Beneath the white linens in her little fiefdom, Layla Sullivan pulls the phone away from her ear. "Toni, please, don't yell. I have such a hangover."

"Hangover? But, Sully! It's picnic day!"

Layla squints against the sun as Hudson remotes the blind. "I've got a good excuse. Remember I told you Hudson and I were gonna have a nice dinner last night?"

"Yeah?"

"It was better than nice."

Toni hears her friend start to squeal. "Slow down, I can't—"

"We got engaged!" Layla says. "Hudson proposed last night!"

Toni's expression drops. She stares out at the blue-gray ocean. Then, *splash!* It feels as if she's been thrown in.

"Toni?"

She fights to swim up for the light. She's gonna make it . . . there! She emerges, choking on water.

"Yeah, I'm here. Just a bad connection, that's all. You know how reception is out here." She flops onto her butt. "That's so amazing," she hears herself say. "I'm so . . . happy for you."

"Thanks. It was the corniest thing. Candles. Music. Roses. Can't wait to tell you."

"Can't wait to hear," she says.

At this moment she hates herself. Her best friend in the world is sharing what is probably the happiest news of her life and here she is, feeling resentful, envious—and petty as hell.

"Did he get you a ring?" Stupid question. No man who ever got within a hundred yards of Layla Sullivan didn't immediately want to spend three months' salary on her. She already had two broken-engagement diamonds reset into the world's most expensive belly button ring.

"He sure did . . ."

"What's it like?"

"Well . . ."

A long quiet beat plays out as Layla examines the five-carat cushion-cut sapphire set in ornate yellow gold. "It's too big, for one thing."

"How can an engagement ring be too big for *you*?"

"I mean the size." She spins it around on her finger.

"That's no problem. You can get it resized. What's it look like?"

"Um . . ." Layla peers toward the doorway. "It's kind of gross."

From the kitchen, Hudson says, "I heard that."

"Just kidding, baby!"

He walks back into the room. "You ungrateful little tart." He taps two aspirin into her palm and she grabs the stale champagne from the bedstand to swallow them back.

"I just mean it's unique, that's all. It's a family ring, right, baby? Your grandmother's or something?"

"*Great*-grandmother." Hudson crawls back into bed with her. "My great grandmother Lily."

"Sorry. *Great*-grandmother Lily . . . as in Munster." Layla laughs and Hudson yanks the sheet down, diving playfully toward her naked body.

On the beach, Toni listens to them laughing and squealing. All she can think about is how long it took her to squeeze the Sorrento lemons.

And reduce the cherry syrup . . .

And knead the dough for pretzel bread . . .

More kissing sounds.

"God, I didn't even congratulate you." She forces enthusiasm into her voice and says the word. "Congratulations."

"You sound mad."

"I'm not mad. Why would I be mad?" *It's just our first picnic of the year, that's all.*

A tradition for fifteen years. "We'll do this another time. You just got engaged. That's more important."

"Yeah, 'nother time . . ." More shuffling sounds. "You're gonna be my maid of honor, right?"

A smile relaxes Toni's face. She feels the tears start to come. "Of course I'm going to be your . . ." She shakes a Pottery Barn napkin out of its holder to dab her eyes. "Of course I will."

"Good. I promise I won't make you wear puce or anything. And we don't want to wait. We've already set the date. It's going to be down on the beach at Hudson's place. Labor Day weekend."

"Wow, that's so—"

More giggles. "I should go, Tone. We have to tell Hudson's parents."

"Good luck with—"

But Layla is already gone.

Toni surveys what's left of her perfect picnic, then calls to the workers on the dune.

"Hey, you guys hungry?"

Chapter 8

In her nine-bedroom co-op on Fifth Avenue, Didi hangs up the phone. She sits at her writing desk and watches the blue-green vein throb on the back of her hand.

God, she hates her hands.

The age spots, the stretched skin, that incessant hangnail on the inside of her left ring finger. How many times did she have to switch manicurists before she found someone who could fix it? Was it too much to ask?

She turns her head at a forty-five degree angle. "Estella," she calls.

Nothing.

"*Estella.*"

A moment later, a stout woman with a black ponytail, brown eyes, and mocha skin leans in the door. She wears a blue cotton housedress and seems out of breath. "Yes, miss?" It was always "miss" with Didi.

"Would you fix me a drink, please."

Estella walks to the crystal decanters on a credenza not five feet from Didi's desk.

"A double."

"Of course, miss."

Didi stares out the tall window at her view of Central Park. The trees, still mostly bare, look dry and gray, like an old cotton field spread out in front of her. She opens a gold cigarette case and places an Eve Menthol 100 carefully between her lips. She lights it using a lighter inscribed with the initials of her maiden name: D.E.B.

Didi allows herself one cigarette a day, usually not before seven o'clock. She'd given up her pack-a-day habit years ago because smoking wreaked havoc on her skin. For a woman who could afford any bauble in the world, this single cigarette had become her one true luxury.

"Anything else, miss?" Estella sets down the martini glass.

"Do you know where Mother is?"

"With her petunias, I imagine."

Of course. With her petunias.

Didi waits until she hears Estella's foam-soled shoes squeak into the hall, then she gulps back her martini in three large swallows.

She turns to face her living room: silk sofas, lamp shades, pillows, moldings, everything done in shades of white. Splashed with crystal lamps and icy chandeliers, the room glistens like a glacial cave. She only finished having it decorated last year but was already thinking of redoing the whole thing in pink. Her husband refused to walk into a room that was pink.

Her bedroom was pink.

At the top of the grand staircase on the second floor, she walks to the end of the paneled corridor and knocks on the very last door. She drags on her cigarette, tapping it into her palm-sized ashtray.

"Mother?"

Nothing.

She turns the handle and braces herself for the assault on good taste that is her mother-in-law's bedroom. Faded flowers and morbid tartans and an explosion of chintz.

She can smell the cats too. Their fur and their litter boxes. She sees the gray Persian asleep on the window box. But where's the Siamese? The skinny Siamese with the blue eyes and the crooked fangs.

God.

She hates cats.

The french doors are open and Didi walks through them to a small terrace. It's a gray day, and seems even grayer from up here because the terrace is in shadow, surrounded on all sides by other white-glove buildings. They'd put

Henry's mother in this bedroom because she was old and it was quiet. She rarely looked up from her flowers anyway—no use wasting a view.

Beatrice Anne Flagstone, a plump silver-haired woman in a floral tunic and old sunhat, leans over a string of red petunias in plastic pots. Last season it was yellow mums. Didi couldn't think of a single more common flower than yellow mums—until she saw red petunias.

"Mother?"

Bea looks up from her flowers, her cheeks round and pink, her face unselfconsciously wrinkled. "Isn't it a little early for your cigarette, dear?"

Not even a breath pause. *Isn't it a little early for your cigarette?* The smile makes it worse—matronly, saccharine, annoying.

Like too much chintz.

"I just got off the phone with Hudson."

"Oh?" Bea keeps pruning her flowers, using shears big enough for box hedges.

Snip, snip, hack.

"When did you give it to him?"

"Give what to him, dear?"

"Oh, Mother. Let's not. You know what I mean."

Bea sighs loudly. "That's what it's *for*, Deirdre. That's why Mother wanted him to have it in the first place. For when he met the right girl."

"Operative term being '*right*,'" Didi says. "Don't you think this is something we should've talked about?"

"Hudson wanted it to be a surprise."

"I hate surprises."

"Well, he doesn't."

Didi grits her teeth at this hint that she, Bea, has Hudson's best interests at heart. Old battle-ax. All of them waiting for her to die and leave them her money and you think she would? Every six months she comes back from her colonoscopy or blood pressure test or suspicious mole check and every time it's the same: "Doctor says I have the heart of a twenty-year-old. I'll outlive you all!" And then a happy cackle.

"Just tell me, is that why we were at the bank the other day?"

"I'm not going to lie to you, Deirdre."

"Not again, you mean."

"Use your head. He's almost thirty years old. Why on earth would he need his high school transcript?"

And that was the worst part about it. That Hudson had lied to her. When

Didi left Bergdorf's to meet him at the bank that day she knew there was something fishy—why would he need his high school transcript for work? But she didn't press him about it because it made her feel like a bad mother that she didn't know more about his job.

But she trusted Henry. He told her Hudson was lucky to meet up with those boys. A trio of magna cum laudes from his graduating class who wanted to start an Internet advertising agency.

Or some such thing.

So Hudson gave them the money—and two floors of the warehouse on 12th Street—and in return they made him president of the company.

But Didi never felt good about the job. The Internet wasn't something she could touch or feel. Yet it was in all the papers, young people making billions of dollars working out of their basements, so it must've been real. And he *did* have a nice linen business card. She kept it in her wallet right behind her Centurion Card so she could see it often and be reminded of his success.

But she should've asked, "Why, Hudson? Why do you need your transcript?" If she had taken him by the shoulders and looked into his eyes she knows he couldn't have lied to her then. She would've said, "Let's just think about this before we do anything rash," and he would've put back the ring and thanked her for being such a good mother and they would've gone to Swifty's to share baked Alaska.

And eventually, the girl would go away.

The gold digger.

She hasn't used the term out loud yet. But she's been thinking it ever since they met for brunch at McMullen's over a year ago. That white shirt undone to her breastbone, no bra, of course, and jeans. Her wrist full of those cheap silver bangles, mismatched beads, and what was that? An old shoelace? On her wrist?

Disgusting.

Even so . . . she was so beautiful.

And so *young.*

Not even Henry, who'd been fuming (the girl was half an hour late to meet them), could stay mad when he saw her. Everyone in the restaurant turned to stare at this carefree beauty loping toward their table. Nobody even knew who she was, but she was with them, wasn't she? She must've been somebody.

"We don't know anything about her," Didi said in the car afterward. "*Or* her family."

"No," Henry said. "But she's a real looker." Then he gave a high-pitched whistle and went back behind his newspaper.

On the terrace, the wind picks up. Not having her view—but only this wedge of Central Park through the other buildings—makes Didi feel depressed.

"We're not finished talking about this," she says. "But it's time for my nap."

"Of course, dear."

Didi turns toward the french doors—and that's when she sees the Siamese sitting in the doorway, licking its paws. The cat with the crooked fangs and the blue blue eyes, blocking her only means of escape.

"Mother?"

Bea makes a kissing sound with her lips. "Come here, Mooch."

Mooch and Smooch.

Gawwd.

The cat runs past Didi and under the table.

"Thank you," says Didi. She disappears into the nightmare of chintz.

Memorial Day Weekend

East Hampton

Chapter 9

If it's high-end shopping you crave, it's difficult to beat Main Street and Newtown Lane in East Hampton. The tree-lined streets were once home to surf shops and family-run delis, but now you're just as likely to find a designer handbag as a beach pail. In twenty years, East Hampton has gone from a sleepy resort town to Rodeo Drive on the beach.

—*The Guru's Guide to the Hamptons*

"Is it getting worse?" Toni asks. "Or are we just getting old?"

"Both." Layla blows cigarette smoke out the window.

It's Friday of the first long weekend and they sit in traffic on Main Street, Toni behind the wheel of the 1973 Volkswagen Westfalia. It's the same old van the Fratellis drove out to the Hamptons when they left New York more than twenty years ago. The thing is almost comical, painted every shade of the rainbow, blue eyeballs, yellow moons, purple flowers. It looks like something straight out of Haight-Ashbury during the Summer of Love.

The tinny voice on the radio announces they're listening to The Wolf, 102.1 FM. "The beach report is up next...."

"Are you thinking buffet or sit-down?"

"It doesn't matter," Layla says. "Just totally casual. What do you think?"

"For the beach? Buffet, probably. Depending on the guest list. Maybe a clambake? I saw this great idea for a cake. Don't ask, though. I want it to be a surprise. See anything yet?"

"Not yet."

They search the curb for precious parking spots. Toni's dad always complains about the slumping economy, but you'd never guess from all the Mercedes, Land Rovers, and Porsche SUVs.

They inch past Starbucks, and Toni says, "Do you ever wonder how many gallons of iced coffee they serve every summer?"

"Not really. But that sounds delish. Green-tea lemonade, half sweet?"

Toni reaches for her wallet.

"My treat," Layla says. "See you around back."

They peck kisses at each other and Layla slips out the door. As she cuts through traffic, a dozen heads turn in her direction but she's oblivious to the attention.

Toni creeps past BookHampton. The sidewalks are dense with people carrying shopping bags from white clapboard shops like Tory Burch, Coach, and Calypso. She tries to ignore the pang of resentment she feels when she notices how many of them are paired off, holding hands. She never used to worry when she saw couples on the street, but lately she only has a second of peace when she wakes up in the morning before reality sets in and she remembers—she's still alone.

The one-minute drive to the parking lot beside Waldbaum's takes more than ten, and by the time she gets there, buses and luxury cars have turned it into Midtown gridlock. A man in a convertible yells "Get the fuck out of my way!" to no one in particular. And no one in particular listens.

There are no fifteen-minute spots open, so Toni keeps looking, inching along. She takes out her red notebook and rests it on the steering wheel. She's been invited to Concordia for the Flagstones' Annual Spring Dinner and she wants to bring something special. She jots:

Ricotta.

Marsala.

Chocolate chips.

Shopping carts rumble by ahead of her, and she can guess the stories behind each one.

Plastic bags from Citarella and paper bags from Park Place Liquors: New Yorkers throwing a party. Beer cases, charcoal, and a skid of Waldbaum's toilet paper: frat boys at a share house.

Everyone looks bleary-eyed and pasty, hung over from last night. Toni wonders when Memorial Day—a holiday to honor the men and women who died for their country—turned into an extended spring break.

Chapter 10

"Enough zeros for you, Johnson?"

Yuri Orlokov leans in the office door, all bulging neck muscles and fake tan. His blond mullet looks greasy and there's a cardboard moving box under his arm.

"Can you ever have enough zeros?" Christopher Ohm slides the check back into the envelope.

"We're all going to Harry's for pre-tirement drinks. You coming?"

"I'll be there."

Yuri heads off, calling, "Hey, Johnson! Enough zeros for you?"

Chris's office is empty except for his chair and a clean glass desk, the surface of which he hasn't seen in two years. He turns to look at his view of the river and the pack of gray buildings huddled around Wall Street.

What the hell was he going to do now?

His BlackBerry sits in front of him, not ringing for the first time in weeks. There's a chip out of the corner where he dropped it that day. He runs his finger along it. It's become a habit of his.

He stands up and walks into the hall. He passes the mayhem of people lifting boxes or emptying file cabinets. Marcy is wearing jeans and a sweatshirt, cleaning out her desk.

"Hey."

She blows hair out of her eyes. "Hey."

He slides an envelope over to her. "This is just a little something from the guys. For saving our asses so many times."

"Oh. Thanks." Marcy doesn't even look at the check before putting it in her bag. She goes back to work.

He just stands there, rapping his fingers on her desk. "So are you gonna be okay?"

"Are you kidding? I'm a temp. No benefits. No job security. No retirement plan. I'm an extremely sought-after individual in this market."

"That's . . . good." He's now jingling keys in his pocket.

"Is there something I can do for you, Chris?"

"Actually . . . maybe. I just seemed to think of something the other day." He tries to act casual. "You know that woman who fainted up on—where the hell were we that day?"

"Ninety-second Street?"

"Yeah. Ninety-second Street. Right, right. Did you happen to . . . uh . . . get her name?"

Marcy looks at him. "Did you join a twelve-step plan or something? Want to make amends?"

"Nah, just . . . did you?"

"No. Why?"

"Nothing, really. Just, uh . . . all right, no problem." He's backing away. "Good luck . . . with everything."

"You, too," she mumbles. "You'll need it."

The bar is already half full on a Friday afternoon. Two tables at the back are pushed together for a group of men laughing and drinking. A forest of hands goes up.

"Hey! Ohmster! Over here!"

He sits down, feeling not unhappy exactly, but uncomfortable, as if he's waiting on line to board a bus but has no idea where it's going.

They're all talking about what they're going to do with the money—and the time.

Verner bought a chalet in Aspen. Willard's getting a bigger boat. Frank Broward's renting a place in the Hamptons.

"You should come with us, Johnson," says Yuri. "Lincoln's coming too."

Chris thinks about it. "The Hamptons? Nah. I don't like it out there. Nothing to do."

"There are girls," says Yuri. "Lots of girls."

Chris smiles. But he hasn't thought about "girls" in the plural since that day. When Marcy got into the town car, she said, "I always knew there was a reason you never lasted more than a couple of dates with anyone."

"Huh?"

"You were a total jerk back there."

"Was I?"

"You just better hope you never run into her again."

It was the first time he had a chance to consider he'd done anything wrong. Afterward, he couldn't stop thinking about her. He kept imagining he'd see her on the street, and his heart would pump a little faster.

He remembered how she stopped ahead of him that day on the sidewalk. How she turned to stare at something with such fear in her eyes it seemed she was witnessing a crime. But she just watched a little girl and her mother as they passed by. Then her knees started to buckle and she went down so fast.

Thank God she wasn't bleeding, he thought when he got to her. *Thank God.*

He remembers how she looked, her eyes closed, her lips parted, her head lolled back as if on a pillow. When she came to, her hair brushed across his face. It smelled like a cake shop.

Then she looked in his eyes.

And he *felt* something.

For the first time in as long as he could remember, he felt something besides anger or frustration. It was shocking to him. And maybe the main reason he had to get out of there that day.

But he'd never done that before, had he? Been the first one there to help someone? Not for years.

Chapter 11

Every hamlet along the forty-four miles of the South Fork has its own flavor. Montauk is rugged and outdoorsy. Bridgehampton is quiet and traditional. East Hampton is for artistic and media types. Southampton, the oldest English settlement in New York State, is where the Old Money goes. The "Summer Colony" started in the 1870s when a successful Manhattan gynecologist recommended the air and waters of Southampton to his wealthy clients. Before long, enormous "cottages" went up along the soft white beaches, with the very best of them on a storied road called Gin Lane.

—*The Guru's Guide to the Hamptons*

Didi stands in the dining room of the Blackhart ancestral summer home. She wears a white silk caftan and Velcro rollers in her hair (someone from Kevin Maple would be back to comb it out before the party).

A team of caterers sets the long Chippendale table that juts into the conservatory overlooking the beach. Housekeepers polish the silverware and florists look as busy as volunteers at the Rose Bowl parade.

For four generations the Blackharts—protected from the ups and downs of the market by several hundred million dollars in stodgy bonds, Treasury bills, and inheritances—have summered at Concordia, all eighteen thousand square feet and nine acres of oceanfront property on Gin Lane.

The original house, built in the 1880s, had been Queen Anne, but was replaced with a three-story Georgian mansion in 1924. Every year, some new renovation project kept it in peak condition, everything from the small (fresh white paint on the shutters) to the large (a new pool palladium inspired by Marie Antoinette's private palace at Versailles). On the eastern grounds were the Har-Tru tennis court and a six-car garage. The geometric pool sat in an L-shaped courtyard of french doors on the west.

Inside, Didi didn't favor the standard chintz of old Southampton, but fresh stripes and toile de Jouy. Her new Clive Christian kitchen was a showcase of ivory moldings and chandeliers. Up the curving staircase, eleven bedrooms could be found, each one redecorated often and named for its color scheme: Lilac, Daffodil, Rose. It was her great-grandfather who had named the place Concordia—the Latin term for harmony—but Didi does not feel harmonious right now.

She stares down at the one thing on her table that doesn't glisten or gleam. At the head place setting, on top of her grandmother's Coalport china, is something crusty and beige.

A starfish?

She sees several more scattered about the table and a pile of them in a big paper bag from Blooming Shells in Sag Harbor at her feet.

"What's this?"

She searches for a familiar face and finds it when she sees Estella holding the ladder for her husband, Jorge, who is up on the top rung polishing the wall of windows overlooking the beach.

"It's a starfish, miss."

Didi tells her she can see what it is—but what is it doing on her grandmother's Coalport china? Estella says it was the girl's idea. Didi asks why on earth she would bother hand-polishing the sterling silver scallop shell finger bowls if she thought crusty old starfish would be all right for the table. Estella says she's not quite sure—though she doesn't remember Didi helping to polish those bowls.

"Where is she?"

"On the beach, miss."

On the beach. Of course.

Outside, the wind is strong and the sun is bright. Didi puts up a hand to make sure her rollers are secure. The front patio, as it is modestly called, is as wide as the house and arranged with white Weatherend furniture. Beyond Spanish marble tiles is a narrow strip of lawn, the rough grassy slope to the beach, and beyond that, the unstoppable Atlantic.

Chewing its way toward the house.

She sees Hudson and the girl lying on a blanket on the expansive private beach, he in navy swim trunks, the girl in a tiny bikini lying on her stomach much too close to him. Didi feels that momentary slip of helplessness she sometimes feels when she sees Hudson in a situation that doesn't involve her. When she realize he isn't hers anymore. She'd been so lucky he decided to stay in New York for high school. Henry yelled murder he wasn't going to Andover like he and his own father had, but Dalton was an artsy school and there was all that acting nonsense.

But then she lost him to Harvard. And ski trips. And surfing.

But never to girls. Girls seemed to bore Hudson.

Until now.

"Sonny!" she calls. Her pet name for him when he was growing up—a play on the last syllable of his name. But the waves are loud and he doesn't hear her. She sees him stroke the girl's back and it makes her want to vomit. She has to stop them. Her gold Dior slipper—Didi never goes barefoot in the sand—finds a foothold on the path.

She doesn't come out to the beach much anymore. It's so wild out here. Nothing grows but chunky dark green shrubs and those faded dune grasses. It's usually too windy, and of course there's the sun. The dreaded UV rays. UV no longer means ultraviolet to Didi but Ugly Vampire—because that's what they'd turned her into.

As she makes her way down the steps she has strange recollections. Eight years old and skipping along in a seersucker dress. A teenager in a bikini carrying magazines. A young mother in a red maillot trying to hide her stretch marks. . . .

"Darling," she says, half laughing and a little out of breath when she gets to them. "Don't you think it's time for you to get ready?"

The girl looks up. "Hey, Didi."

"He . . . hello there."

"But we have hours, Ma."

"Still, I want Jorge to rake the sand."

Layla looks at Hudson. *Rake the sand?* He makes a groaning sound, then springs to his feet. "I have to wash off," he says. Didi tries to call him back, but he dashes across the beach and dives into the waves.

It's just her and the girl now.

Her honey blond hair is knotted into itself, white-blond fronds skim her unlined forehead. She looks so young. Hudson said twenty-nine, but she barely looks twenty. Or maybe all young women barely looked twenty to Didi now. She sees a strange tattoo on the small of the girl's back, an Asian symbol of some kind; it repulses her, the look of tattoo ink on a woman's skin.

"Look at you," Didi hears herself say. "How lucky you are to just lie out here like this. When I was your age, we used to—"

"Use Johnson's baby oil?"

The girl sits up then and Didi is shocked to see something she doesn't expect to see.

The girl's breasts.

Her nipples.

The girl is sunbathing—topless?

Didi glances toward the Meechford place, but the beach is empty, thank God.

Layla turns the bikini top over in her hands. "Isn't that what you were going to say?"

Didi doesn't know where to look. It was the same at Farmington. All the girls running around the shower rooms and dorms half naked. Didi's own breasts had always been small and neat, the nipples more like another pair of eyes on her chest than sex organs. But this girl is so lush, nipples soft and pink as rosettes on a store-bought birthday cake.

"Baby oil. Y . . . yes. We were so stupid back then."

Layla motions to the bottle in the sand. "I still use it," she says with a grin. "Could you tie me up?" She turns around, offering the bikini strings.

"I saw what you did with the starfish," Didi says, as she starts to tie the bow. She's taken aback by how soft and warm the girl's skin is. "I appreciate the help, but I think we should save them for another time." *We've had this discussion. It isn't an engagement party. It's the Annual Spring Dinner. A tradition for almost a hundred years.*

"All right?" Didi steps back.

Layla shrugs. "Whatever. Maybe we can use them at the wedding then," she says. "Thanks." She turns and runs toward the water, diving in like a twelve-year-old at summer camp.

Didi watches them swim toward one another. She'd been dodging rumors about the engagement for weeks. "You know, my son told me" or "I just happened to hear." But Didi would just laugh and say it wasn't official. In her circle, it hadn't been as difficult as she might've thought. Not everyone lived and died by gossip blogs or Page Six.

She watches the two silhouettes swim toward one another. She feels that slip of helplessness again. As if she's dropped something very important and can never get it back.

The water is a drumroll in Layla's ears. Cold water punching and pushing. She emerges, face-first, fingertips already numb; the water wouldn't be warm until August. It makes her teeth chatter.

Drrrr . . . drrrrr . . .

She tastes the water in her mouth, salty as chicken broth. Hudson marches onto the beach, calling to her, but the waves are too loud and she can't hear him. She sees Didi make her way up to the house, white caftan billowing. The scene looks like a vintage postcard come to life.

Layla knows people—writers, artists, poets—have always talked about the light in the Hamptons. How special it was. Vivid and gauzy at the same time. Even Toni seemed to understand what everyone meant, always wanting bigger and bigger boxes of Crayolas so she could draw every flower and rock and leaf the exact shade she saw them.

Layla pretended she understood, but she was born here, grew up here. Light was . . . well, it was just light, wasn't it?

But on Gin Lane, she understood. The light was softer than anywhere else, almost powdery, like viewing the world through a pale sheet of vellum. On calm days when the mist was low, all but two hundred yards of this beach disappeared and it looked as if nothing else in the world existed—or ever had.

She remembers her parents' old bungalow on Underwood Drive. The sagging roof line. The crooked shutters. She used to think it must be the ugliest house in the Hamptons. She wouldn't even let the rich summer boys drive her home. She'd get off at the corner of Springs Fireplace Road and walk because she didn't want them to see how much of a Bonacker she was. "Bonacker" was the name for people from Springs, a wooded tangle of roads near Accabonac Creek where Jackson Pollock used to paint—it meant hillbilly.

And here she was . . . a Bonacker on Gin Lane.

You are cordially invited to

The 99th Annual
Spring Dinner at Concordia
Saturday, May 30th, 2009

7:30 P.M.
810 Gin Lane
Southampton, New York

Attire: Garden Formal

Chapter 12

In the small dimly lit kitchen where she learned to cook, Toni sits at the table holding a pastry bag over a tiny cannoli shell. She concentrates, squeezing just the right amount of cream into the little tube.

She hears a slam from the next room. It makes her jump and the plastic nozzle crushes the shell. She shakes the crumbs and cream off her hand onto a piece of wax paper full of other imperfect shells.

"Dad, could you please take it easy in there?"

The bathroom door off the kitchen is open and her dad had just closed the medicine cabinet. He comes out wearing black pants and a fresh white shirt. Vic Fratelli has a horseshoe of black hair, bushy eyebrows, down-turned jowls.

"You shouldn't make them so small," he says.

"I like them like this."

"Why?"

"Because they're easier to eat—and they're cute." She sets a finished cannoli down in a row so perfect it looks like a display in a Lilliputian bakery. She was up half the night making the pastry, and three different kinds of filling: chocolate, mocha, and vanilla cream. She whipped the ricotta until it was as smooth as butter, getting rid of those little chunks she didn't like.

He stands over her, squinting through his bifocals. "You care too much what those people think," he says. "What time do you think you'll be back?"

"I don't know. I'll call."

"Are you going to make it for closing? I could use you. It's a busy weekend. I can't believe it's Memorial Day already. That's it." He claps his hands. "The summer's almost over."

"Dad, the summer hasn't even started yet."

"Might as well. Once Memorial Day hits, you know how fast it goes."

She sighs. "I still wish you wouldn't say it."

He's at the mirror tacked behind the back door putting on his tie. Toni can't believe that mirror is still there. When her mother first hung the thing, it was too high up for Toni to use, but there it is—like everything else in the house. The collection of salt and pepper shakers. The blue tin canister set. The living room furniture that somehow seemed too big for the place. The whole house had become a time capsule of Toni's life—and her dad was sealed up in it too.

"I notice you didn't cash my check last week," she says.

"Sure I did."

"No—the money's still in my account."

"Must've overlooked it."

"You? Overlook a check? Gimme a break."

"Honey, I'm your father, not a banker. If I expected it back, I wouldn't have given it to you." He kisses her head. "Stay on the main roads, bella."

"I will."

"Liar."

The back door slams behind him and Toni jumps again. She shakes the goo off her hand and starts over. She sees the nozzle of the pastry bag and remembers the first time she used it, in this very kitchen, to pump frosting onto a Duncan Hines cake.

She was halfway through fourth grade when the Fratellis finally managed to sell their apartment in New York. They packed everything they could into the old VW van and headed east along the expressway. It had been almost five years since Toni's accident. She thought they were moving into the slant-roofed saltbox on Gardiner's Bay—the one the Fratellis had bought years earlier as a summer house. Some of her happiest memories were from that little cottage, standing on the big deck outside, watching the sailboats through her telescope.

But they had to sell that too to buy the restaurant. Vic Fratelli said they were "starting over."

Someplace safe.

They sang "Ninety-nine Bottles of Beer on the Wall" and "Hey Bus Driver" all along the LIE.

She'd never been to the Hamptons in winter before, each village decorated with a different color of Christmas lights. She smelled fireplaces burning and it made her stomach twist with excitement. The snow on the trees and the gingerbread houses made her think of nursery rhymes. *Over the river and through the woods, to Grandmother's house we go. . . .*

Handmade Christmas decorations still hung in the windows of East Hampton Primary the day her mother took her to enroll. All the children's artwork was low-down on the walls: she remembered seeing one that would hang in the hallway for years, a pastel-crayon drawing of a unicorn flying through a blue sky, and the messy printing in the corner:

Layla S.

The first thing Toni noticed when the classroom door opened was a skinny blond girl in the very back row. Even sitting down, the girl seemed too tall for fourth grade—about the same height as Toni. She wore a blue sweater that had pilled and pants that showed her ankle socks.

The teacher introduced Toni at the front of the class, and it made her feel like something called in for Show and Tell. When she sat down, it was in the second-to-last seat in the row beside the girl. There was a chunky pink pen hanging on a shoelace around her neck and Toni wondered what it was. The girl met her gaze with frank blue eyes. Toni half expected her to say, "Take a picture, it might last longer." But she didn't.

Because the girl was tall, Toni felt as if they belonged to a secret society of Amazonian women dropped down onto a planet of dwarfs; it gave her the kind of nerve she didn't usually have with new girls. The next day, when the girl rubbed the chubby pink pen on her lips, Toni turned around and whispered, "What is that?"

"Bonne Belle Lip Smacker. Tastes like strawberries. Want some?"

Toni shook her head.

"I got it at White's."

Toni nodded as if she understood.

That night Toni approached her father as he did the books in the dining room. He'd developed lines on his forehead in the last few years. "Mom said you have to buy me Bonne Belle Lip Smacker. You can get it at White's."

"Sure, honey," he said.

That evening he took her to White's Chemists and Perfumers, a white clapboard drugstore on Main Street. A sign out front said the shop was founded in 1873. When Toni saw the cosmetics section, her esteem of the blond girl shot through the roof.

The next day Toni had her own Bonne Belle Lip Smacker attached with a purple ribbon around her neck and a long tube with six different glosses in it. They tasted like strawberries *and* grapes *and* everything in between.

"I'm Layla," the girl whispered. "Where'd you get *that*?"

After school that day, they bonded in the cosmetics section of White's, a place where they would spend many more hours over the years. Layla stood at the mirror next to the counter and brushed tester on her cheeks. She said she was partial to CoverGirl makeup and talked about how she was going to be just like Christie Brinkley when she grew up.

When they left the shop that afternoon, they both sensed they had found a soul mate. Two girls brought together by lip gloss and the fact that they were both five feet tall in the last grade of elementary school.

What Toni didn't know at the time was that Layla would grow another eight and a half inches—and she would only grow another four.

Chapter 13

Expressway? Chris Ohm thinks. Not even close.

The root word "express" seemed to suggest speed, ease, and directness. But stuck bumper to bumper in traffic on the Long Island Expressway, he understands why they call it the LIE.

The top of his metallic gold '67 Mustang convertible is down. Flanking him on one side and pulling up the rear are three other cars. All the drivers are wearing headsets.

"This is part of the experience," Frank Broward III says behind the wheel of his dark green Range Rover. "Is it easy to climb Mount Everest? No." A Yale man with fair skin and glasses, he's more buttoned-down than his Brooks Brothers collar. "But that's the point. The challenge of it."

A high-pitched whistle from behind the wheel of a black Maserati. "Check out one o'clock, boys. That's about a million bucks' worth of why we get up in the morning." Lincoln Jacobs points to a Ferrari Enzo ahead of them. He has a shaved head and a trimmed goatee. A graduate of Morehouse, one of the best historically black colleges in the country, Lincoln can always spot nice cars, good clothes—and distressed businesses.

"This is taking too long!" Yuri Orlokov pounds his steering wheel. "I am wasting my life out here!" He pulls his yellow Jeep into the HOV lane and roars ahead of the others. It's a cardinal sin to enter the HOV lane if you're not carpooling, and the afternoon becomes a din of honking horns, but Yuri ignores them. There are several universities on his CV, from Saint Petersburg to Princeton, where he claims to have "minored in business and majored in girls."

"Back to the list," Frank says. "Ohm? Do you copy?"

The headset is quiet.

"You better not be checking e-mail."

Chris rubs the little nick on the top right corner of his BlackBerry. He tosses it to the seat. "Who, me?"

"Can't do that, Ohm," Frank says. "It's on the list. As soon as we get out there, we have to turn in our Bluetooths."

"Don't you mean blue *teeth*?"

"Damn, Johnson!" says Yuri. "Smoky on my six!"

The men watch a police cruiser pass them, siren blaring.

"Going dark," Yuri says.

"Don't forget to turn when you see the POW signs," Frank says.

"Copy that." Yuri clicks off his headset.

The men watch in their rearview as the Jeep is pulled over by a police cruiser.

"Did he actually say 'Smoky'?" Lincoln asks.

"Burt Reynolds must be big in Mother Russia," Chris says.

"Back to the list," Frank says. "No e-mail. No texts. No work-related calls at all, in fact. No checking stock quotes. No e-trades."

Lincoln says, "Broward, I will see your no e-trades and I will raise you no *Wall Street Journal*."

"How're we gonna know what's going on if we can't read the papers?" Chris asks.

"That's the point," says Frank. "We're on an extended vacation."

Lincoln says, "I like this. Most people get paid to work. We're getting paid *not* to."

"What about the sports section?" Chris asks.

"Sure. Sports are okay, I guess. But first one to get caught with his nose to the grindstone has to pick up the lease. Deal?"

A moment of silence as everyone realizes how much they paid for the beach house. "Deal," they finally say.

Chris smiles to himself; they're the only people in the world who could turn relaxing into a competition.

Chapter 14

With a vintage serving dish of four dozen perfect mini-cannolis, Toni winds the old van past a cornfield. The sprouts are just starting, bright green and barely a foot tall. It makes her happy. There was so much summer left.

Her father had been right—she didn't stay on the main roads. She knows all the shortcuts and scenic routes too well. She even drives down Long Beach Road and rolls down the windows. She leans her head out and takes a big long breath. The bay has a different scent from the ocean; the briny air seems more salty and dense.

She drives through the winding streets of Southampton and turns onto Gin Lane to see hedgerows towering more than fifteen feet on either side. It makes the street feel like one long maze she could never win. Some of the hedges are bowed, others flowering, others boxy, but none are as tall or straight as the one outside Concordia: it looks like one long green marble wall.

At the front door, a woman in a navy suit consults her clipboard. "Fratelli . . . Fratelli . . ."

Two security guards flank the high double door and a single closed-circuit camera blinks at Toni. The columns on either side are ringed around with pink peonies and red roses. Men and women in pastel dresses and suits wait behind her with linen invitations.

She *really* should've bought that dress. She saw one in the window of Ralph Lauren, but she couldn't find a parking spot. So her black V-neck cocktail dress would have to do, as it had "done" for every special occasion for three years.

"Here you are," says the woman, checking off her name, not typed but handwritten in Layla's loopy script with an arrow pointing to the space underneath Dr. and Mrs. Lawrence Fairweather and Mr. Samuel B. Fenwick III.

She steps into the foyer, double high with a chandelier and marble flooring. A custard white corridor runs straight through to a large gathering hall overlooking the ocean. Elegant guests disappear through french doors on her right. Somewhere a string quartet is playing. She smells flowers, canapés, and candle wax.

She's greeted by two servers wearing fresh white polo shirts with the LDV logo and navy pants. They smile at Toni and offer their wares, but with the cannolis, a bottle of wine, and a gift bag, her hands are full.

"Toneeeeeeeeeeee!" She hears pounding on the stairs as Layla bounds down in jean shorts and a tank top.

"Thank God," Toni says.

She gives Toni a big kiss. "I *told* you not to bring anything."

"I didn't want to show up empty-handed."

"Estella, will you take these for her."

"Not this." Toni keeps a little blue gift bag, but watches as her cannolis and wine are carried away.

Layla grabs two champagne flutes off the tray. "Come on. Still getting ready."

Upstairs there are family portraits framed on the walls. Some are ancient and sepia-toned, others more modern, showing Hudson and his cousins playing on the lawn like the Kennedy clan.

"I can't believe this place. The guesthouse is bigger than my dad's."

"No kidding," Layla says. "You could get a villa in Tuscany for what they paid for Didi's new pool house." She takes Toni into a room with a plaque over the door that reads Bluebell. "It's the only room that hasn't been decorated since 1978," she says.

There are two single beds covered in gingham shams and duvets. A cane rocker. An antique dresser. Makeup, clothes, and shoes are strewn everywhere like backstage at a fashion show. Layla and Toni had been roommates for years in New York and Layla's housekeeping habits were one of the few things they fought over.

"I'm not a slob. You're a clean freak."

"Just because I'm a clean freak, that doesn't mean you're not a slob."

Layla licks her finger and tests her big curling iron.

"I wanted an ocean room," she says. "But Didi gave me a view of the garage instead. And Hudson's bedroom's all the way over on the other side of the house. She's trying to keep us apart. She's still calling me Lila, if you can believe that. She hates me."

"I'm sure she doesn't *hate* you."

"You'll see."

As Layla strips down to her tan lines, Toni walks to the window and sees Susan Schumacher's vans hidden near the service entrance. Just seeing the navy logo makes her feel a rush of nerves. La Dolce Vita Foods is going to be her biggest competition this summer.

"I wonder what's for dinner?"

"I saw live lobsters being trucked in. And foie gras. Didi just loves torturing defenseless animals. We're probably having baby seal for dessert." She slips on a silky red minidress by Michael Kors. The front falls in an elegant drape. "What do you think?"

"Smashing. And decidedly demure. Good choice."

"Not quite." She turns around. The dress is backless, dipping past her tailbone. "Gotta show the tramp stamp for the boys."

Toni notices her finger is bare. "What happened to your ring?"

"Hudson's having it resized before the wedding."

"Speaking of which. Have you talked to Didi about the food yet?"

"What for? *I'm* the one who's getting married. Don't worry, it's not gonna be a big thing. Fifty, sixty people on the beach. You'll blow everyone away. The dresses are going to be easy. I'm making mine. And you could wear *that* if you want. I'd love to have a black wedding. Didi hates black in the Hamptons."

Toni blinks. "Why didn't you tell me she hated black?"

"Toni, if I started listing everything Didi hates I'd be going strong until Christmas."

Toni drops to the bed. "I knew I should've bought that dress."

Layla sees the gift bag. "What's that?"

"Just a little something . . . until you register."

"Awww, Tone. You didn't have to do that!"

But she bounds over and bounces on the bed next to Toni anyway. She lifts out a small box with seashells glued on top. Inlaid is a photograph of the two girls sitting on Main Beach when they were about twelve. Toni sniffs a bit.

"You're not going to cry, are you?"

"*Nah.* Of course not . . ."

Layla opens the bag and holds up a small plastic statue of Smurf in a top hat and Smurfette in a white wedding dress, holding hands and smiling.

"Oh my God!"

"I saw it on eBay," Toni says, dabbing her eyes. "Bought it ages ago. Couldn't resist."

"I love it! We're so totally putting it on the cake!"

Toni doesn't mention she bought the little statue for Kevin and herself last year. The stupid thing was better for Layla, anyway. Saturday mornings after sleepovers they'd sit on the floor eating Froot Loops and watching cartoons. Toni always related more to the girls in *Josie and the Pussycats* or *Scooby Doo.* Smurfette didn't seem to do very much except look pretty and prance around in her high heels. The other Smurfs fawned all over her anyway, the way boys fawned over Layla. Layla basically *was* Smurfette—and had been all her life.

It's right that she have it.

The tears start to come and she has to dig for tissues in her purse.

Layla says, "Aw, Toni, please don't—"

But a loud knock interrupts them. A young woman in her midtwenties leans in. Long straight dark hair, green eyes, deep tan. Her minidress is mint blue and the sandals are silver.

"*Hola, amiga!* Sorry. *Amigas!*"

"Toni, this is Hudson's cousin, Tabitha Schick. Tabitha, this is Toni Fratelli. My MOH."

"Pleased to meet you, MOH," Tabitha says.

"You too," Toni says, blowing her nose. "I'd shake your hand but—"

Tabitha's already talking to Layla. "Sweetie, you remember those 'dorable little drop earrings you had on the other night? May I borrow them, pretty please?"

Layla wonders aloud where she put them and starts digging through her jewelry. Toni starts to rewrap the Smurf cake topper.

"Omigod!" Tabitha says. "The dwarfs!" She hurries over and snatches them out of Toni's hands.

"Smurfs, actually."

"I know that, but my nanny could never get the hang of Smurfs. She always called them the dwarfs. So"—Tabitha shrugs helplessly—"so do I."

"Oh . . ."

"Found 'em!" Layla holds up a pair of long silver earrings.

Tabitha throws the Smurfs over her shoulder; Toni lunges after them before they hit the floor. "*Gracias tanto, mi amiga!* Fab dress, by the way. See you ladies downstairs!" She gives a wave of her manicure and twirls out of the room.

After she's gone, Toni says, "Schick? Any relation to the razor blade people?"

"Probably. They're all related at some point." She grabs Toni's hand. "Come on. Let's show these people how to party."

Chapter 15

"Commit this to memory and then destroy the originals." Frank hands everyone a white card with the combination for the front door of an enormous glass and steel postmodern mansion overlooking the beach. "This code should not fall into the wrong hands—by penalty of a very large security deposit."

Lincoln wheels his luggage inside and looks around. "Maybe happiness can't be bought," he says. "But it sure can be rented."

The main room is double-high with a sunken sitting area; the furniture is a mix of midcentury and modern and the open-concept kitchen is a showcase of stainless steel.

"It's worth twenty million at least," Frank says. "Forty before the recession. I saw the floor plans, so I've assigned bedrooms." He takes two neatly folded papers out of his pocket and straightens them on the dining table. "I like to be up early, so I've taken the one on the east. I drew straws for the other ones. Yuri, you're the animal, so—" He looks up. "Guys?"

Yuri comes in from the pool deck. "Where are the girls, Johnson?"

"There are no girls."

"But I am told all about Hamptons house shares, and they are telling me about the girls."

"This is a luxury rental, Yuri. There's a difference. We're civilized here."

Lincoln comes down from the second floor. "No girls? That's not civilized."

Frank says, "Who wants sixty kids sleeping on wall-to-wall mattresses? You want to know what you're really sharing? Genital warts. Herpes. Pubic lice."

"Ha," Chris says. "Louse share. That's funny."

Yuri says, "But I told the police officer there would be girls. I don't think he would want to come if he knew there was no girls."

Chris says, "You bribed a police officer not to give you a ticket?"

"No, he still gave me the ticket. I invited him anyway."

"Forget all the partying," says Frank. "We're going to commune with nature. Rediscover what the great industrialists used to love about the Hamptons."

"By great industrialists," Lincoln says, "I presume you mean the robber barons of the nineteenth century. The ones who raped and pillaged the land and oppressed everyone in their paths to be the first on the block with a horse-less carriage?"

"Uh . . . yes," Frank says. "But without the, um . . . nasty parts."

"Did the robber barons have TVs in their fridges?" Chris asks. He leans next to the stainless Sub-Zero, playing with the buttons.

"They didn't even have fridges," Frank says, turning off the LCD screen. "And we agreed no TV."

"That wasn't TV. That was Bloomberg."

"No Bloomberg. No CNN. No CNBC. They're all on the list."

"What about *Playboy*, Johnson?"

"Yuri, can't you live without pornography for ninety days?"

"I agreed no competition. I agreed no disclosure. But I did *not* agree no *Playboy*."

"Okay, fine. *Playboy*." Frank grabs a teak bowl and begins circling the group. "All right, everyone, ante up. BlackBerrys. iPhones. Whatever other form of twenty-first-century technology you may be addicted to."

Chris stares at his phone longingly, then tosses it in the bowl. Everyone follows suit.

"I'm bored already," Yuri says, flopping on the sectional.

"Maybe this wasn't such a good idea," Lincoln says. "It's so quiet out here. I can hear waves."

"That's because we're by the ocean," says Frank.

"But I can *only* hear waves. I need traffic sounds to sleep. You know those Bose Wave machines? You think they have them with traffic sounds?"

"They have them with waves," Chris says.

"It'll be good for you, Linc," Frank says. "Waves have a positive impact on your alpha rhythm."

"So do car horns," he says.

Chris looks around at his friends and wonders how he'll manage to spend three months with them. He'll give it another two days, then drive back to the city.

He remembers the traffic.

Fly back, more like.

Chapter 16

"I see everyone else got the memo about Didi hating black in the Hamptons," Toni says.

She looks around the living room at all the shimmering dresses and floral gowns on the women. The men wear navy blazers, pale gabardines, and bright-colored ties.

"Don't worry about it," Layla says. "You're hot. Look, there's Hank." She points to a silver-haired man with a weathered face standing outside smoking a cigar. In a navy jacket, kelly green pants, and madras tie, he looks like he just stepped off a Highlands links course.

"He's older than I thought," Toni says.

"All that red meat and golfing."

"Where's Hudson?"

Layla motions through a wall of french doors to the pool deck. Toni sees Hudson and Didi standing with guests, everyone posing for a group photo. Didi's gown is acid green, strapless with a swooping train. Her hair is up and her lipstick is bright red. Several photographers from the local magazines work their way through the crowd.

A server stops by with a tray of lobster dumplings. They each grab one and Toni takes out her notebook.

"You're not going to take notes, are you?"

"Gotta keep up on the competition." She chews, savors, jots: *too much dill.*

Layla motions to a skinny woman dressed in head-to-toe Chanel.

"See that dress? You could build a school in Africa for what she paid for it. Two schools. Not that anyone cares about Africa around here. And what about her? She's had so much work done she should have construction pylons around her. . . ."

Toni feels a time warp closing in on them.

They're back at their senior semiformal, glommed together in the smelly pink bathroom at East Hampton High. Layla is blowing cigarette smoke out the window. The other prettily dressed girls are leaning against the sinks, fixing their makeup.

"Watch this," Layla says.

Patti Newscombe is at the end sink, wearing red taffeta, digging through her clutch. Layla takes the tip of her burning cigarette and touches the edge of the big bow on the back of Patti's dress. Toni slaps her arm, *no.* But it's too late. A corner of the bow turns brown like a leaf in the fall. Patti walks out, completely unaware.

Patti got into Layla's bad books after she started the Teen Abstinence Program in tenth grade, preaching that sex before marriage was not only immoral but dangerous. Just say no to drugs. Just say no to alcohol. Just say no to sex.

Layla didn't say no to very much. She lost her virginity when she was fifteen to a lifeguard the girls had been ogling for weeks. They both worked Main Beach during the summer, Layla as a lifeguard, Toni in the Chowder Bowl snack bar serving ice cream and grilling hotdogs. Toni remembers warm nights around bonfires, all the lifeguards and summer kids singing songs, the white guard towers empty, the signs barely legible in the dark.

Swimming Is Prohibited. No Lifeguard on Duty.

Toni fell for a lifeguard that summer too, a skinny one who wore glasses at night. He was farsighted, which was fine for saving lives, he said, but not so good for life.

As for Layla, she went through lifeguards and rich summer boys the way Toni went through recipes. Things only got worse after Layla's parents died. She basically lived at Toni's house for months, crying herself to sleep at night, and every morning before school. When people look at Layla now, all they see is a glamour girl. But Toni knows better.

———————

"Here comes the Wicked Witch of the South," Layla says, nudging her.

Didi walks over in a cloud of shushing silk. "Lila, how *festive* you look."

"It's Layla, Ma." Hudson releases his mother's arm and kisses his fiancée—a little too deeply. He looks handsome in a navy suit and white tie. Now that Toni sees them together, she realizes how much he looks like his mother.

"Glad you could come, Toni," he says, pecking her cheek too. "You look gorgeous."

"This old thing. And I mean it—this old thing." She checks Didi for any reaction to the black dress, but Didi smiles blankly.

Layla says, "Didi, this is Toni Fratelli. My B-F-F."

"Which stands for bachelor of . . . ?"

"Best friend *forever*."

Didi smiles. "I knew that. So nice to meet you, Toni." She extends a cold hand. "Will you be staying for dinner?"

"Uhhhh . . . not if it's a problem."

"It's not a problem," Layla says.

"Of course not," says Didi. But Toni notices she's begun to flick her fingernail.

Layla says, "Toni's going to be my MOH, Didi."

"Moe?"

"My maid of honor."

"Really? You work quickly, don't you, Lila, dear? You just got engaged and—"

"Ma, it's *Layla*."

"Isn't that what I said?"

Two blond women approach, one wearing peach peau de soie, the other in sea-foam shantung. They're so pale they remind Toni of ice-cream cones that wandered off from the snack bar at Main Beach.

"Didi, what a fabulous party!" says Peau de soie.

"Just perfect!" says Shantung.

The compliments continue to pour. The dress. The food. Those shoes. Then everyone just blinks at each other for a moment. When it's apparent Didi is not going to introduce them, Layla says, "I don't think we've met. I'm Layla Sullivan. Hudson's fiancée."

Two pairs of eyes widen. Glance at Didi. Congratulations and well wishes are disbursed. Didi just flicks her fingernail.

Shantung points to the small of Layla's back. "We couldn't help but notice your tattoo from across the room, dear. Is that Chinese?"

"Japanese, actually," Layla says, arching her back to look down behind her. Several men glance over, distracted by the curves. "I got it when I was modeling over there."

"And what does it mean?"

"It's the kanji symbol for fertility."

"Oh?" asks Shantung. "You hope to have a lot of children, do you?"

"Not really." She leans into Toni and whispers, "But I hope to have a lot of *sex*."

Toni gives her a little nudge and Layla tries not to laugh.

Tabitha inches up. "May I steal you guys for a minute? There's someone I want you to meet." Without waiting for an answer, she propels Layla and Hudson out to the pool deck. Toni watches them sail away like a life raft.

"She's so beautiful, Didi," says Shantung.

"Yes, where is she from?"

Didi just sidesteps the question with a blank smile. "Will you ladies excuse me for a moment? I have to see about dinner." She turns on her heel and disappears in a shush of silk.

Toni is suddenly alone with the ice-cream cones.

"And what do *you* do, dear?" asks Peau de soie.

"I'm a cook," Toni says. "Chef, actually."

And she *was* a chef once. Not a sous chef or a saucier, but an executive chef in her own restaurant.

Once.

"I'm running a catering company with my father now."

"How interesting," says Peau de soie.

"I'd *love* to know how to cook someday," says Shantung, shivering as if it's some dangerous sport she's been working up the nerve to try.

Toni just smiles and looks around for more champagne.

Chapter 17

Didi stares down at her perfectly set table. Bowls of red and white roses are set so closely together they look like one dense garland down the center. Since 1910, Spring Dinner at Concordia has been served on Didi's grandmother's Coalport china, bright blue with gilding and scalloped edges. Didi knows the pattern is old-fashioned and ornate. If there were sixty people for dinner, it would be too much. But there are never sixty people for dinner because Spring Dinner at Concordia is always for fifty. *Always.* Since 1910. In fact, there were only fifty place settings of Coalport in the first place, and in all that time not a single teacup or bread plate has ever been broken. But now, for the first time in almost a century, Spring Dinner would be for fifty-one.

Didi feels the bile rise in her throat.

She'd have to drag out the Spode.

"Hey, Toni."

Toni's mouth is full of beluga caviar as she turns to see a tall man with a scruffy face standing behind her. There's a camera strung around his neck.

"Three hundred dpi," he says. "Bill Mitchell usually works too."

She swallows. "Bill, hi! I'm so sorry! You have to forgive me. I'm terrible with faces. I have prosopagnosia."

"Proso-what?"

"I never recognize people. Hardly ever, anyway. Unless I've already met them a few times. Alec Baldwin came into my dad's restaurant once and I thought it was the man who cut our grass. I was nice to him, thank God—I liked the man who cut our grass. But if I had known it was him, I would've spilled minestrone in his lap."

Bill laughs.

"What're you doing here?" she asks.

He tells her Mrs. Latham fell off a ladder planting her window boxes last week and broke her hip.

"Oh no!" Toni says. "Not again! How bad is it this time?" She's already planning to bring her pineapple upside-down cake.

Bill tells her she'll be out of commission for three months, that she'll probably need a hip replacement, that they'll know for sure by the fall. In the meantime, he's taking her job as society editor and photographer. "Do you think I'm underdressed?" he asks, pointing to his cargo shorts and old running shoes.

She motions with her thumb and forefinger. "Maybe just a titch."

"I know, but I thought Memorial Day. Barbecues. Corn chips. Keg beer."

Toni laughs. "Not in Southampton."

A server walks up. "Belgian wren tartlet?" she asks.

"Oh, you have to try these," Toni says. "They're the best."

They both take one and Toni watches Bill for his reaction as he chews. "What do you think?"

He looks at her, eyes wide, cheeks bulging. "Delicious," he says, swallowing.

"I thought it was a bit gamy this time," she says.

"Well . . . maybe a bit."

He notices another photographer dressed in a white dinner jacket snapping pictures of a gaggle of women outside. "*He* knows how to dress the part," Bill says.

"No kidding," she says. Toni looks over at them, the women smiling for the camera. "You know, I lived here for twenty years. There are more magazines than you can count—and never once did I make the society pages."

Bill lifts the camera and points it at her. "Now you will."

———

At 8:30 P.M., the dining room is full of voices and clinking plates. A dinner bell chimes somewhere and the guests, accustomed as they are to being reminded to act when they hear a pleasant ringing sound, look around as if to find the doors back into the opera house.

At the head of the table, Didi smiles and stands up. "Hello, everyone," she says in her clear fundraising voice. "As many of you know, because you've been here before—and so have your parents. Or *grand*parents, as the case may be." Laughter. "This is the ninety-ninth Spring Dinner at Concordia. I always love this time of year. The flowers are just starting to bloom. Old friends get a chance to—"

A tinkle of butter knife on crystal. Didi reacts as if to nails on a chalkboard.

"I'm sorry, Mother," Hudson says. "Can we postpone the flowers-in-bloom speech? I have a special announcement to make."

Didi tries to laugh. "Hudson, it can—"

"It won't take long," he says, standing up.

Didi feels as if she's been blown over by a nor'easter, but she refuses to let the guests know she's perturbed, so she sits down.

Hudson picks up his wineglass and smiles at Layla, who is sitting across from him, the two of them separated by candlesticks and bowls of roses.

"Almost two years ago," he begins, "I walked into the Waverly Inn for a few drinks during Fashion Week."

The string quartet begins to play in the background. Toni sits beside Layla at the only all-white setting. She's no classical music expert, but the song sounds familiar to her.

Mozart? Beethoven?

"And I saw this gorgeous woman standing—at the bar, of course."

Layla snorts a laugh, and a few of the guests chuckle politely.

"She had legs that wouldn't quit, a smile that wouldn't stop, and ever since I looked into her blue eyes, I have not been able to think about anything—or anyone—else."

Hudson walks around the table, behind his mother.

"Four weeks ago, I asked this angel to be my bride . . ."

Some gasps of excitement.

"But there was a *problem* with the ring. So here, in front of all of you, I want to ask her again."

Hudson gets down on one knee as Layla turns in her chair to face him.

"To paraphrase the great Eric Clapton, Lay-la, I'm down on my knee."

The quartet hits the chorus and Toni thinks, *Not Mozart! Clapton!*

"Layla Marie Sullivan, my princess, my angel, my local peach, will you marry me?"

He opens the ring box and presents the big blue sapphire—resized, polished, and sparkling so brightly it's as if someone has turned up the chandeliers. Layla puts the ring on her finger and throws her arms around his neck. Toni feels the tears start to come and thinks twice about using the linen napkin, dabbing her eyes with her fingertips instead.

The crowd applauds and from the opposite end of the table, Henry says, "Hear, hear!"

The couple starts to kiss.

And kiss.

Didi's smile falters. She wants to pry them apart with her bare hands; instead she just lifts her wineglass in a toast along with everyone else.

The two finally release each other, and Layla grabs Toni's shoulder. "Everybody, I want you to meet my maid of honor, Toni Fratelli. She's also gonna do the catering for the wedding. The little cannolis are hers. You should try them. They're around somewhere. She's the best!"

"Caterer?" Didi asks, looking over. She's trying to smile, but she flicks her fingernail so hard, it slams the edge of her bread plate.

Toni, who's been collecting vintage dishes all her life, hears the unmistakable sound of a chip being made in the Coalport china.

June

Chapter 18

Toni was expecting her move home to solve at least some of her problems. She wouldn't have to worry about finding another job in the city after Dash closed.

She wouldn't have to worry about the exorbitant rent on her apartment.

Or where to walk Tucker.

Or how she was going to pay her father back.

Her own place, she told him almost eighteen months ago. Her dream come true. With friends. Just a loan.

When Vic heard she wanted to open her own restaurant, he didn't seem happy, the way Hollywood stars and cops must feel when they hear their kids want to follow in their footsteps.

He had a thousand questions.

"Where was it?"

"West Village."

"What kind of food?"

"Bistro."

"What's it called?"

"Dash."

"Like a dash of salt?"

"Yeah. But it's also an anagram. All the first letters of everyone's names."

Vic counted the partners on his fingers. "David. Amy. Sam. Heather. Where's the *T* for Toni?"

"Dasht doesn't have quite the same ring," she said.

"That's not a good omen."

"You don't believe in omens."

"But I believe in facts. Ninety percent of most restaurants fail within a year."

"Not ninety, Dad. Twenty-six. I've done my research. Twenty-six percent in the first year, nineteen percent in the second year, and fourteen percent in the third year."

"That's fifty-nine percent altogether." Tallying cash register receipts most of his life had turned Vic into a walking adding machine. "That's worse than the divorce rate."

"Well, it's not going to happen to me," she said.

She tried to feel steeled, not discouraged, by the advice her dad and everyone else, including the banks, had given her.

Twenty-six percent of all new restaurants fail in the first year, which meant 74 percent of all new restaurants succeeded! Those were pretty good odds. Layla had finished high school with a lower grade average than that. Toni didn't have to worry. Her life was on schedule. Pretty soon, Kevin would be back from San Francisco and they would get married and the restaurant guides would be giving Dash four-star reviews. Then would come the house, the kids, and happily ever after.

Instead, she's been home a month and still hasn't booked a single catering job. What's worse, she's waking up on faded Beauty and the Beast sheets in her girlhood bedroom, staring at a poster of John Cusack, and listening to the same clock radio that used to wake her up for high school.

She reaches to turn it off and sees her mauve ballerina lamp.

She needs a new radio—*and* a new lamp.

Tucker sniffs along the sidewalk cracks of Church Street as she takes him for his morning walk. The canopy of trees is so lush and dense it feels as if she's strolling through an apple orchard.

Practically every house she passes looks like her father's: an old shingle style with shutters and a white picket fence. She notices a few people have painted their trim a different shade and there are newer cars in the driveways, but otherwise the street looks the same as it did when she was growing up.

Other places changed over the years, especially in New York. Her bistro had already been turned into a flower shop. The vacant store on 51st Street was a Chase bank now. Even the Hamptons were changing quickly—too quickly as far as Toni was concerned sometimes, with old family-run businesses like the Pork Store being replaced with upscale boutiques.

But here on the residential streets of East Hampton, things were different. Just as the beach, the light, and the ocean would always be the same, it seemed as if the historical sections of town had been sealed up in a Mason jar two hundred years ago and opened again perfectly preserved.

It was all the building regulations and architectural reviews in town. You needed a permit to so much as paint your shop or put up a satellite antenna. Her dad resented all the rules—Nazi Mayberry, he called the place. But Toni understood. A part of her longed to hang on to the past, even as the rest of her tried to move on.

An elderly man drives by in a Chrysler, waving out the window at her. She waves back. She wonders how many times she's seen Mr. Fitzgerald head off to work at Town Hall. He was always so friendly to her—all the neighbors were—but even after twenty-two years on the same street, she didn't feel like a local. To be a local, you had to be born here—and she had been born in New York. She was "from away."

When she moved back to Manhattan for cooking school, she thought it would cure her of this feeling of not belonging. But in the city native New Yorkers didn't let her forget she grew up somewhere else, so she never felt totally New York or totally Long Island. Sometimes it seemed as if mismatched pieces of herself were strewn all along the expressway. If she could just pick them up and bring them to one place, maybe then she would feel complete.

Maybe.

Chapter 19

Didi sits alone in the pool pavilion decorated exclusively with French antiques. She pores through more than five pounds of newspapers and glossy magazines printed in the Hamptons every week like a high school junior searching for her photo in a yearbook.

"It was Escada couture," she says, closing *Dan's Papers*. "Not Dior."

She opens *Hamptons* and approves of Jason Binn's spread in "The Flash." A nice write-up, a flattering picture. The handsome soul. She'd have to send him flowers.

She likes the Hot Shots photo in *Social Life* too, and Parties and Benefits in *HC&G*. There's nothing in the *Independent* or *Vox*, but she's not surprised. At least the *East Hampton Sun* did something. A whole spread on Spring Dinner. Wait, who was that horsey woman wearing her dress? She doesn't remember—

But then she realizes who the horsey woman is.

Worse than not finding a shot of herself in the weeklies is finding a *bad* shot—and this one is the worst. The left side of her face. The side that made her look more like her wealthy golf-playing, scotch-drinking, game fisherman father than his *Mayflower* bride. Her shoulders are bony, her cheeks are drawn, her neck looks as scrawny as an apple core.

She wants to scream.

She would never knowingly turn that side to a camera. If she sensed a photographer moving in, she could perform conversational pirouettes to get into position. Chin held slightly out to minimize the jowls, shoulders back, hips slung forward. Any sane photographer would know better than to print an unflattering photo of her.

But there it was, under the caption, "The hostess wore green."

Simply—green?

She sees the byline: Bill Mitchell. The Rolodex of grudges she holds in her mind spins to M, and she viciously finds a slot for Bill Mitchell of the *East Hampton Sun*.

She's still recovering from this shock when she's dealt an even worse blow. A photo of her darling Hudson, looking handsome and dashing in his suit, with his arm around . . . *the girl*. That little hussy hangs off his neck as if he were a stripper pole.

But then comes the coup de grace. In the corner, a photo of a woman in a black cocktail dress standing in front of the french doors as if she owns the place. The caption reads, "Caterer Toni Fratelli enjoying a moment of peace."

Didi snaps the paper closed.

Chapter 20

In 1899, when East Hampton celebrated its 250th Anniversary, a flag was raised on Main Street and only the children who were at least eighth-generation descendants of the first settlers could participate. In the Hamptons, there's only one group more elite than the rich summer people— and those are the folks who've been there all along.

—*The Guru's Guide to the Hamptons*

Susan Schumacher is on her knees in a patch of edible flowers in the middle of fifteen acres of Further Lane property. The morning is a din of lawn mowers, sprinkler systems, squawking hens, and buzzing bees. Her short red hair is tucked under a large sun hat. She's a small woman, only five-foot-one, with pale skin and blue eyes; she wears a pink tunic from Scoop Beach and her iPod, which plays a downloaded meditation recording.

"*Om mani padme hum* . . ."

She chants softly along, working her spade into the rich dark earth; it's the same soil that attracted so many settlers years ago, including her late husband's family. Susan herself is from a long line of accountants in Islip, but the Schumachers had been farmers for six generations and they had a saying: Put a kernel of corn in the mud in East Hampton. Two months later, you'll have a whole field.

Beneath the chanting of her zen master, Susan hears her cell phone. She sees Didi Flagstone's number on the call display.

She grits her teeth and hits Ignore.

Again.

She plucks one of the flowers from the field, rubs a little dirt off it, puts it in her mouth, chews. After a moment, Susan listens to the harried message. The apology about the misprint. The silliness of all these "rags." The decline of the media in general. And, of course, how wonderful Spring Dinner was.

Susan hits Delete.

Then she takes a moment to scroll through her iPhone contact list, admiring the famous names. It warms her heart to see them. As if all those important people in her hand were actually there at a big dinner party. She finally tucks her phone away and goes back to her edible flowers.

Chapter 21

"What's the problem?" Hudson asks. He's at the marble island eating a bowl of granola as Estella refills his coffee cup. "It's not the *best* picture you've ever taken, but—"

"It's not that," Didi says. "At least, not *just* that. This photo makes it seem as if your girlfriend's *bee-eff-eff*"—she jabs the paper—"catered my Spring Dinner. Susan Schumacher isn't even returning my calls."

"So?"

"So, who is she? This little Fratelli girl? Nobody knows her. She hasn't done any big parties. Has she?"

"Actually, she just opened up."

"That's even worse. Sonny, I *always* hire Susan. You know that. She's more expensive, but she's worth it. If people see this, they'll think I've had a falling-out with her. Or that I've gone liberal. Or worse, that we're"—Didi chokes on the word—"broke."

"Ma, you always complain about the weeklies. They usually make some mistake or other. It used to be a game for us, remember? Find the Misprint."

"This isn't a misspelled name, Hudson. This is serious."

"In whose galaxy?"

Didi crosses her arms. "I'm not sure I like your attitude, young man. And while we're on the subject of inappropriate behavior, the next time a photographer points a camera in your direction, could you please refrain from feeling up your girlfriend in public?"

"She's not my girlfriend. She's my fiancée."

Didi's just about to say "Don't remind me" when she sees the girl standing at the door, wearing only Hudson's faded Nirvana T-shirt and bare feet.

"Peaches!" says Hudson, spinning on his stool.

"Morning, baby." She pads to him, resting her forearms on his shoulders. They kiss and nuzzle until Didi can't watch them anymore. Estella continues wiping the same spot of counter she's been at for five minutes now. She knows this is one of those conversations she can hear but that she shouldn't be listening to.

"How'd you sleep?" he asks.

"Like a pussycat." She goes to the cupboard for a coffee cup. Didi resents the fact the girl knows where the cups are; it would take her twice as long to find them.

"You made the papers, my dear," Didi says. "Since you're almost part of the household"—she can't bring herself to say "family" yet—"I feel it's my place to give you some insight into being photographed."

"I don't think she needs pointers, Ma. She used to model."

"Bikini shots are one thing. This is different. When there are photographers around, please keep your wineglass at a right angle, here by your waist." Didi motions. "Better yet, find someplace to put it down."

"I never put my drinks down. Roofies were going around when I was in Tokyo. You should've seen what happened to some of my friends."

Didi looks around in confusion.

"She thinks you're talking about Indian currency," Hudson says.

Layla's blue eyes widen when she sees the shot of Toni. "Omigod! Toni finally made the papers! She's going to die!"

"And so might I," Didi says. "The next time you talk to her, please ask her to stop masquerading as my caterer. There must be better ways to get free publicity than lying."

"Toni wouldn't do that. She doesn't lie. She hates liars." Layla squints and brings the newspaper close to her face. "Didi . . . is that *you*?"

Chapter 22

"Only you could think this is a bad thing," Vic says.

Toni and her father are in the big kitchen at the back of the restaurant. She's making fresh noodles with the pasta machine. He's seasoning the marinara sauce. Around them, several prep chefs, the sous chef, the pastry intern, and the bussers get ready for the lunch rush, chopping, tasting, cleaning, and generally trying to stay out of each other's way. Rhonda, the pretty blond hostess (and a dead ringer for Layla when she had the same job) sits at the staff table folding red napkins and answering the phone.

"Good morning, Fratelli's. . . . Sorry, no, we don't take reservations . . ."

The swinging doors to the main restaurant are open and a handful of servers gossip and laugh, setting tables with red-and-white-checked tablecloths. Literally a mom-and-pop business, Fratelli's looks much the same as it did before Mom and Pop got a divorce.

"It *is* a bad thing," Toni says. "Sully told me Didi's completely pissed off. She thinks I did it on purpose."

"So? Rich people have to be pissed off at someone. Otherwise they don't feel rich."

"Still. It's just my luck. I finally make the papers and this is what happens.

Susan's probably mad too. If she doesn't sue me, she'll at least go through the roof."

"Let's hope she goes through the roof of her chicken coop. She'd get SARS or E. coli from all that fancy chicken shit of hers. They'd have to put her place up for sale and I'd buy it for half price and open the best B & B on the East End."

"You've put some thought into this."

"One can always dream."

"Anyway, I don't *hate* her anymore. Those days are over. As soon as people start hearing about us, things will pick up. There's more than enough business in the Hamptons for everyone."

"There used to be," he says. "Not anymore. Do you know how many tables I turned away last night?"

"Yes, Dad. I was there, remember?" Unfortunately for Toni, her promising catering business has turned into extended shifts waiting on tables. "About fifty. Right, Rhonda?"

"Something like that," Rhonda says.

"Sure, fifty. Thank God people have to eat. But I used to turn away two hundred every night. It's only a matter of time before we all go under now."

"Stop being such a pessimist," she says. "Do you think I should go over and apologize or something? Maybe send flowers?"

"Because of a mistake you didn't even make? Do I have to remind you of all the nights you came home crying from her shop?"

"No, you—"

"Theresa, how many times did we tell her not to take that job?"

A woman with salt-and-pepper hair looks up from the counter where she has made tiramisu every day—excepting the births of her grandchildren—since Fratelli's opened.

"*Lotti,*" she says.

"See? *Lotti.*"

"I was eighteen when I worked for Susan, Dad. I was stubborn back then."

"You still are," he says. "*Testardo.*"

The phone rings again and Rhonda picks it up.

"Fratelli's?"

Toni says, "This isn't a summer job anymore. I'm in business now. *We're* in business. There's a lot more at stake than a reference for college."

"You have to remind me?"

Rhonda holds out the phone. "Toni, it's for you."

"That better not be a personal call," Vic says.

"Do you think you could possibly say *one* thing today that didn't make me feel like I was twelve?" She takes the phone. "Hello? . . . Yes, this is . . . just a moment, please." She puts the call on hold and excitedly motions for a pen. "Someone saw my picture in the paper! They want us to cater a party for the long weekend!" She gets back on the call. "Yes . . . I think we can handle that."

Vic turns to Theresa. In Italian, he says, "I told her it was good news. She's such a pessimist sometimes."

Chapter 23

Susan Schumacher teeters down Newtown Lane carrying a gift basket wrapped in blue cellophane. Her ensemble, from the polka-dot dress to the platform shoes, is from Betsey Johnson's summer collection. Betsey is her close personal friend.

Of course, everyone in the Hamptons is her close personal friend. Which is what really irks Susan about the misprint in the *Sun*. In a part of the world where everyone was a celebrity, the real stars were the locals who managed to get the rich summer people addicted to some vital service they provided. There was the hardware store salesman, the dry cleaner, the owner of the Monogram Shop, and dozens of others. But above them all, there was Susan Schumacher, owner of La Dolce Vita Foods.

How could anyone, especially a social writer, think Didi Flagstone would hire a little nobody like Toni Fratelli to do Spring Dinner? Susan practically *invented* modern-day Hamptons. Everyone knew she was the one who had turned it from the provincial beach town past its prime into the elegant country retreat it was today. Before Martha Stewart; before Diddy's mother, Janice Combs; even before Ina Garten's *The Barefoot Contessa*—there was La Dolce Vita Foods. She was the one who figured out that the more you charged for something in the

Hamptons, the more successful you were. Not even the real estate brokers could compete.

Where were they getting these hacks, anyway?

Bill Mitchell is at his computer working on an article about the piping plover regulations for the Fourth of July when a small woman walks in the door. She hefts a gift basket onto the counter that all but obscures her from view. Bill looks over at George Comfrey, the sports editor, who quickly picks up his phone.

Bill goes to the counter himself. "I'm sorry, but Mrs. Latham's still in the hospital. If you . . ."

"Oh, this isn't for Margaret. It's for you. Pleased to meet you. I'm Susan Schumacher."

"Thank you. That's very sweet of you. But I'm sorry, journalists aren't allowed to accept gifts."

Susan gives a soft laugh. "I think we're both overshooting the terms here a bit, don't you, Bill?"

"Have we . . . met before?"

"Not officially. But I recognize your picture from the paper." She retrieves a folded copy of the *Sun* from her bag and opens it to the offending article. "Do you know what I do for a living, Bill?"

"Uh—"

"I own La Dolce Vita Foods."

"That's . . . good."

"*I'm* actually the one who catered the Flagstone Spring Dinner." She slides a page of neatly typed letterhead toward him. "Which is why I'd like you to print this retraction to correct your mistake."

"I'm sorry? A retraction? I've never printed a retraction in my life. Let alone over a silly dinner party."

He hears a wincing sound from George's desk. Dinner parties in the Hamptons could be "lavish," "simple," or "extravagant in the extreme," but they were never "silly."

"Obviously, I didn't mean—"

"No need to apologize, Bill. I wish I were just talking about a dinner party. But I'm not. Have you ever heard the proverb, 'A butterfly flaps its wings in China and there's a hurricane in LA'?"

Bill nods.

"In the Hamptons, information is a lot like a butterfly. This one mistaken piece of information in your newspaper is like a butterfly flapping its wings on Memorial Day. The hurricane it could very well start is that La Dolce Vita Foods will be out of business by Labor Day. You wouldn't want that, would you, Bill?"

"Uh..."

"Do you know how many people I employ?"

"Uh..." Bill is reduced to monosyllables.

"Thirty-six full-time. Sixty part-time. How many local farmers do you think I rely on? Let alone the fishmongers and runners and gardeners."

"Um..."

"It would be almost impossible to calculate the economic trickle-down effect of La Dolce Vita Foods in the Hamptons, but I think it would be safe to say that three, four, possibly five hundred people might be out of a job this summer because of something *you* wrote. Do you want to take responsibility for that, Bill?"

"Uh..."

"I didn't think so." She pushes the page toward him again. "Thank you so much for your kind attention. By the way, that was a *lovely* picture of Didi Flagstone you took. You have real talent."

Correction

Please note that the following information in the June 6 edition of the East Hampton Sun *wrongly identified Ms. Toni Fratelli as the caterer of the Flagstone Spring Dinner on Memorial Day weekend. Susan Schumacher, longtime owner and operator of La Dolce Vita Foods, one of the oldest caterers in the Hamptons, provided all the services for the event.*

Chapter 24

Layla steps out of Springs General Store, unwrapping a fresh package of cigarettes. The straps of a white bikini are visible at the neckline of her sundress. She crosses the road to the green banks of Pussy's Pond. A flock of ducks waddle about the water and grass. She takes one bite of her lunch—a blueberry muffin—and then pulls it apart, scattering the crumbs for the ducks. They come quacking and paddling over. She watches them eat for a few minutes, then gets back into her car.

She pulls the white convertible Beetle onto the shoulder of Underwood Drive, gravel crunching beneath the tires. She looks across the street at the old bungalow. Someone has painted the shutters and planted hydrangeas out front. But the grass is still patchy, the pine trees look scraggly, and the shingles are the shade of mud.

She lights a cigarette and stares at it, hoping the people who live there now don't see her. Sometimes there's the silhouette of a woman's head in the window above the kitchen sink.

When she was a young girl she began to notice the difference between her house and the ones closer to town or on the beach. But her parents always taught her how lucky she was to grow up here. Not everyone lived in a place where people like Steven Spielberg had summer homes. She was like a princess, they told her, in a fairy-tale kingdom. She just let the rich summer people borrow the place sometimes.

She was about twelve when she started to realize that her mother complained about how the rich summer people treated her when they shopped at the grocery store. And that they yelled at her father over problems with their cars. By the time she was working as a hostess in the restaurant—where the female customers ignored her while the men leered—she had figured out the truth. Her parents had lied to her. The summer people weren't part of her fairy tale. She was part of theirs.

Chapter 25

Khahn's Sports is a small colorful shop in East Hampton specializing in sporting and casual clothes. The crammed racks and dim lighting reminded Chris so much of the beach shacks in Malibu when he was growing up he couldn't resist coming in.

He's trying on sunglasses when a woman comes up behind him, holding a T-shirt. "Do you have this in a medium?"

"Uh..." He looks at her, frowning. "I don't work here."

The clerk behind the counter says, "There should be some on the sale rack."

She smiles thanks and walks away.

Chris glances at himself in the mirror. *No wonder she thought he worked there.* He barely recognizes himself. His hair was always long for Wall Street, but it hasn't been trimmed in months and looks positively shaggy; there's at least a week of scruff on his face, and he's sunburned from being out on the water too long yesterday.

What was happening to him?

His first vacation in five years?

Six?

No BlackBerry. No contracts. No meetings. Nothing to prop up who he had been in the city. *Was it the surfing?* One long pipeline right back to his childhood?

"You're gonna love it," says the clerk behind the counter, a young man with sun-bleached hair. "The chop at Ditch Plains Beach is awesome. What do you got?"

"Eight-and-a-half-foot longboard," Chris says, getting out his American Express card.

"Nice. I'm a boogie boy myself."

On the counter between them is a small stack of T-shirts and board shorts. Chris only had two pairs of gym clothes to get him through the summer, so he decided to stock up. First he went to Gucci. Then Elie Tahari. Then Ralph Lauren. He didn't find anything that seemed right—until this cornucopia of inexpensive Quiksilver and Billabong on Park Place.

"Are these really only twenty bucks?" he asks about the sunglasses.

"Yup."

"Sold." He tosses them on the counter too.

The clerk looks at his credit card. "Ohm. That's so chill. *Om* is the sound the universe makes. You get a free gift for that." He tosses a tin of surf wax on the counter. "Must be your lucky day."

Outside in the sun, the sidewalk is crowded and the large parking lot is jammed with sports cars and SUVs. He's waiting for a break in traffic when a woman with dark hair walks toward him. She wears a peach blouse, shorts, and flip-flops. "Tucker, *no* . . ."

There's a stack of magazines clamped under her arm and a black dog pulling on its leash ahead of her.

"Tucker, I said *no* . . ."

He holds his breath as she passes him.

Was it her?

Ninety-second Street?

She's so preoccupied with her dog, she doesn't notice him. He takes off his sunglasses to get a better look, but a bus full of tourists unloads next to him and she's lost in the crowd. He takes one step toward the parking lot and his gold Mustang. He remembers Marcy's words—"You better hope you never run into her again"—and he hesitates one long moment. Then he finds himself doing an about-face and hurrying after her.

He gets to the lane beside Starbucks and stands on his toes to find her, but she's gone. He doesn't know if he's disappointed or relieved. It probably wasn't her, anyway. He thought he'd seen her dozens of times in the city. What were the odds she'd be out here?

He hears a little whimper beside him and looks down to see the black dog sitting on the walk.

"Uh . . . hi," he says.

The dog sniffs his Reef sandal, then hunkers down as if prepared for a wait. Chris sees a mountain-climbing carabiner attached to his leash. He remembers that heavy red schoolbag with the carabiner attached. It *must* be her. His heart starts to pound like a fist inside his chest.

The glass door to Starbucks opens and he hears a woman's laugh; he peers in the shadows to see her standing on line. A flood of relief rushes through him. And then nerves.

Should he really try to talk to her?

Maybe even apologize?

All he knows is that he doesn't want to lose her again.

The shop smells like caffeine and warm sugar; tables of people linger over lattes and iced drinks. She's at the counter, ordering.

"Green-tea lemonade, half sweet, and a mocha frappuccino, double whip, double caramel sauce."

"Sure thing, Toni." The barista marks the cups.

Toni?

His heart still thrums as he gets on line two people behind her. He watches her move down the counter to wait for her drinks. She leans against the wall and opens one of her magazines. He sees that beat-up red schoolbag. It's definitely her.

"Yes?" The young cashier looks at him.

Chris glances at the menu board. When he wants coffee he runs down to the diner on the corner and brings back a black, no sugar, in a Styrofoam cup. He hasn't ordered a caramel macchiato in his life.

"Do you have just plain coffee?"

The barista points to a sign with different flavors, from Breakfast Blend to Kenyan. "What kind?"

"Um . . . normal. Regular. You decide," says Chris.

The barista pours a cup and rings him through. He pays and then realizes he's just standing there with no reason to hang around. And she's still waiting for her drink.

The blender whirs.

He steps to the little creamer station behind him. He sneaks glances at her every now and again, to see her still flipping idly through her magazine. He adds sugar, then cream, then Sweet'n Low, stirring in between. He tastes his coffee and winces. It's awful, and he feels like a stalker.

He should just go. This is stupid.

He heads toward the door—and at that precise moment so does she. They stop in front of each other, blocking each other's way. She smiles at him—right at him—and the thump of his heart stops for one long beat.

"Excuse me," she says. She pushes her shoulder against the door. "Tucker, come!"

Outside, the dog follows her across the sidewalk, dragging his leash. She stops outside an old VW van parked on Main Street. With her hands full, she can't open the door easily, and Chris comes up behind her.

"Can I help you with that?"

"Oh, thanks," she says. She gives him another big smile, but this time she frowns a bit. He meets her eyes, wondering if she'll recognize him, preparing himself to get reamed out on the street. But she seems to shrug it off, smiling again.

"This is great of you. I always try to do too much."

"No problem," he says, opening the side door.

A delicious aroma wafts out at him like a five-star Meals on Wheels. He sees a picnic basket and a beach blanket on the seat. She's leaning to put the drinks in cup holders when the dog bounds into the van, wrapping the leash around her legs.

"Whoa, Tucker!" She spins around.

The magazines slip out from under her arm, falling to the sidewalk in a flutter of pages. She twists and turns, laughing, trying to get untangled, but Tucker climbs into the front seat and that just makes it worse, flattening her against the van. Chris tries to hold the leash so she can step out of it, but her purse strap gets caught.

"Let me just take this off," she says. But as she lifts the bag over her shoulder, the flap opens and something heavy—and very hard—falls onto Chris's baby toe.

"Ow!"

"Oh my God! I'm soooo sorry!" Her eyes are wide. "Are you okay?"

"Yeah . . . I mean, I think so . . ." He looks down to see that his baby toe is pink—and there's an antique pressing iron sitting on the sidewalk beside it.

An iron?

"I hope that's not going to bleed," she says worriedly. "I've got a first-aid kit in here somewhere." She starts digging through her bag again and Chris finds himself backing away from any more potential shrapnel.

"It's fine. . . . Really."

"Are you sure?"

"Absolutely." He wiggles his toe for her. "See?"

She exhales in relief. "Don't ask. The kitchen sink isn't in here, but it might as well be." She picks up the vintage iron and shoves it back into her purse.

Somebody walks by, kicking one of her magazines.

"Don't you just love the tourists," she says.

He laughs awkwardly and bends to help her pick them up. They're crouched so close to each other on the sidewalk that he can smell her hair. *The cake shop.* He looks at her again, searching her brown eyes for any indication she remembers him, and she hesitates, staring back at him, giving him an uncertain smile.

When she doesn't seem to recognize him, the relief that floods over him is tangible. He's just about to introduce himself and finish what is probably going to be one of the most ignominious introductions in the history of girl-boy relations when he sees the covers of the magazines:

Modern Bride.

Today's Bride.

Martha Stewart Weddings.

His smile fades.

"Pardon?" she asks.

"Huh?"

"You were going to say something?"

"Uh . . . nothing. No. Never mind."

She frowns and puts the magazines into the van. Her smile has faded too.

"Well . . . thanks again for all your help. I really hope your toe's gonna be okay. You should put something cold on it. It'll help keep the swelling down." With one last worried smile, she climbs into the van and closes the door.

Chris stares after her as she drives away.

Chapter 26

"Thanks for all your help with that," she says to Tucker. "Only decent guy on Main Street and you practically made me cripple him."

Tucker, who's got his head out the window, whimpers as if to apologize.

"Did he seem familiar to you?"

But Tucker's looking out the window again.

"He did to me."

Maybe she met him at a party once? Or a barbecue out here? Could be. He looked like he lived at the beach.

And was it her imagination—or did he seem to be interested in her? For a second there, anyway. Smiling and looking so deeply into her eyes. But the moment she tried to reciprocate, he cooled off.

Men.

Maybe she was acting too available or something. Giving off those desperate vibes she was so afraid she was giving off since Kevin. Which only made her more worried she was doing it.

At the Main Beach parking lot, she nudges the van back and forth, squeezing into the very last spot. Years of driving in the Hamptons have made her a quantum physicist when it comes to parking cars.

She grabs everything, including Tucker's leash, and does another clumsy bellhop routine across the parking lot toward the beach. She passes Layla's white Volkswagen, top down, empty cigarette packages littering the seat. And no beach sticker, of course. It's why they had to come to the public beach in the first place. As usual, Layla had not applied for a parking sticker in time. She missed the "sweet spot" (what felt like a forty-eight-hour window where the limited number of beach parking permits were available from Town Hall) and had to pay for public parking like the tourists. As for Toni, she had her beach sticker before Memorial Day.

Main Beach is crowded, dense and colorful as a flag laid out on the pale sand. She steps around beach blankets, umbrellas, coolers. Children pound up the steps to the broad deck of the Chowder Bowl snack bar. Lifeguards wearing yellow T-shirts and red shorts stand on their towers overlooking the waves. Toni remembers seeing Layla up on those towers when they were younger. Wearing her red bathing suit and Wayfarer sunglasses. More than a few summer boys faked their own near-drowning accidents to get her attention back then.

And still would today.

She's the hottest girl on the beach.

"Hey!" Layla whistles and waves her arm in the air. She wears a white bikini and sits by the very edge of the cordon. Tucker tugs even harder, kicking up sand as he tracks across blankets toward her, then tramples all over her gleaming legs when he gets there.

She just laughs and rubs his ears. "Hey, fella."

"You're early," Toni says.

"And you're late."

"I had to pick up your homework." Toni drops the wedding magazines on the blanket. "And then, oh, I don't know, I thought I'd hobble the cutest guy on Main Street."

"Huh?"

"Never mind." She strips down to a navy one-piece she bought for a romantic getaway with Kevin that never materialized. She tries not to feel depressed about it—even though any woman lying next to Layla in a bathing suit would.

She grabs her SPF 50 bottle and begins rubbing lotion on her arms and legs.

Every morning, Toni puts on sunblock—double when she's at the beach—and here's Layla slathered in Johnson's baby oil, and Toni knows she'll get wrinkles first.

She motions to one of the magazines. "I saw this great recipe for spicy crab cakes. I think they'd be perfect for . . ."

Layla groans.

"What's wrong?"

"Do we have to talk about the wedding *now*?" she says. "It's still three months away."

"More like two. Tucker, no." He sniffs Layla's drink. Toni digs out a bowl for him, pouring fresh water from a bottle, keeping his carabiner clamped under her butt so he won't run away. Between Memorial Day and Labor Day, dogs can't be off-leash on the beach.

"You at least have to start thinking about themes," she says. "For the invitations and things." She grabs the wedding binder, divided by little tabs: Menu, Seating Plan, Dresses, Favors. "You probably want something beachy. Starfish. Seashells. What about sandcastles? You love sandcastles."

Layla opens one eye. "You really do have it, you know that?"

"What?"

"Now What Syndrome. You can't relax. Even when we're at the beach, you're working on *my* wedding."

"Somebody's gotta do it, Sully. A wedding's not like a pregnancy. It doesn't pop out fully formed nine months after conception."

"I know. It's just that I didn't want it to be such a big deal. And it's all anybody talks about anymore. Even Didi's on my back about it. Speaking of which—and I mean that literally: witch—she wants us to go into the city to shop for dresses."

"Like wedding dresses?"

"Uh-huh."

"You're kidding?"

"Not just mine. The bridesmaids', hers, all of ours."

"And you're going?"

Layla just shrugs and Toni stares at her, confused.

She remembers all the nights they spent in the home ec room at East Hampton High, the lights turned down except for one over the stove, where Toni learned to make béchamel sauce and soufflés for the first time, and another over the sewing machines, where Layla sat making her own patterns or customizing a pair of jeans. Layla had dreamt of going to design school when she was younger—and had more than enough talent to do it, if it hadn't involved actual *schooling*—but the one thing she dreamed about more than anything was designing her own wedding gown.

"I can't believe it," Toni says. "You're seriously thinking about *buying* a dress?"

"Huds wants me to go. Just to humor her. I probably won't find anything. She'll have to get off my back then. But you guys need dresses, right? I mean, I want my bridesmaids to go barefoot, but I don't want you to go bare-*assed*. Will you come?"

Toni looks down at the binder, then smiles and closes it. "Of course I'll come. I'm your MOH."

"Awesome! You rock the cash bar!" Layla seems visibly relieved, sitting up and checking her tan lines. "I'm baking out here. I gotta cool off."

She stands up, straightening her bikini bottom with two snaps. She walks slowly toward the water, weaving between blankets and umbrellas. Everyone she passes turns to stare. Women flipping through magazines. Men reading paperbacks. Lifeguards on their towers. She takes three long strides into the water and disappears beneath the waves. When the girl in the white bikini is just another head in the surf, life returns to normal on the beach.

But Toni knows something has shifted, like the subtle movement of the sun in the afternoon. With the obvious exception of hearing the news about her parents, Layla did not let things get to her. Not failing math. Not missing senior prom (even though she was voted queen). Not broken hearts. It was one of the things Toni admired most about her. But to be coerced into shopping for a wedding dress she'd always dreamed of making herself?

This wasn't just a record. It was a sea change.

Chapter 27

"I just don't see what the rush is," Didi says. She and Hudson are on the court battling the Tennis Tutor ball machine.

"There's no rush. We just want to get it over with."

"It's your wedding, Hudson, not the LSAT. Take your time." She lobs one out of bounds. "You should consider putting it off until next year. Even Christmas. How inconvenient is it to have a wedding on the last long weekend of the season, anyway?"

"Why? Are you busy? Going to Diddy's White Party?"

She turns to face him. "Are you making fun of me?"

"Watch it!" he says, as the machine beams one over her head.

"You better not be," she says.

"Of course not. I'm just saying we're not postponing it. Peaches wants to do it Labor Day weekend, so we're doing it Labor Day weekend."

Didi rolls her eyes.

Peaches.

His local peach. Cheap. Dirty. And picked up by the side of the road, probably.

She gets back to the game, and they take turns striking the balls, expertly dipping in and out of each other's way. Didi and Sonny Flagstone had been one of the top-seeded mixed-doubles partners at the Meadow Club for years (and if fashion sense were taken into account, they would've been Wimbledon champs). But Didi's stamina isn't what it used to be. And of course, there are the dreaded UV rays, so after a few more lazy volleys, she goes back to the shade of the umbrella—and her martini glass.

"I just wish you'd get to know her better, that's all," she says. She sits down to put on more sunblock, watching Hudson on the court. She admires the length of his legs as he lunges. The taut strength of his Achilles tendons as he jumps.

"I *do* know her."

"Know her *better*, I said. You've only been going out a year."

"Almost two."

"Ex*cuse* me. Two."

The balls stop popping out.

"Jorge!" Hudson calls. *"Bolas, por favor!"*

Jorge materializes from behind a hedgerow, scooping tennis balls into a wire basket. They don't pay any attention to him. But they don't pay any attention to the handful of gardeners on the grounds either.

"What about her family? You don't know anything about them, do you?"

"I'm not marrying her family."

"But you are, Sonny. That's the point. A wedding is a coming together not just of two people, but of two entire generations of people. All their DNA and traits and . . ."

"Someone's been watching PBS again."

"Don't be smart."

She walks to the court and holds out her sunblock. "Do my neck. And don't get any in my hair." She turns around and Hudson rubs lotion onto the nape of her neck. "Did you know her father was a mechanic?"

"Something like that."

"No, not something like that. Exactly that. And her mother was a cashier at the IGA."

"Who cares?"

"Okay, Meester Flagstone!" says Jorge.

The machine pumps another ball and Hudson rushes to return it. Jorge has to duck not to get hit.

"Is she pregnant?" Didi asks. "Is that how she roped you into this?"

"She didn't *rope* me into anything."

"I wouldn't doubt it. Her parents didn't get married until she was two years old. Did you know that? She was born into bastardy, Sonny."

He laughs. "Bastardy? What is this, act 1, scene 4 of *Lear*?" He stops playing and looks at her. "How do you know all this, anyway?"

"Never mind. I'm just saying she's illegitimate. Doesn't that bother you?"

"Not at all. And I don't know why it would bother you. Big deal. Her parents were kind of hippies." He goes back to battling the balls.

"Sometimes I think it's my fault," she says, watching him. "That I sheltered you too much. I never wanted you to be a snob, Sonny. But that doesn't mean I didn't expect you to use good judgment. I feel sorry for the girl, really I do. Losing her parents the way she did. But because they didn't die of natural causes, we really have no idea what diseases might run in her family. And I'm worried about my grandchildren."

"We're not even sure we're having children," he says, returning a hard backhand. "So why talk about the hypothetical diseases"—he runs across for a ground stroke—"that our hypothetical children"—he's winded now—"might hypothetically get?" He drops his racket to his side. "What did you do, anyway? Hire a private detective?"

"He's not a detective. He's a genealogist. And he's been working for the family—"

"Oh, yes." He goes back to volleying. "Dear Mr. Beecher. Did you have him spy on *all* my girlfriends?"

"I didn't have to. I knew everything about your other girlfriends."

"I'm not sure you did, Mother. You didn't know Isabel Slokum was a kleptomaniac. Remember that Christmas your Fabergé egg disappeared? You should've checked her dorm room."

"Isabel comes from a very good family. And there's help for that kind of thing."

"Oh, Mother, please. Let's play. Who am I?"

"Sonny, I don't feel like—"

"Come on!" He returns a volley, then shakes his fist angrily at the machine. "Who am I?"

"McEnroe," she says with a little pout.

"Good guess!" He hits the ball and twirls his racket expertly, running his hand through his hair.

"Federer," she says, laughing a little.

He takes a hard forehand, then delicately puts his hair behind his ear, batting his eyelashes.

"Sharapova!" She laughs out loud.

She doesn't know if it's the martinis or their beloved old game, but suddenly she's feeling better. She drains her drink and rushes at the ball machine, taking a hard swing.

"Billie Jean King!" he says.

Chapter 28

"Did they say *why* they wanted to cancel?" Toni is up to her elbows in pastry dough.

"Um . . . not really," Rhonda says.

"You told them about the forty-eight-hour notice?"

"They're still going to pay the deposit. They just don't want you to cater it anymore. They're calling Susan Schumacher."

"They *told* you that?"

"No. But when I hung up, the phone rang again and it was them asking if I had her number."

"And you gave it to them?"

"Uh-huh."

"That was considerate of you."

"I thought so." Rhonda swings back through the doors into the restaurant.

Toni sighs out loud. Her first booking—and her first cancellation—end up being one and the same. The Hendersons must've seen the correction in the *East Hampton Sun.* She has no idea what she's going to do with the six hundred votive candles she bought for it.

The prep cooks, dishwashers, and servers all sneak glances at her. The only people not watching her are Mike and Lisa—the sous chef and the pastry intern—who are flirting with each other by the walk-in fridge.

Toni keeps seeing couples everywhere.

Mike and Lisa.

Layla and Hudson.

The swans.

Even the deer.

She saw a doe standing by the side of the road last night. It was her first deer of the season, so she actually pulled over to take a picture of it. The doe stood quietly as Toni snapped shots with her phone. They stared at each other for a long time, like single sisters commiserating over their spinsterhood. Then a stag came along, protectively stepping in front of her. Toni felt the pumping of their hooves and heard the cracking of branches as they ran off into the woods together. She looked at the photographs, but they were nothing but smears of green and brown.

She realizes the futility of what she's doing. She unties her apron, folds it neatly over the chair, then goes out to her van to cry.

Fourth of July

East Hampton

Town of East Hampton

Est. 1648

Public Notice

Regarding the upcoming Fourth of July celebrations, owing to the delicate nature of the piping plover and least tern nesting grounds along the beaches, and the ongoing threat to these endangered species in the area, the Town of East Hampton's public fireworks display has been postponed again this year.

All unauthorized private fireworks demonstrations are prohibited. Violators may be arrested and fined pursuant to section 11-0303 and 11-0321 of the Fish and Wildlife Law, New York State of Environmental Conservation.

A tentative rescheduling has been set for Labor Day. Thank you for your cooperation.

Happy Independence Day!

Chapter 29

"Hey." Toni is surprised to see Vic up so early, especially after a long weekend.

"Morning, bella." They kiss cheeks. "I thought it was your day off."

"It is. But lots to do." She ties on an apron. "What about you? Anything wrong?"

"Why?"

"Because you only make the mozzarella when something's wrong."

He strains a large batch of cheese curd through a metal colander. "It relaxes me."

"Why do you need relaxing?"

"I dunno. Things."

He backs away from the vat and she steps forward to sprinkle salt over the cheese.

"Thanks for being so specific."

Toni looks around the kitchen for clues. There are several slit-open envelopes on the staff table.

"Have you sent in the application yet?"

"You asked me that already."

"Have you?"

"I'm not even sure we're going to do it this year. Registration's so expensive." Vic presses the curd through a sieve. It emerges smooth and stretchy. Toni takes one side of it and they begin to tug on it like pizza dough.

"The most important food festival of the year? Of course it's worth it."

"You never know. Could be a total waste of money. I bumped into Larry O'Gorman yesterday. He's got to be out of the place by the end of August."

"What?" Toni feels a tug in her heart. The O'Gormans owned an ice-cream parlor on the highway; Toni worked there for a summer years ago and still loved their dipped cones. "What happened?"

"They expanded last year. Maybe they were having a little trouble before that, I don't know. But their mortgage company went under and some hedge fund bought it out. Probably for fifty cents on the dollar. I bet they'll turn it into a condo or night club or something. The vultures. They'll own half the island by next year."

"You see? That's what I mean. It's more important than ever to do F-4. People have to know we're out there, Dad. If you're not going to do it, I will."

"All right, bella. If it makes you happy, go ahead." He rolls off a tiny ball of fresh mozzarella and holds it out for her. She nibbles it and utters the first Italian phrase he ever taught her: *"Cibo degli dei."*

Food of the gods.

Chapter 30

Well before the eastern tip of Long Island became known for astronomical real estate prices and Gunite pools, it was responsible for more fishing than its relatively small coastline would suggest. Old South Fork families have been relying on the sea's bounty since the 1600s—in particular, the very eastern tip of the island: Montauk. Unlike the rest of the Hamptons, Montauk does not submit so easily to sod. The tended lawns and classic homes of the western villages are replaced by overgrown trees and surf shops. Only the most adventurous New Yorkers go all the way to "The End."

—*The Guru's Guide to the Hamptons*

Chris Ohm opens his eyes and is surprised that he doesn't recognize where he is. More than once since he got to the Hamptons he's found uninvited guests passed out in his bed and he's had to find somewhere else to sleep. But this room seems even stranger than most. The ceiling is pink—and very high.

Then he hears seagulls.

He sits up and looks around. He's in the backseat of his Mustang staring at the rolling green of Hither Hills State Park.

He'd been playing poker for how long last night? Eight, ten hours? The numbers on the cards had begun to smear. Frank's attempt to make the perfect mint julep had been replaced by the convenience of keg beer.

Lots of keg beer.

The hours passed. Guests came and went. He made some money. Lost some money.

He got into the Mustang around three, with his surfboard bungeed in the trunk; he drove east along Old Montauk Highway, taking hills and knolls. The sky was sugared with stars above him. He came to a sandy clearing on the south side of the road and a sign that read, THIS IS AN OVERLOOK, NOT A BATHING BEACH. ONE-HOUR PARKING. Beyond a crop of grasses, he saw the dark slate of the Atlantic. He climbed in the backseat and fell asleep.

The sky is like cotton candy pulled apart above him as he opens the trunk. He strips out of his shorts and into a wetsuit. Grabs his yellow longboard and steps down through picky grasses to the beach.

Two men in high boots and frayed sweaters stand in the surf with fishing rods. They look as if they've been peeled from a package of frozen fish and pasted on a Whittemore canvas. The sky has changed, more orange than pink now. He hears the spinning and clicking of their lines.

The water fights him as he climbs on his board and paddles out. He pumps toward a break, lifting his head, waiting to feel the water rise beneath him. But the wave closes out and never materializes. He paddles farther. His heart pounds as he rises to his feet, trying to catch the next break. But the wave subsides quickly and he falls in, not fighting it, just letting the water take him. He emerges into yet a different color dawn. He tries to stand several times but can't catch a break, falling headfirst, then feetfirst, then butt first into the waves.

He can almost hear his father's voice: "Surfing is an utter waste of time. Worse than golf."

"It's not a waste if I like doing it," Chris would say. But his logic was lost on Dr. Ohm.

Back then, nothing could make him forget about girls more easily than surfing. But he's still thinking about her.

Maybe hasn't stopped thinking about her.

He straddles the board, catching his breath, and looks back toward shore. The men are slivers along the sand. He's already come too far.

The current takes him closer to the fishermen than when he went out. He hears them chuckling at him. One of them wraps his catch in old newspapers. He can't imagine how ridiculous he must've looked to them in his neoprene suit trying to hang ten.

"How's the fishing?" he asks, a little winded.

"Better than the surfing," the tall one says. His face is craggy and he has a patchy beard. Captain Gorton himself.

"Maybe I should lose the board next time. Pick up a rod."

"Maybe," says the Captain, laughing.

Chris heads back across the sand. He doesn't see the other man drop a flounder onto a back issue of the *East Hampton Sun*. The man's weathered hands fold up the society pages one by one. By the time the photo of Toni wearing a black cocktail dress and a big smile on her face comes into view, Chris is already back at his car.

Chapter 31

"Are you okay?" An elderly woman peers over the top of her glasses.

"Yes, absolutely. Something in my eye, that's all."

"Need a tissue?" Mrs. Mayhew holds up a box from her desk.

"No, I'm fine." Toni stares at the pretty box. It has purple flowers. Flowers make her think of the wedding. The wedding makes her think of food. Which makes her think of catering. Which makes her think of failing—again.

"Well, maybe just one . . ." She plucks one out. "Or two."

The woman types on a keyboard as Toni dabs her eyes.

How many times has she been in the Town Hall Permits Office? For parking, for signage applications, design changes, driver's licenses, and, of course, registrations for various festivals, like F-4. In fact, Toni had been here for almost every kind of permit on the big sign next to Mrs. Mayhew's desk except the first one on the list: Marriage License.

She blows her nose.

"You sure you're okay? My coffee break's coming up. I'm all ears."

"No, I'm fine. Thanks. It's my day off. I've got tons to do."

Mrs. Mayhew hits Print. "Registration fees went up this year," she says. "Susan Schumacher still bought four booths."

"So I heard."

Mrs. Mayhew presses a stamp into her blue ink pad, squaring up the edges. "Good luck, Toni. Wonderful to have you back."

There are no secrets in the Hamptons. That's the one thing Toni had forgotten about the place. Everyone knows everybody's business. Who's dating who. Who's divorcing who. Who's having an affair with whom. Who's pregnant, and is it a boy, a girl, or twins. Who's having money problems. Who scored big in hedge funds or lost it all in real estate. Who's suing whom for what and how much, and who's representing them. All the way through the list of life's many secrets, up to and including how many booths the competition has at the Seventh Annual Foodies for Fibromyalgia Festival.

That's one of the things Toni misses most about the city: the anonymity of it. In New York she could cry in public without someone asking if she's okay. She remembers being on the subway after the last time she saw Kevin. She stood pressed shoulder-to-shoulder with other passengers. Some held briefcases, some shopping bags, others had their hair done for holiday parties.

She let herself feel what had just happened to her. That she had sat across from the man she thought she was going to marry for the first time in six months. That his firm had been so impressed with his work for the ballet company they were going to make him a partner. So what if they hadn't met for those sexy trysts at the Holiday Inn in Boise like they said they were going to? So what if he had stopped answering her texts and e-mails right away?

He was back and it was Christmas and he was going to make everything better. The restaurant. The money problems. The fear. She might even confess to buying that stupid Smurf wedding cake topper on eBay.

Maybe he even had a ring.

But then he started talking about meeting someone new. He kept using her name—Nadia—as if Toni knew her.

Nadia thinks, Nadia said, Nadia likes.

Toni's hands were remarkably steady on the stem of her wineglass when he said, "I thought I should tell you in person" and kissed her forehead. She couldn't believe it. Her life was blowing up like a plateglass window in front of her eyes and she just stared at it without even backing away.

She wasn't sure exactly when she started crying, only that by the time she was on the subway the tears were streaming down her cheeks. Nobody around her turned to stare. They all held firm to their own grip of the train—and the world—and let her cry in peace. It was as if they understood that sometimes you just have to cry on the subway. No harm done. But not in East Hampton. Here, if you shed a tear, someone held out a Kleenex box and asked you for coffee.

Even though it's her day off, she drives to the restaurant and oversees a shipment of root vegetables. Then poultry. She places an order with the linen supplier. Takes Tucker for a walk. She drives to Lotus Blossom Yoga in Wainscott for her first chance to "relax" in two weeks. She keeps a notepad on the corner of her mat and jots down things that occur to her. It makes the instructor laugh.

She calls her father and tells him she's going to Mulford Farm to look for that trivet. He tells her to use a bag of sugar like everyone else. She says it doesn't look as nice.

She finds a parking space across from Hook Pond just outside the white tents of the Mulford Farm Antiques Show. She looks at the cygnets, wobbling along the banks behind their mother, still traveling single file.

She turns toward the fair with her heavy red schoolbag. She doesn't notice she's parked directly behind a gold Mustang with a yellow surfboard bungeed inside the trunk.

Chapter 32

Mulford Farmstead on James Lane is a collection of some of the most important colonial farm buildings in New York State. Originally built in 1680, it's listed on the National Register of Historic Places. Ten generations of farmers lived and worked this land. To visit it, across from the site of the first church in East Hampton, is to step back in time.

—*The Guru's Guide to the Hamptons*

The white tents are high and peaked as if for a traveling circus. Toni steps into the first aisle, following the same pattern she's used since she was twelve years old. The other customers browsing the tables move slowly. The smell of furniture polish mingles with the scent of grass. She walks from booth to booth, checking prices, provenances, invariably putting things down. Her gaze moves from trinkets and knickknacks to the faces of the vendors. She's known most of them for so many years that she has no problem recognizing them and calling them by name.

"Hey, Toni," says a slim man in a bow tie.

"Hey, Mr. Cavanaugh." She gives him a smile as she handles a vintage Anchor Hocking trifle bowl. She has a thing for bowls. So decorative, yet so useful.

She's inspecting the stamp on the bottom just as Chris Ohm passes behind her to look at an old Gibson guitar.

"Just browsing?" asks Mr. Cavanaugh.

"No, something particular actually."

She takes out the vintage smoothing iron and explains that she has to find a matching trivet for it. She lost the original months ago during her move out of Dash and has been carrying the iron around ever since in search of a replacement.

The man inspects her iron, an Archibald Kenrick with a decorative shield, six pounds, circa 1895, then begins looking through his collection of vintage appliances. He finds a trivet—the low three-footed pedestal the iron would originally have rested on over a hot stove or fire. Toni puts her iron on top of it; it's the same material as her original one—black wrought iron—but it's in the shape of a diamond, not a heart.

"It's close. But not quite right."

"I can give you a good price on it."

"I'd love to, but I really want to find the right match. The one I had was perfect. In the shape of a—"

She stops when she hears the opening chords of a familiar song. She turns to see a man with a wrinkled T-shirt and baggy board shorts curled over the neck of a six-string guitar. His hair is shaggy and there's scruff on his face. Spread out around him is a miniature orchestra of vintage mandolins, saxophones, and clarinets. A small crowd has gathered to listen to him play. The acoustics of the tent make the fair feel like a country church.

Toni loves that song. "Eye of the Hurricane" by David Wilcox. It was one of a few she tried to learn during summer nights around a bonfire.

The man is lost in concentration, licking the corner of his lip. He doesn't seem to be aware of his audience as he looks up to twist a tuner knob—then he sees her. He freezes.

A smile comes to Toni's face. She's pleasantly surprised she recognizes him from that day on Main Street. "Hi, there," she says. "I remember you."

Chapter 33

As a rule, Chris Ohm does not believe in fate. He's never had his palm read or his chart done. The metaphysical world has held no fascination for him since a philosophy class at Harvard, and he stopped saying his prayers when he was eight.

Yet looking up from the strings of the Gibson and seeing the girl from 92nd Street smiling at him in the soft white light of the tent makes him realize how soldiers must feel waking up in the infirmary to see a pretty nurse smiling down on them, telling them everything's going to be okay.

The audience gives a little round of applause and starts to disperse. He just stares at her.

"How's your toe?"

"All . . . all better," he says, coming to his senses. "I'm sorry." His hand goes out. "I didn't introduce myself properly last time. Chris Ohm."

Ohm, she thinks. A yoga instructor once told her that's the sound the universe makes. *Ommmmmm.* Though she's never heard it herself.

"Toni Fratelli," she says. She likes the feeling of his palm and fingers around hers as they shake hands. Warm and rough-soft like an old beach blanket.

"So, you interested?" asks the man at the booth. "It's a steal at five hundred."

"I'll take it." Chris hands over the guitar.

"There's no case for it."

"That's okay." He pulls out his wallet and begins counting bills. "Oh . . . uh, do you take credit cards?"

"Sorry . . . no."

"I don't seem to have enough cash right now. . . . I'll come back for it," he says.

The man shrugs and puts the Gibson back on its stand.

Toni feels embarrassed for him being short of money and changes the subject. "You're good at that," she says. "I don't know many people who can play David Wilcox."

"Too many nights on the beach," he says.

He motions to the grounds as if asking permission to walk with her; she smiles and nods. He tries to sneak a glance at her ring finger as they walk. He's never been afraid to back down from a fight, and he just wants to size up his competition. But her left hand is down at her side, holding her big red schoolbag.

"Where's your dog?" he asks. *Stupid question, stupid question.*

"You've heard of the saying, 'A bull in a china shop'?" she asks.

"Yeah."

"They've got nothing on my crazy dog at an antiques fair." Her eyes widen when she sees some vintage toasters.

"Hi, Toni!" says a plump gentleman behind the booth. "How're things in the restaurant business?"

"Like my dad says, people have to eat. You?"

Mr. Newell shrugs. "Not bad. All things considered. What about the wedding plans? How's all that coming?"

Chris's stomach drops; he watches her closely.

"Slow," she laughs. "As you can imagine."

"I bet."

She finds an antique trivet and holds it next to the iron. "Almost. But not quite."

"That's my Toni. Always the perfectionist. I'll keep an eye out for you."

She thanks him and then continues walking with Chris slowly through the aisles. To be the slowest-moving couple at the Mulford Farm Antiques Show is no small feat, but they're doing it. Retirees with walkers are passing them on the outside.

He asks her if she collects vintage irons.

"Not really," she says. "I collect dishes. I love old plates, cups, silverware, seltzer bottles, bowls especially. But I need the iron and trivet to make sandwiches."

"You need an iron to make sandwiches?" He seems confused.

"It's a long story," she says.

They find themselves standing in the sunshine at the very edge of the market. She didn't find a trivet, but she did end up with the Anchor Hocking trifle bowl. She couldn't believe Chris *Ohhhm* actually had the patience to wait while she debated buying it for fifteen minutes. Kevin wouldn't set foot in an antique market. He said old things gave him hives.

As she puts the bowl into the back of her old VW van, Chris wants to tell her she's probably marrying the wrong man. But he can't tell her she's marrying the wrong man; he just met her. So he settles for, "So when's the big day?"

She gives him a curious look.

"The wedding."

"September fifth." She frowns. "How did you know?"

"Everyone keeps asking you. And I saw all those wedding magazines you had before."

"Riiiight." She hefts her purse on her shoulder again and points to the street. "I'm going into town. Are you—"

"Absolutely," Chris says.

She smiles, shocked by how happy she is that he didn't say good-bye at the car.

They cross the street, stepping over the little wooden bridge by Hook Pond, past the worn old gravestones on toward Main Street.

Chris searches for an appropriate question for a bride-to-be. "So . . . um . . . did you get your dress yet?"

"We're going in to shop for them next week."

"Oh? That's . . . nice."

They get to the short tree-lined blocks leading to the village shops. He goes to look at his watch, hoping for some way to hint about lunch. But he stopped wearing a watch when he left New York. So he just plunges right in: "I don't suppose you're hungry, are you? I was thinking of grabbing something to eat."

"Actually, I'm saving my appetite for popcorn."

They're on the crowded sidewalk now, stepping around gaggles of models and playboys and sunburned kids.

"You see a movie on a hot summer day?" he asks.

"It's the best time. On a rainy day, you'll be on line for hours. When it's sunny, nobody wants to sit in the dark for two hours. They're all down at the beach."

"Or window-shopping," he says, sidestepping a pair of well-coiffed women.

"Exactly."

Chris feels the heat of the summer day baking down on him. He wonders if it's actually the sun—or just his nerves.

"Are you meeting anyone?"

She shakes her head. "I like going by myself. That way I can cry in private."

"Do you usually cry in movies?"

"I cry at coming-soon trailers," she says, laughing. "I cry at commercials. But romantic comedies? They're the worst. I was a complete and total wreck for six months after *Say Anything*." And then she stops and wonders why she told him that.

She's feeling the sun today too.

Chris wants to keep her talking; maybe she'll miss the beginning of the movie and they can go for lunch.

"So . . . the lucky man," he begins, "what does he do?"

"Oh. It has something to do with the Internet. Advertising. Something like that. Anyway, he doesn't *have* to do anything. You know how Ron Perelman and Donald Trump are rich?"

"Yeah."

"They've got nothing on Hudson. His family owns half of New York. Below Fifteenth Street, anyway."

"Wow, lucky girl."

"No kidding."

Outside the large white brick building on Main Street with a big sign on the wall that reads East Hampton Cinema, Toni begins digging for her wallet. The posters and marquee announce *Saving Face* as being "The Date Movie of the Summer."

"I'd ask you to come," she says, "but I don't know if you're into romantic comedies."

"Wouldn't your fiancé mind?"

Toni's eyes widen. "My *what*?"

"The one who owns half of New York? Below Fifteenth Street, anyway."

Toni starts to laugh. She actually has to bend over at the waist and put her hand on the wall to steady herself. She tells him she's not getting married—her best friend is. She's the caterer and maid of honor—but *no*, it's not her wedding.

He gives a big smile. "I love romantic comedies then," he says.

Five minutes later they sit beside each other watching the coming-soon trailers. They each have cold drinks and on the armseat between them is a large box of popcorn with double butter. As the lights dim and they take turns digging for handfuls of popcorn, Toni shakes her head.

Fiancé.

What a joke.

He offered to pay for her ticket, but she insisted on buying her own. The poor guy. His board shorts. His shaggy hair. He should save his money for that Gibson.

As the credits start, Toni thinks the day feels strange and familiar at once. She doesn't know how many dates with boys she's had in this theater. Or how many movies she's seen here with Layla when they were growing up.

Shouldn't she feel awkward? Sitting with a stranger? Shouldn't her hands be shaking? But instead, she feels filled with warmth and lightness, like a whole body sigh.

Their hands brush occasionally as they reach for the popcorn. The first few times they look over at each other and smile apologetically. But after a while, they get into the rhythm of it, letting each other take turns, and when their hands do brush, they don't stop and smile apologetically at each other anymore.

They just let it happen.

The movie is halfway through when Toni realizes some of the actors look familiar, but the turns in the plot have stopped making sense. She hasn't been paying attention. She's been thinking too much about—has in fact been completely absorbed by—the rush of heat that runs up her arm every time she touches his hand.

Chapter 34

Didi sits in her private office in the pool pavilion staring down at the genealogy report for Layla Marie Sullivan. She rips it up and tosses it in the garbage can.

The main room of the pool house is fit for a queen, naturally. But Didi's private office is different, almost monastic. It smells like cedar from the custom cabinets. The walls are plain. A dehumidifier and ionizer hum quietly in the corner, and there are UV filters on the windows overlooking the woodshed.

On a large table in front of her is a roll of parchment paper held down with Tiffany paperweights. Little leaves and vines are drawn here and there; hundreds of names branch out in all directions written in Didi's small, slanted calligraphy.

The family tree.

Didi took up the hobby ten years ago when she was forced to give up tanning and horseback riding during the summer. She and Percy Beecher of the Empire Genealogical Society had actually traced her side back to twelfth-century Brittany.

And now Hudson was trying to insert an illegitimate Bonacker in the space next to his name.

Not if she could help it.

She made a mistake with him somewhere. She sees that now. Maybe many mistakes. It's almost as if he had been a decorating project that she didn't get a chance to plan as she went along. So all the Louis XIV tables and Imari vases and Le Corbusier chairs coexisted in the same room at the same time—and it was a clashing mess. A child was basically a living testament to all the mistakes one made as a parent. The only difference was with a child, you couldn't rip everything out and start over again.

Chapter 35

"What can I say?" Toni says. The crowds on the sidewalk are heavier and the sun has shifted in the sky. "I love romantic comedies. Must be because my love life is such a joke."

"I probably have you beat."

"Don't count on it. Let's see. My first boyfriend ended up being gay. He's traveling the continent with his boyfriend right now. We're still really good friends. Every time I broke up with somebody, I would go to him and cry: 'You're not supposed to be gay! I'm supposed to be with you!'"

"I had one of those too."

"A gay boyfriend?"

He laughs. "Girlfriend. In college. She left me to join the Peace Corps. Speaking of romantic comedies."

"Not bad," Toni says. She counts on her fingers. "But I've also had a doctor who ended up being a drug addict. A family therapist who was afraid of commitment. An investment banker who was married—twice. And most recently, an entertainment lawyer who left me for a ballerina. And not even the prima ballerina. Just one of the girls in the chorus line."

"Remind me not to take you to *Swan Lake*," he says.

They stand outside the old VW van across from Hook Pond. "I meant to ask you before," he says, "where'd you get this? Hippie eBay?"

She laughs. "*Hair* was our school play in sophomore year. Layla and I painted it."

"Wow. I'm impressed. I was Berger in eleventh grade and all we did was wear headbands."

"I'm an A-type," she says.

There's an awkward silence. He shuffles his feet, looking down. She shuffles hers, looking up. She's trying to figure out how to ask him for lunch without seeming too desperate when he says, "Are you hungry? I was going to get something to eat."

"Starved," she says, exhaling in relief.

They take the Mustang east along Montauk Highway, driving with the top down. Toni points out shortcuts along the way, restaurants like the Lobster Roll, crab shacks, and ice-cream parlors where she used to work.

"Remind me to take you to Joni's," she says. "They have the best breakfast wrap on the East End."

"You worked there too?"

"Not unless you count standing on line for two hours work. But worth every second. Anyway, that's all behind me."

"What?"

"All of it. Everything I did wrong in New York. I worked eighteen, twenty hours a day for years, and what did it get me? Dumped and in debt. I'm so over it. I'm making a fresh start out here. I want to relax more and enjoy my life." She stretches back, putting her hands behind her head.

"I like the sound of that," Chris says. "Can I play too?"

She laughs, looking at his shaggy hair and rumpled clothes. "I don't think you need any pointers in that department."

When Toni and Chris get to the Meeting Place Restaurant, it's full—as usual—so Toni suggests a picnic in Amagansett Square. They go back to the car to grab a blanket, and Toni sees the pillow in Chris's trunk.

Is he so broke he sleeps in his car?

But rather than feeling a surge of judgment toward him, she's filled with intense curiosity—and an attraction she has not felt in many years.

He notices the look on her face. "I'm not homeless," he says. "I'm staying with friends, but the place has become kind of Animal House Redux. I've had to pass out in the backseat a couple of times."

"Poor you," she says. She can't imagine a laid-back surfer dude trying to find peace in a share house.

As they wait on line for dosas from the Chutney Company and pizza from Astro's, she tries to learn more about him. She finds out that he was born and raised in Malibu. That he went to Harvard Business School. That he's in the Hamptons for the summer with friends. When she asks what he does for a living, he seems uncomfortable, shuffling his feet and looking down. He tells her he's "between gigs" right now and she wonders if he got laid off. Maybe he's too embarrassed to talk about it, and she doesn't want to press him.

He seems more interested in her than talking about himself, anyway, so she tells him the story of the rise and fall of Dash. He seems supportive and sympathetic in a way that Kevin never did.

She wonders why their occasional silences feel so comfortable to her already. Why they can just stand there on line, smiling at each other or letting their hands touch. She feels pulses of heat moving through her. Up through her chest and into her head like a sugar rush, then back down again in a wave.

They spread the blanket on the clover-filled grass of Amagansett Square. Lone readers enjoy the latest from BookHampton sitting in Adirondack chairs beneath the shade of chestnut trees.

"I'm glad I got a chance to show you this," she says. "Amagansett's not changing as fast as some of the other towns. This is kind of the way East Hampton used to be. Except you can get iced coffee now. Which I like. I'm not waving a placard against *all* progress," she says with a laugh.

They unpack the food and open a bottle of wine. "I just love it here. It's one of my favorite places in the world. Mind you, I have a thousand favorite places out here. I should take you to Chester Drive some time. We used to rent a cottage there when I was a little girl. The sunsets are absolutely—" She stops and watches him for a moment, narrowing her eyes.

"What?"

"Nothing. It's just that you seem so familiar to me. Like I've met you before or something. It's almost like déjà vu."

Tell her, Chris. Tell her now. "Toni . . . what if we have met before?"

"You mean, like in another life?"

He laughs. "No, not in another life." He stops, swallows. "I mean, like in this one."

She flaps a hand at him. "Oh, I know. That time on Main Street. That was so sweet of you. None of those New York guys would've stopped to help me. Especially outside a van that wasn't worth five grand. I'm so totally over those guys. All those self-absorbed jerks in the city who just care about their careers. My ex was like that. Everything was work, work, work. Funny thing is, I was too busy myself to even realize it." She laughs to herself. "But you're not like them, are you? You're so . . . relaxed. I really envy that."

He watches her for a moment. *Tell her, Chris.* "Toni . . . it wasn't just on Main—"

A voice from the walkway. "Toni?"

Toni turns to see a young woman pushing a double stroller with twins.

"It *is* you!" says the woman. "I heard you were coming back!"

"Hey! Hi, there!" As Toni gets up, she leans into Chris, whispering, "I went to high school with this woman. It's bizarre. I can remember her face—but for some reason I always forget her name. And it's too awkward to ask now. Can you introduce yourself?"

He nods and Toni runs over to meet the woman, giving her a big hug. Chris watches them chatter about how big the kids are getting. He walks over, feeling sheepish.

"Chris Ohm," he says.

"Claire Rafferty."

Of course! Toni thinks. *Claire!*

And then they begin to reminisce about high school; Chris doesn't know if he's disgusted with himself or relieved that he missed his chance to confess.

Chapter 36

"What do you want?" Vic asks Tucker. The dog stares at him from the braided rug in the dining room. "I just walked you."

Tucker whimpers.

Vic sits at the table in front of his ledgers and a large stack of envelopes and bills. He looks at the clock.

"What happened to her? She's been gone all day."

Tucker's tail makes a thumping sound on the floor.

"I don't know. I think I'm going senile already. I feel like grounding her. Why doesn't she just pick up her cell and call me? Let me know she's okay?" He remembers how responsible she was when she was young. She'd call from the public phones at Main Beach every hour after ten o'clock. He thanked his lucky stars that she wasn't like Layla. He loved the girl, but with her short skirts and her high heels and her makeup? He'd mark the bottles in the liquor cabinet when she came over. He thought Layla would be the one to be single forever. That Toni, the organized, sensible one, would settle down first.

He looks at his watch again. "Oh, what am I doing? She's a big girl, right? She can look after herself."

Tucker makes a sound in his throat, half whine, half growl.

"Can I ask you something?"

Tucker shifts his weight on his paws.

"They say it's a dog's life. What does that mean exactly?"

Tucker looks around, then back at Vic and whimpers.

"I didn't think so. Listen, you ever tried my espresso? You'd like it. Double shot. That'll put hair on your chest." With one last look at his watch, Vic gets up from the table.

Chapter 37

The sun is going down, the sky a wash of pink and peach, as Toni drives the Mustang down Bridge Lane, a picturesque road flanked by cornfields, drooping elm trees, and black-eyed Susans. Enormous mansions are set back on broad lots, looking more like hotels than summer homes, some of them with FOR SALE signs out front: Corcoran, Sotheby's, Randall.

"This isn't real estate," Chris says looking around. "It's surreal estate."

"No kidding."

"But I bet we're looking at several hundred million dollars of distressed debt."

Toni frowns at him. *Distressed debt?* That seemed pretty technical for a surfer. But then she remembers he did say he went to business school.

She drives across a small wooden bridge and pulls onto the shoulder. She points out a large rambling shingle-style mansion with white shutters and a peaked roof sitting on a private pond. The water reflects the image of the house and the sunset above it until it seems like a study in photorealism, a Howard Kanovitz canvas come to life.

"That's my favorite house in the Hamptons," she says. "Besides the one on Chester Drive, I mean." She leans back and stares at it. "Don't you just love it? It looks like a fairy tale. As if nothing could ever go wrong in a place like that.

I used to wonder what it was that I loved so much about that house. Or any of the places out here. Do I want to live in them now? Or do I want to be baking cookies in them with my kids ten years from now? Do I want to be a grandmother in them? Or do I wish I had been a little girl in them?"

He just watches her.

"I used to believe people who lived in a house like that couldn't have any problems. But now I think they have more problems than anyone else."

"Toni . . . can I see you again?"

The question is so sudden, she actually gasps.

"Tomorrow, maybe?"

She feels her cheeks get warm. "I . . . I don't think so. We're going into the city to shop for dresses."

"What about Wednesday?"

"Oh, I don't know. It's so crazy at the restaurant right now."

"All day? I thought you were trying to relax."

"I'm still working on that."

"Working on relaxing? That doesn't sound right."

"I'm just too busy to relax right now. See?" She takes out her notebook and flips to her To Do List. "Wednesday, I have to get up at five to meet the fishmonger. Then I walk the dog. The rest of the deliveries start around six. Then we have to prep for lunch. Then I have to work the lunch rush. I walk the dog again at two. Then I have to write a script for Plum TV."

"What's that?"

"I didn't tell you? I'm actually going to be on Plum TV! It's a local television station out here. Layla knows the guys who started it. She got me an appearance." She goes back to the list.

"At three I go for my yoga class. If I didn't do yoga, I'd go crazy. At five, depending on how busy it is, I might have to work dinner. After my shift, I have to *practice* whatever it is I'm making for Plum TV so I don't screw it up on air. That should take me until at least one in the morning and then I have to—"

"Walk the dog."

"Yes."

"I'm sorry I asked."

"I should've warned you. Sully says I suffer from Now What Syndrome. That it's an actual disease that I have to keep busy all the time."

"I think Sully is right. Is there any time between six forty-five and, say, two in the morning that I could take you to dinner?"

She looks at him. "I don't think it's a good idea."

"Why not?"

"I'm not . . . ready."

"For dinner?"

"For . . ." She motions around. "All this."

"What's this?"

"You know," she whispers. *A relationship.*

"What about Joni's? And Chester Drive?"

"Some other time maybe?" she says. She's surprised by her own reticence, but she can't help herself.

"All right. But for the record I think ballerinas are scrawny and have too many veins."

She smiles at him, then opens the driver's-side door. "Thanks for letting me drive your car."

"You're welcome." He gets out and they meet in front of the hood. "I never let anyone drive my car."

"I feel privileged," she says. She tries to walk past him, but he stops her gently.

"Toni, no matter how busy you are, you still have to eat."

"That's true. If I don't eat I get dizzy. My blood sugar. I'm gluco-sensitive."

"You told me at dinner."

"Oh, yeah. You should stop me when I talk too much."

"Okay."

He takes her arms in his hands and urges her closer to him. She feels the world shift beneath her feet.

"Are you going to do what I think you're going to do?" she asks.

"That depends." He stares at her mouth, a small smile on his face. "What do you think I'm going to do?"

"Kiss me."

"Okay." He leans forward and presses his lips against hers. They both feel it. A slight swoon toward the car. That tumbling rush of heat. He stops and looks at her.

"That wasn't an order," she says.

"Semantics." He kisses her again, more slowly this time. They're still kissing when he lifts her easily onto the front of the car. The metal hood beneath her legs still feels warm from the engine.

"You know we just met," she says through their kisses.

He presses toward her, separating her thighs slightly with his to get closer. "You don't kiss on the first date?"

"Was this a date?"

Through his kisses he says, "It started out with antique shopping at Mulford Farm, lasted through one date movie . . ." He's still kissing her. "Popcorn, soda, a picnic on the grass . . ." More kisses. "Iced coffee from Sylvester & Co. . . . Ice cream from Snowflake . . . and a drive to your favorite house." He stops and looks her in the eyes. "I think that qualifies as at least two dates. Possibly three."

"You're right," she says, wrapping her arms around his neck as they start to kiss again.

Chapter 38

"Don't worry," Hudson whispers. "He won't come in here. He never comes in here."

Hudson and Layla are in the living room when Henry walks in the front door stamping his shoes. They're on the couch, completely naked, their clothes on the floor beside them.

"Nice timing, Dad," he whispers.

Layla holds her breath. The chandelier in the hall turns on. She sees the furniture around them begin to glint. Their bodies are in shadow from the sofa back as they lie perfectly still. Henry opens the hall closet, takes off his shoes. Hudson starts to move again, thrusting slowly.

"Stop," she whispers, slapping him.

"It's okay, he won't care."

The library light turns on. Crystal decanters are opened. The sound of ice cubes. Then:

Pock.

Brrrrrr.

Henry is practicing his golf putting again.

"He left the light on," Hudson says. "Good. I can watch you."

He spins her around and she eases onto him, sitting up. She feels so exposed in the light of the hall chandelier. His strokes become deeper. She has to bite her lip to stop from crying out. One of Didi's six-hundred-dollar silk pillows tumbles to the floor. They don't pay any attention to it.

When Layla's cell phone starts to ring on the coffee table—they don't pay any attention to that either.

Toni tiptoes up the steps to her bedroom. "Hey, Sully, it's me," she says into her cell. "Sorry to bug you so late. I just wanted to ask if you're still doing my makeup on Friday. I hope so. And they told me not to wear patterns. But is a white blouse too plain?"

She turns on the light in her bedroom. The mauve walls. The posters of Madonna and John Cusack. The ballerina lamp, which for the first time in two months hasn't depressed her.

"Anyway, that's not really why I called. I called because . . ."

Because I miss talking to my shrink.

Because I miss talking to you.

"Because I met someone today," she says. She curls herself into bed, hugging her knees. "He was the guy on Main Street when I made such a doofus out of myself that day. I saw him at the antique fair shopping for guitars. He actually went to an antique market voluntarily. Can you believe that?" She shakes her head in astonishment. "Anyway, he's just this really cool, laid-back surfer dude, and it looks like the only thing he has in the world is his car and I don't even care. I had so much fun with him. It was kind of like being with you, except—"

Beep.

"—we kissed."

The Mustang and the VW were the only cars left on James Lane when they got back to Mulford Farmstead. She felt so close to him, so comfortable with him already, it baffled her to think that just that morning she had actually cried in Town Hall.

He walked her to the driver's-side door. They looked at each other for a long time, their hands entwined. The swans were asleep somewhere in the darkness. He pressed his thigh against hers as if to hold her still for a moment. She felt the muscles in his legs, the bone of his knee against hers; it was shockingly intimate. Then he leaned in and kissed her again. She felt a catch in her breath. The ground rocked unpredictably beneath her feet. The kiss went on and on, until she had to grab him to stop herself from falling.

"I'm glad you're not getting married," he whispered.

"Me too," she said.

Chapter 39

In the morning Didi finds her pillow on the floor beside the coffee table. She picks it up and puts it back on the couch, adjusting the fringe. There's a creamy smear on her custom-made toile de Jouy. It's been a long time since Didi Flagstone has seen the detritus of love on any surface in her house, even a bed—but she recognizes it immediately and it makes her want to vomit.

"Estella!"

Her hands shake as she lights an early cigarette in her Petit Trianon. She should have the sofas reupholstered.

Stripes, maybe.

Or a nice floral.

The whole idea nauseates her. Didi had been forced to give up sex years ago because of her bad back—at least that was the story she told Henry. But it had as much to do with her fear of growing old as with her sciatica.

She had to stop horseback riding for the same reason. The last time Didi had taken a horse on a gallop—at a fox-hunting party at a friend's estate in Leicestershire—she had literally felt her cheeks snap every time the hooves hit the earth. Her cosmetic surgeon had told her to stop her daily jog on the treadmill because the jarring impact of her feet hitting the ground placed undue pressure on her newly tightened cheeks. Eventually, it would make her face fall.

Again.

Didi knew that if running on her treadmill jeopardized her face-lift, then trotting across the English countryside on a hunting pony would completely unravel it. She dismounted right there and walked back to the estate. The resentment she felt when she realized that yet another pleasure of her youth was forbidden, like smoking and tanning, was enough to make her cry.

But as painful as the idea of giving up riding was, it was definitely preferable to falling cheeks. She told her hosts that her back was acting up and stayed indoors for the rest of the weekend. That night, in a grand bedroom of antiques and brocade, Henry told her how tired he was of her "damn sciatica." It was ruining his life.

His life.

As if *he* was the one who suffered from it. But she knew what he meant.

Sex.

For their entire relationship, Didi and Henry had always used the missionary position. As far as Didi was concerned, it was the only acceptable position for sex. Like frontal lobes, opposable thumbs, and art, it was one of the things that separated people from the animals. But having Henry on top of her pumping toward his sluggish orgasms hurt her back so much that afterward she'd turn over in agony and whimper into her pillow.

"Oh, for God's sake, Didi, it wasn't that bad. Why don't you get on top if it hurts so much?"

A few of her more liberal friends told her the same thing.

On top?

Didi had never been on top in her life—but for the first time she started to consider it, if only because she resented any of life's pleasures being withheld from her for any reason, and sex was supposed to be pleasurable, wasn't it? So one night in a tone she usually reserved for agreeing to go to a dreaded social obligation, she told Henry that she would try it "on top."

She was shocked by the little gleam in his eye.

She was nervous about it all week. Not only did being on top seem primitive and pornographic, but she didn't like the idea of her breasts and naked body being so exposed. So she bought a new peignoir. It took her two hours to decide which one. Black or red seemed right for a night of passion, but both were too tacky for a woman of forty-five, so she decided on a sheer lacy maroon.

On the given night, Henry was in the big king bed waiting for her. When he saw her open her boudoir door, he turned off the television. As she crawled into bed and swung her leg over him, it reminded her of mounting her pony those mornings long ago at the Topping Club. When Henry started to buck and move around, it felt so much like riding a horse, she almost laughed out loud.

But the giddiness was short-lived. Because thinking about horseback riding made her think about her face-lift, which in turn made her think about getting old. Could being on top like this, moving up and down, dislodge her face-lift too?

She looked down at Henry to see if he could tell she was worrying about her wrinkles and not sex. But his eyes were tightly closed.

He was almost sixty at the time and just seeing him made her feel old.

The shaking fat on his belly, the gray hair on his chest, the spindly arms, pale from shoulder to elbow, then leathery brown from wearing golf shirts most of his waking life.

Suddenly she wasn't thinking about sex at all anymore but face-lifts and getting old. She tried to focus on something else. The headboard. Mint green tufted satin.

But was that a loose button on it?

Several minutes into "it," Henry's movements became erratic and stiff. The grunting finally stopped and he went limp beneath her. Didi didn't know if he had climaxed—or just given up. When he let out a long sigh and patted her thigh, she closed her robe and crawled off him.

"Was that better?"

"I suppose," she said. She leaned into the headboard. "This button is falling off. I think we should recover it. Pink, maybe."

They slept in separate bedrooms after that.

Chapter 40

"Where were you yesterday?" Vic asks. "*And* last night?"

Toni is in the kitchen at the restaurant, shucking a bucket of fresh clams. She doesn't realize she's smiling to herself—that she has been smiling since she got up.

"Out."

"I figured that." He notices she's wearing a new white blouse, a beige skirt, earrings. "Do you have a date or something?"

"No. We're going into the city to shop for dresses." She keeps smiling to herself, sliding the knife under the hinge of the shell. "Ow!" She nicks her finger, stops to check it. "Didn't break the skin."

Vic is grateful. He can't stand the sight of blood. It opens a pit in him the size of Accabonac Harbor. He goes to the walk-in fridge and takes out a pot of stewed tomatoes. He sits down across from her.

"All right," Vic says. "Who is he?"

"Who is who?"

"I know that smile."

"What smile?"

He motions to her face with his paring knife. "*That* smile."

Toni touches her cheeks, aware now that they're aching. "Oh."

Vic sighs. "What does he do?"

Toni stops and looks at him. "Why is that the first question out of your mouth? What does he *do*? Why can't people just, you know, *be*?"

"Sorry. How old is he?"

"Thirties somewhere, I guess."

"Okay. *Now* what does he do?" He points at her. "You can't say anything this time. That was my second question."

She smiles to herself again. "He's a surfer . . . I think."

"A professional surfer?"

"Nooooo . . ."

"So he's a beach bum?"

"Dad!"

"Let me clarify. When I ask what he does, I'm asking whether or not he's gainfully employed."

"You-know-who was gainfully employed and look what happened with him."

"That's not an answer."

She stands up to drain the clam juice for soup. "He said he was between gigs. I didn't want to press him about it."

"That doesn't sound good."

"He didn't seem too concerned. I just don't think he's into that sort of . . . stuff."

"Jobs, you mean?"

"I mean, he's a bit of a wanderer. A free spirit. He doesn't even have a cell phone. Or a watch. He plays David Wilcox songs on old guitars."

"David who?"

"I'm just saying he's different from all the other guys I've known. I've had it with those self-important New York jerks who do nothing but think and breathe work twenty-four/seven."

"So he's an unemployed bum, is that what you're saying?"

"Dad!"

"Toni, if you want to swear off high-powered entertainment lawyers, you have my blessing. But you don't have to go all the way to unemployed bum for a change of pace. There are a whole bunch of jobs in there before you actually hit unemployed bum."

"Like what?"

"Like police officers. Insurance salesmen. Carpenters."

"Carpenters?"

"Yes, carpenters."

"You want me to date a carpenter?"

"What's wrong with carpenters? You have something against them?"

"Of course not. I don't have anything against any of them. But my whole point is, it doesn't matter what he does. Not to me—and it shouldn't to you." She changes the subject. "Am I working tomorrow night?"

"Why? You have a date?"

"What if I do?"

"Then you're working."

"Dad, I'm not fourteen anymore. You don't have to put me on the late shift to protect my chastity."

"I know, bella," he says. "I just don't want you to get hurt again . . ."

And she feels that one like a punch in the chest.

She's still thinking of his words when she stands at table 3, staring down at her order pad. *I just don't want you to get hurt again.*

The restaurant is full for the lunch rush, everyone laughing, talking. In the background, Dean Martin sings "That's Amore."

There's a skinny blonde at table 3. "Did you hear me?"

"I'm sorry," Toni says, coming back to reality. "Yes. Chef's salad, dressing on the side. Thank you." She takes the menus and ducks through the swinging door to the waitress station.

"Layla's here," Rhonda says. "She's outside having a smoke." Then, "Uh-oh."

"Uh-oh what?"

"Uh-oh that." She points to tomato sauce on Toni's white blouse.

"Shit!"

And it was a new blouse too! She knew she shouldn't have worn new clothes to work. She douses a rag with soda and rubs at the stain.

Damnit.

How many stains had she rubbed off blouses in her life?

How many salads with dressing on the side had she delivered to skinny blondes at table 3?

Too many.

She wasn't supposed to be doing this anymore. She was supposed to be a celebrated chef! The one thing that had given her any pleasure in months was the idea of this "new man" in her life, Chris Ohm.

And now her father was ruining even that with his paranoia.

She gives up on her blouse and grabs two fresh salads from the fridge. She turns to Jerome, a red-haired high school senior who busses tables. "Can you take these to table three? Dressing on the side for this one. Keep the tip."

Toni hurries through the busy kitchen, feeling as if she's stepped back in time.

They were eighteen years old, getting changed in the staff restroom after a Friday night shift.

"I figured out why I can always spot the richest guy in any room," Layla said, her voice muffled from bending over to brush her hair.

"I'm not sure I want to hear this," Toni said.

Layla flipped her hair back and went to work on her mascara. "You know how pool players say it's all in the wrist?"

"Yeah."

"For me, it's all in the nips."

"Now I'm *sure* I don't want to hear this."

"It's true. My nipples twitch whenever a rich man comes into the room."

"Ewwww."

"I wasn't sure about it at first. I thought maybe I just liked nice cars or expensive watches or something. Which I do, don't get me wrong. But just because a guy has a nice car doesn't mean he's really rich. He could be some schmuck who sells nice cars. But I've always been able to spot the imposters, and lately I've been noticing it's because of my—"

"I get the picture," Toni said.

"The problem is, there are so many rich men around here that I walk down the street and my nipples twitch so much it's like I'm living in a walk-in fridge." She stopped and regarded her reflection. "Do you think I'll ever find him, Toni? A man who makes my nipples twitch forever?"

"Don't worry, Sully. I'm sure you'll marry twitch."

Then they went out to the dance at the Maidstone Club and Toni watched Layla get hit on by practically every man in the room.

If there was anything Layla's taste for rich men did it was make Toni aware that money didn't matter to her at all. At least not very much. She knew the most important qualities about her Prince Charming couldn't be defined by his bank account. She's not sure what *would* define him, of course, because when she thought about him all she saw was the Christmas card.

Her, her husband, three children, and a dog posing in front of the tree. They would all be wearing variations of tartan or forest green. The tree would be draped with gold ribbons and bells. Framed photographs on the mantelpiece behind them would be an infinite reflection of domestic bless.

That the face of the man in the photograph was just a fuzzy blur didn't bother her. She knew he was out there, smiling for no reason at other people, waiting for her to come along. And she knew that he would come along at just the right time (in other words, "in time") and that they'd be together forever.

When she met Kevin Pritchard that night, she thought he was The One.

He had a nice smile. A square jaw. Neat brown hair. He wore a tie to work. Ties symbolized something to her back then, that a man was responsible. Her father always wore ties. That's why she hadn't been afraid to serve breakfast in bed for Kevin that first morning he slept over. Or show him her "hope locker," as Layla called it, of vintage china in the basement. She knew she had found her Prince Charming. The only things missing were the kids, the dog, and the tree.

Which was why it was so devastating when Kevin came home—at Christmas no less!—and told her about the ballerina. It was the first time she was ever worried that she had been wrong all along. Maybe Prince Charming wasn't out there at all.

Chapter 41

"Get *out*! You kissed him?" Layla's blue eyes are wide. They stand in the sunshine on the back steps of the restaurant waiting for their ride. "Was it hot?"

"Extremely hot."

"Did you guys do it?"

"On the hood of his car on Bridge Lane? No."

"But if he's a good kisser, he's a good lover too."

Toni feels herself swoon a bit. "Oh, he's a good kisser, all right."

"So do it! I think half your problem is that you need to get laid. You're thirty years old, Toni. You're almost at your sexual peak. You should get some practice in or you won't know how to climb it when you get there."

Bee-beep!

A pale blue Mercedes pulls in and angles across two parking spots, a pounding dance beat drifting out the windows. *"Hola, amigas!"*

Layla grabs her bag. "So are you going to see him again?"

"I don't know . . . he asked me."

"And what did you say?"

"I told him I was busy."

"Wrong answer."

Tabitha turns down the music and makes affected kissing noises over her shoulder—*Mwah! Mwah!*—as Toni climbs into the cluttered backseat.

"Just move all that aside. I'm a pig. So sue me."

Toni shoves some shopping bags and juice containers out of the way. She notices Tabitha is almost opalescent, glistening like mother-of-pearl from lips to brow bone. Her Cynthia Rowley minidress is so of the moment, she immediately makes Toni feel as if she just stepped out of a Talbots ad.

"What were you guys doing *there*?" Tabitha asks, pulling out of the parking lot.

"Toni had to work."

"You *work* there?"

"My dad owns it."

Layla says, "You've never been there? It's practically an institution. We both worked here growing up. Tan all day, work all night, party down on the beach. Right, Tone?"

"The good old days," Toni says.

"Sounds . . ."—Tabitha searches for the word—"fun."

At the red light at Hook Pond, Tabitha rifles on the seat next to Layla for something.

"Check out page seventy-six." She throws a copy of *Hamptons* in Layla's lap.

Toni leans over the seat to see that Layla and Tabitha have made The Flash, this time for the Art for Life benefit at Russell Simmons's estate. There they are, smiling and linking arms like best friends.

Toni sits back, trying not to feel jealous. She doesn't know if it's the clashing perfume, the lunch shift, or the dance music, but she's already getting a headache.

The light changes, but traffic is so bad that they're practically at a standstill. Tabitha flips down her visor to check her makeup, and Layla follows suit. Layla has always been on good terms with her reflection, but today it seems worse than ever. Toni barely recognizes the self-absorbed expression in her eyes. She stares at herself, picking at her eyelashes, slathering on more lip gloss.

Layla suddenly senses someone watching her. She meets Toni's gaze in the mirror. A smile breaks out on her face. "Want some?" she asks, holding out her YSL lip gloss. "Tastes like strawberries."

Toni smiles, remembering.

"What tastes like strawberries?" Tabitha asks.

"Inside joke," Layla says.

Tabitha turns up the music again. It's obvious she doesn't like inside jokes.

Chapter 42

The average number of fittings needed for a society bridal gown at Marc Leblanc's atelier on Fifth Avenue is six. Bridesmaids—or simply *filles*, as he refers to them—need at least three. His sumptuous shop is done in so many tones of off-white and champagne only someone who designed wedding gowns for a living could have conceived of it.

Didi stands in front of the mirror in her dressing cubicle. She's always dreamt about this moment. Shopping for her mother-of-the-groom dress. But it just depresses her. "I feel like I'm ready to spawn," she says, kicking off a salmon pink fishtail gown.

Toni opens the door of her dressing room and a young sales associate smiles at her approvingly. "I like that. Very simple."

"Thanks." Toni smooths the silk around her hips. It's a sleeveless navy V-neck gown.

Tabitha whisks by in her bra and panties. "Boh-ring."

Toni feels her spirits sink and goes back into the cubicle. The gown looks a lot like the black cocktail dress she's had for three years. "How do you say 'rut' in French?" she mumbles. She brushes her hair down over a series of faint scars on her forehead.

She hears squealing from outside—a haphazard cacophony of women's voices all in a similar pitch.

"Sorry we're late!"

"You look gorgeous!"

"No, you do!"

A flurry of kisses. The soft thump of expensive handbags dropping to chairs.

"God, I missed you."

"How was the flight?"

Didi's voice joins the fray. "I thought I heard someone familiar."

"Aunt Didi!"

More kisses.

Softening voices. Whispers.

"Getting ready." A knock. "Layla? You okay? The girls are here."

"Out in a minute," Layla says. Toni's heard this tone before. A minute usually means an hour.

"Don't be long. Everyone's dying to meet you."

"I said in a *minute*."

Toni takes a deep breath and opens the door. She wears a mustard yellow floor-length halter dress.

"Oh, good," Tabitha says. "This is Toni. The MOH."

A tight fan of expensive jeans and shining hair opens in front of her. Hands extend, clattering with rings and bangles.

This is my sister, Penelope, just call her Poppy. This is Auden. This is Elle. And this is Lorne.

Lauren?

No, not Lauren. Lorne.

Lorne, sorry.

They step back and look down at Toni's dress. The white monotony of their smiles fades.

"Oh," says Tabitha.

"I'm not sure I like that color," says Auden.

"It bunches up around the hips," says Poppy.

"That cut's not right," says Elle.

"I hate it," says Lorne.

In her double-large cubicle, Layla sits in a cloud of white tulle. Her image multiplies around her until the world seems like nothing but blond hair and white silk. She hears Toni trying to fend for herself out there. She drains her champagne and stands up.

"Here comes the bride," she says.

The introductions are a five-car pileup of chattering voices: *So nice to finally meet you! Sonny's said so much about you. Poppy, you guys met. Christmas, remember? And you remember Auden. Hi again . . . Auden. And this is Lorne. Lauren? No, Lorne.*

The sales associate, like a handmaiden, leads Layla to a raised platform, the lone bride on top of the wedding cake.

"You see," says Didi, "now that dress is lovely."

"Stuh-ning," says Auden.

"Gorgeous," says Elle.

Layla says, "I hate it. It looks like a pom-pom imploded on me." She jumps off the platform and disappears.

A few minutes later, she comes out in a filmy slip dress of bias-cut silk.

"I love that one," Toni says. "It's definitely more you."

"It's okay, I guess," Layla says.

"I'm sorry to embarrass you, Layla, I really am, but you're pooching." Tabitha pats her tummy.

"This is stupid. I'm making my own dress."

"You are *not* making your own dress," Didi says. "We've talked about this before. It's completely infra-dig."

"Infra-what?"

"*Infra dignatum.* It means 'beneath dignity.' You know the term infra-red, well—"

"Oh, Deirdre. Enough with the Latin lessons." A different voice enters the fray, this one sharp. "Who the hell's expected to know what that means anymore?"

Everyone turns to see Bea Flagstone stepping into the elevator vestibule with a stiff purse hanging off her arm.

"Gram!" everyone yells, running toward her.

Bea holds up her arms. "Not all at once. I feel like a bowling pin."

When she sees Layla her face brightens into a smile.

"You look like a princess! But with that figure and that face, you could put a bread bag on this girl and she'd still turn heads."

After a big hug, Layla eases Toni forward. "Bea, this is Toni Fratelli."

Bea takes Toni's hand with her warm gnarled fingers. "The *chef de cuisine!* Layla's told me so much about you."

Toni feels her first natural smile since she got into the backseat of Tabitha's car.

"You've opened your own business, haven't you?"

"Just starting out, really. Haven't had any *official* jobs yet."

"Well, don't you worry. From what I hear, you'll be double-booked in no time."

Toni blushes and looks down, shocked by how flattered she feels. Didi breaks in. "Let's keep going," she says. "My back is acting up."

The atelier takes on the din of a girl's locker room.

"Too tight."

"Too short."

"Too schoolmarm-y."

Layla stomps back to her dressing room murmuring things like "screw this" and "Las Vegas" under her breath.

Toni keeps looking for bridesmaid designs but starts stalling over the actual wedding gowns. Each time she finds one she really likes, she sees a flash of Chris Ohm's face, smiling at her. She feels a rush of uncertainty and puts it back.

This is stupid. She just met him.

She finally sees one she thinks Layla might like and knocks lightly on her door. "Sweetie?"

Toni opens the cubicle. Layla is a heaving mess. "Holy shit. I've never taken so much rejection in my life. Considering I modeled in Paris, that's saying something."

"Who *are* they all?" Toni closes the door behind her.

"Cousins. Friends of the family. Who knows? I've only met them a few times. And I don't think I've *ever* met Lauren."

"Lorne."

Layla snorts a laugh. "Whatever."

Toni helps her on with the dress. "So you don't know all of your own bridesmaids?"

"Weird, I know. They're like my evil step-bridesmaids or something. It's these people. They have to have everyone since Sunday school stand for them. Hudson has nine groomsmen so far and counting. I can't just have you and my sister. Who, incidentally, might not be able to even come because she'll be too pregnant to fly. If you're my only bridesmaid, I'll look like a loser." She stops. "Wait. That didn't come out right."

Toni just grins at her.

"What I mean is I'll be so *proud* to have you as my MOH, Toni. But if it's *just* you and he's got a kabillion groomsmen, it'll feel like I'm on Wedding Facebook or something and I don't have enough friends."

Toni just laughs. She does the last of a covered button on the dress. Layla straightens the material and looks at herself in the mirror.

Toni waves her hand in the air, sputters, looks around for a tissue.

"What's wrong?"

"Nothing . . . it's just . . . it's The One."

Layla emerges from the dressing room. The chattering stops.

"Perfect!"

"Stuh-ning!"

"Ohmigawddddd!!"

"It's The One, isn't it?" Toni says.

"Absolutely!"

Bea, who had decided long ago that all these dresses were too young for her and had fallen asleep in a chair, snorts awake and beams that Layla looks like an angel.

Layla turns quarter profile, looking at herself in the mirror. It's a fitted gown, with a plunging **V** at her décolletage and sheer cap sleeves appliquéd with seed pearls, the same pattern running down the long train. It's high fashion, yet somehow beach-y. Layla has donned a thousand wedding dresses for catalog shoots over the years, but she's never seen anything she likes better.

"Yay!" Tabitha says. "We finally found the Oh Mommy Dress!"

"Oh Mommy?" Didi asks.

"You know. You try on the dress. You turn to your mom. She starts crying. You start crying. You go 'Oh Mommy!' because you both know it's The One."

"Where *is* your mother, by the way?" Poppy asks.

Toni makes a wincing face.

Tabitha widens her eyes.

Poppy says, "Oh, yeah, right. I forgot. Sorry."

Layla just gives a polite smile. "Thanks. It happened a long time ago." She goes back to her reflection. "This one's not bad, I guess. But it's just so . . . wedding-dressy."

Tabitha says, "Of course it's wedding-dressy. It's a wedding dress!"

Didi breaks in: "I'm sorry, but I don't like it at all. I think she looks like a French hooker showing that much cleavage. And look, you can see her tattoo in the back."

Layla turns and looks over her shoulder at the plunging back. "Now *that* I like."

"Don't be a prude, Auntie," says Tabitha. "Sexy dresses are totally in right now."

Didi hesitates slightly. She doesn't like being out of the loop about what's in. "Really?"

"Tooooootally," the girls say in one synchronized chorus. Obviously, they've had much practice pledging their allegiance en masse to God, the country, and their various sorority houses.

"Everyone's doing sexy dresses," Tabitha says. "They're a little ahead of the curve, but you'd rather be ahead of the curve than—" She leaves an ominous silence.

"Exaaaaaaaactly," the chorus chimes in minor key.

"You have to get it, Layla!" says Tabitha.

"You *need* to get it!" says Lorne.

"What I *need*," Layla says, "is a cigarette. Back in a sec." She jumps off the platform and leaves the room.

After she's gone, someone whispers: "How did her parents die?"

"I never asked," Tabitha whispers back.

"Car accident," Toni says. "They were hit by a drunk driver. Layla was sixteen years old."

"Ooooooooooh." The chorus is in minor key again.

"Excuse me." Toni hitches up the hem of her pink ball gown and leaves the room.

When she's gone, Didi asks Tabitha, "Are you sure they're doing sexy dresses now?"

"Absolutely. The hotter the better."

"Do you like the one she has on?"

"It's super cute."

"But is it hot?"

"Super hot."

Didi flicks her fingernail. She had decided that if the girl was going to get married at her home, she would at least wear a fabulous wedding dress.

"Tabitha, go get her," Didi says. "She's probably making a scene out there. Tell her that I don't mind the dress she has on. If they close the cleavage a bit and fix the back. Then tell her . . . tell her I'll pay for it. We can't have her looking like a country bumpkin at the . . . on the day." Didi still can't bring herself to use the word "wedding." "Just no tattoo."

Out on the busy street, New Yorkers in black, gray, and beige stream by Layla in her white gown like a muddy river around a lotus blossom.

"Hey." Toni makes her way Frogger-style through the pedestrians.

"You really like it?"

"I hate to say it. I always wanted you to make your own dress too—but it's perfect."

"It's just not what I pictured, y'know?"

"I know."

"And it's so damn expensive . . ."

Tabitha taps out of the shop wearing a powder blue Empire-waist gown. The three women meet in a pastel triangle on the sidewalk. She happily announces that Didi likes the dress. With a few modest changes, she's even willing to pay for it.

Layla looks from Toni to Tabitha, then back again. "Rock the cash bar," she says. She drops her cigarette and puts it out with her shoe, then skips back into the shop.

Toni smiles. Didi has already discovered two of Layla's major weaknesses—the first for compliments and the second for anyone who picks up the tab.

Chapter 43

Toni jerks awake, disoriented. She relaxes when she sees where she is.

The bus is relatively empty this time of night. Traffic is light and the western sky is a wash of maraschino red behind them. Layla is asleep on her shoulder, snoring lightly. Toni thinks of all the times the two of them have ridden home—drunk, passed out, or just plain tired—like this in the backseat of the Jitney or Luxury Liner.

After Didi put a down payment on the wedding gown, the other girls announced they wanted to check Vera Wang. Then they went to Bergdorf's, then Saks, then back to Marc Leblanc. The day became a kaleidoscope of billowing silk and pastel swatches.

Eventually, exhaustion reduced everyone to a strapless gown in a shade they could all agree on: a misty blue somewhere between robin's egg and aqua, called seabreeze, which seemed fitting for the beach. The dress cost $1,100, and that didn't include the custom-dyed shoes. Toni had no idea how she was going to pay for it.

When everyone left the shop, Didi said she was seeing her back doctor in the morning and driving out tomorrow afternoon. Tabitha said she was staying in the city with her sister for a few days. Without their ride home, that left

Toni and Layla in a spot they had been many times before: fast asleep on the bus.

She stares out the window at the vast fields and dark trees. The city had long ago faded off behind them. A shimmering heat works its way from her heart, into her every breath. She can't stop thinking of Chris *Ohmmmmm*.

Chapter 44

The tall privet hedges on either side of Gin Lane remind Layla of beanstalks as the taxi slows down outside Concordia. The car inches through tall white gates and past the convex mirror. She sees the grand house in the distance. The fountain with its uplights. The topiaries guarding the place like sentries.

She can't believe how hard it was to get off the bus before Toni. When they used to take the Jitney, Layla's stop in Amagansett was always after Toni's in East Hampton. But getting off first tonight and then searching the windows to wave good-bye made Layla feel like a nervous kid on the first day of school.

She pays the driver and he tells her to "have a pleasant evening." Layla thinks it's funny. When cabbies used to drop her off on Underwood Drive, they'd tell her to have a nice night. But it's "pleasant evening" on Gin Lane.

She opens the front door. It amazes her that the Flagstones leave their door unlocked at night. It's as if they don't think anything bad could ever happen to them. But millions of dollars' worth of antiques and art would be up for the taking if only burglars had the nerve to try the front door.

Light from the library shines into the hall. As usual, Henry is up practicing his putting for a life now spent at Shinnecock Hills Golf Club.

Pock.

Brrrrr.

The room is lined with dark paneling and built-in bookcases; Layla stands in the doorway.

Henry hits the ball. *Pock.*

Brrrrr. It rolls across the floor between his desk and the fireplace.

Thump. It hits the wall.

"Hi, Hank."

Henry looks up. "Hello, little girl."

"Anything to drink?"

"Help yourself."

Pock.

Brrrrr.

Thip.

He misses the cup.

"Shit."

Layla walks to the wet bar. The only thing more valuable than the assortment of Steuben and Baccarat decanters is what they contain: thousands of dollars of rare scotch. Layla knows rich people prefer some things old: their furniture, their money, their art, and their booze. Otherwise, everything should be new.

Especially women.

"Where's Hudson?" She takes a seat on the desk, dangling her feet.

"He was moping around here so much without you, I told him to go out with some friends."

Pock.

"I got my dress."

Brrrrrr.

"What's it like?"

"White."

Thump.

"Sounds nice."

Two large-screen TVs are on, one tuned to Bloomberg, one to the Golf Channel.

"Did it take long?" His limbs crack as he bends over to fetch a ball.

"The bridesmaids' dresses were worse."

"I imagine Deirdre didn't make up her mind."

She shakes her head. "Can I ask you something?"

"Sure."

"Maybe you'll walk me down the aisle?"

He looks up from his putter.

"I mean across the sand."

"I'd love that," he says.

She walks to him and he offers his cheek, which she kisses. "Thanks . . . Dad."

As she leaves the room, the grandfather clock in the foyer starts striking midnight. A moment later, several clocks throughout the house follow suit. She grabs a hard candy from a dish in the hall and pops it into her mouth. There are bowls of expensive bonbons sitting next to flower bouquets all over the house. Layla knows for a fact that local businesses buy hard candies in bulk, pour them into pretty cellophane bags, tie them with ribbons, then sell them at five times the price. Bluebooks would never consider buying discount humbugs; the more expensive something was, the better it must be.

And she means Bluebooks, not just blue bloods. That's what she and Toni called the people who made *The Blue Book of the Hamptons*. Published annually under much secrecy, this social register cum telephone directory was how old-money people found each other at their other houses during the year. The Sullivans never made the *Blue Book*—even though her family had been in the area for centuries.

The grandfather clock stops chiming.

Upstairs she sees the door to the Rose Room open at the end of the hall. She knows Didi's spending the night in the city. She tiptoes down the hall and turns on the light. The room glows in tones of dusty rose silk.

She sits on the edge of the four-poster bed. The sixty-thousand-dollar Hastens mattress gives beneath her weight. She runs her hand along a duvet that feels as soft as a bubble bath. An ancient book with a ribbon bookmark is angled on the nightstand. *War and Peace.* There's a portrait of Didi when she was younger framed in gold over the bed.

Layla stands up, still sucking on the hard candy.

She goes to Didi's dressing room. There are full-length mirrors and a large vanity overlooking the fountain and the grounds. Clothing racks are three high. Entire chests for her scarves and jewelry. Scores of clear boxes for shoes.

She sees a pair of silver Ferragamo mules and slips one on. It fits snugly and feels cool like a piece of jewelry on her foot.

She hears a car come up the drive. She goes to the window to see Hudson get out of his black Aston Martin. She starts unbuttoning her blouse.

Mumbled voices in the distance as he talks to Henry.

Pock.

Brrrrrr.

She pulls off her jeans. She hears creaking on the stairs. His voice as he comes down the hall, looking for her.

"In here," she says.

By the time he's at the door, she's already wet. He stops in his tracks when he sees her wearing nothing but his mother's Ferragamo mules.

"I've got an idea," she says.

He makes a growling sound. They meet halfway across the room. The bed sinks beneath them as they slide onto it.

Hudson drags kisses down her skin. She moans out loud as he flicks his tongue along her skin, down between her thighs. She hears a voice in her head: *That dress makes your stomach pooch.*

She guides his hands away from her tummy and turns her head on the pillow, trying to get into it. But the satin puffs up around her face like coffin padding. She feels the portrait of Didi watching them.

She sits up, crunching the last of the candy.

"I can't do it," she says. "Not in here."

Chapter 45

"My sciatica was acting up."

Didi is on her back in a leather reclining chair. "I thought while I was in the city I'd . . ." Her voice stops as the needle pierces her skin. She enjoys the painful prick and subsequent rush of toxin into her forehead like a junkie in a fix. ". . . I'd stop by. Thank you for seeing me on such short notice."

"Of course," says Dr. Aldren. She smells like rubbing alcohol and expensive perfume. Her patients call her the Genius of 72nd Street and she's just as likely to be featured in the style section of the *Sunday Times* as any of her clients. She has a summer house of her own in Bridgehampton, but the keys to private homes all over the world are hers for the asking. There are few things wealthy New York women love more than being on good terms with their dermatologists.

"I'm surprised you had the time," the doctor says. "You must be so busy with the wedding."

"Oh." Beat. "Yes."

"Congratulations, by the way."

"Thank you." Didi's eyes begin to water and a nurse dabs at the tears. Her lips are already swollen from several cc's of Restylane. Not one of those big messes of stewing beef many of her friends have where their mouths used to be—just enough to keep her lipstick from feathering. "H . . . how did you find out?"

"Other than the fact that it was on Page Six?" The doctor laughs. "The girl is very beautiful. What does she do?"

"Oh, these kids. It's not how it was when I was young. She hangs around half the time. They both do. PR I think."

"Where's she from?"

Didi swallows, a loud sound.

"Mmm?"

"East Hampton. An old family there."

"What does her father do?"

"Dead."

Thank God, Didi thinks. No questions.

"So sorry to hear that. What was her name again?"

"Sullivan."

"Any relation to Milandra?"

"Not that I know of."

"Dodi Sullivan-Schwitzer?"

"I'm not sure."

"What about—"

"To tell you the truth, it's all happened so quickly, I haven't gotten to know her family as well as I'd like."

"Well, Sullivan is a common enough name, anyway."

"Yes." Didi grips the armrests. *Common.*

July 15

50/50 Day

Chapter 46

Toni's in her bedroom, rifling through every T-shirt and blouse she owns. Her voice is muffled as she holds her phone to her shoulder, pulling off a rejected top. "I told him I had to go shopping for Plum TV and he said he wanted to come."

"I love a man who shops. It's almost more important than his—" Layla's sentence is drowned out by the din of a Cessna taking off.

"Where are you?"

"The airport."

Layla stands outside the East Hampton Executive Airport. Behind her the small terminal, made almost entirely of smooth gray logs and surrounded on all sides by wide fields, luxury cars, and private planes, has the air of an expensive hunting lodge.

"Didi's still in the city. But she's flying Huds and me in. She says she wants to take us to register for wedding gifts."

"Are you kidding me? The ice queen melteth?"

Layla tosses her cigarette away in an arc. "I know. My alarm bells are going off too."

———————

Toni dabs on lip gloss, then fluffs her hair. She can't believe how excited she is. In the past, 50/50 Day was usually bittersweet for her because it marked the unofficial midway point of the summer. But today, she feels no bitterness— just the dizzying rush of sweet.

She hears the characteristic rumbling of an engine out front. She runs to the window and sees the gold Mustang pull up to the curb. Her heart turns over on itself.

She hurries down the stairs, hopping the last three steps to the floor. She lands with a thump on the hall rug, skids out, and grabs the banister so she doesn't fall. She takes a moment to get her bearings. It's been at least ten years since she's done that.

The front porch is full of old wicker furniture and once-dying spider plants she's nursed back to health. She feels her heart dip when she sees him raise his hand to knock on the screen door.

"You didn't have to come to the door," she says, breathless.

"I thought honking was adolescent."

You should've just seen me on the stairs.

There's an awkward moment where she doesn't know if they should kiss or shake hands. And then she has that rush of being lost in time again. That she couldn't have just met him. While this soup of emotions roils in her head, he kisses her. The confusion falls away.

Chapter 47

Carolyn Lester was barely in her teens when her father helped her set up a roadside stand to sell cucumber and corn from her family's 250-year-old farm. In the last 40 years, that simple stand has become a popular Hamptons landmark: Round Swamp Farm, a produce, bakery, and fish market still run by the extended Lester family.

—*The Guru's Guide to the Hamptons*

Toni points to a small wooden cottage shaded by chestnut trees. Luxury cars and SUVs have spilled out of the parking lot onto both shoulders of Three Mile Harbor Road. Their footsteps crunch in the gravel as they approach the entrance, where big pails of sunflowers and gladioli sit on benches next to pints of blueberries and strawberries and baskets of fresh tomatoes.

The dim low-ceilinged room is jammed with men and women waiting patiently on line. Fans blow warm air filled with the smells of apple pie, banana bread, and spices. The busy cashiers call out Toni's name as she enters, and she waves to them.

"This is another one of my favorite places," she says. "Especially back here."

She takes Chris's hand and leads him to the far corner of the shop. She opens the glass door of a large walk-in cooler and Chris steps into a room that overwhelms his senses. The first thing he notices is a wall of fragrance: herbs, fruit, and, vaguely, the earth. It smells like paradise, like the Garden of Eden itself—but with air-conditioning. There are pineapples and asparagus in baskets, huge mushrooms and bins of watermelon; mint, rosemary, tarragon, chives, all freshly picked and bundled on shelves.

She's telling him how much she loved coming here when she was a kid when he suddenly kisses her. She feels that dip in the ground beneath her feet as their mouths touch. She puts her arms around his neck, letting her basket drop to the floor. She doesn't know how much time has passed when the door opens and a red-haired woman walks in.

"Hi, Toni." Carolyn Lester grins at her, setting a basket of corn on the floor.

"Hey, Carolyn," Toni says, blushing. They hurry out of the room.

"Is there anyone you don't know out here?" Chris asks as they wait for the cash register.

Yes, she thinks. *You.*

Chapter 48

In the backseat of the Bentley illegally parked on Lexington Avenue, Tabitha puts her head on Hudson's shoulder.

"What's taking her so long?"

"Who knows?" Hudson says. "When she goes to the 'back doctor' "—he makes air quotes—"she's gone for hours."

"And then comes back with Botox bullet holes and fat lips," says Layla.

"The heartbreak of sciatica."

"Don't tease," Tabitha says. "There's nothing wrong with a little maintenance."

"That's right. Ma just loves to redecorate."

Tabitha slaps him playfully.

Layla stares out at the wall of gray buildings in Midtown. But she thought Didi went to the Genius of 72nd Street. What were they doing here?

She feels bored. She craves a drink and a cigarette. She can't believe registering for her own wedding gifts has been such a chore.

At Tiffany's she dragged her feet like a kid being trucked through a carpet store. Everything she chose—the china, the crystal, the silverware—was overruled by the others. Hudson and Tabitha seemed to agree on everything, walking arm in arm through the displays and chattering so happily, several of the sales-people asked *them* when the "Big Day" was.

When Layla suggested a set of white Calvin Klein dishes for everyday, Hudson balked.

"White's so boring. What about this Royal Copenhagen?" and he pointed to a set stenciled with simple blue flowers. That's when she turned on her heel.

"I need a cigarette," she said.

"But don't you want to help? It's your wedding."

"Doesn't feel like it."

The glass doors on the building flash open and Didi emerges wearing a bright red suit. A thin gray-haired man follows behind.

"About time," Layla says.

"So great seeing you guys," Tabitha says. "I'm staying with Poppy for an-other couple of days. But I'll be back out on the weekend. *Mwah! Mwah!*" She air-kisses them both and slips out.

She and Didi whisper on the sidewalk for a moment, then Tabitha hails a cab.

The driver holds the back door as Didi and the gentleman climb inside. The man holds a big black briefcase on his lap. Layla checks for the telltale signs of one of Didi's "sciatica treatments"—the pinpricked forehead, the swollen lips. Judging from the shine on her skin she's obviously had something done recently. But not today.

"Sonny, you remember Edgar Barston."

"Absolutely." Hudson shakes his hand. "This is Layla Sullivan. My fiancée."

A shift of gray eyes behind bifocals. "So pleased to meet you." He opens his briefcase and takes out a thick legal-size document.

"Mr. Barston is our family attorney," Didi tells Layla. "We just have a little something we want you to sign."

The man plunks the thick document on Layla's lap. Her first emotion isn't shock—or even anger. She picks it up as if to weigh it in her hand. "I was look-ing for a beach read," she says.

Prenuptial Agreement Between

Henry Hudson Flagstone IV

and

Layla Marie Sullivan

Chapter 49

The top of the Mustang is down and Toni gives directions, priding herself on being able to get around most of the South Fork without making a left turn. Turning left in the Hamptons in the summer can double the length of a trip because of the traffic.

"Just like L.A.," Chris says.

She watches him closely, eager to learn more about him. "It must've been great," she says. "Growing up in California . . ."

She asks about his parents and finds out his father was a "rather accomplished" heart surgeon (Toni takes this to mean brilliant) and his mother was a doting stay-at-home mom. Unlike Toni, his parents never discussed divorce— "but maybe if they talked once in a while in the first place, it would've come up."

She laughs, encouraging him to go on.

He says his natural attraction to Malibu surf culture—partying, sitting on the beach, playing his guitar—was not appreciated around the Ohm dinner table. His father didn't see the benefit of sport or play. Life was about serving others. Too many people needed help to waste time. Chris says he hardly saw his dad when he was young; he can almost count the number of times they had a real discussion about anything but work or school or future plans.

As she listens, she tries to piece him together from the disjointed anecdotes. Again she asks what he does for a living and the term "between gigs" comes up.

She narrows her eyes on him. "Are you a trust-fund baby or something?"

He laughs and says, "I wish. No, I put myself through school mostly. Tending bar, waiting tables."

"Join the club," she says. She wants to press him about it, but he suddenly seems quiet, a red flush on his cheeks.

He must *have been laid off,* Toni thinks, *and he's too ashamed to talk about it.* She feels sorry for him and doesn't push it.

What did it matter, anyway? Money had never been that important to her. Kevin had a good job. He was responsible and clean-shaven. So were all of her old boyfriends, and it had always ended in a disaster.

Chris *Ohmmm* was so different. So relaxed and laid-back. She feels a physical draw to him as tangible as the tide. Like watching land from her tire ring in Gardiner's Bay when she was child, letting the waves carry her back in.

O'Gorman's is a big white Victorian house with a wraparound porch and gingerbread moldings. Kids at picnic tables sit licking ice-cream cones as Toni and Chris climb the steps.

"I used to work here too," she says. "I still love it. The dipped cones especially."

The two main rooms are filled with ice-cream counters and a little gift shop with shelves of beach souvenirs. The place smells as sweet as a cotton candy machine, almost as good as her hair, Chris thinks.

"Hi, Toni!" says an elderly man behind the counter. "The regular?"

"You bet."

Chris just smiles and says, "Same for me. I trust her judgment."

As they pay for their chocolate-dipped cones, Toni grabs extra napkins. Chris thinks she needs them for the ice cream but as they walk out to the car, he notices her eyes are watering. She dabs at them. "Poor people," she says.

"What happened?"

"My dad told me their mortgage got bought out by some big hedge fund or something. They have to be out by the end of the summer. Those guys are making so much money—and it's all off the misery of other people. It just breaks my heart." She looks up at the old house and sighs heavily. "Some things should never have to change."

He watches her for a moment, then looks up at the house too. He feels an emotion that's very foreign to him when it comes to floundering businesses: sympathy.

They sit in traffic behind a sputtering old fruit truck. Toni stares at the exhaust pipe. "It looks like a backfirer," she says.

"Backfirer?"

"I don't like the sound of backfiring trucks. I was in an"—she hesitates— "accident once." She self-consciously smoothes her hair over her forehead, and the faint network of scars.

"A car accident?"

The light changes and the truck turns off.

"No."

"What kind of accident?"

She stares out the window for a moment and wonders whether she should talk about it. Then suddenly her voice opens up and she's telling him about her "accident." Cars around them are loaded down with water toys and picnic baskets. Shoppers dawdle along the sidewalks. The sun is brilliant above them.

And she's talking about a bomb.

She doesn't remember much of it. . . . She was only three years old. . . . It was when they lived in New York . . . a hundred stitches . . . there was a lot of blood. Everyone said it was a miracle she survived. She hates being held down now, because that's the one thing she remembers most: the doctors had to hold her down to take the stitches out.

She tells him that afterward her parents squired her from doctor to psychologist to specialist worrying how the trauma would affect her. Sometimes she thought the whole incident was harder on them than it was on her.

Her dad tried to make some sort of sense of what happened by handling the case himself. It was four years before they made it to court, and by then, the charges were dropped because the young protestor who had built the bomb had been too young at the time of the incident to stand trial.

Shortly after that, Vic resigned from the law firm. The Fratellis put a down payment on the restaurant, sold their Volvo, and packed everything they had into the old van.

Starting the business seemed like such an idyllic notion at the time, and Toni remembers that the first few years were happy. Her new neighbors and school friends didn't handle her with kid gloves like everyone had in New York. She was glad people stopped asking her parents how she was doing. Only her father continued to seem shaken. Always hovering over her, wincing at the slightest cut or scrape she got. Sometimes she thought the accident had made him overprotective of her, almost blindly supportive. If young Chris was expected to get A pluses on his report cards, Cs were fine on hers as long as she was happy.

But the Hamptons didn't end up being the end of the rainbow for the Fratellis. Her mother's heart was not in the restaurant business; she got tired of the cooking and the hours and working with her husband all day and night. She had never liked the beach. She didn't know how to drive. And the long isolating winters were hard on her. Eventually, to keep herself sane, she picked up photography, a hobby she'd been interested in as a girl. Local galleries started showing her work.

And then collectors in New York discovered her.

Toni doesn't know exactly when the fighting started. Possibly her parents had been fighting all her life and she was just too young to realize it. When they finally filed for divorce, Toni had just started high school. Her older brother and sister were already in college. The youngest by seven years, she was the only one left in the house.

When custody became an issue, as difficult as it was for her mother, it was decided Toni would stay in East Hampton with her dad. She had friends there, her teachers liked her, she was thriving in school. The doctors felt that another move, changing schools and especially moving back to New York, would be too much of a shock for her. So Toni became the only person she ever knew whose mother packed her bags, kissed her hard, and then left home.

Toni knew what other people thought: that her mother was selfish. But Toni always wanted her mother to be happy. If her mother could find something that made her happy, it meant happiness was possible for all of them too. It also meant Ruth Fratelli knew her daughter was strong enough to handle it.

"That's why you don't like loud noises," he says.

They're in the front yard surrounded by the flowers her mother planted when they were all younger—hydrangeas, daylilies, and lavender roses. *They're perennials, Toni. It means they'll bloom forever.*

"Backfiring trucks," she says. "Thunderstorms. Fireworks. I wasn't all that disappointed when the Fourth of July fireworks were canceled again this year.

I like the way they look, but the sound?" She winces. "Breaking balloons too. They're almost the worst. Sort of unfortunate for someone who is now going to spend half the summer working at birthday parties and barbecues." She laughs. "Well, not that many parties, I guess."

She unhooks Tucker's leash and he bounds around the yard in crazy circles.

Chris watches her. He remembers seeing her on 92nd Street—how she stared so intensely at the little girl with balloons.

He wants to tell her he was there on the sidewalk, even opens his mouth to do it. But then he sees her trusting smile and the timing doesn't feel right. In fact, it feels worse than ever.

Instead he pushes a strand of hair behind her ear. "You can hardly see the scars."

"Children are resilient," she says.

"Lucky for us."

In the kitchen, Toni slices a round loaf of fresh white bread in half.

"I like to get everything ready before I start cooking," she tells him. "Have it all measured out and organized. Pain bagnat—or pan bagnat, as it's also called—is an old recipe for a sandwich from Provence—Nice, in particular—and it literally means bathed or wet bread in French."

Chris looks over his shoulder. "Are you talking to me?"

"Of course I'm talking to you."

"Because it didn't seem like you were. You were looking"—he points to the wall—"over there."

"Well, I *was* talking to you." She grabs her bag of tomatoes. "Heirloom tomatoes are always the best to use," she says, looking at the wall again. "I just think they give a better flavor. We're really lucky to have so many good—"

"See! You're doing it again! Like you're doing your own cooking show or something! The way you're talking and explaining everything out loud."

"Doesn't everyone pretend they have their own cooking show when they cook?"

"I don't know. The most talking I do when it comes to food is usually 'I'll have fries with that.'"

She laughs.

"Just keep going. I won't change the channel."

She smiles and takes fresh onions, putting them on the chopping block.

"One of the great things about the Hamptons is that there are so many good local organic farmers. But the one thing you still have to go to Italy for . . . is this." She holds up a dark green bottle. "Cold-pressed, unfiltered, extra-virgin olive oil."

"Extra-virgin?"

"That's right."

"Sounds intriguing." He gives her a suggestive grin. "Can you be an extra virgin?"

"If you're an olive, apparently you can."

She laughs and turns around to rinse her hands in the sink, catching a glimpse of herself in the old mirror beside the door. The smile on her face is so broad. She doesn't remember ever seeing herself look so happy.

Chapter 50

"I knew it was coming," Layla says. "But to do it that way? To make us think we're registering for wedding gifts? And then drag out the prenup?"

Toni sits in a director's chair in a makeshift TV field studio at the Bridge-hampton Historical Society. On a patch of green grass, surrounded by gardens and trees, is a little vignette with a gleaming outdoor kitchen and a camera. Layla is doing Toni's makeup, dabbing powder on her face.

"Feels like we're getting ready for a Friday night, doesn't it?"

"Except you weren't worried about prenups back then."

"Maybe I should've been."

"Did you sign it?"

"Of course not. But she wanted me to. That's why we had to go into the city to register. I could've done most of it out here. But she wanted to plan this whole 'fun' afternoon, she said. What she needed was to see me sign the thing in front of her lawyer. She was so peeved when I told her I wanted your dad to have a look at it. You think he will?"

"You kidding? He's chomping at the bit."

Toni sees Chris heading over from the parking lot with Tucker.

"That's *him.*"

Layla looks over and fans herself. "He's a hottie. Have you guys, you know, done it yet?"

Toni gives her a light slap. "Shut up."

Chris walks up and kisses Toni on the lips. It's so lingering and intimate, she nearly falls over in her director's chair. Layla widens her eyes in approval.

Toni gets her bearings. "Chris, this is Layla Sullivan. Layla, Chris Ohm."

Ohhhhhmmm. She can't say his name without thinking about the universe that has never spoken to her.

"Hi there, surfer boy," Layla says. "I've heard so much about you."

Toni expects some sort of reaction from him—there was always some blush or stammer or quick head-to-toe glance from her boyfriends when they met Layla—but Chris's smile is natural. "And you." He motions to the dish in his arms—a pie plate, covered in a cookie sheet, topped off with a half-full bag of sugar and Toni's vintage iron.

"Can we eat this yet?"

"Almost."

"Close your lips," Layla says. She starts dotting on lipstick.

An attractive woman with a floaty linen dress walks over. "Layla!"

They kiss cheeks. "Anna, you remember Toni."

"Of course. We met at the Great Chef's Dinner last year," Anna says.

"Oh, ribe. Grape do zee ya." Layla is still doing Toni's lips.

"We're so happy we can finally have you on. Layla's been singing your praises for ages."

Toni tells her she's glad to be here, and no, she's not nervous, not really, and yes, she'll be ready in five.

"What're you making?" Anna holds a clipboard ready to make notes.

"Pain bagnat."

Anna blinks at her. "Come again?"

Toni spells as she jots along. "What's that?"

"Well . . . fish sandwiches."

"What kind of fish?"

"Tuna."

"So you're making tuna salad sandwiches?"

Chris laughs. "Don't insult her."

Chapter 51

"Now, *this* is how to have a wedding," Didi says.

She and Henry stand side by side on the pastoral grounds of the Meadow Club watching the Frybrook-Garner wedding party pose for pictures in front of the sprawling shingle-style mansion. The bridesmaids are in buttercup yellow. The groomsmen are in navy suits, with yellow ties. The bride is stunning in a simple white sheath. The ceremony at Saint Andrew's Dune Church had been perfect. And everybody—absolutely everybody—is here.

A server comes by with a tray of Belgian wren tartlets. Didi plucks one off the plate, the only hors d'oeuvre she allows herself at any benefit or party. She can't imagine her son's wedding without Susan's pièce de résistance.

She balances the plate expertly between her left ring and middle fingers, a cocktail napkin resting over her baby finger, her champagne glass supported with her thumb and the cocktail plate. Most of the women—and men—she knows were taught this simple trick of cocktail etiquette by their mother or nanny when they were young. It leaves one's right hand free to shake during introductions and chats.

But not Henry.

He has a scotch glass in one hand and with the other he pops a whole tart straight into his mouth. Didi tries not to be embarrassed as she dusts crumbs off his lapel.

She knew when she met him that eventually his roots would begin to show. Dirty. Smelly. Grimy. Texas oil money.

Not the clean hard shine of Blackhart steel. The same grit and audacity that had his great-grandfather digging through the mud only 130 years ago still ran through Henry's veins. There was a reason they called oil "crude"—if there was one word to describe the whole sordid business that was it.

She supposed she married him because he reminded her a little of her rough-and-tumble father. And her mother told her she could do much worse. He came from a good family, good schools. Everyone knew how much money they had.

"A girl can't be too fussy," her mother told her. "Otherwise a girl finds herself alone with her thoughts." Then Trudi Blackhart gave a little wink, as if being alone with one's thoughts was the worst thing that could happen to a girl.

When the engagement was announced, her mother told Didi she mustn't give in to her husband's taste. It always pained Trudi that she hadn't been married on the lawns of Concordia, like her mother. That she'd let John Blackhart talk her into that ceremony aboard his father's yacht in the Aegean.

"It had seemed so glamorous and bohemian at the time," she said. "But I've regretted it ever since. A girl's wedding is the most important day of her life. People will remember it forever. A wedding is a social obligation, Didi. An outward expression of who we are. Never forget that."

But it was 1976 and Didi was a sophisticated New York debutante. As much as she loved Concordia, she didn't want a country wedding. She wanted a Plaza wedding—and she got one. It had been a three-day-long affair with six hundred guests, and it had been perfect.

She remembers only one lonely moment in front of the mirror before the ceremony. Her mother had just tried to give her "something old"—a custom-designed Van Cleef & Arpels bracelet of all the family's birthstones. But Didi was wearing platinum and she thought the bracelet clashed. She told her mother she already had "something old"—her pearl necklace. Her mother seemed hurt by the rejection, but smiled bravely anyway. When she left the room, Didi couldn't help it; she succumbed to the wedding day jitters she'd been holding at bay since the engagement. She wasn't sure she loved Henry. She wasn't sure he loved her. Was she making a mistake? Twelve years was a big age difference. And she wondered if they were compatible . . . in bed.

Despite the outward marks of 1970s liberalism—a mood ring, gauchos, a well-thumbed copy of *Love Story*—Didi Blackhart was still a prude. When they did consummate their relationship later that night, she remembered it being more uncomfortable than pleasurable. Henry was snoring the next morning and she actually cried.

But then she saw the wedding photos.

Hundreds of them, thousands maybe, some color, some black-and-white, with not a single bad shot of her. As for the groom, Henry was handsome in his black tuxedo—and he knew how to hold a cocktail plate back then.

Didi sighs and watches him slurp his scotch on the rocks. Were his manners getting worse just to spite her? Or at some point is everything a husband and wife do to each other out of spite?

"Didi!"

Didi sees Helen and Nicholas Pullbridge heading over to chat. She gives Henry's lapel a cursory check.

"If they don't ask about the wedding," she says, "don't bring it up."

Chapter 52

"Extra-virgin olive oil?" Anna says. "I always think that sounds naughty."

Toni glances over at Chris, who grins back.

"I know what you mean," she says.

Her voice sounds to her as if it's echoing in a tin can. She feels the weight of the microphone on her blouse collar, sees the two-shot of Anna and her on the monitor off to the side. But she still can't believe she's on TV.

"Pain bagnat is such a wonderful summer dish because you can make it ahead. In fact, it's better if you do. Originally, sardines or anchovies were used because cured fish keeps so well. But I prefer canned tuna, mixing the herbs to taste."

She sprinkles olive oil on both sides of a round loaf of bread cut in half horizontally, then lays down fresh lettuce leaves.

"You should look for seasonal ingredients wherever you are. This version is essentially salade niçoise on a loaf of fresh bread."

"Which smells wonderful," says Anna. "Did you bake it yourself?"

"Are you kidding? We went to Breadzilla yesterday. They still have the most wonderful bread. This is my theory on bread: if you absolutely don't have time to bake it yourself, why bother? Good cooking is all about delegating.

I'm sorry, but who needs to knead dough that badly? Not me. I'm not that kneady."

Everyone laughs.

Toni feels herself relaxing. She glances over at Chris. He smiles at her and gives her a thumbs-up. Then he crouches down with Tucker, pointing to her as if explaining how proud he should be.

As for Layla, she got on her iPhone five minutes ago and then waved good-bye, blowing a kiss.

Afraid she might lose her train of thought, Toni concentrates. But even as she's explaining how to customize the recipe—"You can use chopped egg if you want or salad dressing instead of olive oil"—and even as she sings the praises of Spanish olives or how delicious the heirloom tomatoes are this time of year— "the Simple Tomato Sandwich at Breadzilla? On a Squishy Roll?"—she smacks her lips—"the best"—she's thinking of last night.

Live dangerously, he said.

She had finished assembling the sandwich in her dad's kitchen at the house, layering lettuce, shallots, capers, tomato, olives, basil, and tuna chunks on the bread. She pressed it together and wrapped it in wax paper. She placed a cookie sheet on top of the flat round loaf, held out the vintage iron, and set it on top of the whole lot.

"The weight compresses the sandwich and lets the flavors mix," she said. "But the iron isn't quite heavy enough. It was the perfect weight with the matching trivet. Not only did it work, but it looked so cute."

"That's what you were looking for at the market that day."

"I lost it moving out of Dash last year." She sighed and took down a rolled-up bag of sugar from the cupboard. "You can use anything to weigh it down. Potatoes. Bricks. Flour. But I've never tried anything but my iron and trivet before." She plopped the sugar bag on top and gave a playful pout. "Not quite the right effect. But I hope it works."

"Live dangerously," he said.

She chewed her nails in mock fear.

"I'm starving. How long's it going to take?"

"Oh. We can't eat this now," she said, putting it in the fridge. "Not until tomorrow."

He seemed confused. "Why make a sandwich you can't eat right away?"

"Some things are worth waiting for," she said.

As the sun was setting they got in the Mustang and wound back out to Montauk Highway. On the Napeague Strip, a straight stretch of road lined with scrub pines and rolling dunes, they pulled into the gravel parking lot of Cyril's Fish House, a busy, raucous beach shack with a thatched roof.

When they got to the entrance, Cyril walked over, his arms wide. He had bleached-out blond hair and sunglasses and looked like a cross between a professional surfer and Neptune himself. He welcomed Toni by kissing her hand, and when she introduced Chris as a fellow surfer, Cyril clamped him in a big bear hug.

The restaurant was busy and the sun was going down behind them. They sat outdoors at white plastic tables. Bob Marley wailed "No Woman, No Cry" on the sound system, and a large mural of an underwater seascape filled the far wall. They ordered macadamia nut–encrusted mahimahi and lobster salad on paper plates. They drank too many Bailey's Banana Coladas to drive. As the sun drained the color from the sky, they carried their BBCs in plastic glasses back behind the restaurant. She told him she wanted to take him to the Walking Dunes. He grabbed his guitar and the old blanket from the trunk and they walked behind the restaurant over the tracks.

The dune grasses shuffled around them like Hawaiian skirts as they climbed a sandy slope. Toni explained they were called the Walking Dunes not because you could walk on them (in fact, they were protected) but because the whole range of dunes shifted—literally "walked"—in the wind. Chris looked out over the sandy hills and grasses. It felt as if they were the only two people on another planet.

They skidded down rough red sand to a curved beach strewn with seaweed. She spread her arms as if introducing a guest of honor: the view of Napeague Harbor. They sat cross-legged on the blanket and watched the sun set as Toni told him about her childhood memories. How much she missed places like 411 on Montauk Highway, with the iguanas in the cage out front, or Squires, with their blackened steak. Or being on the beach with her dad playing paddleball. She had so many memories of the Hamptons when she was young that she couldn't disconnect the things she remembered from the things she saw today.

After a while, she stopped and looked at him. "I'm talking too much. Why don't you talk for a while?"

"Because I'd rather listen to you."

She narrowed her eyes on him. Their plastic cups were empty. She couldn't tell if it was the melancholic tug of her sugar crash or a misguided instinct, but she felt a shiver of mistrust. She fought it for a while, then lay back on the blanket and watched the sky. He put his guitar on his lap and began to play David Wilcox songs. She looked up at the sky, unable to tell the fireflies from the shooting stars.

Live dangerously, she thought.

Chapter 53

On any given day during the season, Susan Schumacher had between five and ten events. She traveled between them in a gleaming white RV. With its bank of closed-circuit TV monitors and vanity mirror, the back of the truck looked more like a mobile television station than a catering van.

The monitors betrayed the understandable paranoia she felt after having clawed her way to the top of the catering heap in the Hamptons. She was rarely out of visual connection with her shop on Newtown Lane, her chef's kitchen, her house, and her rare-poultry coop. But the monitors also helped her keep abreast of popular cooking shows.

Her SUV is parked near the kitchen entrance of the Meadow, where she's catering the Frybrook-Garner wedding. She's just about to freshen her green eyeliner for the reception (Susan loves making appearances at "her weddings") when she hears a familiar "Tah-dah!" from one of the monitors.

She looks up to see Toni Fratelli presenting an exquisite pain bagnat on Plum TV. Susan remembers how everyone used to swoon over her pain bagnat in the shop all those years ago—and everything else she made. Susan resented the girl's talent, as she had resented Vic Fratelli when he opened his restaurant—*Ha! Pizza parlor more like!*—on Main Street. Susan only hired his daughter to learn more about how the place had become such an overnight success. But Toni didn't reveal any of her dad's secrets. Instead, she stole everyone's heart—and stomach. She had a natural ease with people, a relaxed attitude in the kitchen, and she was a perfectionist when it came to presentation. She became a favorite with customers and staff alike.

Susan fired her after six weeks, accusing her of stealing *James Beard's American Cookery*. Toni swore she was innocent—she already had that book, she said—but Susan stood firm.

She thought she had gotten rid of the girl all those years ago, but here she was, back in the Hamptons, starting her own business and laughing on Plum TV.

Little upstart, Susan thinks, and snaps her frosted green eyeliner in two.

"Oh-em-gee!" says Anna with her mouth full. "That is delicious!"

Toni cuts pieces of the finished pain bagnat and hands them out to crew members.

Anna turns to the camera. "I wish you could taste this."

"Well, it's on the menu at F-4."

"You're going to be there this year?"

"Absolutely. Booth 21."

"Booth 21. Remember that, everyone. Fratelli's Restaurant and Catering. Don't miss it. And when we come back, we'll be checking what was in the gift bags from the Denim and Diamonds gala and God's Love We Deliver."

Everyone smiles at the camera. Toni becomes aware that her cheeks are aching.

"That's it. We're out. Thank you so much for coming. You were fabulous!"

"Was I?" People gather around her, some cleaning the counter, another taking off her microphone.

"You truly were. Will you come back, *please?* Everyone loved you."

"They did? I don't even remember what I said."

"You were perfect."

"That's good," Toni says.

Toni looks around at the green trees, the blue skies, and the bizarre mix of television studio and country garden. She sees Chris walking toward her with Tucker—or rather, Tucker dragging Chris like a workhorse pulling a cart.

Chris is laughing when he gets to her. "You were amazing," he says, giving her a big kiss. "And you're right. Some things are worth waiting for."

Chapter 54

Vic pushes his large green ledger out of the way and drops another heavy document on the table with a thump.

Layla rubs her shoulder and says, "Felt like I was carrying around the September issue of *Vogue*." She sits down and lights a cigarette.

Vic opens the prenup. "Are you still smoking?"

"Not still—again. I quit for a while."

"You keep it up, you'll be dead by the time you're my age."

"Think of the money I'll save on my 401(k)."

"You're an attitude case. Always have been."

"Always will be."

"That's what I love about you."

Toni comes into the family dining room with a glass of wine for Layla and a coffee for her dad. Vic puts on his bifocals and begins flipping through the document.

"I can't believe I'm reading your prenup. I used to help you girls with your math homework at this table."

"Enough to make you tear up, isn't it?" Layla says. Toni watches her take her first big gulp of wine.

As Vic reads, making notes on a yellow legal pad, Toni shows Layla ideas in the bridal magazines.

The ring cushion with the blue ribbons she wants to make.

The imprint of a sandcastle for invitations and name cards.

The hydrangea and delphinium bouquets she thinks would look great on the tables.

Layla just watches her, saying, "Great . . . great . . . Whatever you think."

The little cuckoo clock in the kitchen strikes three. Toni brings her dad more espresso and Layla more wine. She makes a plate of cheese and cold cuts, but Layla doesn't eat. The friendship bracelets and bangles look loose on her wrist and her collarbones jut out.

Has she lost weight?

Layla had always been the type of person who could eat anything without gaining a pound (a source of chagrin for most women who knew her). But when she started skipping meals for whatever reason, she dropped weight like ballast from a sinking ship. Toni starts to feel worried.

The clock strikes four. Vic sits back and rubs his eyes. "It's been so long since I've read one of these, I thought I'd forget."

"Hope it's like riding a bike," Layla says.

"Bike doesn't quite cut it in this case. More like a Harley Electra Glide Classic."

"I'll take the crib notes."

"Between Hudson's property, his trust funds, his stocks, his T-bills, his inheritances, *and* his cars . . ." Vic points to a figure.

Layla whistles out loud. "I knew he was rich, but I didn't know he was *that* rich."

"And this is you." He points to a line that reads $16,345, the resale price of her white convertible Beetle and her former engagement rings.

Vic says, "In the event of a divorce, you're only entitled to two million, provided there's been no hanky-panky."

"Who says I'm getting divorced?" She picks up the pen.

"You're really going to sign it?" Toni asks.

"Why not?"

"Hope you're ready for this," Vic says. "They say money changes everything."

"That's what they say." The pen hisses along the page.

Outside, Layla throws the contract carelessly in the passenger seat of her car. "How's the surfer boy?"

"Good," Toni says. Then, "Great, actually."

"You sound surprised."

"I guess I am. A little. You know me. But so far, so good. Knock wood." She looks around for something to knock on.

Layla points to the white picket fence, but Toni thinks it would be a little desperate to run all the way down the driveway. Layla gets into the car and checks her makeup in the rearview mirror.

"We really have to try to get together to work on this stuff," Toni says. "At least get the invitations out. I can't believe you haven't sent them yet."

"We're still working on the guest list."

"I thought you did the guest list."

Layla puts the car in gear and starts backing slowly down the driveway; Toni follows alongside. Since Layla got her driver's license, their good-byes on Church Street weren't complete without this walk down the driveway, a double honk, and the peace sign at the corner.

"We did *my* side. But you should see Hudson's. Try cutting five hundred people down to fifty."

"And what about the menu? I still need you to sign off on it."

"We will."

"When?"

"I don't know. Soon."

"What about tomorrow night?"

"I can't tomorrow night."

"Why not?"

Layla squints. "Something's going on. I forget. But something."

They're at the end of the driveway now.

"But I miss you," Toni says. "I've hardly seen you at all this summer."

"I know. It's all this wedding shit. But I'll call you soon. We'll go for dinner or something."

"Yeah. I'd love that."

"You, me, Tabitha, and the boys."

Toni just smiles. She hadn't meant Tabitha and the boys.

"Love you," Layla says.

"Love you too." They kiss cheeks, and Toni notices she smells like Tabitha's perfume. She watches the white Beetle back out of the driveway. "Eat something!" she says.

Layla just waves, roaring down the street. A beat passes. At the corner she honks twice—and gives the peace sign. Toni exhales in relief. It would've broken her heart if she hadn't remembered.

As she heads back up to the house, she sees the white picket fence. She glances around to make sure no one's looking and gives it a quick knock.

Chapter 55

Money changes everything....

Layla sits in traffic on Main Street, her convertible reflecting in the gleaming windows of the shops as she inches along. She passes White's chemists and wonders how much of her "prenup fortune" she had spent on makeup in that store.

Too much, probably.

But she loved it there. To be around all the makeup and hair products and pictures of supermodels on the packages. Long before she and Toni bought their Bonne Belle Lip Smackers, Layla remembers seeing Christie Brinkley on the package of an eye shadow trio in White's. Her mother was shopping for aspirin and tampons and ended up gossiping with some women at the counter. Young Layla migrated to the cosmetics section. Although today you were far more likely to find deluxe lines like Estée Lauder and Bobbi Brown at White's, back then she remembers standing transfixed before a wall of Christie Brinkley's blue eyes and blond hair. She felt like a novice before an image of the Virgin Mary.

She would see many more pictures of Christie over the years, but it was that first one that made her start to feel that the best thing in the world a girl could be was pretty and perfect and preserved forever in a photograph. She didn't admit it to people. It was her secret. She had taken her first hit of Christie and was instantly addicted.

She followed Christie's career from CoverGirl to *Sports Illustrated;* bought her makeup and exercise equipment; read about her doomed marriages and her art career. Divorce battles, custody suits, sex scandals—nothing could tarnish the pure adoration she felt for her idol. She was only seven years old the first time she saw the video *Uptown Girl* on MTV. When Christie made her debut in the big black hat and chandelier earrings, Layla stood transfixed in front of the television. After that, she made her big sister, Leslie, dress her up and teach her all the lyrics and dance steps. When Leslie moved on to Cyndi Lauper and Boy George, Layla was still hooked on Christie. She listened to "Uptown Girl" so many times it became little more than a series of distorted notes and scratches. For Christmas, her parents bought her a tape player and a cassette of the whole album, *An Innocent Man* by Billy Joel. When Christie married the Long Island singer and became a local celebrity, Layla thought she and Christie were destined to become Uptown Girls together.

Even though she wasn't exactly sure what that meant.

It wasn't until a ninth-grade field trip to the American Museum of Natural History in New York City that she found out. As the school bus drove out of the shade of the Queens Midtown Tunnel, Layla was shocked to see the signs UPTOWN and DOWNTOWN, with arrows pointing right and left.

She was usually embarrassed asking people when she didn't understand something, but not with Toni. So Toni explained what they meant.

Uptown people were rich, she said.

Downtown people weren't.

"But my mom says everyone in New York is rich," Layla said.

"Yeah," Toni said. "But uptown is a special kind of rich." She thought about it for a while, then said: "Uptown means you were born rich."

It was then Layla realized that she could never really be an Uptown Girl. The way summer people could never really be locals. Even now, with Hudson's family ring on her finger and the wedding date set, she didn't feel like an Uptown Girl.

She glances at the prenup on the passenger seat. That wasn't helping either.

Chapter 56

"I still can't believe you went to business school," Toni says. Her voice is muffled as she searches through a stack of boxes in the back of the garage on Church Street.

"One of my dark secrets," he says. He's just outside in the driveway, looking through a dusty white telescope at the night sky. "Do you know anything about the stars?"

"Not really. I used to watch the fishing boats with it. Ah, finally!"

She comes out of the garage lugging an old Singer sewing machine—a hand-me-down from Layla when the zipper foot broke. Chris helps her set it up on the picnic table in the backyard, beside a small pile of red-and-white-checked tablecloths from the restaurant. The little shell-shaped patio lights she had strung across the yard for a dinner party years ago are dusty and faded, casting a glow like Christmas lights.

Chris brings the telescope back into the garage. He sees an old ten-speed bike with the front tire missing; shelves full of vintage hurricane lamps, colored seltzer bottles, and boxes carefully marked: CRYSTAL, SERVING BOWLS, SILVERWARE.

"This is one of my dark secrets," she says. "My Hope Garage."

He just laughs.

They sit at the table as Toni sews two tablecloths together into one long one for the booth at the food festival. It's the only surface large enough for her to work at—and it's such a perfect summer night. They had been discussing their most embarrassing moments when the topic of business school came up.

"I don't see what's so embarrassing about Harvard."

"It's not school," he says. "It's my first big interview after graduation."

She threads the machine expertly, and he watches her; it's his job to keep the fabric off the grass.

"My father arranged for me to have an interview at this very conservative firm in Hong Kong. I guess I partied too hard before the flight"—he hesitates—"and *on* the flight . . . and after the flight . . ."

She laughs.

"I had just graduated!" he says in his defense. "So I showed up at my interview at this very conservative Chinese firm, and I was taken to the top of what I think they said was the third-tallest building on the planet, but I don't remember for sure. I was led into this very large office that I remember as being all gray. The view would've been incredible, but all I could see was smog and clouds—which were also kind of gray. So this very conservative president of this very conservative firm sits across from me at this very big gray desk and asks me what I could do to improve productivity at his company. And . . ." His voice trails off.

"What did you say?"

"I'm not sure. Because the next thing I remember was him standing over me, trying to shake me awake in the chair."

"You passed *out* at a job interview?"

"Passed out cold. Snoring. Drooling. Probably talking in my sleep."

She laughs. "Okay, that *is* embarrassing. I guess I don't have to ask if you got the job."

"Good guess."

"What did you end up doing?" She keeps her voice light and casual.

"Before or after my father stopped yelling?"

"For work, I mean."

"This and that," he says with a shrug.

"Come on. You must've had to do *something* for money. I'm sorry. I don't mean to pry." She looks at him, smiling. "I'm just curious . . ."

"I don't know. After I graduated, I got a job selling photocopiers. For a while. I tried working at a brokerage firm, but it bored the hell out of me. I've done some . . . investment work."

"Investment work? You're kidding? I can't even picture you in a tie."

"You'll just have to take my word for it. I wore a lot of them."

He seems uncomfortable again, almost ashamed.

"Well, I'm glad you don't wear them anymore," she says. "I can't tell you how relieved I am that you're not one of those uptight Masters of the Universe who only care about their jobs. I'm so over those guys."

"So you keep saying," he says, quick to change the subject. "All right, you heard my most embarrassing moment. Your turn."

She takes the fabric out of the machine and cuts the loose threads. "Besides showing you my Hope Garage?" She smiles and thinks about it. "Okay. Here's one. Sticking with the job interview theme, last year I had to see the loan officer at my bank. I was applying for a business loan to help get the restaurant started. I had this nice tweed suit and I thought a pair of really good black stockings would be perfect with it. But I was sick and tired of buying hose that ripped the first time I wore them, so I decided to buy a really good pair. So I went into Fogal's, thinking it might cost me forty bucks. I ask the saleswoman for her most reliable pair, and she sings the praises of these ones from France. I say fine. I go to the cash register and she rings me up and the things come out to over two hundred bucks. Just to make a joke, I asked her if that was in francs."

Chris laughs.

"She didn't think it was funny. So I asked if she had a slightly *less* fantastically snag-free pair of stockings, and she showed me the cheapest ones she had in the store. They were still ninety bucks, but I bought them anyway because I felt too stupid for going into the place and not buying anything at all."

"That's not that embarrassing."

"I'm not finished yet." They roll the fabric over the dowel, creating an awning; Toni adjusts a neatly scalloped edge to hang off the front. "So I meet Sully for lunch because she's going to help me practice my pitch. I want to rehearse what I'm going to tell these people. How I always wanted my own restaurant. How trustworthy and dependable I am. How great my business plan is. We go to one of my favorite bistros in the entire city and I sit down on the wicker chair—I repeat, wicker—and I hear these loud snaps and rips from my butt. I try to get up—and the chair comes with me. The damn wicker has snagged my brand-new ninety-dollar French stockings in about seventeen places. Layla had to help me extricate myself. I went to the interview with so many runs in my stockings I looked like an extra from *Oliver*."

Chris laughs.

"I didn't get the loan," she says. Her smile fades a bit. "I ended up borrowing the money from my dad. Which is what I'm doing here," she says looking up at the house. "Back home."

"I'm glad you're here," he says. She feels his arms around her.

"Me too," she says. She can't believe that for the first time in months, she actually means it.

7TH ANNUAL

FOODIES FOR FIBROMYALGIA FESTIVAL

JULY 24–26

MULFORD FARMSTEAD

$500 PER PERSON

2 FOR $900

ATTIRE: HAMPTONS CHIC

Chapter 57

There are so many charity events in the Hamptons that many people are actually starting to suffer from fundraising fatigue. But that doesn't stop the most fashionable summer people from donning pretty frocks and heading out to at least a couple of parties to drink and dance and donate. In the Hamptons, as everywhere, charity is as much for the benefit of the rich as it is for the poor.

—*The Guru's Guide to the Hamptons*

"Good food travels fast," Vic says. He wears a chef's hat and white uniform, and dishes out a plate of baked ziti. "We're the busiest booth here."

"I know," Toni says. "I just hate making people wait so long." She looks at the line snaking away from Booth 21.

"Be thankful. It's better than the other way around."

"True . . ." But her voice still sounds worried.

They stand beneath one of a string of large white free-span tents filled with several hundred guests sipping drinks from plastic glasses and nibbling food from booths sponsored by other Hamptons restaurants: The Palm, Della

Femina, Nick & Toni's, Almond. A Dixieland jazz band plays on a small stage nearby.

"Oh when the saints . . ."

People laugh, gossip, and pose for photographs for the local magazines. Despite the charity exhaustion, attendance is high, as it always is for F-4. Fibromyalgia is a painful bone and muscle condition that is sometimes so severe, just getting dressed can be an ordeal. If there's any disease close to a socialite's heart, it's one that prevents her from trying on new clothes.

Toni's checked tablecloth and awning make her booth stand out amid the others, but it's the food that has people waiting twenty minutes or more. She tries not to worry about the guests at the back of the line. She remembers her parents trying to teach her about gratitude when she was younger; how Thanksgiving was all about being grateful for what she had. She remembers digging in her dad's jacket pocket every day for two weeks before she found the bleacher tickets for the Macy's Thanksgiving Day Parade every year. Thank you thank you, she said up into the ether. For her, Thanksgiving was as much about the parade as anything else.

A tall attractive man samples her eggplant parmigiana, licking his lips. "This is unbelievable! Are you married?"

Toni says, "Um . . . no, but we just met."

He laughs, says good-bye to Vic, and heads off into the party.

"I can't believe you can be so cool," Rhonda says. "That was Ed Burns."

Toni stares after the handsome guest. "I guess I do have prosopagnosia."

"Propro-what?"

"Never mind."

She continues to serve and smile. Almost everyone greets her by name, congratulating her and taking copies of the menu. She can't believe she's actually having a successful night. She feels lucky and nervous at the same time, as if she's halfway across an extension bridge and doesn't want to look down.

A bright flash nearly blinds her. She looks up to see Bill Mitchell. "Hey, Toni! I saw you on TV the other day."

"God, I was so nervous, I don't even remember what I said."

"I'll vouch for you. You were great. Tuna salad sandwiches never seemed so tempting."

Toni just smiles, remembering Chris's words: *Don't insult her.*

"Thanks."

"Look at that," Vic says, motioning to Booth 16. "Susan Schumacher, ten o'clock. She's fuming."

Toni looks over to see Susan yelling at her employees; both her Asian and her Continental booths are vacant. She keeps glancing over at Toni, who can almost hear her screaming voice over the band.

Vic puts his arm around her. "Did I ever tell you how glad I am to have you home?" He kisses her cheek, then slips around back for more lasagna.

A man steps forward, next in line. "I've been on line for a while, but I hear it's worth the wait."

Toni is shocked to see Chris wearing a white button-down shirt and jeans, his hair brushed back and his scruff trimmed. He looks . . . *successful*.

And so handsome. She just stares at him.

"Listen, I'm gonna split," Bill says, sensing Toni's mood. "I heard Kelly Ripa is here. I have no idea how she gets to so many events every night."

"Clones," Toni says. "Each one cuter than the next."

He laughs and slips off through the crowd.

"I'm surprised to see *you* here."

"Supporting the local socialites," he says. "And *you*. What would you suggest?"

"Everything," the woman behind him says. She has flashy red hair and a Long Island accent. "I'm Georgia Randall. Pleased to meet 'cha." She turns to Toni. "Can I have anothuh scoop of those roasted vegetables? They're delish."

"Absolutely, Georgia." Toni dishes out the food.

"So how's business?"

"So far so good."

"And your fath-ah?"

"He's good too."

"Good to he-ah. But I want you to take this. Just in case." She slips Toni her business card. "If you ev-ah need a place on your own, you know who to call. The house on Chester Drive is still vacant. Needs a little TLC, but you can handle that." She winks and walks away with her food.

"Don't tell me," Chris says. "Realtor?"

"Used to be farming out here. Now it's real estate."

Vic walks up carrying a fresh pan of lasagna. "Make room for the cow huggers. This one's vegetarian." He sets the pan down, immediately noticing the newcomer.

"Uh, Chris, this is my dad, Vic. Dad, this is Chris Ohm." She feels slightly uncomfortable, as if Chris has shown up at the door for her senior prom.

Chris gives a polite smile. "Nice to meet you, sir."

"Uh-huh." He lets a beat pass. "You must be the surfer."

Toni cringes. He always did that.

You must be the baseball player.

The artist.

The drummer.

She starts to blush.

"I guess I am, sir."

"Uh-huh," Vic says again.

Afraid Vic will start grilling him about his job, she says, "Dad, can I have a minute?"

He shrugs and starts to serve the next customer.

Chris has a nervous look on his face. It makes Toni uneasy. "Can I see you later?" he asks. "There's something we have to talk about."

"I won't be out of here for hours."

A whoop goes up from the crowd. Chris looks back over his shoulder to see Frank Broward in a seersucker suit being lifted above everyone's heads by Yuri and Lincoln. "You know how they say you can judge people by their friends?"

"Yeah?"

"Don't." He smiles. "What about tomorrow?"

"Maybe," she says. She hands him his plate. He hesitates as if he wants to kiss her, but then looks at her dad. "Good luck," he whispers. "We'll talk later."

She watches as he licks a bit of tomato sauce off his thumb. She's convinced it's the sexiest thing she's ever seen anyone do to her food, including seeing Ed Burns lick his lips.

Vic watches him as he leaves. "Nice-looking guy, I guess. But he seems to do pretty well for a surfer."

"I know," Toni says, sounding confused. "And the tickets are so expensive."

But she didn't like the sound of that. *There's something we have to talk about.* That's exactly what Kevin said the last time she saw him.

The Dixieland jazz band starts playing "La Vie en Rose."

Layla stares down into her St-Germain cocktail. She's unsteady on her feet, her four-inch Jimmy Choos stabbing the grass. Tabitha, Lorne, Poppy, and Auden are behind her, also being sucked into the lawn by their heels. Between them so many diamonds flicker and flash when Layla lets her eyes go out of focus, she feels surrounded by a swarm of fireflies. Photographers keep herding them into a little group to take photographs. People stop by to chat. Air kisses are exchanged. Invitations offered. Compliments disbursed. Layla is introduced as "Hudson's fiancée, Layla Sullivan."

Never Layla Sullivan first, then Hudson's fiancée.

She feels her stomach rumble. Hudson paid almost a thousand dollars for their tickets and she hasn't eaten a thing yet. Neither have any of the step-bridesmaids. It always baffled her: all the money in the world to eat anything they want, and most of the socialites preferred to starve themselves.

Her spirits brighten when she sees a camera flash at Booth 21.

"Hey. That's Toni's booth. We should go over and say hi."

Tabitha says, "She looks busy. Let's walk around. I hear Christy Turlington is here."

Layla feels herself propelled through the crowd. She meets Christy Turlington and Ed Burns, Beth Ostrosky and Howard Stern, Billy and Katie Lee Joel, and a dozen other people she thought she wanted to meet all her life. But it just makes her miss Toni even more.

Chapter 58

Bill Mitchell is at his desk, flipping through the hefty document provided by the East Hampton Environmental Society on the Piping Plover and Least Tern Protection Project. He's convinced that his life as a journalist must consist of more than herding socialites at food fairs. He's determined to snap at least one photo of the endangered piping plover before the end of the summer.

The door opens, letting in a slash of light. He's pleasantly surprised to see Tucker drag Toni in.

"Tucker, stay . . ."

But Tucker sniffs around the room, dragging his carabiner.

"Hey, Toni."

This time he leans right over to kiss her on the cheek. She backs away automatically, but then realizes what he's trying to do. There's an awkward moment where she leans forward smiling and they kiss cheeks.

"Hey," she says. "I wanted to thank you so much for that nice write-up you did on F-4."

"No problem. You deserved it. You guys kicked butt for fibromyalgia." She's filling out a form. "More staff?"

"If you can believe it." She smiles with excitement. "We got such great feedback from the fair, I even have an *official* birthday party next weekend."

"Congratulations," he says. He watches her for a moment. "You look good."

"Thanks. You too."

"No, I mean really. You look different lately. You're tan. And kind of . . . shiny."

She frowns at him.

"No, not shiny. That's not what I mean. I mean . . . you know. Happy. Relaxed. Glowing!" Bill is relieved to find the word. "Yes, glowing."

"Thanks. I'm a summer person. Always have been." She keeps writing.

Bill clears his throat. "You know, I never got a chance to apologize to you over all that trouble at the beginning of the summer. All that retraction stuff."

"Oh, *that.*"

"It was Susan Schumacher who made me correct it."

"I'm not surprised. I know Susan. She makes the people at Town Hall look like the ACLU."

He laughs. Shifts his weight a bit. "I've always wanted to make it up to you. In fact, I was hoping to, um . . . uh . . . I just wondered if you . . . um . . ."

"Um?"

"If we could go for dinner or something."

It's Toni's turn to um and uh.

"What about this weekend?"

"Uh . . . sorry . . . I'm busy."

"Next weekend?"

"Busy."

"Thursday?"

"Sorry." She winces.

"Are you always this busy?"

"Actually . . . yes."

"Well, if you ever get a night off, maybe you could call me and we could go for drinks or something."

"That sounds . . . um . . . er . . . good. When things slow down for me." She rummages through her bag and slaps a ten on the counter. "Nice seeing you again, Bill. Gotta run. Very—"

"Busy?"

"Right." She grabs Tucker's leash.

"Wait a second. Let me give you my number. Just in case."

"Yeah, sure." She takes his card and stares at it. "That's a very . . . nice number. As far as numbers go." She backs toward the door. "Okay, Chris—I mean, Bill—nice to see you again."

"Nice seeing you too."

She gets to the door, grabs the knob, stops. She closes her eyes and slumps back toward the counter.

"Uh, Bill?"

"Yeah."

"I'm probably not going to call you."

"What?"

"I didn't want to say anything. I have trouble saying no to people. It's one of my problems. And usually why I'm so busy all the time. But I should just tell you. I probably won't be calling. Because . . . I'm seeing somebody else . . . I think."

"You think?"

There's something we have to talk about.

"It *feels* like I'm seeing somebody, anyway. You know, all the butterflies"— she pats her tummy—"and the fireworks"—twirls her arms in the air.

"Was he the guy I saw at the fair?" Bill's tone is soft and slightly hurt.

"Yeah. . . . How'd you know?"

"Just . . . the way he looked at you."

"Really?" She can't help but smile. Then she remembers herself. "Anyway, the reason I'm telling you is that I don't want you to be waiting for me to call when I probably won't. It's a small town. We're going to bump into each other for the rest of the summer, and I'll be trying to avoid you and you're going to be wondering what's wrong with me and the summer's so short and it goes by so fast and it's such a happy time of year, who needs that extra stress, right?"

"Right . . . I guess."

"I just thought I'd tell you that in case you're waiting for my call. I hope you don't think I'm rude."

He smiles kind of sadly. "I don't think you're rude."

"Good." She smiles at him. "Well . . . have a nice day. Or summer. Or . . . never mind. You know what I mean." She gives him a smile and turns to the door, thinking, *In the Hamptons, when it rains, it pours.*

Chapter 59

With its loamy soil and near-ideal sun exposure, it was only a matter of time before a new fruit was added to the bountiful crops of the Hamptons—grapes. In only twenty-five years, viniculture on the North and South Forks has grown from a single vineyard to over thirty operating wineries. The East End is now considered to be one of the country's most exciting wine-producing regions.
—*The Guru's Guide to the Hamptons*

Didi stands bony elbow to elbow with three friends on the terrace of Wolffer Estates for the annual Parrish Art Museum benefit. The winery has the aged-stone appearance of a European villa, and the fields spread out in all directions like tight green stripes in an awning. A keyboardist and bassist play smooth jazz in the corner as guests mingle and nibble on canapés, the women in floral dresses or pastel suits, the men casual, without ties. Didi tries to avoid questions about the wedding, but it's impossible.

"You can't have a wedding without a planner," says Livonia Havisham.

"Or at least a consultant," says her sister, Nemone.

"You can't expect to do it on your own," says Margaret Wainwright-Bankes. "You're much too busy."

"Much, much too busy."

"We all are."

"The summer," the sisters opine together.

"It's so busy you need a vacation to get over it."

A server walks by with a tray of smoked salmon. The women look over the hors d'oeuvres as if seriously considering eating more.

"I'm so stuffed."

"My eyes are bigger than my stomach."

"No, thank you."

The server walks away.

Didi tries to keep her voice casual as she asks: "Do you happen to know any good planners?" She hates not "knowing" someone she should know.

"Let me ask Winnie," says Margaret. "Her daughter's wedding was lovely."

"Just beautiful."

"And what about florists? Have you thought about that?"

"Or music?"

"Or food?"

"Well . . ."

"You're hiring Susan, aren't you?"

"Well . . ."

"You *have* to hire Susan, Didi."

"The girl's friend is a caterer and—"

"What's her name?"

"Toni something."

"Who's she worked with?"

"Um . . ."

"Has she done any big parties?"

"I'm not exactly sure."

They blink at her. Blink at each other. Raise their eyebrows. Sip their wine.

"Excuse me, ladies," says an attractive young man with a camera. "Would you be so kind?"

"Oh, delighted!" The women fall in line, standing in a little semicircle. Didi jostles Nemone out of the way, making sure her horsey side stays out of the shot.

"Say cheese, ladies!"

Didi looks at her friends, holding what's left of her facial muscles in a smile. *Don't you mean extra-old cheddar?* she thinks.

Chapter 60

Toni drives slowly along Middle Lane, careful not to upset her precious cargo: several coolers, bins, baskets, and a bubbling silver vat of liquid nitrogen. Rhonda and Jerome sit straight-backed, watching the tank as if it might explode.

Her cell phone rings. The call display says it's a pay phone. "Fratelli's Catering."

"Toni?"

It's him.

Chris *Obbbbbm.*

She feels the smile brighten her face. "When are you going to get a cell?"

"I'm roughing it, remember?"

Rhonda points out a sign. "There!" Toni takes a left at a professionally painted banner that reads: David and Duncan's 7th Birthday Party.

"I just wanted to wish you luck," he says. "Maybe later we can go out for dinner and celebrate."

She lets out a breath of relief. She thought he was going to say "talk."

———

"It's not that big," says Rhonda as they pull up to a five-thousand-square-foot modern home by the road. Everyone imagined the producer and his wife would've had a much larger place.

"It's still nice," Toni says.

She turns left through the gate and sees Sammie and Tootie, a husband-and-wife clown team, juggling bowling pins on the front lawn. She knows for a fact that the duo are one of the most popular kids' acts around.

And they're relegated to the gate?

A dwarf dressed as a rhinestone cowboy rides a mini-horse over to the van. "Love the car," he says in a squeaky voice. "You'll need this." He hands her a map of the grounds, where ten acres have been subdivided like an amusement park.

They ease up a winding drive, passing a full-size merry-go-round and a puppet show in rehearsal. Finally, the main house comes into view, looming over the property like an ancient pyramid.

"I guess the one down at the gate is just a guesthouse," Rhonda says.

"Yes, I have dijon." Toni smiles at a mother who has a small demon child by the wrist. Toni spreads a dollop of mustard on a mini-cheeseburger, then watches the woman drag the screaming child away.

She's staked out on the raised deck of the Gunite pool, behind a granite counter and an outdoor kitchen. More than a place to barbecue and store beer, this version of the latest Hamptons status symbol has a professional six-burner cooktop, a Sub-Zero fridge, a built-in wok, a vegetable sink, and a garbage compactor—which the kids keep dumping twigs and flowers into because they like the sound it makes.

There are about sixty guests, half of them children. Toni recognizes most of the parents from television, the sports pages, or local society magazines. There are very few nannies in attendance. For people who are without their children 99 percent of the time, a birthday party is an opportunity to show the world that you actually know how to take care of your kids.

The attire is typical Hamptons garden party: floral dresses and sandals for the women, pale gabardines and button-down shirts for the men. There are very few shorts and except for the kids and a bored-looking lifeguard, no bathing suits. You'd never know you were five minutes from the beach on a hot summer afternoon.

As for the children, they all look like they're decked out for a Best & Co. photo shoot. Unfortunately, the perfection ends there: the party feels more like a page out of *Lord of the Flies* than a high-end catalog. Everyone is screaming and fighting, scratching and crying. The guests of honor, seven-year-old tow-headed twins in matching powder blue Victorian seersucker jumpers, are the worst of the bunch. Every time Toni has to go inside the house for supplies, one of them blocks her way.

"What's the password?" he says, digging a toy gun into her stomach.

"Um . . . I don't know the password." Her hands are full but she tries to play along.

"Then you can't get by."

It takes her ten minutes to get anywhere.

At least the food is a hit. That's what everyone keeps telling her, anyway. She made mini everything last night. Mini-hotdogs and cheeseburgers. Tiny cupcakes, bite-sized croque-monsieurs, and her mini triple-chocolate cannolis. The liquid nitrogen is particularly popular. Rhonda freezes strawberries in the bubbling fluid, then dips them in chocolate and freezes them again, or uses chunks of frozen candy bars for mind-numbing chocolate kebobs.

Toni's astounded at how much money this birthday party must've cost. There's an eight-foot-high soda pop fountain. A petting zoo. Cotton candy machines. On the far side, a clown is being dunked in a six-foot tub. Winners of the contest run around with full-size stuffed animals by Steiff. Toni remembers begging her mother to buy one of their little four-inch teddy bears from FAO Schwartz when she was a kid. "We're not made of money," her mother said. And here they are giving away a full-size menagerie as party favors.

She's on the pool deck serving up a platter of toothpick-size french fries when she notices a cluster of kids at the edge of the deep end. Some of them wear bathing suits, others their day clothes, but they're all looking into the water. That's when she sees a form on the bottom of the pool.

Without thinking, she tosses her fries and jumps straight into the water. The world becomes nothing but turquoise bubbles and the taste of chlorine. She hears her mother's voice.

Hurry, Toni, hurry . . . You'll miss the light.

Don't panic, she thinks, *don't panic.*

She pumps toward the figure at the bottom of the pool. It's a boy, one of the twins. His arm is slippery when she grabs it, tugging him toward the surface. They both emerge into sunlight, coughing on water. The boy glares at her, his eyes red from chlorine.

"What're you doing, you stupid dummy?" he yells.

She hears a splash behind her and sees the lifeguard, a tanned blond college boy, swimming overhand toward her.

"You okay?" he asks when he gets to her.

"I'm okay," she says. "Is he?"

The boy dog-paddles to the edge of the pool, the other kids laughing at him.

"Ah-hah!" says the second twin, jumping up and down. "I knew you couldn't do it!"

Toni looks back at the lifeguard in confusion.

"It was a game," he says. "I'm teaching them to hold their breath."

Everyone on the deck is now looking at her as she treads water in the middle of the pool with all her clothes on. She feels her cheeks flush. She takes a few clumsy strokes to the ladder and pulls herself out. The parents are still staring, all looking so calm with their drinks and their food. She peels wet hair off her face and wrings out the tail of her blouse.

"Better safe than sorry," she says, then slops across the deck for a towel.

Chapter 61

"Forget it, Johnson. Don't say a word."

The men are on the beach in front of the house, a volleyball net strung across the sand. A smattering of people Chris doesn't know files in and out of the house and down to the beach. There are beer cases, barbecued hotdogs, and several bikinis.

But Chris doesn't notice any of them.

"I'm just feeling so damn guilty," he says.

"For what?" Yuri asks. "It's not your fault she has propas . . . pro-pat—"

"Prosopagnosia," Lincoln says, coming out of the dune with the lost volleyball. He tosses it over to Yuri's teammate, a tall leggy redhead in a purple bathing suit.

Yuri says, "That's what I meant. Stop mopping about it."

"Moping," both Chris and Lincoln say.

Lincoln turns to Chris. "So tell her if it's bothering you that much."

"I've been trying to," Chris says. "But every time I go to say something, either somebody interrupts us or she's too busy. Or she says something that makes the timing all wrong." He serves the ball over the net. "It's driving me crazy."

Yuri watches his teammate set it up; he spikes it back hard. Chris is so preoccupied he misses the return.

"Point!" Yuri hugs the redhead and they slap each other's butts. He turns to the guys: "I love this country," he whispers.

Frank comes down from the house with a tray of Gatorade. "Rehydration time."

"You got anything stronger than that?" Lincoln asks.

"Alcohol dehydrates you. Especially in the sun."

"That's what ice is for," Lincoln says.

Frank offers his tray to Chris, who shakes his head.

"What's wrong with him?"

"Ninety-second Street," Lincoln says.

"Still?"

Chris shrugs.

"You didn't tell her?"

"Not yet."

"I thought you were going to at the food festival."

"She was busy."

"Or he wimped out," Lincoln says.

"Do you blame me?"

Frank says, "You probably shouldn't say anything until the deal's over, anyway. It's not like you have a choice. When it all comes down, if she's half the girl you think she is, she'll understand."

Chris turns to Lincoln. "What do you think I should do?"

"You don't want to know."

"Nothing, right?"

"My feeling is, you had a bad day. Big deal. We all know how much pressure you were under—we were *all* under. If she doesn't remember, you got a get-out-of-jail-free card. Just go with it. I sure wish I could take back a couple bad days." He tosses the ball up to serve.

"But what if she finds out?"

"How can she?"

Chapter 62

"There you are."

Layla is on a lounger by the pool when Didi steps into her sunlight.

"Are you busy?"

"Sort of." She's on her iPhone trying to book guests for a party at the Surf Lodge that night.

Didi says, "Well, the sun's not going anywhere. I want to show you something."

Layla sighs and gets up, ignoring the outstretched hand. The heads of two gardeners appear over a shrub to watch Layla wiggle by; they vanish again when Didi glares at them.

The pool pavilion is cool and quiet; the sound of lawn mowers is muffled by classical music.

"I'm so glad we get a chance to talk like this. I wanted to thank you for making such quick work of all that"—Didi opens a small armoire—"legal nonsense."

Only after she grabs a bottle of white wine does Layla realize it's a lovely mini-fridge.

"Lawyers run the world, don't they? They certainly run mine."

"No problem. Till death do us part, right?"

Didi hesitates as she pours the drinks. Her greatest hope is for an early divorce. "That's such a—refreshing—attitude for a young person to have about marriage." She hands Layla her glass.

The sound of Baccarat against Baccarat chimes like the high C on a church organ.

"Speaking of nuptials, I was at the most marvelous wedding at the Meadow last week. I wish you could've seen it. It would've inspired you." She goes to the door of her private office and inputs the code. "The gardens, the orchestra, the flowers." She raises her voice to be heard as she disappears inside the office. "It was sensational. And absolutely everybody was—" Didi turns around to see Layla standing in the doorway.

"What is this place?"

"My office." Her arms are full of photo albums as she tries to block Layla from entering the small room. But Layla walks around her.

"Smells like a hamster cage."

"That's the cedar. To prevent moths. The entire room is done to archive specifications. I have some very valuable documents in here. Why don't we—"

"Why are the windows tinted?"

"To protect from UV rays." She motions with the photo albums. "These are what I want to show you. But let's go outside. We don't want any accidents with the wine."

Layla sidles away and leans over the table. Didi watches in horror as a single drop of condensation builds on the rim of the glass and starts dripping slowly down the stem.

"So this is it, huh?"

"The family tree, yes. I've been working on it for years."

Layla sees all the names, the birthplaces, the spouses, the offspring, and often the name of the officiant—usually an Episcopal priest—at each wedding date.

"You're related to all these people?"

"Yes. I've traced one branch of the Blackhart bloodline back to the twelfth century. You know we were part of the first passage. Do you know what that is?"

"Sounds familiar."

"The *Mayflower*," Didi says.

Layla thinks: *My family has been here just as long as yours. Only we've been working for a living, not sitting around on our asses all summer. I was born in the Southampton Hospital, by the way. Down the hall from where Jacqueline Bouvier was born.* But she imagines Didi Flagstone would not be impressed with her slim connection to Jackie O., both of them being good Catholic girls. So all she says is . . .

"What's the *Mayflower*?"

Didi laugh-coughs.

"I'm just kidding," Layla says. She notices the blank spot next to Hudson's name and it reminds her of a double plot headstone that has yet to be engraved. "How come I'm not on it?"

"Not until *after* the wedding," Didi says, scooting her out of the room.

They sit together on the blue divan. "These are from *my* Big Day." Didi opens a large white album on her lap.

"I've seen some of these around," Layla says.

They flip through the shots of Didi in her snug strapless gown, tiny veil, dark lips. "You were so pretty," Layla says.

Didi sighs. "You have no idea, my dear. The gift of beauty is not worth the curse of losing it."

"Oh, come on. Don't talk like that. I hope I look as good as you when I'm your age."

Didi hesitates; she doesn't know if that's a compliment or an insult. "Thank you," she says.

"What's that one?"

Didi opens a second, older album, covered in tapestry. "These are from my mother's wedding. She was married aboard my grandfather's yacht in the Aegean. The ship's captain married them."

Layla sees Didi's mother, a slim girl with dark eyes and hair, wearing a gauzy gown; the groom is tall and broad with a large mustache.

"It was a whirlwind romance," Didi says. "Must've seemed very bohemian at the time. My father was not the most reserved man who ever drew breath, let's face it. It was a bit of a *scandale*, actually. I'm not sure my mother ever lived it down. She always shared with me her regrets that she didn't have her wedding here on the lawn at Concordia like her own mother. She even tried to convince me to marry Henry here. But young women, they have their own ideas."

Layla notices that the last half of the album is empty, and Didi quickly closes it, as if a lack of photographic evidence of something made it less important.

"This is my grandmother's wedding." Didi opens the third album, this one leather with black pages. The photographs of women in pale gowns and bonnets and men in tight-fitting suits are cracked and sepia-toned. Layla recognizes the slope of the lawn and the back of the house, the shape of the windows and fountain.

"I remember my grandmother showing me these when I was young. I don't know how many times we went through them together. I think it was one of the greatest joys of her life, the perfect wedding." Didi turns to face her. "Now, you're a beautiful girl, and from what I've seen you take a marvelous picture. Well, of course. A model. I would love to have modeled when I was young— but my mother wanted me to get an education."

Layla gives a little roll of her eyes.

"If you have the wedding on the beach, think about the photographs. It could be Martha's Vineyard. It could be Newport. Good God, it could be Mexico! Why would you want such generic pictures on your wedding day when you have such a beautiful house here that I know you love so much?"

"But I thought we *would* take some shots up toward the house."

"And get all that scrap fencing in there? All those scraggly weeds? It will be so depressing to see nothing but grass and sand. What about the lawn? And the gardens?"

Didi says they'll rent some nice tents and have a dance floor on the tennis court and champagne fountains and great columns of flowers everywhere. Didi asks her what her favorite flower is and Layla says she likes daises and Didi says, all right, daisies it is! Probably. And if there aren't enough daisies on the East End, they'll have them shipped in from India or wherever it is that they grow daisies in bulk.

Layla turns away from the albums. "But a garden wedding is so fussy."

"Not *fussy*. Elegant. Maybe it's time for you to expand your aesthetic horizons a bit. And now that you have the perfect dress, why not the perfect wedding?" She hesitates for a moment, then pats the girl's knee. Layla almost shivers from the weight of her cold hand.

"Just consider it. That's all I ask. If you do decide to do something a little more . . . traditional, I want you to know that Henry and I would be happy to pay for it."

Layla's jaw drops open. "Are you serious?"

Didi nods.

"That would be so—nice—of you." It's not a word she's ever associated with her future mother-in-law before.

Chapter 63

Sag Harbor is a small village built on the north shore. Settled in the early 1700s, within a hundred years it became one of the most important whaling ports in the world. Today, the gingerbread shops on narrow winding streets still evoke the charm of an old English fishing village. Sag Harbor is so architecturally significant, in fact, that the entire business district is on the National Register of Historic Places.

—*The Guru's Guide to the Hamptons*

Toni stares at the black-and-white photograph on the wall of the Tulla Booth Gallery: a dandelion growing out of a crack in a sidewalk. Then another: a simple air duct against a brick wall. There are wide shots of New York City. Several shots of her mother's old neighborhood in Brooklyn. She looks at these black-and-white images of New York and decides she's not missing the city as much as she thought she would.

She feels arms go around her waist. "I hope you're not bored," says Ruth Fratelli.

"Not at all. I'm so proud of you . . ."

"And I'm proud of *you*. Come on. Let's walk. I need a breather."

Ruth puts her hand in Toni's arm and leads her out of the gallery, past a respectable handful of people sipping wine and studying her photographs. Ruth is a young-looking fifty-nine with shiny shoulder-length auburn hair. She wears a white tunic and black leggings, which look much more sophisticated than the aprons she used to wear cooking in the restaurant. Toni notices a flat package tied with a bow sticking out of her tote bag.

Out in the sunshine, Ruth takes a deep breath. "It still smells like fish out here."

"I like that smell," Toni says. "It's not just fish. It's flowers and earth and sand and fruit and—"

"Still smells like fish to me," Ruth says with a laugh. They walk arm in arm down Main Street. "I wish I could stay longer. I'd love to meet your new man."

"I wish you could've met him too. I tried to call him, but . . . he doesn't have a cell."

"Mmmm."

"He kind of dropped out of the world."

"So you said."

They continue past the large gingerbread verandah of the American Hotel, where Steven Gaines does his NPR talk show every Sunday. Toni remembers reading about old Sag Harbor in high school when they studied *Moby-Dick.* She imagined the streets filled with merchants selling harpoons and whale oil and dried cod. Back then it felt to her as if the whole East End was a history book and she was tucked into its pages somewhere.

Ruth says, "I happened to get your father on the phone when I called. We had a nice talk."

"Nicer than the old days?" Toni says with a grin.

"That wouldn't be hard. He says he doesn't know what the boy does for a living, and it concerns him."

"By 'boy' I assume you mean Chris?"

"Sorry. Chris."

"He's not a boy, Mom. He's a man. He went to Harvard Business School. He's just . . ."

"Between gigs," they say together.

"That's right."

"I don't want to pry, sweetie. Neither of us do. I'm totally into free spirits and wanderers. But it's your dad. You know how he worries about you. We just want you to be happy, that's all."

"But I *am* happy," Toni says.

Ruth turns to face her daughter. "Are you?"

"Is everything perfect? Do I wish my phone was ringing off the hook with more business? Do I wish I didn't have to wait tables at night? Uh, yeah."

"But the boy—I mean, Chris—does he make you happy?"

Toni thinks about it, her pace slowing. "He makes me feel like nobody ever has. He listens to me when I talk. He makes me laugh. I don't know. I just feel this connection to him. It's weird . . . he's so familiar. As if I've known him all my life. And yet . . . I'm still kind of nervous about it. As if something's going to go wrong any second."

She sees her mother's worried eyes and quickly changes the subject.

"I mean, everything's great. Really it is. Never mind. I hardly ever get to see you. Let's just do our thing today. Forget the boys."

Ruth smiles and kisses Toni's cheek. "You're right. I have an idea. Ice cream?"

"Perfect!"

They stop at the Ice Cream Club and take their cones to walk down Long Wharf, passing white yachts and sport cruisers at the marina. Toni thinks there's nothing more perfect than strolling the Hamptons with an ice-cream cone. Except when she can do it with her mom.

"Have you been out to Chester Drive?" Ruth asks.

Toni makes a little wincing face. "I've been avoiding it. It's too hard to see it in such bad shape. Georgia Randall says it's for sale, but that it needs some TLC. You know what that means in Realtor's language. Just this side of the wrecking ball."

"If there's anyone who could get it into shape, it's you."

"As if I have the money," Toni says. "Who's that for?" She points to the gift sticking out of Ruth's bag.

"I was wondering when you'd get curious."

Toni's eyes widen with excitement. She hands off her ice-cream cone and they go to sit on a nearby bench. Ruth watches, smiling, as Toni unwraps a framed black-and-white photograph. Her eyes fill with tears when she sees a little dark-haired girl in profile looking through a white telescope, a tiny hand fixed on the focus wheel. Behind her are wooden railings and a long curved beach.

"I found it when I was cleaning out some old photographs last week," Ruth says. "I thought you might like to have it."

Toni just flutters her hand in the air. She motions for the ice-cream cone again, and Ruth goes to hand it back to her, but she just wants the napkin to dab her eyes.

Ruth puts her arm around her daughter and kisses her. "You are sooo sensitive sometimes," she says with a laugh.

Chapter 64

Toni has been in a love-hate relationship with August all her life. The weather is still beautiful. The trees are lush. The streets and beaches are busier than ever with a special brand of tourist: the August People.

But each day the sun sets a bit earlier and the shadows seem longer, even at midday. The pumpkin patches are dotted with orange and the nights start to get cool. Toni knows the calendar specified thirty-one days in August—one of the longest months of the year—but not one of them went by more quickly for her.

She's walking Tucker when she sees a postal carrier she's known for twenty years whistling down the sidewalk. He asks after her and her father, as he always does, hands her the day's mail, then whistles on his way. Toni flips through it as she walks back up to the house.

What she sees makes her stop in her tracks.

Layla's wedding invitation is mixed in with bills and a flyer from Citarella. A thick white envelope almost as soft as Egyptian cotton sheets is calligraphed in silver ink.

Miss Antonia Fratelli and Guest.

It's printed on Mrs. John L. Strong stationery, the most exclusive papery in New York. There are no seashells or sandcastles or anything else that reminds Toni of Layla. It is very formal, it is very expensive—and it is very Didi.

But she feels a rush of excitement when she thinks about bringing Chris. Whatever he wanted to "talk" about before couldn't have been that serious. He hasn't brought it up again, and they've spent every spare minute together for a week. Going to the beach, trying her favorite restaurants, just taking Tucker for a walk.

"At least I have a guest," she says. Tucker barks and wags his tail as if he's the one who's just been invited.

Mr. Henry Hudson Flagstone III

and

Mrs. Deirdre Elizabeth Blackhart Flagstone

request the honor of your presence
at the marriage of their son,

Henry Hudson Flagstone IV

and

Miss Layla Marie Sullivan

On Saturday, the fifth of September
Two Thousand and Nine
At four o'clock
In the garden of Concordia
810 Gin Lane
Southampton, New York
Reception to follow

Chapter 65

In the large kitchen of her shop on Newtown Lane, Susan Schumacher separates six dozen small organic eggs. Around her, a small army of chefs and prep cooks get ready for all her events that day. Two garden parties. Four birthdays. A bar mitzvah. A barbecue. The Annual Running Charades Game at Concordia. Susan wouldn't be going to Southampton herself—the forecast was for bad weather—but she'd definitely be on hand Labor Day weekend for the wedding.

That would teach that little upstart.

Susan cracks another small egg into the bowl and sees a tiny splotch of red in the yolk. She looks over her shoulder, then leans forward to pluck at the clot with her latex-gloved finger. It slides out of her grasp like soap. She takes off her glove and nudges the clot up the side of the bowl with her bare finger. She exhales in relief when it's safely on the outside rim of the bowl and then goes back to cracking her eggs.

Chapter 66

Toni and Chris spread out a picnic blanket on the grass of Herrick Park. Around them, basketball, tennis, football, and baseball each claim a corner of the vast green sporting field. The trees of Dayton Lane behind them seem as tall and dense as a mountain range as the late afternoon sun sinks toward them.

"This feels so weird," Toni says. "I don't know how many times I played touch football here when I was a kid."

"You sure you want to?" he says. "We can just go for dinner."

"No, it'll be fun. Sully and I could hold our own in Ultimate."

"A woman of many talents," he says.

He leans over to give her a light kiss. It's innocent and natural at first, until he stops and looks at her mouth. They start kissing again, more deeply. She feels his arms go around her waist as he pulls her closer to him. Before long, she forgets that they're in public—until she hears a voice call across the field.

"Johnson!"

A group of people head over from the parking lot. Toni and Chris pull away from each other, both seeming a little shocked at how quickly an innocent peck on the lips could turn into something else.

"So this is her," Lincoln says. "We've heard so much about you. Great to finally meet."

Yuri says, "No wonder we never see Johnson anymore." He gives Chris a high five. Toni just laughs.

"Frank Broward the third," says another man. He wears glasses and almost dips in a bow.

Chris points to the rest of the group. "That's Amanda and Joyce," he says about two attractive women, one with long blond hair and another with short curly dark hair. They stop walking and linger near the edge of the field, clearly locked in an intense conversation.

"I have no idea who the others are," he whispers. "They just crashed at our place last night."

Toni sees a gaggle of tanned men and women carrying a beer cooler and blankets.

"Life at a house share," she says, trying to ignore the sting of jealousy she feels. "There's food if anyone wants it." She points to her picnic basket.

"'Food' is an understatement, by the way," says Chris.

Yuri turns on a boom box and George Michael's "Faith" blasts out. Some of the newcomers jeer.

The Day-Glo green Frisbee starts going back and forth between the players as everyone warms up. Toni catches her shots easily, zipping them off to Chris, who stands about twenty feet away. As the shots get harder, she's able to keep up, and when she misses, she just laughs. Chris starts getting into it too, jumping and taking dives. He complains he's getting hot and pulls off his T-shirt, revealing his bare chest. Toni fans herself playfully, and he just shakes his head and laughs.

Obviously everything is fine between them, she tells herself. He's even introducing her to his friends. For a guy, that's tantamount to meeting the parents.

She feels whatever nervousness she had about him finally start to unwind.

When did she become such a pessimist?

Has she always been like this? Or did it just happen last year?

"Duck, Toni!"

She hears Chris's voice, and she automatically dips to her knees. The Frisbee whizzes over her head.

"Sorry, Johnson!" Yuri says.

And then—*thock*—on the other side. She turns to see Frank turn at the last second and take the Frisbee in the forehead. His glasses go flying. He buckles to the ground.

Without thinking, Toni runs toward him. Her breathing is shallow and panicked.

Don't faint . . . don't faint. . . .

Frank is on his back, moaning. There's a little gash on his forehead, turning purple but not quite bleeding. The other players run over, Chris pushing in front of them with a take-charge look on his face.

"How you doing, buddy?" He sees the cut, gets up, and runs to the cooler, coming back with a can of Budweiser.

Toni frowns. *Odd timing for a beer.*

The can is cold and dripping as Chris kneels next to Frank. "That's not so bad, Frankie. You'll live."

Frank is coming to, his eyelashes fluttering.

"Put this on your head," he says. "It'll help keep the swelling down."

Chapter 67

She feels the ground warp beneath her feet. A flash of images. Him kneeling beside her on the sidewalk. The feeling of his hands as he helped her up.

Where'd you learn that? Boy Scouts?

A million things run through her mind in the next second, but all she can say is, "You?"

"Toni . . . I was . . . I . . ." His voice trails off.

Lincoln looks from one to the other. "Uh-oh."

"That was *you* that day?"

Chris sighs and looks down. He seems guilty and, for the first time since she met him, afraid. Without saying another word, she turns on her heel and heads back to her van.

Her head pounds. If she doesn't keep walking, she thinks she's going to faint.

She can't believe it. It's him?

She hears the scrape of his shoes behind her in the stone archway between the field and the parking lot. "Toni, please . . ." He takes her arm. They stop in the shade of the archway, so cool and dim; her heartbeat seems to echo off the walls. "I *wanted* to tell you. I tried telling you. I really did. But every time I went to explain, somebody interrupted us. You know everyone out here."

"Not *everyone*, apparently." She jerks her arm out of his grasp and keeps walking.

"Toni, please . . ." He follows her again.

The parking lot is busier than ever with August People. Cars, buses, pedestrians, the smell of exhaust. People honk as she walks in front of them without looking.

"Toni, please talk to me. I can explain."

"Explain what? That you're one of the biggest jerks I've ever met?" She's at the van, fumbling with her keys. "I knew you looked familiar. I knew I'd met you somewhere before. Prosopagnosia or not." She gets into the van and slams the door.

The window is open and she tries to roll it up, but he holds it with his hands. "Toni, I know I was an asshole that day. But I was so stressed. You can't believe what was happening. I had such a splitting headache from—"

"Yeah, I know. You were hung over from karaoke. Don't remind me." Her hands shake as she tries to get the keys in the ignition. She wills herself to have the calmness she had that day in the restaurant with Kevin. *I thought I should tell you in person.*

"I know I should've said something, Toni. I know. But—"

"You were too ashamed of yourself?"

"Well . . . yeah. But it's not just that. There's a legitimate reason I couldn't say anything before."

"Don't you mean *excuse?*"

"A reason is different from an excuse."

"Depends which side you're on."

She finally gets the engine to catch and the van lurches as she puts it in reverse. She tries to back up, but there are cars clogging the lane behind her. *So much for the dramatic getaway,* she thinks.

He lets out a big breath of air. "I'm actually glad it's out now," he says. "I can't believe it, but I'm relieved. It's been bugging the hell out of me all summer."

"Poor you. I could really tell." She leans on her horn and a BMW behind her is so shocked he stops and lets her in. But traffic is still slow and Chris is able to keep up with the van at a walking pace.

"Toni, the truth is, I manage money for a living. My company—our company"—he motions back to the park—"is called Eastwood Investment Funds."

"Let me guess. After Clint Eastwood, right?"

He gives a little shrug. "We're all fans."

"You think everything's a joke, don't you? Was *I* a joke too?"

"Toni, *no.* . . . Please listen to me. I'm not finished. That's where I was working the day I saw you on Ninety-second Street. That's why the suit and the town car and—"

"The attitude?"

He sighs. "We had just got an offer from Federal Alliance Investments. They wanted to buy us out."

"I'm getting the business report now?"

He perseveres. "It all went down a few weeks later. But one of the stipulations of the deal was that we couldn't work for a competing firm for ninety days. That's what we're doing here—doing nothing."

"Between gigs," Toni says. "But to think I actually felt sorry for you. I thought you were laid off or something. And you were *bought out*?"

"Toni, I know it's stupid. I know it is. But we weren't allowed to talk about it. The deal was totally confidential. We actually had to sign an NDA. Do you know what that is?"

"Of course I know what an NDA is. My dad was a lawyer, remember?" She takes a tiny dig. "And so was my ex."

"So you understand then. If I had told you what was really going on, I could've been sued."

"Welcome to the Hamptons," she says. "Everybody's afraid of getting sued!" She finally gets a break in traffic and screeches away.

Chapter 68

"I wasn't going to beg," Didi says. She follows Estella up the steep stairs to the rooms over the garage.

"Of course not, miss."

"Nothing but wedding planners from Westhampton to Montauk and I can't find *one* who's going to help me without asking a bunch of stupid personal questions. What business is it of theirs how much I want to spend? Don't they know how rude it is to ask people about money?"

Estella opens the white door at the top of the steps. A broad room with small gable windows is dim and dusty. Estella turns on a bare lightbulb, scattering some moths. The room is full of old furniture, broken mirrors, lamps with no shades.

"I'm sure it's in here somewhere," she says. "Try over there." She points to a stack of boxes in the corner, and Estella moves an old rocking chair to get to them.

Didi says, "I can't tell you how much I resent this. Why do I always have to do everything myself? As if I'm not busy enough in the summer without having to plan a wedding too."

"You don't *have* to do it, miss." Estella pulls over an old stool to reach the boxes.

"And what's the option? To let *the girl* do it? I don't want my Sonny married at some scruffy ceremony on the beach. What would people think? Maybe it's that big one there." Didi points to a box.

"The wedding is going to be beautiful no matter what happens, miss," Estella says. "The house is so lovely and they're both so happy that—"

Thump!

The box lands on the floor, kicking up dust.

Didi is just about to snap at Estella to be more careful when she sees the black marker on the side. "That's it," she says. "I knew it was here. We kept all our old junk here."

Estella carries the box to Didi.

"Open it."

Estella rips brittle masking tape and pulls back the flaps. Didi peers down into the box as if looking over a high cliff. She sees a large flat white box tied with ribbon.

"Oh my God," she says. "Keep looking." She picks up the white box and carries it to the rocking chair. She unties the ribbon and pulls back tissue paper.

A soft gasp catches in her throat. Her bridal gown is slightly yellowed after so many years, but folded neatly. She hasn't seen it since her wedding night.

"Is this it?" Estella holds up a slim pale book with a sketch of a pink cupid on it. Didi tosses the dress to the side.

"I knew I'd find it!" she says, grabbing her original copy of *Emily Post Weddings*. The spine cracks as she opens it to the bright pink title page and her maiden name written in the top corner. Deirdre Elizabeth Blackhart.

Estella continues looking through the box, taking out silver spoons from France, Italy, and Spain. "What are these?"

"Souvenirs. From my honeymoon."

"And this?" Estella lifts out a black velvet ring box.

Didi laughs. "My engagement ring," she says.

"But I thought *that* was your engagement ring." Estella points to the four-carat pear-shaped diamond on Didi's finger.

"I picked this out later. That one was Henry's idea of a joke."

Estella opens the box and sees a large dark gray stone on a tarnished band. "Is it valuable?"

"God, no. Worthless. It's a mood ring. Do you remember those? Did they have them in Peru?"

"I'm from Tijuana, miss. And yes. We did."

But Didi's not listening anymore.

She can still hear him cackling by the door.

They were on their way to the Waldorf for dinner that night. Henry asked her to get his keys from his pocket—and she found a black ring box instead. She remembers the jolt of nerves and nausea she felt when she realized what would happen next.

Henry chuckled and said, "Let's get old together, Didi!"

She felt her bottom lip quiver. He noticed the look on her face when she saw the oval-shaped gray stone and insisted it was a joke. That they'd get a real ring in the morning. But he put it on her finger anyway and made her wear it to the restaurant. Bea and his father were there waiting to celebrate.

Henry kept guffawing all night, elbowing his father, who laughed too. Even Bea thought it was a marvelous joke. The whole restaurant stared.

Crude.

"It's supposed to turn blue when you're happy," Henry said. "Why is it still black?"

"Let me try it," said Bea, slipping it on her finger. Within moments the ring started to turn green like cat's eyes. She passed it to Henry's father, and the oil man's finger turned it bright blue. They handed it back to Didi, who put it on and watched it turn green, then gray, then black again.

"Cold hands, warm heart," Henry said. Everyone laughed.

Didi excused herself and went to the restroom. She held the ring under warm water and watched it turn purple. She dried her hands and watched it turn gray again. She slept with the ring that night, hoping that in the morning it would turn blue or green, but it was darker than ever.

It depressed her so much. When the world saw nothing but the perfect girl with perfect breeding and a perfect education and perfect manners and a perfect family, this worthless bauble had seen something else. There was something wrong with her.

Later that day she went to Winston's with Henry to pick out the pear-shaped diamond she still wore. Years later, she remembered it was also called a teardrop cut in some circles.

A teardrop. On her wedding finger.

It was fitting.

Chapter 69

Toni is in the front yard pruning the roses. She should've done it earlier. But she had been too busy deciding what she would wear, blow-drying her hair, getting the picnic ready. She throws the big mauve flowers into a basket. Tucker runs over, sniffing through the petals.

"Tucker, *no*." Her tone is so firm that he actually sits back and listens.

What really bothers her is that she had finally relaxed about him. Why did things go wrong just when she let her guard down? What was wrong with her?

When she sees a yellow Jeep pull up to the curb, she quickly wipes the tears from her eyes. The car is still rolling when Chris jumps out of the passenger seat and hops the picket fence to see her. He carries her picnic basket, putting it on the front steps.

"You're too kind," she says sarcastically.

"Toni. Come on. I really tried to tell you. I just didn't know what to do." She doesn't even look at him, snipping away at the flowers. "It wasn't just the nondisclosure agreement either. Or the fact that I was such an asshole on the street that day. That was what it was at first, sort of—but then you kept talking about all those New York hedge fund guys. What jerks they were. How could I tell you I was one of them?"

"Excuse me?" She turns to face him. "You're in hedge funds?"

He sighs guiltily and nods.

"What kind of hedge fund?"

"Distressed debt."

She narrows her eyes. "Which means exactly what?"

"We buy up the mortgages of distressed businesses or people having trouble with their—"

"Wait a sec. So you're a *vulture*?" She motions at him with the gardening clippers and he has to step back not to get snipped.

"Pardon?"

"That's what my dad calls you guys. Vultures. Buzzards. Faceless beasts!" She mimics him by pointing her finger in the air. "Do you know O'Gorman's mortgage was bought out by a distressed-debt hedge fund?" She stomps to the other side of the yard. "I can't believe this. You're even worse than I thought!"

"See? How could I tell you that? How could I tell you what I did for a living? Especially when you had this incredible idea of me. That I was some laid-back cool surfer dude. I wanted to be that for you, Toni. I really did. I didn't want to burst your bubble about me."

"*My* bubble?" She lets out a blurt of a laugh. "Don't worry about my bubble, okay? Keep your eyes on your own bubble, mister."

"But I *am* worried about your . . . bubble," he says, trying to sound dignified. "Sometimes I think I worry too much about you."

"Don't bother. I can look after myself."

"Can you? Fainting if you get too much sugar? Or not enough or whatever it is? Crying at coming-soon trailers?"

"You're one to talk. Pretending you've devoted your life to hanging ten and folk songs. I bet you just bought that surfboard this summer." She picks up the flower basket and faces him. "Was the guitar part of the ruse too?"

"Toni, there was no ruse. . . . I just didn't want to lose you. The main reason I didn't tell you was because I knew you'd be mad."

"I'm not mad," she says. "I'm *busy*!" She pounds up the steps to the screen door. Just before she disappears inside, she says: "Enjoy the house share, fellas!"

And Frank, who still holds the Budweiser can to his head, says, "It's not a house share."

Chapter 70

In the days before hurricane warnings, telephones, or even radio, severe storms—"easters," as they were then known—could catch the summer colony without notice. In August of 1893, the *Panther*, a large tugboat bound for Massachusetts with a load of coal, was sunk by the breakers of a severe hurricane. Of six hundred vessels stranded off the coast of Long Island, the *Panther* is the only wreck that ever foundered directly off the sandy shore of Southampton. Wealthy summer residents were forced to watch helplessly as the vessel sank within view; a few braved the storm to help carry in the bodies as they washed ashore.

—*The Guru's Guide to the Hamptons*

Toni drives the van down narrow Sagg Road, flanked at turns by cornfields, wildflowers, and big summer homes. The sky is heavy with orange-gray clouds. The Hamptons begin and end with the light: when it's bright and vivid, the world seems like a fairy tale; but when it's dark and brooding, you can't help but feel the same.

A hedge fund manager? It all made so much sense now. . . . That's why he could afford his expensive muscle car. And the ticket price at F-4.

Stop thinking about him.

It's not like you've been going out for a year.

Were they even going out at all?

A few dates, that's all.

So what if he was cute.

So what if she could talk to him.

And that he listened to her.

So what, so what.

So what?

On the radio, the Beach Report predicts rain and thundershowers for the night.

Thunder.

Great.

The cornstalks on either side of her are almost six feet tall, crowded and dark green, casting long shadows on the road. By Labor Day, it would be harvested, the wedding would be over, and the summer would be gone. It makes her feel more depressed than ever.

She wishes she could talk to Dr. Weinberg about everything. But it was August and all the New York therapists she'd ever known took the whole month off. Most of them were probably in the Hamptons.

But she wishes she could've heard his calm voice, or even better, been able to sit in his cluttered office on 92nd Street, talking through her anger at Chris Ohm. She knows Dr. Weinberg would tell her—as he always did—that she worried too much. That she was being too much of a perfectionist. That she wasn't ready to be happy when she moved to the Hamptons at all. He would make her talk about the little girl on the street that day, the one with the balloons. *What color was her hair? How old was she?* He would remind her that she was so young when her accident happened, she never had a chance to deal with it in an adult way. That's just starting to happen now. He would tell her that maybe by being on the street that day, Chris Ohm stepped right into the nightmare and was hit with the shrapnel himself.

Maybe he would say all those things.

Or maybe he'd just let her talk.

Whatever the case, she knows she would not stop staring at the framed poster on the far wall, that explosion of black and gray drips. Strangely, the house where Jackson Pollock painted the original is one of the few Hamptons landmarks she has never seen.

Chapter 71

Chris and the others stand in the crowded entryway of Fratelli's. The people on line ahead of them look well dressed, sunburned, and rich.

"Why don't we go somewhere else, Johnson? You really feel like Italian that much?"

"He feels like a specific Italian," Lincoln says.

A young blond girl with a name tag that reads RHONDA greets them. "Sorry, we don't have anything available."

"Can we wait? Maybe out there." He points to a small patio with a trellis of vines where people are smoking and drinking aperitifs.

"They're already waiting for tables."

"What about there?" Chris points to the bar.

"Sorry. We're at capacity indoors right now."

Vic stands at the cash register, noticing the stubborn clog of young men at the door. He walks over, not smiling.

"Hi, Mr. Fratelli," Chris says.

Vic nods. "Uh-huh."

"When can you squeeze us?" Yuri asks.

"Squeeze us in, he means," Lincoln says.

Vic looks around the crowded restaurant. "How's Labor Day for you?"

"It's Toni, sir," Chris says. "Do you know where she is?"

"She's spending the night with friends. You mind telling me what happened?"

Chris sighs. "I'm sorry, sir. It made so much sense to me at the time . . . I don't know why. But I'd like a chance to explain everything to her first."

"Then we're booked, boys. See you in September."

Chapter 72

Hudson is just coming out of the house, twirling his car keys, as Toni heads toward the door with her overnight bag, a cake box, and a bottle of wine.

"Hey, Toni!" They kiss cheeks and he helps her with her things. "So glad you could make it. You get to meet the whole gang."

She thanks him for inviting her and tries to smile as they carry everything into the foyer. The place looks even more beautiful than it did for Spring Dinner. Houses in the Hamptons were a lot like flowers: they seemed to bloom and brighten as the summer went on.

"You okay?" he asks.

"Sure, why wouldn't I be?"

"You just look like you've been crying or something."

She sniffs. "Hay fever."

He gives her a sympathetic look. "That sucks. I'll put all this away for you, okay? You make yourself at home. Layla's upstairs getting ready. I'm just running out for her cancer sticks. You need anything?"

Toni shakes her head. He kisses her cheek and tells her he'll see her in a few.

———

Upstairs the corridor drones with activity. Bedroom doors open and close; there are muffled voices and laughter. A silver-haired woman in a Lilly Pulitzer dress passes by, smiling at Toni as if at a stranger in a B & B.

Toni knocks on the door of Bluebell. "Sully?"

Nothing.

She opens the door onto stale dimness. The curtains are drawn. The room smells of cigarettes and hair spray. She's just about to back into the hall when she sees a form on the unmade bed. Layla's facedown on the pillow, motionless.

"Sweetie?" Toni tiptoes over. Gives her a gentle shake. "Hey . . ."

Layla lifts her head, looking around.

"Rise and shine, Sleeping Beauty."

"What time is it?" Her voice is groggy.

"Almost seven."

"Shit," Layla says, sitting up. "I need a shower."

Toni goes to the window and opens the curtains. She sees one of Susan's vans parked by the garage and ignores the pang of jealousy she feels. Then she steps on a stack of papers on the floor. Binders, pamphlets, wedding magazines. "What is all this stuff?"

"Just wedding crap. There's so much paper flying around I feel like I'm going back to school." Layla pads barefoot into the en suite.

Toni sees what looks like a seating plan for at least three hundred people on the back lawn. She follows Layla into the bathroom, her eyes wide.

"When did sixty people at picnic tables turn into this?"

Layla turns on the faucets, testing the water. "Talk to Didi. I'm tired of fighting her. I just don't care that much." She steps into the shower, closing the curtain.

"Well, *I* do. I'm the one who's gotta make everything. I have to know how many people are coming, Sully."

"We'll figure it out, okay? Don't worry. I'm just so friggin' glad you're here. The whole family's on deck—and they're playing charades. Sorry." She pokes her wet head out of the curtain. "*Running* Charades. Judging from all the calls and e-mails, these people take their charades very seriously."

She goes back behind the curtain, and Toni half listens, toying with the makeup and expensive French soaps on the ledge.

"They're all so goddamn competitive. They actually played touch football on the lawn last night. Only 'touch' is not the . . ."

Her voice fades into the background as Toni sees an amber prescription bottle on the sink next to the makeup. She reads the label—diazepam—and the doctor's name.

"You saw my *shrink*?"

There's just the sound of running water.

"You saw Dr. Weinberg?"

Layla pulls back the curtain. "Toni, I—"

"When?"

"When I was in the city for a fitting a couple of weeks ago."

Toni blinks a few times. "I don't know who I'm more angry at. You or him. Why didn't you tell me?"

"Because I didn't want you to worry about me." She goes back behind the curtain.

"Well, of course I'm going to worry about you. I'm your best friend. That's my job. But I'm the one who goes to shrinks. Not you. You're supposed to talk to me about your problems."

Layla pulls open the curtain. "But you can't write a prescription for Valium, can you?"

Toni sighs, puts the bottle down. "What the hell do you need Valium for, anyway? You're Novocain on heels."

"It's this damn wedding. I don't know how I'm gonna get through it. Did you get the invitation?"

"Yeah . . ."

"Doesn't it suck?"

"It's beautiful," Toni says. "It's the *plus guest* part that sucks."

"Did something happen with the surfer?"

"He's not a surfer," Toni says.

Chapter 73

In the big postmodern on the beach, Frank cranks down the umbrellas on the deck. "Storm's a-brewin', mytie! Gotta batten down the hatches."

"Or close the cantilevers, as the case may be," Lincoln says.

Chris looks at the dark, uneasy ocean. The waves sit straight as cowlicks. He feels a dull ache in his stomach. As if he's just gone ten rounds with his trainer. That's the only thing that would help right now.

Boxing.

Sweat until the floor was slippery beneath his feet. Then he'd go home, have a beer, check the quotes, and pass out. It would all be better when the alarm went off.

"Johnson, where the hell are you going?"

Chris holds his surfboard over his head as he jogs across the picky grass to the beach. "Surf's up!"

Frank says, "But you're not supposed to swim alone!"

Toni stands in the conservatory overlooking the beach. The long table is laid out with a floral cloth and a buffet fit for a five-star all-inclusive resort.

Layla puts her arm around her, making her jump a bit. "Did you hear if there's going to be thunder?"

"I doubt it," Layla says, but she doesn't look convinced. She pours herself another drink.

"Darn!" Didi's voice rings out across the living room as the first droplets of rain patter on her french doors. "I suppose it could be worse. At least Running Charades is an indoor sport!" There's a crisp glassiness to her optimism.

Clusters of people gather by the food, by the bar, by the fireplace, as voices and laughter escalate. The step-bridesmaids are on hand, as are several of the boyfriends. Arturo, the handsome Argentine, is there, unable to speak a word of English, but with the biceps and hair of a young Fabio it doesn't seem to matter much to Tabitha or anyone else. There are aunts and uncles and cousins skidding about in stocking feet. Everyone wears bright cotton or cashmere, and they all seem to know each other—except for Toni, who only says hi to a few of the caterers she recognizes from La Dolce Vita. Even Layla is having fun, laughing more loudly than anyone else—and drinking more than she should.

"Don't get *Valley of the Dolls* on me," Toni had said.

"But that's half the fun."

Toni wishes she could find an excuse to leave, but the rain is getting heavier and the fog is moving in. She knows how dense the fog can be on a night like this. She remembers nights on Main Beach when she couldn't see the sand beneath her feet. She and Layla would cling to each other, looking for the dull glow of the bonfire. It was terrifying to be so disoriented in such a familiar place.

Toni's stomach feels nauseous. She hopes there isn't thunder. And tonight of all nights, when she's already so depressed. She munches on a carrot stick with a dip that could use a little more cayenne and stares out the window at the waves.

Chris tastes the salt in his mouth.

Never surf alone.

Never surf in a storm.

Never surf in unknown waters.

All the things he ignored as a kid. And still did.

The breakers toss him into the ocean. There's a hard slap of sandy water against his face. Then behind, a wave with the power of a football linebacker drills him. He feels himself grinning through the water he spits out of his mouth and gets on the board one more time.

Didi stands in the living room in front of the fireplace. She blows on a silver whistle that she wears on a cord around her neck. The sound carries through the house like a scream.

"Teams, everyone! Teams!"

All the houseguests move toward the living room, stopping to check a chart on a silver stand outside the door.

"I hope everyone worked hard on their clues this year!" Didi says. "Remember, ten clues and be specific! No boring old movies or proper names!"

Toni is happy for the distraction of the game. Maybe it'll take her mind off Chris—and the storm.

"I think we should go with romantic comedies," she says. "It's supposed to be specific, right?"

"Whatever," Layla says.

"I'm going to miss you, baby!" Hudson says, coming over to kiss Layla.

"Miss me?"

"I'm in the library. I'm on the Green team."

"What color am I?"

"Brown, baby."

"Blech. Who else is on Brown?"

"Check the chart. Gotta run! Aunt Miranda's here and she wants to unseat the champions! Which"—he points his finger in the air—"she will not do!"

"Which she most certainly will!" says a thin dark-haired woman tickling his side.

And then Hudson introduces his Aunt Miranda, a celebrated playwright for forty years. Somewhere in the distance, a whistle sounds. Didi says: "Twenty minutes, everyone!"

Layla and the Brown team are holed up in the Palm Room—Didi's informal sitting room near the front of the house, done in rattan and shades of pea green. Layla sits draped in the wingback chair, sipping her drink.

"I'm bored already," she says.

But Toni is working on the clues. The game is focusing her. Like a To Do List.

"Ten-minute warning," Didi says, coming into the room with her stopwatch. She leans over Toni's shoulder like a schoolmarm. "No, no. I said be specific."

"It *is* specific. Romantic comedies."

"Obviously, you don't understand the rules for Running Charades." She gives Toni a list of sample categories: it looks like an admissions test for Mensa.

"Oh, crap," Toni says.

"Ten minutes, everyone," Didi calls, leaving the room.

Toni taps her pen for a moment. "I've got it!" she says. "Romantic comedies with a cooking theme!"

The pandemonium of the annual Running Charades championship at Concordia is enough to keep Toni occupied until she sees the first flash of lightning at nine o'clock. She stops in the hall, a little out of breath from running back and forth for the different clues.

One-steamboat, two-steamboat . . .

She runs back to the living room, where she picks up another clue, then skids into the hall, passing other teams at work.

"Three syllables, first syllable sounds like . . ."

"Oscar Wilde!"

"C-D-E-F!"

On her way through the hall she almost bumps into one of the servers from LDV. The table is so spotless it seems as if they were never there.

"We're on our way," says the girl. "We have to get on the road before the storm gets worse. Hope you enjoyed everything."

Toni stops herself from saying the dip needed cayenne.

Considering the house is full of every intellectual in the family, the Brown team is at a decided disadvantage. Toni can't believe the names were picked randomly. The Brown team consists of herself, Layla, Jorge, Estella, Arturo—and Uncle William, a doddering white-haired old man in a smoking jacket who seems permanently attached to a glass of sherry. He mutters things under his breath—Toni thinks about a war though she's not sure which one—while laughing to himself, raising white eyebrows, and pounding his neighbor's back.

In the library, Brown faces off against Maroon—last year's second-place team, made up of the playwright, a journalist, two lawyers, and a professor emeritus.

The professor acts out his clue—and there's another lightning strike.

Toni closes her eyes: *One-steamboat, two-steamboat . . .*

It was her mother who had taught her to count the seconds between a flash of lightning and the thunderclap. It helped her judge how far away the storm was and be prepared for the loud noise when she heard it. But tonight it doesn't help. The storm is getting closer, and when the thunder cracks it's so loud that it threatens to split the house like an egg.

One-steamboat, two-steamboat . . .

Just before 10:00 P.M. the Red team is eliminated.

By 10:15 Blue, Brown, and Purple fall by the wayside.

At 10:25 it's just Green and Maroon facing off in the living room. The runners-up look on, drinking and cheering.

Toni curls up on a sofa holding a pillow to her chest and trying not to tremble.

At 10:38, Didi cries, Foul! That clue is incomplete!

At 10:41, Hudson collapses with relief when they squeak through a round of Shakespearean comedies.

At 10:44, the lights go out.

Chapter 74

In the library of the big postmodern, Chris reclines in a leather chair by himself. The reading lamp beside him flickers. He watches it for a moment. The throbbing music, pounding feet, and laughter from the rest of the house eases for one tense moment, then rumbles with a cheer as the electricity comes back on.

The library is full of well-thumbed paperbacks for the renters. Romance novels and true crime and biographies of people nobody really cares about. This morning he got up early and scoured the shelves, looking for something he could get into. He decided on the detective novel—

Or was it spy?

—but keeps having to start over again. Nothing makes any sense to him. He wonders where she is right now. He knows how much she hates thunder.

The initial gasps and screams after Concordia was plunged into blackness turn to a stream of excited murmurs as eyes adjust and people huddle together waiting for the candles to be lit.

Estella and Jorge lead the charge, braving the blackness with flashlights and matches. The house becomes pools of golden light and gray-brown bodies and glinting furniture.

The thunder pounds on. It sounds like a war to Toni: the stutter of gunshots, the rumble of distant bombs.

"This will definitely put a crimp in Running Charades," Didi says.

"Who'll join me in the library?" says Henry. "I have a hankering for a cigar."

"I need a smoke too." Layla grabs her cigarettes and looks around for her matches. She sees Didi's gold lighter and grabs it quickly. She tucks her arm in Henry's as several of the guests follow Uncle William and him into the darkened hall like an expedition party for the East India Company.

Another flash of lightning.

One-steamboat, two-steamboat, three . . .

Toni forgot how violent storms could feel out here, huddled so close to the sea. In New York, when the power went out, it seemed half the world was outside your window waiting to turn it into a street party. But out here, a bad storm threatened to shake you off the edge of the earth.

A half-hearted game of Monopoly ends quickly because nobody can read the clues. Guests begin to yawn and complain of being tired. Groups of two and three peel off from the crowd and head toward the bedrooms or gather in pairs beneath umbrellas to run to the guesthouse.

By midnight, the storm is still raging. Toni's forehead glistens with sweat. Layla sits next to her on the sofa, rubbing her back. A small group has gathered in the living room around a flickering fire, which Jorge tends like the Olympic flame.

Uncle William has started talking about the hurricane of 1938. At least Toni's pretty sure that's what he's talking about. She remembers sitting cross-legged on the gymnasium floor in East Hampton Middle School with Layla. A screen at the front of the room played old black-and-white footage of the aftermath of the big storm. The unsteady camera panned across splintered homes and broken fences, big elm trees pulled up from their roots, old black sedans crushed beneath branches.

"It was a miracle anything survived," the teacher told them after she turned off the projector.

There was that word again.

Miracle.

The one all the grown-ups used to use about her.

"I hope my Trianon will be okay," Didi says, standing by the french doors overlooking the pool. Expensive topiaries are draped in burlap, but big trees bend at angles against the wind.

"I'm hungry," Hudson complains.

"Me too," says Tabitha.

"I'll make something," Toni says, jumping up.

"No, no. I'm sure Estella—"

"No, please." Toni grabs a candlestick. "If there's anything that'll take my mind off the storm, it's cooking."

Toni pushes open the cut-crystal doors to the kitchen and half a dozen people follow behind her. She's been dying to see this room. But Didi's Clive Christian showpiece is only shadows and glinting chrome. It slowly comes to light as candles are set down.

"Get ready for the magic," Layla says, pulling a stool to the island. Her face is a pan of perfect features as she lights a cigarette.

Didi takes out another cigarette too. She's had half a pack already today. "Where's my lighter?"

Layla winces and slides the lighter across the counter. "Sorry."

"I'll do a little menu first," Toni says. "So that I only have to open the fridge a few times."

She talks half to herself, half to the others. "In a bind like this, you automatically think you have to make something cold. But if you have a gas range, you might get"—she turns the knob on the cooktop and a circle of blue light appears—"lucky."

Everyone cheers.

She opens cupboards and drawers, glad for the distraction. She's never seen such a well-stocked kitchen. As she gets things ready, the guests tell ghost stories. Tales of pirates with hooks and sitting around a campfire with a serial killer on the loose.

Toni listens to them as she putters about. She makes a platter of vegetables and pâté. Cream crackers, cheeses, pita bread. Her famous grilled-cheese sandwiches with tomato and cured ham. Fresh strawberries and pineapple chunks and clusters of green grapes. Everyone sits at the island, munching and laughing. Toni feels brief happiness as she watches them eat.

Another lightning flash. *One-steamboat, two-steamboat . . .*

"How's the hummus? Is it too chunky? I didn't have a processor."

"It's delish!" Tabitha and Hudson say in unison. They look at each other, eyes wide: "Jinx!" they say together, giggling and slapping each other, trying to "undo" the curse by saying their full names quickly—Tabitha Samantha Jane Henry Hudson—until it starts to sound like a roll call.

Another loud bang from the sky. Windows rattle in their panes.

"How much longer can it last?" Toni asks.

Tabitha says, "When I was little, I was afraid of storms too. But my father told me it was just God playing with his polo ponies, and that made me feel better."

"Never heard that one around my house," Toni says.

"It's not just the storm, anyway," Layla says. "It's loud noises. Bursting balloons. Backfiring trucks."

Another crack.

"Thunder," the girls say together.

"How come?" asks Hudson.

"It's nothing. It was so long ago."

"Come on," Layla says. "It might help to talk . . ."

"I know, it's just—"

Another loud clap. Toni feels her heart jump along with it and suddenly she's there on the street.

"Row, row, row your boat . . ."

She can see her mother ahead of her on the street corner.

"Hurry. Hurry up, Toni. Or we'll miss the light . . ."

And then she hears another voice—"I was walking home with my mother"—and realizes the voice is her own. "I was three years old at the time."

"Three and a half," Layla says.

"That's right. The therapists all say that's important. How old I was at the time." Toni begins to clean up, crumpling linen napkins and scraping plates, talking to drown out the storm. "I'd just come from a birthday party. Hilary MacAllister had turned four. Her mother had given us each balloons as party favors and mine was red. . . . I remember my mother and big brother walking ahead of me. He was all dressed in his football equipment. . . . He'd just come from practice. . . ."

He looks like a spaceman *in his green-and-white uniform, padded shoulders and helmet. . . .*

"Peter, no need to wear that now, aren't you sweltering?"

Toni looks at her mother's hand flapping toward her.

"Hurry, sweetie. We don't want to miss the light."

"We'd done a singalong at the party. I'd just learned a new song. "Row, Row, Row Your Boat." I was humming it to myself. Ignoring my mom, who kept telling me to hurry."

Another flash of lightning.

"I remember we were on East Fifty-first Street. We didn't live far from there. There was a small wall in front of a row of town houses. It wasn't very high. I always used to walk along it, balancing like I was in the circus. I had to jump down between the stoops and climb back up again."

"Come on, honey. We don't want to miss the light."

"There was a vacant shop on the corner, not far from the United Nations. . . . My mother was standing there, waiting for me."

Jumping down . . . and the wall seems so high . . . clinging to the string of the balloon . . .

"Toni, don't dawdle. . . ."

"The vacant shop had a big glass window out front. I never really paid much attention, but that day I looked over and saw my reflection."

"Hurry, honey . . ."

The light was green.

She jumps off the wall one last time. She sees a flash of light, like a huge mirror, as the glass window bows out to reflect the sun in the split second before—

"And then it happened."

The world comes apart.

Trees and cars and sky turning over and sparkling glass like raindrops falling in every direction . . .

Then the afternoon goes very still and quiet. Toni is on the sidewalk. The balloon is gone. The taste of something salty and metallic in her mouth. . . . A smear of dark red as she blinks hard trying to see . . .

"I don't remember any pain—not then."

Her ears are ringing. Her mother is crouched next to her on the sidewalk. Toni tries to touch her own face, but her mother takes her hands away.

"No, no, sweetie . . ." Her mother's voice is calm. So strong, like the Rock of Gibraltar . . .

A man across the street runs through traffic to try to help. She remembers him saying he'll call an ambulance and her mother saying there wasn't time.

"It'll be okay, sweetie, it'll be okay. . . ."

She hails a cab and it pulls up to the curb. Climbing into the back, her mother holding her in her arms, burying Toni's head in her shoulder so she won't see the blood.

"My mother held me in her lap when we got to the hospital. She wouldn't even let them bring me into the operating room until the anesthetic had taken effect."

"What on earth happened?" It's Henry's voice now.

Layla turns to him. "A bomb."

The room responds with a beat of shock.

"A young boy made it," Toni explains. "We were so close to the UN. He was trying to protest one of their policies in Africa—but he got me instead."

Toni looks around at the staring faces, trying to fit her jagged memories into a place that makes sense right now. She's told this story so many times in her life it feels as if she was talking about something that had happened to somebody else. It was a terrible story—but it was a *story* nonetheless.

"She got a hundred stitches," Layla says. "In her *face*."

"Seriously?" Hudson's voice. "I've never seen scars."

Toni touches her forehead. "If you look really close."

"What happened after that?" Tabitha asks. "Was everything okay?"

Lorne looks at her and curls a lip. "Does it *sound* like everything was okay?"

Toni laughs softly. "The worst part was getting the stitches out," she says. "I remember them having to hold me down. All these people in masks and big lightbulbs. Afterward, there were lots of shrinks and child psychologists." *Her father having to work harder to pay for the bills. The fights over money. The absolute fear.*

"Eventually," she says, "we moved out here."

Someplace safe.

Aunt Miranda shudders. "Goodness, Toni. It sounds like a miracle you survived."

"That's what they said."

Toni doesn't mention that for the longest time she thought a "miracle" was something bad.

She sits straight up in bed, her heart hammering. She's in the extra bed in Bluebell. The electricity has flashed back on and three lamps, the bathroom light, the curling iron, a ceiling fan, and "Vampire Weekend" on Layla's iPod dock all blare to life.

She waits for her heart to slow down.

She looks over at Layla, who sleeps right through the commotion, her foot hanging off the bed. Toni gets up to turn things off. She hears whispering and creaking in the hall as Jorge and Estella do the same. One by one, lamps go off, the curling iron, the music.

When she climbs back into the bed, she settles into sheets that smell like lavender. She listens for any sound of the thunder. But the storm is over. The night is so still. The only light comes from the full moon, shining through the half-open curtains.

She turns on her side and sees her cell phone on the end table glowing with a new text message. She reaches over to read it and feels a small tug in her chest.

"Just thinking about you. I know how much you hate thunderstorms. I hope you're okay. Chris xo"

Toni holds the cell phone, just staring into the darkness. Nobody's ever done that for her before.

Chapter 75

Bill Mitchell feels like an early pioneer or an explorer rifling through the grass and shrubs. Only he's armed not with a musket or a machete but with a camera and binoculars. He wears a multipocketed vest, a Tilley hat, and has zinc ointment on his nose.

The storm last night seems to have turned the world upside down. Seaweed and driftwood on the beach below. Branches on the ground. He follows a sandy path toward the water, passing scraggly weeds and dune grasses. He consults the information pamphlet from the Piping Plover Project and then his old copy of *The Guru's Guide to the Hamptons.*

He comes upon another path and has to stop at the fork in front of him. It's a dried-up creek bed and the clearing beside it is overgrown with weeds. He takes out his voice recorder and tries to formulate his opening paragraph. But all he can think to say is, "They're gone," and it seems so pointless that he puts away the device.

He hears the ocean, so calm compared to last night, like soft breathing. He steps through the grasses onto the white beach. The waves slide up the sand and bow away. He lifts the camera and takes shots of the dried-up creek bed and then around on the west side. There's a cord strung along the beach and up through the grasses, and a sign: PRIVATE PROPERTY—NO TRESPASSING.

He sees the roof of a large mansion just visible over a dense hedgerow. He hears the distant whir of lawn mowers, the peeping of birds and cackling of hens.

"It was a terrible storm," Didi says. She leads two people across the pool deck littered with leaves and overturned planters. Jorge and other workers are up on ladders, dragging branches down from the top of the pool house.

"It was bad in the city," says Mr. Beecher. "But it seems catastrophic out here." He wears a neat navy suit; he has small shoulders and a shiny bald head. His assistant is a pear-shaped woman in a beige dress.

"It was," Didi says. "I can't thank you enough for coming out so soon. I was horrified when I saw it."

She leads them into the pool house and through the open door of her private office. Her finger shakes as she points to the family tree on the table. The man holds a magnifying glass over the yellowed parchment. This is the first time he's seeing the concrete evidence of all his research for Didi Flagstone—the esteemed parchment itself—and he's suitably impressed, with both her lineage and his work. Then he looks up to see a water stain in the ceiling; he *tsks* three times.

The assistant sets down a hygrometer, and everyone watches it for several minutes. "Seventy-eight percent," says the woman.

Mr. Beecher actually gasps. "How long has your dehumidifier been broken?"

"I didn't know it was," Didi says. "Is there . . . mold?"

"Not yet," says Mr. Beecher. "But I'm glad you called when you did. I'd like to take it into the city for a week or two. We'll clean it up and it'll be as good as new. By then you'll have the ceiling repaired and the dehumidifier replaced."

Didi watches them both put on white cotton gloves and carefully start rolling up the long piece of paper.

"I hate to send it out. It hasn't been out of my sight since my mother died."

"Two weeks at the most, Mrs. Flagstone."

Didi watches as they slide the document into a tube marked EMPIRE GENEALOGICAL SOCIETY: DOCUMENT AND TEXTILE REPAIR.

"You sure it'll only be that long? I was hoping to give it to Hudson as a wedding gift."

"Mrs. Flagstone," says Mr. Beecher with great reverence, "I shall guard it with my life." He tips an imaginary hat and they're gone.

***

Didi lights a cigarette several hours early for the day. She picks up her copy of *War and Peace* and settles in for a chapter. Every summer she dragged her $16,000 antiquarian copy of the tome to Concordia, determined to finish Volume One, at least. But she never did. *Too much war,* she'd think, *and not enough peace—like the Hamptons themselves.* Russian troops are occupying the villages of Austria when she sees a figure approach the door of the Petit Trianon.

Toni raps lightly on the glass and gives a little wave. Didi's less annoyed at the interruption than she normally would be, grateful to put down the book.

"Hi, Mrs. Flagstone," Toni says.

"Didi, please." The wide hostess's smile.

"Didi, I mean. Sorry. I just wanted to thank you for last night."

"Mmm. Yes. It was an adventure, wasn't it?"

"Yeah," Toni says with a laugh. "I hope this isn't a bad time. Do you have a minute?"

"For what?"

"I can't seem to get Layla to sit still long enough to talk about the menu."

Chapter 76

Toni bears down on the gas pedal as she roars toward East Hampton. "When were you going to tell me!" she yells into her cell.

"Oh, God . . ."

"I have to hear from Didi that Susan's already been hired?"

In her single bed in Bluebell, Layla holds her head. "Sweetie, please, calm down. . . . I have such a headache."

"Good! We're even." The reception is bad and the line crackles in and out. "When were you going to tell me? The wedding's less than three weeks away!"

"I just found out myself," Layla says. "Just the other day. I wanted to tell you, and then I don't know. I just . . ." She groans. "I didn't want to hurt your feelings."

Toni makes a growling sound. "I really wish everyone would stop worrying about my feelings so much. Because it's really starting to piss me off. I end up getting my feelings hurt *and* being pissed off."

"Baby, I'm sorry, really I am. I'll make it up to you. I just couldn't say no to her. . . ."

Toni says, "Funny how easy it is to say no to me." And hangs up.

———

In the reception area of Lotus Blossom Yoga, Yuri leans on the counter.

"My name is right there on the card, beautiful. You want my number too?"

Tammy McCann, an instructor at the studio, looks down at his Visa card. "But this is an advanced class, Mr. Orlokov. Have you ever done yoga before?"

"Maybe you could give me a private lesson." He pumps his eyebrows.

Chris keeps his eyes glued on the entrance of the studio as women of various sizes and ages file in, everyone wearing Lycra or organic cotton and carrying yoga mats. The place smells like enforced relaxation: incense, green tea, and just a little sweat.

When he sees Toni with her hair pulled back and a harried look on her face, he leaps toward her. "Toni, please. I knew it was yoga day. Please talk to me." His expression is soft and concerned. "First of all, were you okay? With the storm?"

She manages to cover her shock at seeing him. "I was fine," she lies. She stomps into the studio with her yoga mat and begins unrolling it in her spot near the back of the room.

Chris and Yuri follow, outnumbered by women at least five to one. The guys grab their own mats from a stack by the door and Chris sets his up so close to Toni's that it actually overlaps hers.

"I can't believe you're doing this," he says. "I can't believe you're going to throw away everything we had because I made one little mistake."

"Ha! One?"

"Or two," he grumbles.

"What did we have, anyway?" She flips his mat off hers. "A few tours of the Hamptons? A couple of little kisses in the countryside?"

"You know damn well those"—he lowers his voice, looking around—"those dates counted for a lot more. And the term 'little kiss' didn't cross my mind when it came to what happened between us."

"Okay, friends," says Tammy from the front of the class. "If we could all move into hero's pose . . ."

They move onto their knees beside one another as the room hisses with the sound of deep respiration.

"Breathe in," says Tammy. "And breathe out. . . ."

"Please try to understand. I wanted to tell you, but it was getting so awkward. Every day that went by it got harder to explain. Hasn't that ever happened to you?"

"No," she says firmly.

Tammy says, "Now exhale into downward-facing dog. . . ."

Toni and the rest of the class expertly follow the pose. Chris tries to, but loses his balance. Yuri just dips up and down, watching the upturned bums of the other class members.

"What about that woman with the twins?" he says. "In the square that day. The one you went to high school with."

"Claire Rafferty?"

"*Now* you remember her name. But you said you always forgot it before and you'd known her too long to ask now. It was too awkward."

"Are you seriously comparing us"—she motions between them—"to forgetting someone's *name?*"

He gives a helpless groan.

"She wasn't even in my class!"

"Okay, everyone, let's move into cobra pose. . . ."

As the others change positions, Toni and Chris stay in downward-facing dog. People are starting to look over.

"It's not like you've been completely honest with me either," he says. "Planning your best friend's wedding as if it doesn't bother you. Pretending you're over your ex-boyfriend when obviously you're still hung up on him."

"I'm not *hung up* on anyone," she says through clenched teeth. "I'm *relaxing.*"

"Oh, you look really relaxed."

"I would be if you weren't here."

"Don't forget to breathe, everyone. . . ."

"You keep saying you want to relax, but you're the most uptight anal-retentive person I've ever met. You carry an antique iron in your purse, Toni. We went halfway across the island for tomatoes. You're the only person I know who can turn a simple tuna sandwich into a four-course meal."

"Toni, is everything okay back there?"

"Just fine, Tammy." They're in proud warrior now, the rest of the class looking on from triangle pose. "What about you? With your cue ball stick shift and your mint-condition muscle car. Mr. Hedge Fund Manager buying used guitars and singing folk songs on the beach."

"I didn't see you complaining about the guitar when I was playing it for you!"

"And I didn't see you complaining about my pain bagnat!"

"Toni, if you guys have something to—"

"No problem, Tammy. I was just leaving." She grabs her mat and turns to Chris. *"Namasté!"* she says, then stomps out of the room.

"What does that mean?" Yuri asks.

"I think it's yoga for fuck off."

Chapter 77

Usually held midsummer in Water Mill, "Super Saturday" to benefit the
Ovarian Cancer Research Fund is one of the season's most anticipated
events. A sort of designer garage sale cum family picnic day in a sprawling
park called Nova's Ark, guests rummage through clothes and accessories
by over two hundred designers, everyone from Donna Karan and Marc
Jacobs to Diane von Furstenberg and Michael Kors. It's a match made in
the Hamptons: shopping and charity rolled into one.

—*The Guru's Guide to the Hamptons*

Layla is on her phone trying to call Toni for the fifth time that day. Around her,
half-clad celebrities and Upper East Side social X-rays slip off flip-flops to try
on new shoes and fight it out with each other for the size 2 sundresses.

Layla paces as she talks. "Toni, please call me. This is so stupid. I'm so depressed I can't even shop—and it's for charity!" She listens to the dead air for
a long time as if listening to Toni breathe. "I love you, baby," she says. "I'm so
sorry. Please forgive me . . ."

Layla can't remember Toni being this angry before. Not even when they
were roommates. There had been arguments over their different housekeeping

habits or when Toni would come home from working all day and see that Layla hadn't taken Tucker for a walk. But they had never really fought a lot. Unlike other girlfriends, they were never interested in the same type of men, so they didn't fight over boys. They hadn't been the same size since fifth grade, so they didn't fight over clothes. Toni had grown up listening to too many arguments in her own family to fight for no good reason, and Layla was just so grateful for any kind of family after her parents died, she didn't like picking fights either. Whether forged over bonfires, Bonne Belle, or everything in between, their friendship was closer than sisterhood. The one thing Layla can't handle right now is for Toni to be mad at her.

Chapter 78

The sun is not quite up the next morning when Toni gets into the van with Tucker and a thermos of her dad's espresso. She barely slept all night. She listened to Layla's messages—twice—then saved them so she could listen to them again. She deleted the few messages Chris left. She can't remember being this angry at two different people in her life, not even when her parents divorced.

She drives east along Three Mile Harbor Road. Tucker is in the passenger seat, his head out the window. She slows down to take the shortcut past Layla's old bungalow on Underwood, but then lifts her foot off the brake.

She doesn't want to see the old house this morning. She hates doing it at the best of times, let alone today.

The Hamptons are a terrible place to be when you're sad, she thinks.

Every time she passes that house, she feels a thud in her heart remembering the night they heard the news. They were coming back from the beach. They'd stayed out longer than they should have, sunburned and exhausted.

It was the wash of red against the trunks of the trees they saw first. A tangle of police cars parked in front. They rode their bikes past two officers standing at the edge of the driveway. Neither of them could look the girls in the eyes. Sergeant Griff Davids, a tall motorcycle officer with a mustache and blue eyes, was waiting on the steps for them. Toni remembers only a few words from that night.

Drunk driver. Pronounced dead at the scene.

It was the first time she had ever seen Layla cry.

The Hamptons were no place to be when there was bad news because it almost hit you harder than anywhere else. You weren't prepared for it. Not in a place that was so beautiful. If you were sad in the Hamptons, where everyone else seemed to be having so much fun, you felt like the only kid crying at the circus.

She turns onto Chester Drive, into the peach and pink sunrise over Accabonac Harbor. Even more vivid than she remembers, the sky is opalescent with mist from the water and ponds. The old van finds its way along a narrow spit of land. Large pink boulders hold back the tide on one side; clam diggers are faint figures in the still water of the harbor on the other.

She sees it in the distance: the slanted roof of the old cottage her parents used to rent. It sits on pilings, hovering over the water. When she was young, the beach ran for twenty feet to the harbor; now the water licks up right under the front deck. She doesn't know what she's doing here now. Trying to cheer herself up?

Or make herself feel worse.

She pulls onto the small lot behind the house. Tucker climbs out after her, sniffing around. The wood shingles are silvered with age and a couple of windows are broken. There's a bright Georgia Randall Realty sign tacked to the back wall. Small seashells crunch like gravel under her shoes as she walks around to a wide rocky beach, and a line of similar 1930s beach cottages lined up on pilings along the curved shore. Out in the bay, she sees fishermen in boats, and across the harbor, the dark green hills of Gardiner's Island. Tucker runs back and forth along the rocky beach chasing the biggest black-and-white seagulls on the South Fork. The water is so clear, the rocks and shells below are magnified, the little shells turned upward like tiny pink mouths.

She climbs the side steps and the wood cracks beneath her weight. She automatically tries the brass padlock on the door, but it's locked. She rubs the grime off the windows and peers inside.

She feels the world shift, a dark film go over her eyes, then brightness. She sees her mother at the kitchen table next to the door cleaning ears of corn. Her father kneels by the fireplace stacking wood. The doors facing the water are open and she sees a little girl out there on the deck looking through a white telescope. There are Adirondack chairs and a picnic table beside her. Her older brother and sister are away at day camp.

"Stay away from the railing," her mother says, her voice so young and clear, her old Nikon camera on the counter behind her.

It is the summer after Toni's accident. The scars are still very fresh. Toni doesn't realize that people stare at her because of them. She likes to be here at the house where it's just her and Mom and Dad.

She grabs the telescope with her tiny hands and peers through the lens at Gardiner's Island. Her father told her stories about how the Indians had given that island to the Gardiner family hundreds of years ago. How the Gardiners were one of the oldest, richest families in New York State.

Toni remembers wondering if they had a castle on that island.

It was her dad who bought her the telescope and set it out there for her; he'd help her focus it on the distant shore. The first time she looked through it, she actually got scared. Everything looked so close, as if it could jump out at her.

But then she understood. She liked shifting the scope back and forth, focusing in on the big house on the hill or the white windmill on the shore. Then she'd look for fishing boats on the water. Or twist left to trace out the pink-beige boulders along the S curve of the road. A little boy or a bicyclist or a car would get bigger and bigger, until it seemed as if it would fly through the lens; but all she had to do was step away and see how small and distant it was. She liked the feeling of power it gave her. Holding that telescope was the only time she felt in control of what came into her life.

She heard several clicks and turned to see her mother with the camera, smiling and taking photographs. Toni felt shy in front of the camera lately. She'd seen pictures of herself and it confused her how the scars looked on the side of her face. Her mother came around to her side, taking a few more shots, and Toni looked back into the telescope.

She finds a piece of driftwood and sits on the beach in front of a depression in the sand, a permanent hole from decades of bonfires. She remembers roasting marshmallows on branches her father carved sharp on one end.

God, she loved the taste of roasted marshmallows when she was a kid. Still does. Even in the city she used to turn on the toaster oven, line the pan with tinfoil, and set a half dozen marshmallows flat side up, then watch them turn the perfect shade of brown. She could never understand people who let their marshmallows catch fire and turn black. Sugar burnt so quickly, there wasn't even time to turn off the oven. The cusp between perfect and ruined was so slim. She'd slide them out at just the right second. Leaning against the counter, she'd eat them with her fingers. They were so gooey and sweet and warm. Afterward, she'd feel her sugar crash and fall asleep.

The Hamptons are no place to be sad, she thinks again.

It's almost as if in the city, you were prepared for bad things to happen. You walked down the street steeling yourself against rude tourists or busy strangers. You hurried to your apartment door at night. In the city, you lived with armor and it helped to protect you—at least a little—when bad news hit.

But in the Hamptons you were soft and vulnerable. Was it the light? The beauty? The ocean? Whatever it was, you put your armor down and walked around with ice-cream cones or roasted marshmallows and a permanent grin on your face. Everything was sweet and soft and peaceful. Then, when you heard something terrible happened—a car accident, a fire, a drowning—it slugged you in the stomach. Toni has thought about it many times, and she thinks the extra layer of emotion she feels when bad news hits out here is . . . loneliness.

She sees Tucker digging up sand and chasing birds.

"Tucker, come."

He leaves the gulls and lopes over, wagging his tail. Right now he feels like her only friend in the world. She hugs him around the neck and bawls for half an hour into his fur. He just stands there and lets her do it. He is used to this.

Chapter 79

The gifts start arriving at Concordia even before the RSVPs. Didi sets them all in the Lily Room overlooking the ocean. Layla thinks it's ironic the gifts get a better view than she does.

She's been depressed all week. Nothing feels as if it's going right without being able to talk to Toni. She went to the house to bring a bouquet of flowers. She knocked for ten minutes, but Toni didn't answer. If she was at the restaurant, she didn't come out front. She tried calling and texting. Recorded "Jack and Diane" and "Wind Beneath My Wings" on Toni's voice mail. She'd even cried during a message last night:

"You're my family, Toni . . . my mother, my sister, my best friend . . . I'm so sorry . . . Sometimes we do things to our family that we wouldn't even do to anyone else. Please, Toni, please don't be mad at me. . . ."

But Toni had not called her back.

"Let's get started," Didi says.

Layla looks around the Lily Room. "On what?"

"On the thank-you notes."

"But I haven't even opened anything yet."

"So, open them."

"Before the wedding?"

"Yes, before the wedding. A proper bride opens the gifts as soon as they come and writes the thank-you notes immediately."

"But I thought I had three months."

"You certainly *don't*. Some of these gifts have come all the way from Europe. You have to let people know they arrived safe and sound." Didi retrieves a stack of custom note cards and a pen. "Let's start with that one." She points to a box wrapped in yellow tissue. "Of course you can't use anything until after the wedding. In the dire circumstance that it doesn't go through, you have to send everything back." Didi smiles.

Layla slumps down on the floor and grabs the yellow box. She opens it tiredly. It's a Limoges butterfly vase.

"Adorable!" says Didi. "Now write a little note about where you're going to put it in the apartment."

"I'm *not* putting this anywhere in the apartment. It's not my style."

"Well, you can't tell them that."

"You want me to lie?"

"I want you to be polite. There's a difference. Here, let me help." Didi excitedly opens another box. She lifts out a Wusthof knife set with everything from a three-and-a-half-inch paring knife to an eight-inch hollow-ground carving blade.

"These will come in handy when you finally learn to cook," she says.

Layla looks from the gleaming blades to her soon-to-be mother-in-law. "They could come in handy now," she mutters under her breath.

One Week Before the Wedding

Chapter 80

Toni drops Tucker's leash to the floor of the reception area of the *East Hampton Sun*. A thin white-haired woman in a yellow pantsuit hobbles over on a cane.

"Mrs. Latham! So glad you're up and about."

"Hallelujah to that." Toni and Margaret Latham kiss cheeks. "Thank you for the cake, Toni. It was delicious."

"Pineapple upside-down. I remembered you always loved it."

"It was the best ever. I don't know how you can keep getting better all the time. What can I help you with?"

"I should've tried to do this earlier. But I was wondering if I could change the wording in the ad I've got running."

Mrs. Latham gives her a curious look.

"I had a . . . change in my schedule. I don't need more catering staff, but my dad could use a couple of bussers for the long weekend."

Mrs. Latham says she'll call up the account and goes to a nearby computer. "How's it going with Layla's wedding?"

"Okay, I guess."

"You don't sound convinced."

"I haven't talked to her in a while."

"Oooooh." Margaret Latham frowns. "What happened?"

"I guess the whole thing mushroomed out of control. Fifty people on the beach turned into a garden extravaganza for more than three hundred, and Mrs. Flagstone said I didn't have the experience. She hired Susan Schumacher instead."

Mrs. Latham laughs. "Well, a bride always gets carried away planning her wedding. You'll see. It'll happen to you someday."

"Riiiiiigght," Toni says.

The door opens behind her and Tucker barks at the vision looming there. Bill Mitchell's hat is askew, his vest bristles with pencils and notebooks, and his neck is strung with cameras and binoculars.

"You look like you're embedded in a war zone," Toni says.

"I *feel* like I'm embedded in a war zone." Toni tries not to laugh as he awkwardly rubs the zinc oxide off his nose with his sleeve.

"He's looking for plovers," Mrs. Latham says. "I've seen enough of those to last a lifetime."

"I haven't seen one," says Bill. "Not anywhere. I've been up and down all the coasts. Digging through sand dunes. I've haven't seen a single piping plover anywhere. It's like they're that big monster on *Sesame Street.* You remember, the one nobody could see so they didn't believe he existed?"

"You mean Snuffleupagus?"

"Yeah. Snuffleupagus. I feel like I'm Big Bird and everyone keeps telling me Snuffleupagus exists, but I'm the only one who can't see him."

"But Big Bird *could* see Snuffleupagus," Toni says.

"Oh. Right."

Toni just grins and keeps filling out her form.

"You taking out an ad for more help?"

"Actually, I need less help," Toni says. "Just a little change to—" Her phone rings and she sees Layla's cell phone number.

It's the third time she's called today. She even texted "SOS"—the code neither of them ignored.

Toni debates; she knows that if she waits one more split second, she'll miss another call. And somewhere in the deepest part of her, she doesn't want to miss another call.

"What?" Her voice is cold as she answers.

"Holy shit," Layla says.

"What happened?"

"I lost the ring."

Chapter 81

The summer that Toni was thirteen, her parents sent her to summer camp in August. She was gone for the whole month—cementing the love-hate relationship she would have with August for the rest of her life. She always wondered if they had done that to trick her. Or if they were actually trying to work things out. Because that was also the summer they decided to get a divorce.

Toni felt lonely at camp. The different people, the different trees, a lake instead of the ocean. She missed Layla more than anything, wrote letters to her every day. A big envelope would come on Fridays from Layla too, with pages numbered 1, 2, 3 because she forgot to mail them the day she wrote them. Toni would read them with an excitement kids usually had for comic books.

When she came home at the end of August, the trees around Hook Pond showed branches of yellow. She was so excited to tell Layla everything she had learned—archery, canoeing, beading—and gossip about how cute the camp counselors were that when she walked in the door of John Papas Café to meet Layla for milkshakes and fries, she was upset to see a young blond woman sitting at their usual table.

A moment later, she saw the crystal flip-flops. It wasn't a stranger.

Toni forgot all about her archery medal and friendship bracelets and how cute the counselors were. It was clear that whatever had happened to Layla that summer had been a lot more important.

Layla sat in the corner slurping a milkshake and reading *Seventeen*. She wore lip gloss and her hair was curled. Her legs were angled outward on the bench and her flip-flops sparkled like tinsel. Layla lived in flip-flops three seasons a year. They didn't make her too tall—and they were cheap. But she always customized them somehow, gluing beads or tying ribbons on them. These were white with silver sequins. She called them her crystal flip-flops and said that, like Cinderella's glass slippers, they would bring her everything she wanted someday.

When Layla looked up and saw Toni, she scrambled off the bench and hugged her so tightly Toni almost lost her breath. She had to laugh and ease herself out of Layla's grip. They sat down at the table and suddenly their words were falling all over each other. It was as if Toni had not been gone at all.

But as much as Layla had changed the summer they were thirteen, Toni is even more shocked by what she sees now. She thinks for a moment that the blond woman lying by the pool must be one of the step-bridesmaids. Layla hasn't been this skinny in years.

Even so, Toni is filled with relief to see her. She hurries across the deck and nudges her foot. Layla opens her eyes and yanks out her earphones.

"Thank God you're here."

Chapter 82

It is immediately business as usual. There is a dire emergency at hand.

"What do you mean you lost the ring?"

Layla propels Toni across the deck toward the house. "I mean, I *lost* the ring."

"*Hola, amigas!*" Tabitha says. She's coming out of the house with Poppy and two other young women Toni's never met before. They all wear bathing suits and carry magazines and drinks.

"Hey," Layla says, trying to smile. She puts her left hand behind her back.

"*Mwah, mwah!*" Tabitha makes loud kissing noises in Toni's direction. "You guys going to join us?"

"In a minute," Layla says. "I just want to show Toni the gifts."

"Oh, good!" Tabitha says. "I'm sorry we didn't invite you, Toni. All things considered"—she glances at Layla, obviously aware of the argument—"we didn't know if you'd want to come."

"Invite me to—"

Layla just grabs her elbow and ushers her into the house. Estella and the other housekeepers are pulling down crepe paper wedding bells and pink streamers. Toni eyes an endless series of pink balloons with uncertainty.

"They had a shower for me," Layla says.

"They did?" Toni can't hide the hurt in her voice. "But you hate showers. You told me I couldn't even throw you one."

"I do hate showers. It was a complete surprise. Trust me, you wouldn't have wanted to come. Everyone turned into Stepford wives."

"Turned into?" Toni says.

Inside Bluebell, Layla closes the door. She gives Toni another one of the big long hugs she got after summer camp.

"I've missed you so much." Her voice is muffled by Toni's hair. "I've been surrounded by so-called family twenty-four hours a day. And I've never felt more alone."

She releases Toni and looks her in the eye.

"I'm really sorry about the wedding thing. I swear I was going to tell you. I just—I fucked up. I fuck up sometimes. You know that."

"It's okay . . . I guess," Toni says. "But can I still make the cake? I have the most amazing cake planned for you."

Layla actually has to dab her eye. "Of course you can make the cake."

Toni can't help but notice her ring finger is bare. "Okay. When's the last time you saw it?"

"I had it on this morning. I always look at it in the morning when I wake up."

Toni quickly rifles the bedding. Layla looks under the bed. They straighten and shake their heads at each other.

"Did you take it off somewhere?"

She shakes her head. "It must've just fallen off."

"I wouldn't doubt it. Look at you. You're a rake. How much weight have you lost?"

Layla just ignores her. "Do you think it's a bad sign? Losing the ring the week before the wedding? I have to find it. Didi's going to kill me. She'll probably call the whole thing off."

"We'll find it. Don't worry. We'll just retrace your steps. What did you do after you got up?"

"Took a shower."

They hurry to the bathroom. Toni checks the sink and Layla checks the tub drain. They shake out the damp towels. Still nothing.

"What next?"

"I went swimming."

"In the pool?"

Layla shakes her head.

"Shit."

They stop at the front patio. Hudson is on the beach with a clan of his cousins; a couple of them are on boogie boards in the water.

"We can't look for it now," Toni says. "They'll know something's up. What did you do after that?"

"I was in the gift room for a while."

"Gift room?"

Toni stands in the doorway of the Lily Room. The spacious bedroom overlooking the beach is cluttered with tea sets, espresso machines, linens.

"Jesus. I feel like I'm in Housewares at Bloomingdale's."

"No kidding."

Along the big dresser, piled three deep, Toni sees various gift bags Layla has taken home from a busy summer of benefits. Heart of the Hamptons. Quogue Wildlife Refuge. Rock the Hamptons. The Group for the East End.

"I didn't think I was supposed to open them before the wedding," Layla says. "But Didi's even got me doing thank-you notes at night. She checks them for spelling mistakes. Or makes me do them over because my handwriting is too messy. She's worse than Mrs. Naylor from composition class."

Toni sees crumpled cards on the desk in front of the window. The big loopy script, *i*'s dotted with little hearts.

"That's not how you spell 'excellent,'" she says.

Layla just shrugs. "You see anything you like, you can keep it. I'm not gonna use half this stuff. There was this great butcher knife set I think you'd love." She starts digging through the gifts. Toni stops her.

"I don't want your wedding presents, Sully."

"I don't want most of them either."

Layla just stands there looking like a little waif. Toni feels a protective urge she hasn't felt toward her best friend in a long time.

"You should tell Hudson. He has to know."

Toni sits at the desk overlooking the ocean. She sees Layla walk out onto the patio below, down the stairs to the beach. Hudson runs over from the group when he sees her and she leads him away from the others. They sit cross-legged on the sand in front of each other. Layla's head is lowered and she wipes her eyes every now and again. Hudson just rubs her shoulders and strokes her hair.

Toni looks down at all the crumpled Mrs. Strong notepaper. She sets the pens in front of her, the brass stamp on one side, the silver sealing wax on the other, the list of addresses off to the corner. She picks up a Waterford champagne bucket and admires it for a moment before carefully composing the note.

Twenty minutes later, Layla comes up from the beach, skipping into the room. "We're going to Tiffany's! We're going to Tiffany's! See? Everything does happen for a—" She stops when she sees the neat stack of addressed envelopes on the desk. "What are you doing?"

"I'm giving you a hand."

"Toni, no! It's not my algebra homework."

"It kind of is." She gently pushes Layla's hands away. "Go get ready. Tiffany's closes at seven."

"How do you know that?"

Toni remembers looking in the window of the white shop in East Hampton, one of the chicest—if slightly unexpected—additions to Main Street.

"Just one of those pointless pieces of information I have in my head."

Chapter 83

For over 150 years artists have found their way to the east end of Long Island. They're drawn by the land, the light, the history. Winslow Homer painted sunbathers on the beaches of East Hampton in the 1800s; Robert Motherwell started working here in the 1940s; Willem de Kooning bicycled to his studio in East Hampton; and Roy Lichtenstein eventually settled in a house on Gin Lane. As for Jackson Pollock and his wife, Lee Krasner, they immortalized their work—and their lives—in a farmhouse on the back roads of the Springs.

—*The Guru's Guide to the Hamptons*

A silver 1952 Rolls-Royce Phantom IV makes it way along the Long Island Expressway. In the front seat is a thin man with white hair and a brimmed cap. In the back, a plump woman in a floral dress.

Bea Flagstone doesn't come out to the Hamptons much anymore. When she was younger you couldn't drag her away from her family's big Colonial in East Hampton. But the house had been donated to the Ladies Village Improvement Society long ago, and Bea didn't enjoy staying at the Blackhart place for extended visits. She'd rather be on her balcony with her flowers and her cats.

But she couldn't bear not seeing Hudson and Layla married. So Beatrice Anne Flagstone made the trip to the Hamptons as she usually did—in her mint-condition Phantom IV with Phillip, her driver, behind the wheel. Her cats are in separate carriers on the backseat with her. Mooch, the angry Siamese, mewls and hisses, but Smooch sleeps the entire way.

When she gets to the house, she sees the mayhem on the grounds. Gardeners are mowing and planting; another team sets up a wire archway on the lawn. A dance floor is being laid down on the tennis court. The white free-span tents are going up. Ladders are everywhere, like an apple orchard in the fall, with electricians installing decorative lights on almost every branch of every tree.

Phillip carries her bags into the house. Children she's never met scamper past her. Nobody else comes to greet her. She carries her cats upstairs.

She has the key to the Violet Room on a chain around her neck and opens the door onto a musty-smelling bedroom with a purple chenille bedspread and lots of books. In the corner by the window is an old wooden chair spattered with paint, and beside it, her easel. The sight makes her smile.

Chapter 84

Didi and Mr. Percy Beecher sit across from each other in the shade on the pool deck. The roof of the pool house has been repaired and the windows cleaned. Around them, gardeners change the roses in the planters from pink to white in time for the wedding. Didi has spared no expense to impress her friends and relatives.

A wedding is a social obligation, Didi. A chance to show the world who we are.

"You said there were some problems with the family tree?" she asks, nervous.

"You could say that," Mr. Beecher says. He takes a sip of his tea, then retrieves the protective tube from where it leans on his chair. Didi notices he doesn't put on cotton gloves as he pulls out the parchment. He takes a cursory wipe of the table with his napkin and begins to unroll it.

"Please be careful."

"Not to worry," he says. "When I took it back to the office, Mrs. Flagstone, I saw no outward appearance of damage. Beyond that small water stain in the corner. Which was easy enough to rectify."

Didi squints. "But I can still see a faint smear."

"What I found is far more damaging than a water stain," he says. "Or even, frankly, mold. Let me draw your attention to the wedding dates."

Didi sees Hudson's name and the blank space where his bride should be. Her own name with Henry's. He points to the branch of the tree where her mother and father's wedding is noted.

"In all the time I've known you, Mrs. Flagstone, you never once mentioned that your parents were married at sea."

Didi flicks her fingernail. "Oh, yes. *That.* Aboard my grandfather's yacht in the Aegean. Quite a *scandale*, as you could imagine. My mother never quite forgave herself. Though I'm sure it was *très bohème* at the time."

"Yessss," he says. He points to the wedding date where the officiant is noted. "I see here they were married by the ship's captain."

"That's right..."

"I really wish you'd asked me to look into this sooner."

"Why would I ask you to research my own parents? I know everything about them."

"Mrs. Flagstone, what I'm trying to say is..." He clears his throat. Cocks his head. Stammers a bit more. "What I'm getting at is that New York State does not recognize—and has not for at least a hundred and fifty years—weddings performed by ship's captains. Not here—and certainly not off the coast of Greece."

"I don't understand."

He takes his bare hands off the parchment and lets it roll up on its own.

"Didi"—it's the first time he's used her given name—"your parents were never legally married in the eyes of the law. I'm afraid to be the bearer of some shocking news—but you're illegitimate."

Chapter 85

Toni sits across from a young man at the staff table in the back kitchen, a stack of résumés in front of her. He has long sun-bleached hair in a ponytail and a red-brown face from the sun.

"Sort of a last-minute change of plans," Toni says. "But Labor Day weekend is always busy. If we need bussers or bar-backs at the restaurant, can we call you?"

"Absolutely."

"I see you won the sand castle contest this year," she says, looking at his résumé. "My best friend and I used to enter that. Never won anything, but it was always fun."

"I'm a sculptor, actually. I just sling beer to make ends meet."

"I can relate to that," she says. "We'll definitely keep you in mind." She thanks him for coming by and shakes his hand before he leaves.

To Theresa she says, "I think that's it, right?" She flips through the résumés on her table.

Rhonda comes in the swinging door. "There's one more person to see you, Toni." She holds the door and a man steps into the kitchen.

———

Toni covers her initial shock at seeing Chris Ohm by organizing the résumés in front of her. "I can't talk right now," she says, tapping, piling, fiddling. "I'm busy."

"I know that," he says. "And I'm applying." He presents a one-page CV and sits down across from her. "I saw your help-wanted ad."

"Chris, don't be ridiculous."

"I'm serious. And if you knew what it cost me to actually *get* a job this summer, you'd be impressed with my resolve."

"I really don't have time to—"

"Rhonda said I get ten minutes. And that's ten minutes more than I've had with you in weeks. I've had lots of experience," he says. "I put myself through business school doing restaurant and bar work, remember? I can plate and serve and bar-back and I've even learned how to mix a great mint julep this year."

Toni sighs and looks at his résumé. "Very impressive, Mr. Ohm. But I don't hire dishonest people." She gets up from the table. "Theresa, I'm taking five."

She walks out the back door, secretly glad she wore her "breakup jeans" today. Her appetite has dropped to nil and she hasn't been able to wear these jeans since last winter.

But in the sunny parking lot, she nearly trips over a basket of small pumpkins. *Pumpkins? Already?* She forgets how much earlier everything is harvested out here.

She tries to walk away but he takes her arm.

"What was I supposed to do? Please try to understand. After that day on Ninety-second Street, I thought about you so much. I *felt* something when I met you that day, Toni. For the first time in as long as I could remember, I felt something for someone else. When I bumped into you out here, it almost seemed as if I had willed you back into my life. But then I thought you were getting married . . . and I was so depressed. I couldn't believe it. I hardly knew you and I was already fantasizing about pulling a *Graduate* on your wedding day. But then, I found out you weren't getting married . . . and we were actually together. And it was *so* good. I didn't want to lose you, Toni. I couldn't lose you. If I had told you the truth, I thought you wouldn't be interested in me anymore. When we went into O'Gorman's that day you said it was actually breaking your heart what was happening to them. How could—"

But then he stops. He can tell by the look on her face that he's already broken her heart. She shakes loose from his grip and walks around to the front.

"Toni, I know you're mad at me," he says, trailing her. "And I understand. But I'm asking you to try to give me another chance."

She stops in her tracks when she sees her father has set out pumpkins along the front walkway. They remind her so much of the fall, she wants to lie down and hibernate right there.

"I'm sorry, Toni, really I am." He looks down, shifting his weight a bit. "I remember reading on a T-shirt somewhere that love means never having to say you're sorry. But that never made any sense to me. I always wished it was more like, love means never having to do something so stupid that you have to say you're sorry in the first place. And if you do something so stupid that you have to apologize, then at least the other person will forgive you because . . . love means not having to be perfect all the time. That's what I wished it said."

"That wouldn't fit on a T-shirt," she says.

"Toni, I'm telling you I love you."

She feels herself falter. The sun is so hot . . . He takes her hand.

"This doesn't have to self-destruct," he says. "*We* don't have to self-destruct. We can make it work out. I know we can. Please stop expecting the world to blow up on you all the time, Toni. Stop expecting it—or it will."

And that cuts through her uncertainty. She pulls her hand away.

"Thanks for the advice. If the whole hedge fund thing doesn't work out, you can always get into therapy." She walks up the main path.

"Toni . . ."

But she slips inside the restaurant.

She leans against the hostess stand for a moment. Rhonda frowns at her and she forces a smile to her face. The same one her father taught her to use to make everyone feel welcome at the restaurant. When people dined at Fratelli's, he said he wanted them to know God was in heaven and all was right with the world. So, like a Broadway actress on opening night, she holds back her tears and walks through the restaurant smiling. *The show must go on.*

In the kitchen, she keeps up a brave face for the troops, going back to her stack of résumés, filing them away. But with one eye on the Kleenex box and another on the staff restroom, she's got her heart set on twenty minutes of a private bawl session.

Why was she still so mad at him?

Was she just being stubborn? Testardo, *like her father always called her?*

Or was it more serious than that? Was Chris right? Did she feel pro-grammed to self-destruct in every relationship she's ever had?

Rhonda comes in the swinging door. "There's a guy here to see you."

"Tell him I've got his résumé on file. I'll call him if I need him."

"Oh-kaaay." Rhonda backs out the door. Toni heads for the Kleenex box.

A moment later, Rhonda steps back in. "I told him the whole résumé thing, but he has no idea what you're talking about. He said his name's Kevin."

Chapter 86

For the second time that day Toni is shocked to see an ex-boyfriend at her dad's restaurant. Kevin stands in the entrance. He wears a pink Lacoste shirt, the collar up, navy bermuda shorts, and the whitest running shoes Toni has ever seen. His Rolex watch and his school ring glint as they always did, but his brown hair is disheveled and he's unshaven. For Kevin Pritchard, he looks an absolute mess.

When he looks over at her, she feels as if every bone in her body is going to fall apart at the sockets. "Toni," he says. He wears a weak smile.

As she walks over, she finds herself saying his name back. "Kevin?" Only it sounds more like a question, as if she can't believe he's there and needs him to confirm it for her.

"You look great," he says.

And Toni doesn't know how to respond. *Thanks. It's the breakup jeans.*

"I don't know how to say what I have to say," he begins. "So I guess I should just come out and tell you. I've left Nadia."

Rhonda is at the hostess station glancing from Kevin to Toni and back again, like a spectator at the U.S. Open.

Toni looks at her.

"Sorry," she says.

"Let's go somewhere," Toni says. She puts her hand in his arm. The feeling of his skin, the smell of his aftershave—a little strong for a summer day—is all so familiar and so strange at the same time.

Kevin's navy blue Audi is in the parking lot. She can't believe he still has that car. That watch. That cologne. It's almost an affront to everything she's been through since Christmas that so much about him seems the same.

He doesn't hold her door for her. Not that she minds that. It's their lack of timing that bothers her. He climbs in behind the wheel and tries to open her door automatically, but—as usual—she pulls at the wrong moment and has to wait two or three clicks before they can sync up and she can climb inside. When she does, she stares straight ahead.

He starts saying what a terrible mistake he made. How Nadia was never right for him and he supposes he was just scared about how attached he'd become to her, Toni.

Attached. As if she were some puppy he'd adopted from the pound.

"It was all just so heady. The new job. The new title. Frisco."

Frisco? She forgot how much his affectations annoyed her.

He tells her he supposes he went a little crazy with it all and hadn't been thinking straight.

And then suddenly he's trying to kiss her. Her eyes are open and she's just watching him, shocked. Then Susan Schumacher walks into her field of vision.

"Shit."

Susan taps along the sidewalk in front of the restaurant, her nose held high. Toni slides out from under Kevin's grasp. "We can't do this here."

Ten minutes later they're sitting on the overstuffed leather couch in the living room on Church Street. All the furniture her parents bought for the apartment in New York had been too big for the old shingle-style when they moved in, but they kept it anyway, as if somehow or other everything would just start working out on its own. Maybe they were hoping for the same thing when it came to their marriage.

"I don't know what I saw in her," Kevin is saying. "I still don't know. It was—"

Tucker sits by the cold fireplace watching them like a chaperone. He steps forward when Kevin puts his hand on Toni's knee.

"You still have that dog." He tries to smile, but Tucker bares his teeth and growls until Kevin removes his hand.

"It was an infatuation, I guess. Just something new and fresh."

New and fresh? What were women? Bread? Apples?

"And she was so exotic, you know. With that accent. I thought Russian at first but she was actually Romanian. From Transylvania. Did you know that Transylvania is an actual place? Not a made-up vampire country?"

"Yes, Kevin, I knew that. And I don't care." She rakes her hand through her hair. "What are you doing here, anyway? How did you find me?"

"I tried calling everybody. David. Amy. Everybody. They all said you moved back home. But that they hadn't heard from you for a while. I tried the restaurant and asked for you and someone said you were too busy to come to the phone. So I knew you—God, you look good!"

He grabs her and starts kissing her again, trying to push her down on the couch. Tucker walks three paces to the edge, close enough that Toni can feel the moistness of his panting and the individual rumbles of the growl in the back of his throat.

Gr-r-r-r-r.

She looks at Tucker and he turns away as if disgusted with her. She pushes Kevin off and sits up.

"This isn't working either," she says.

Upstairs Tucker stands in the hall staring at the closed door of Toni's bedroom. He makes helpless little noises in the back of his throat.

Toni sits on the single bed with its Beauty and the Beast sheets, her John Cusack poster, and the ballerina lamp watching. Kevin is telling her he loves her. He's actually using the word.

Love.

Before, he only used it when he wanted to have sex—but then, there it is. He does want to have sex.

"I love you, Toni . . . I missed you so much."

But she's thinking about Chris.

Did he actually tell her he loved her today?

Kevin starts kissing her neck, his stubble prickly on her skin. There's a part of her that wants him so badly; at least wants to want him. Wants everything to be normal again, wants the world to feel safe and steady beneath her feet. God, it's been so long. Here was the man she'd gone to bed crying over for so many nights, the man she thought she'd marry, and he's come back, wanting her, telling her he loves her.

She closes her eyes, trying not to let the fact that he never knew what to do with his elbows or his knees bother her, always thumping her with one or the other as he tried to seduce her. She lets out a little moan, as if to coax herself to get into it.

But she's thinking of Chris Ohm.

Not just thinking of him, but *feeling* him.

The way her whole body could fall into him just when their lips touched. The way his rough-soft beach blanket hands felt on her skin. She can even see his face when she closes her eyes. She doesn't know who she's being unfaithful to, but she knows it's somebody, so she puts two hands firmly on Kevin's shoulders and pushes him up.

"This is not working either," she says, sitting up. "Maybe my blood sugar's low. I should make something to eat."

"Aw, Toni," he groans, seeming annoyed. "No cooking tonight. This is a special occasion. Let's go out. I haven't seen you in six months."

"Eight," she says.

Chapter 87

"It's pool candy, right, Johnson?" Yuri pokes Chris in the ribs. He points to two young women circling each other in the pool. "Get it? Like eye candy, but with a pool."

"That's very good, Yuri." Chris edges his lounge chair over a bit so Yuri can't elbow him again and he goes back to his novel.

As the two women in the pool move to the edge, talking very intimately and sharing a kiss, Yuri widens his eyes. He goes to nudge Chris again, but Chris is out of elbow reach.

Frank Broward carries a tray of drinks through the glass doors from the kitchen. He's mastered the art of the mint julep and has moved on to sangria.

"They're not staying here another night, are they?" Frank asks, motioning to the pool.

"Girls are not work, Johnson. For you maybe. But not for me."

A whoop sounds from the corner of the house as Lincoln walks in carrying a load of shopping bags. "Look what I found!"

Behind him are a handful of people. *Were they here last night?* Chris can't remember. They all blur together, a smear of shimmer cream and tans.

Chris tries to get back to the detective—or spy—novel.

He wishes he could surf. But the beach is busier than the pool with all the novices out there trying to hang ten on waves that aren't much taller than a picket fence.

He should just go back to the city.

He wishes he could stop thinking of her.

"What's up?" Lincoln asks, settling in a lounger beside him.

"It's Ninety-second Street," Yuri says.

"Oooh."

"The only reason he's obsessing about her," Frank says, "is because he can't have her. It's basic supply and demand as applied to the male psyche."

"That is one of the stupidest—and smartest—things you've ever said," Chris says.

One of the pool candy girls, the blond one, hangs her elbows over the side of the pool. "You okay?"

Chris puts down his paperback. "No."

She looks back over her shoulder at the new guests. "Me neither. Let's go get something to eat."

Susan Schumacher clicks down the sidewalk of Main Street talking on her cell. "Tell her who it is. And that I've tried calling six times."

"I don't think it's been six," says Estella.

"I exaggerate to make a point."

Susan cranes her neck to see how much of a lineup is on the walk outside Fratelli's. She frowns when she sees Vic has done something new with the entryway, lining the walk and the edge of the steps with fresh pumpkins and sunflowers.

"One moment, Mrs. Schumacher."

While she's gone, Susan takes the phone away from her ear and snaps a picture of the walkway.

"It's Susan Schumacher again," says Estella.

In her bed at Concordia Didi wears an eye mask and earplugs. With the curtains drawn and her duvet pulled up to her temples, she still heard the squeak of Estella's foam-soled shoes.

"Tell her I'm unavailable."

"I tried, miss. She insists on speaking to you. Something to do with the hors d'oeuvres."

The wedding.

All the decorations, all the phone calls, all the gifts pouring into the house—and all Didi can think about is that sham aboard a yacht in Greece.

She rolls over in bed and takes out her earplug. "Yes, Susan? Sorry I've been so—busy lately."

"I've been concerned about you, Didi. Is anything wrong?"

"Of course not," Didi says, even as she thinks, *Everything*.

Chapter 88

Toni and Kevin walk down Newtown Lane. He tries to hold her hand, but it feels so awkward that she breaks off from him to admire a lamp in the window of Shabby Chic.

"She wasn't as smart as you," Kevin is saying. "She wasn't as funny as you. And she had the ugliest feet." He curls his nose. "You hear that ballerinas have ugly feet, and you think you can overlook that, but then when you're in bed with her and you see those feet, all you can think is—" His BlackBerry rings. "Hang on a sec. I have to take this."

He steps away from her, covering his ear. "Kevin Pritchard."

Toni stands in front of the window, trying to get her bearings. She still feels dizzy. Maybe her blood sugar is low, after all. She looks across the street to the vintage donut maker in the window of Dreesen's and Scoop du Jour. She can't believe he talked about being in bed with the ballerina and it didn't even faze her.

"Sorry about that," he says, walking back. "The new gig's cah-razee. I'm working twice as many hours as I used to. But I love it. You should see my new office. Sharp. I even got the Eames recliner. The black leather one? How about you?"

"I didn't get a recliner."

"I mean, how are things?"

She realizes this is the first time he's asked a single question about her life since she saw him. The day has become more about Nadia and him than about his relationship with her. She's just about to say, "Life has never been better" and lie through her bicuspids to even the score, when she sees another couple walking toward them.

Chris and a pretty young woman with straight fair hair. She has her hand tucked into his arm. They're window-shopping, her head on his shoulder.

Today he tells her he loves her—and he's already out with someone else?

"Men," she says out loud.

"Pardon?"

"I mean, amen to that. I'm glad you got the recliner."

"But I asked you how you were."

"We'll see in a second."

As Chris and the new woman approach, Toni grabs Kevin's hand. "You're so funny!" She laughs for no reason and playfully slaps his arm.

"Oh . . . hi." Toni keeps her voice casual and light when they finally come face-to-face on the sidewalk.

Chris's tone is not quite so friendly. "Hi," he says. She feels vindicated by the expression on his face. Shock at first, and when he looks at Kevin, a curious anger just kept in check.

Toni holds out her hand. "I'm Toni," she says to the new woman.

"Toni? How nice to finally meet you!" The woman has an English accent. "I'm Amanda Simms."

Toni's surprised by the friendly greeting. Either Amanda Simms has been crowned Miss Congeniality UK or Chris has been talking about Toni—a lot.

She looks at him, but he's still glaring at Kevin.

"Chris Ohm," he says, extending his hand.

"Kevin Pritchard," he says, pumping Chris's hand.

Chris looks at Toni.

Kevin?

"I see," he says. His expression is now blank.

They're all standing in front of Babette's, staring at each other. The silence goes from awkward to tense.

"We were just going for something to eat," Toni says, pointing to the restaurant.

"So were we," says Chris, holding the door.

The odds that a couple without reservations could step into any restaurant in East Hampton early on an August evening and actually find a table are about a thousand to one. To be able to find two tables is nothing short of record-breaking. But the clog of people at the door are all larger groups and the hostess is able to seat both couples right away.

Kevin moves to sit facing the window (he always took the best seat in any restaurant they went to), but at the last second, Toni scoots him out of the way so she can have a view of Chris's table.

She wants to watch them.

To pour salt on the wounds.

And vinegar.

And a squeeze of lemon juice.

"The time away did me good," Kevin says. "I feel different. Mature. Ready to handle the responsibilities of a grown man. I've got a great new apartment on the Upper West Side. It's fantastic. There's even a little courtyard in the back. I think you'd love it. And I think I'm ready, Toni. To move in together, I mean. What do you think?"

"Do you think she's pretty?"

He's confused. She nods to Amanda. "Yeah. I guess she's pretty. Didn't you hear me?"

Amanda leans forward, looking up into Chris's eyes, tenderly taking his hand.

"Toni, I asked you to move in with me."

She tries to look at him, but another woman has walked into the restaurant. Dark curly hair, a deep tan. She creeps up behind Amanda, putting her hands playfully over her eyes.

"Boo!" Toni hears the faint voice.

Amanda turns around, her face brightening. The dark-haired woman bends down and kisses her on the lips.

"And not just moving in together," Kevin says. "But getting engaged, shopping for a ring—I would never buy you a ring on my own, you're way too picky—and someday, in a couple of years, I'll even be ready for marriage." He sits back in his chair and lets out a big breath of air, as if he just survived a parachute jump. "What do you say?"

"Would you excuse me for a second?"

"What?"

"I'll be right back."

In the washroom, Toni leans against the counter. Her cheeks are flushed. Her heart is thrumming. She turns on the cold water and takes several cool sips with her palms.

The door opens and Amanda walks in. She doesn't walk into a stall. She just puts her bag on the counter and smiles at Toni.

"I don't know what you did to him," she says. "But he can't stop talking about you. He's absolutely besotted."

Besotted? Toni's always loved that word, besotted. She's always wanted to besot someone.

"He's usually not like this with women." Amanda turns to the mirror, fluffing her hair. "All he cares about is work. He wasn't like that when we were younger. He used to be the coolest guy in school. Did he tell you about our sing-along's in the newspaper office? Him with his long hair and—"

"Wait a second." Toni notices Amanda's earrings. Silver peace signs. Then her purse. A green knapsack with travel badges and a FREE TIBET button. She remembers the kiss with the dark-haired woman at the table.

"Were you ever in the Peace Corps?"

"Yeah. For years. Why?"

Toni can't believe how relieved she feels. It's the ex-girlfriend he told her about after their date movie. The opposite of having the rug pulled out from under her, Toni feels as if the rug has actually been put back, vacuumed, with the fringe combed out.

How ridiculous. The man she thought she wanted to be with for the rest of her life is out there proposing to her (well, sort of proposing to her), and she's just so delighted that Chris isn't actually on a date with a cute British girl that she wants to jump up and down.

"He told me what happened, Toni," she says. "I don't blame you for being mad. But I hope you guys can work things out." She stares at the door, as if he's standing there. "He got so, I don't know, *into* himself when he went to Wall Street. Into money more than anything. He changed so much. It's good to have him back. Even for a little while. I think I have you to thank for that, right?"

Toni looks at her reflection, feeling confused.

Kevin is on his BlackBerry again. There are two glasses of white wine on the table.

"It'll just be a minute," he says, holding up a finger.

Toni looks over at the other table. Chris is gone. The brunette sits by herself reading the menu. Toni turns to the broad window and the busy street, but he's not there.

What was she going to do? Go over and say she forgives him? Just because he was having dinner with his ex-girlfriend and not someone new?

When Amanda comes back to the table, she and the other woman hold hands and lean in close to each other.

Kevin puts the BlackBerry down. Then angles the screen toward him so he can see incoming messages. "I ordered you some wine. I remembered you liked Riesling."

"I don't like Riesling," she says, annoyed.

"Damn." He snaps his fingers. "I knew there was one you didn't like. I thought it was Chardonnay. I'll get you a—" He puts his hand up but she stops him.

"This is fine," she says.

"Anyway, as I was saying, the new place is fabulous. You'll go crazy decorating it."

"Who says I'm decorating it?"

"I just thought after you moved in . . ."

"Who says I'm moving in?"

"Don't you *want* to?"

"At this point in my life, Kevin, I can honestly say I have no idea what I want."

"Well, you can't want to stay out here. The summer's almost over. Come back to the city. You can get another job. It'll be just like it used to be."

Just like it used to be.

The words Toni has longed to hear for months—but why does it feel like the worst thing he could've said?

"Kevin, my life is here now. Can't you see that?"

"You actually want to stay here? In your old house? With your dad?"

"I'm paying him back more quickly."

"You don't have to pay him back. I know for a fact he told you that."

"I want to pay him back, Kevin. And I'm doing a damn good job. That's the one good thing about waiting on tables—the tips are great."

Kevin curls a lip. "You're a waitress?"

At that precise moment, the server comes over to the table. "Are you ready to order?"

Toni crosses her arms and looks at Kevin. "Why? What's wrong with being a waitress?"

Kevin looks up at the girl. Laughs uncomfortably. "Uh, nothing. What are the specials today?"

The girl goes to speak, but Toni hands the menus back. "Sorry. We won't be eating."

The server shrugs and leaves them alone.

"This isn't working either," she says. "This. Me and you. And everything. I want it to work, Kevin. I really do. At least I did. But it's just all too much the same. You on your BlackBerry talking about work. Me too busy or preoccupied with something else to even notice. You know what our problem is?"

"No."

"We're all presentation."

He gives her a blank stare.

"When you're plating a dish to take to a table, you make it look as pretty and clean as possible. But if the food's not good, what does it matter how it looks? It's pointless. The whole thing reminds me of the croissants in Susan Schumacher's window."

"*What?*"

"In her shop when I worked there. She had these croissants shellacked so that they wouldn't get stale. They looked perfect, but if you tried to eat them, you'd be at the poison control center in an hour."

"Yuck. I've seen that. Like when restaurants have plastic sushi in the window? I hate that too."

"Exactly. But that's us, Kevin. We're plastic sushi. We look great on the surface, but underneath we're not real. Maybe we never were. All I know is I want more from my life than that."

"But . . . I want more too, Toni. That's why . . . that's why I'm asking you to marry me."

"No, you didn't ask me to marry you. You said you might be ready to start *thinking* about marriage. And that maybe we could shop for a ring because I'm too picky for you to buy one yourself. For future reference, when you propose to a girl, rethink the wording a bit."

She grabs her bag.

"But isn't that what you want? To get married?"

"Marriage isn't a consolation prize, Kevin. It's not a dozen roses that you bring to someone to make everything better. You can't treat a person the way you treated me and come back and expect everything to be okay. I'm sorry, but it's over." She gets up from the table feeling a full six inches taller than when she sat down. "I'm really glad I got a chance to tell you in person." She gives him a kiss on the head, the way he did to her that day at the bistro. "By the way"—she leans in and whispers in his ear—"you don't have the world's prettiest feet either."

Chris sees the gray-brown skyline of the city ahead of him. The expressway had been true to its name this time, and he made it in less than two hours. Or maybe he had been speeding the whole time and didn't realize it.

The sight of Toni with another man—Chris remembers his phony smile, his pumping handshake, his pink collar sticking up, *fuck*—sent him careening back to high school. Especially since it was him—Kevin. The Ex. He wanted to go three rounds with the dude right there on Newtown Lane. But he kept it in check, and here he is, moving in the opposite direction of where he wants to be.

He drives into the gloaming of the Midtown Tunnel. When he emerges, he smells exhaust fumes, gasoline, vaguely garbage. Tourists are everywhere, everyone looking half lost.

He gives the car to his garage and checks for mail in his lobby. So many flyers and bills and junk mail, all of it seeming even more pointless than it did when he left.

His apartment feels like a mausoleum, untouched for almost three months. He grabs his gym bag and heads for the club. It's almost deserted this time on an August night. Everyone's away—most of them in the Hamptons, probably. Just a few overdeveloped Mr. Universe types staring at themselves in the mirrors. He leaves after barely working up a sweat.

He finds himself wandering the crowded streets, fighting the humidity, the traffic. He stops to look in windows at things he's never noticed before. Antique vases, vintage toasters, old-fashioned silverware. Then he sees something he could really use. In the window of an electronics store, a Bose Wave machine.

Chapter 89

In the twilight, Toni sits on the back steps of the delivery entrance, a place she
has been many times before trying to get over broken hearts or bad grades or
fights with her parents. Layla comes out of the restaurant with a big glass of
root beer and a box of Kleenex. She sits down beside Toni on the steps.

"That's a busy day, young lady. Even for you."

"I know," Toni says. "And all I could think about was you-know-who."
Kevin used to be you-know-who for months. Now it's Chris's turn. She wonders if she's just destined to substitute one failed relationship for the next.

"I bet you're all he's thinking about too," Layla says. "He loves you, you
know. I could tell when I met him. I've never seen anyone look at you like that
before. He looks at you the way Huds looks at me."

Toni wilts with hopefulness. "His ex-girlfriend said he's besotted."

"That's good, right?"

"Besotted is good." Toni slurps her root beer. "I just wish I could erase him
from my mind, you know? Like when you're cooking something and you put
cinnamon instead of nutmeg, you can usually work with it. And if you can't,
you can always start over."

"But he's a person, Toni. Not a recipe."

"I know, but . . ."

"Why does every little thing have to be perfect for you all the time? I mean *all* the time?"

Toni's bottom lip quivers. Layla holds out the Kleenex box for her.

"Do you remember when we were kids and you hated keeping a diary?"

Toni sniffles, shrugs.

"Because when you kept a diary everything had to be perfect the first time you wrote it, or you'd have to throw the whole thing out. You didn't like the cross-outs. You thought they were messy."

Toni gives a little laugh. "And I wouldn't rip the pages out either, because they weren't perforated and they'd leave all those jagged edges. I didn't like that either."

"Exactly. So you had to start over with a brand-new diary every time you made a mistake. Just because things weren't absolutely perfect the first time. It's like you're doing that to Chris. Don't you want to forgive him?"

Toni nods, then shakes her head, then shrugs.

"You always forgive *me*. It doesn't matter what I do. Late for picnics, making you write my thank-you cards, canceling the catering."

"But you're my best friend. I'm supposed to forgive you."

"What about Tucker? He's not a perfect dog. God! He's a beast sometimes. But you wouldn't dream of giving him back, would you?"

Toni gives her a wide-eyed look.

"Then why would you dump a perfectly wonderful guy who loves you so much because one thing went wrong?"

Tears start streaming and Layla hands her more tissues. That's when Toni notices the new diamond ring: an enormous emerald-cut solitaire set in platinum. It's one of the biggest diamonds Toni has ever seen—and considering she spent much of her life waiting on tables in the Hamptons, that was saying something.

"You got it," she says. "Your ring . . ."

It's the exact engagement ring Layla had her heart set on. The one that, in the years before Tiffany's was part of Main Street, the girls would sneak in to see at the flagship store in the city. Toni would get lost in the china department, wandering like a kid in a candy shop, and Layla would gravitate to the rings—in particular, enormous square-cut diamonds.

"How do you get everything to work out for you all the time?" Toni playfully shoves her hand away.

"Lucky, I guess."

Toni looks at her. *Lucky?*

You?

She doesn't have to say it.

What about your parents?

Toni remembers the summer it happened. It seemed as if nothing worse could happen to anybody—ever—and that Layla could never be expected to get through it.

Layla gives a sad smile. "Sometimes bad things happen, Toni. Sometimes really, really bad things happen. And you have to deal. But you know what? That doesn't mean things are never going to be okay again. Everything can still be great."

"It can?"

"Yes. It can. So just relax, okay?"

"But I'm trying to. I've been trying so hard."

"*Trying* to relax is sort of beside the point," Layla says.

Toni makes a sound, part laugh, part sob. Layla hands her another Kleenex and they sit together on the steps for a long time.

Chapter 90

Didi tosses in bed. The sound of high tide on the beach is like the rush of Napoleon's army. But even with two Ambien in her system, she can't seem to drift off. She keeps thinking about the word: illegitimate.

She hasn't been able to do anything for days. She hasn't played bridge or tennis. She's letting Estella handle the wedding plans—unaware that she'd been doing most of that already. She just can't bring herself to see anyone for fear they'll know something's wrong with her. That something has been wrong with her all along.

Suddenly, she sits up in bed. The clarity of an idea floods over her.

In her white silk robe and Dior slippers, she tiptoes out of her room and down the hall. She gasps when she feels something brush past her legs. The Siamese flits into the shadows beneath a console table and through the half-open door to the Violet Room. Bea leaves her bedroom door ajar in the city too, so the cats can have their nocturnal run of the place. Didi hears Bea's light snoring coming from the darkened bedroom and imagines she can smell their litter boxes too.

She feels herself shiver and moves on.

She lets herself out the door and creeps across the pool deck toward her Tri-anon. The wind feels cool this late on a summer night. She grabs an armful of glossy magazines, documents, and photographs from her private office. She rolls up the family tree and shoves it under her arm like a baton. She marches outside, through a break in the juniper bushes, and dumps the papers on the grass between the side of the pool house and the woodshed. She goes behind the shed, a place she has not visited since playing hide-and-seek as a girl. The place smells dank, of garbage cans and earth. Moths flutter around a dim lightbulb and enormous beetles cling to the window. She grabs one of the shiny tin bins Jorge uses for lawn cuttings and rolls it away from the shed into a twelve-foot clearing. She gathers an armload of kindling from a pile, then two large cured logs from the cord stacked against the shed. She drops them into the bin. She's never lit a fire herself in her life, but she's seen people do it a thousand times. It's the most basic of human technologies. Surely to God she could manage this.

She fumbles for the gold lighter in her robe. She lights the end of a rolled-up magazine cover and sets it down in the bin.

Things fizzle for a moment, then smoke, making her cough. She takes the big load of society magazines and papers at her feet and piles them into the can. The fire begins to catch. When yellow flames reach up past the rim, she crumples the big parchment into a ball and throws it on top. She has to step back because of the heat.

She pats her robe, looking for her cigarettes. Her hands tremble as she lights one. She's shaking so badly that when she tries to put her lighter back in her pocket, it slides to the ground and bounces away from her feet.

She stands there smoking, watching the fire, feeling a dark sense of relief. She waits until the family tree is nothing but gnarled intersections of black. She throws her cigarette into the can and walks back across the dewy grass to the house. She passes the white tents and the wedding gazebo and the dance floor in the distance. She lets herself in the front door. As usual, it's not locked.

As Didi sleeps in her queen-size bed, dragged down by all her exertion outside, the dried logs kick and snap. The covers of *Hamptons* and *Social Life* flutter, half burned. A single page of smiling socialites lifts from the embers and floats on the wind like a large butterfly. It falls onto the cord of wood leaning against the shed. The wood starts to smoke, then turn orange, then crawl with flames. Within minutes, fire engulfs the whole shed in a closed yellow fist. Embers flit through the air like migrating birds and land on top of the nearest free-span tent. . . .

The alarm at the Southampton fire department sounds twenty minutes later, not because of a 911 call from Concordia, but because the security cameras at the house next door capture a spectacular shot of the flames as they reach above the hedgerow. Private security guards monitoring the CCTVs at their headquarters see the flames and call the fire department immediately. By the time the first fire trucks arrive, a chunk of Didi's hedgerow is on fire, illuminating the way like a lighthouse.

Chapter 91

Toni can't believe it.

She stares at the mess on the kitchen table. A bowl of tiny candied chocolate shells; a box of graham crackers; the recipe for the rosewater fruitcake and pale fondant and frosting. She grabs a small handful of candy-coated shells and pops them in her mouth, chewing in a daze.

Vic comes in the back door with the morning's mail and the newspaper. He seems preoccupied.

"You're not going to believe this," Toni says, and tells him the news.

"What?"

She takes the newspaper and points to the front page. Fire being a communal fear in the Hamptons, there's a full-color photo of the blaze at Concordia.

"Didi says it's too dangerous. The grounds are all burned out. The guest-house was damaged. Two of the three tents are completely gone. Poor Sully. I haven't heard her sound this upset in years."

"Huh," Vic says. He walks through to the dining room.

She puts the paper down and follows him. "Dad, what is wrong with you? I said the wedding's canceled." She watches him put a letter on top of his pending pile. There's a Town Hall logo on it.

"What's that?"

"A cease-and-desist order."

"What do you have to cease?"

"Not just cease. I have to desist too."

"What do you have to cease and desist?"

Vic walks into the kitchen and gets the espresso pot out. "My pumpkins," he says. "In front of the restaurant. Apparently, there's been a complaint from a member of the Business Association." He taps his lips in mock concentration. "Gee, I wonder who *that* could be. Because I didn't send in an application before I set my pumpkins out."

Toni stares at him. "Since when do you need a permit for pumpkins?"

"My sentiments exactly. Whoever it is, and trust me, I know who it is"—he mutters *Susan* under his breath—"says my pumpkins constitute illegal signage-slash-advertising. She's trying to get the Architectural Review Board up in arms."

Toni winces. In East Hampton, where everything from signs to antennas needs approval from one office or another, she knows it's not difficult to get the Architectural Review Board riled up.

"But how can pumpkins be advertising?"

"Because we serve pumpkin ravioli this time of year."

She takes a moment to savor the thought of her dad's pumpkin ravioli. "Mmmm. *Cibo degli dei,*" she says.

"*Grazie.* But because pumpkins are on the menu, having pumpkins on the walk outside constitutes illegal advertising because I did not receive a permit from Town Hall. It's crazy. If pumpkins are advertising, it's pretty damn subliminal. It's her. I know it is. I saw her skulking outside the restaurant the other day."

"So did I."

"Who else would pick on my pumpkins? They're threatening to arrest me if I don't get rid of them."

"Then just get rid of them. Who wants to look at pumpkins in August anyway?"

"I happen to like looking at them."

"More like you don't want to back down from a fight. You're *testardo.*"

"Maybe. But I know my rights. I can prove it to them—and to Susan Schumacher—that sometimes a pumpkin is just a pumpkin."

"That's great, Dad. But don't do anything until we talk, okay?" She grabs her keys. "I have to run."

"Where are you going?"

"Southampton," she says. "I don't think you heard me. The wedding's off."

Didi sits at her dressing table overlooking the half-charred lawn. She's on the phone, watching the bones of two of the tents get loaded into a dump truck.

"It's unfortunate, I know. . . . Thank God no one was hurt, that's all. . . . No, the prevailing winds were from the south. The house was spared, thank God. Small mercies, I know. . . . Yes, we're all just heartbroken about it. . . . Thank you . . . thank you. . . . I'll be in touch."

Didi hangs up the phone, consults the guest list, then dials another number.

"Millie? It's Didi. . . . You heard? . . . Thank you. . . . No, the winds were from the south, thank goodness. The house is fine, but the guesthouse is a mess. And my poor Trianon?" Didi sighs loudly. "What a disaster scene."

That's what really bothered her. Her beloved pool house was ruined. The cedar-paneled walls of her private office went up like charcoal, leaving half of the pool house ready to collapse.

"We just couldn't go through with it—not with everything in such a sorry state. It might be dangerous too. . . . That's what the fire marshal said. . . . Thank you . . . thank you. . . . I'll be in touch with any new plans."

One after the other, she calls family and friends, from New York to England, from Palm Beach to Palm Springs, and in the Hamptons from west to east.

"It's off for now. . . . I know, we're all heartbroken, Sonny especially. . . . We were so looking forward to it, but at least no one was hurt. . . ."

Layla sits cross-legged in the Lily room amid the wedding gifts. She listens to Didi's voice carry through the house. Each hour, each announcement, each conversation spiked with a laugh happier than the last. It's as if her telephone calls were double martinis and she was getting drunker on each one.

Hudson lies on the bed, his chin in his hands, a little pout on his face.

Layla holds the little Limoges butterfly vase in her lap. "I can't believe how much I hate the idea of sending this back."

Chapter 92

"Mrs. Schumacher!" Bill says. He walks up the tree-lined driveway to the parking lot behind Susan Schumacher's house.

Susan lifts Styrofoam coolers into the back of one her fleet of vans. She narrows her eyes on the tall man with the camera.

"Hello, Mr. Mitchell," she says. "What can I do for you?"

He takes out his notebook. "I was just hoping to get a comment from you about the complaint you placed at Town Hall against Fratelli's illegal signage."

"Allegedly illegal, Mr. Mitchell. How do you know about that?"

"There's not a lot of news around here. People tell me these things."

"I have no comment," she says, climbing into the van.

"Then what about the cancellation of the Flagstone wedding? Can you comment on that?"

"I have dozens of events this weekend. It's unfortunate, but it won't put me out of business."

"No, I see that." He watches two other vans pull out of the parking lot. "You made it through, didn't you? The flapping of the wings on Memorial Day didn't bother you all that much."

Susan sits in her van, the window open. "Do you have a point, Mr. Mitchell?"

"Just that it's Labor Day—and we're both still in business."

"Labor Day's not until Monday. Don't count your chickens." She starts backing out of the driveway. "Please show yourself out. I'm very busy today."

Bill flips his notebook closed and watches after her.

Cerulean blue, Bea thinks.

She sits on her paint-spattered wooden chair at the very edge of the dune grasses surrounding the front patio. Her easel is positioned toward the broad angle of the beach. The palette hooked around her thumb is thick with layers of paint, some wet, some dry.

She rummages in her paint kit, through squeezed tubes of zinc buff, unbleached titanium, cinnabar green. A lifetime of Hamptons beach scenes. On the easel in front of her are three stripes of blue and beige—sand, sea, and sky—the composition that has fascinated so many for so long.

No cerulean blue.

She wipes her hands on her smock and walks around the house, past the tennis courts where the lights and equipment for the dance floor are still set up. She walks toward the garage, where she sees a VW van painted every shade of the rainbow. She stops to admire it, a testament to all the hope and joy of teenagers getting ready for a school play.

Toni comes out of the house with a picnic basket.

"Is that yours?" Bea asks, pointing to the van.

Toni laughs. "Yeah. Jackson Pollock by way of sophomore year."

"I'd say more Picasso, actually. Jack the Dripper wasn't usually so literal."

Toni laughs. "Oh-kay. I'll take your word for it. Are you painting?"

"Yes. And I need more cerulean blue. Will you help me? It's dim in there."

The garage smells of old fuel as they step through the doors. They pass Bea's Rolls-Royce, Hudson's Aston Martin, Didi's Bentley, an old Vespa, the space for Henry's Range Rover, and years of bicycles. Bea leads her to the very back corner beneath a dusty window and opens a wooden chest.

"I might have some in here somewhere." As she sorts through a clutter of squeezed tubes and brushes, she knocks a burlap sheet with her hip and the fabric falls to the ground, revealing a stack of canvases leaning against the wall.

"Are those yours?"

Bea nods.

"Layla told me you painted."

"Only dabble."

Toni flips through them, seeing one beach scene after another. "These are so good."

"Thank you. So is your van."

"The good eyeballs and sunshines are Layla's. She's the artist. Mine are the crooked ones."

"You shouldn't be so hard on yourself. We're all artists at heart." She hands Toni a little tube. "What's this?"

Toni holds it to the dusty window. "Sèvres blue."

Bea thinks about it, setting it aside.

"There are no people in any of these," Toni says.

"I never enjoyed painting people. They complain so much about how long they have to sit. And they make things so complicated. I prefer to keep things simple." She hands her another tube.

"Cadmium red."

"That might be nice for a sunset. This?"

"Cerulean blue!"

"French or general?"

"French."

"I'm sure it'll be fine." She pockets her little tubes, noticing Toni still looking at the paintings.

"Choose one if you like. It might be worth something someday." Bea winks. "But not for a while. I'm healthy as a horse."

"Hey, guys." Layla stands in the door, her blond hair and white blouse glowing in the sunlight.

"Hello, angel."

Toni says, "You ready?"

Layla nods excitedly.

Bea helps Toni choose a small painting of a sunrise, and Toni kisses her cheek. "Thank you . . ."

She and Layla get into the van, with Bea waving good-bye to them. Just as they're about to turn onto the road, two police cars pull in.

"Looks like we have company," Layla says.

"*They* have company," Toni says as she hits the gas.

———————

Didi flicks at her fingernail, down to nothing but a sore pink nub now. The fire marshal blows dust off an old VCR beneath the DVD player in the library. He inserts the tape.

"I'm just glad we found this before it looped over the evidence," he says.

Evidence? Didi thinks.

"The point of origin was the tin garbage can by the woodshed," he says. "The fire radiated outward from there. But we think we have a shot of the perpetrator."

He fast-forwards through the tape. The day's festivities flash by in high speed on the screen: a steep angle of the door, the tops of people's heads coming and going. The digits at the bottom of the screen spin through the day: 2:35, 5:51, 8:17. Darkness settles in. The carvings on the white door deepen with shadows. Moths flutter in the light of the nearby bulbs. He fast-forwards through the stillness until he sees a swift blur.

He stops the tape and rewinds.

Didi freezes when she sees the top of her own head coming in the front door.

"According to the recorded images from the security system next door, the fire was visible by 3:30 A.M. Meaning it must've started earlier than that. And this is the time someone entered the house." He points to the digits in the corner: 3:13 A.M. "Did you leave the house the night of the fire, Mrs. Flagstone?"

"Of course not. And we have a lot of guests staying here all the time. That could be anybody."

"Maybe not anybody," he says. He holds up an evidence bag.

Didi exhales in relief—she thought she'd lost her gold lighter or that the girl had stolen it. But her respite is quickly replaced by a cold rush of fear. Even through the black soot the initials are clearly visible: D.E.B.

Chapter 93

Tucker runs on ahead of the women, kicking up sand and chasing seagulls along Georgica Beach. They leave the dense crowd of the public beach behind, carrying the picnic basket and a blanket past the great mansions on the dunes. Mating season is now over for the piping plovers, so they can ignore the signs on the dunes and set up the picnic in their favorite spot in front of Calvin Klein's place.

Their voices are casual murmurs. "Pass me that bowl." "This is delicious." They sit on the blanket and watch the waves unfold on the beach for their first picnic of the year. They drink wine and eat chicken salad sandwiches and triple-chocolate-chip cookies. They tell stories about old boyfriends. They remember Tucker when he was a puppy. They talk about Layla's sister, Leslie, too pregnant to fly, and halfway across the country by train, unable to turn back. They rehash old stories, gossip about old teachers and friends, circling but never quite touching on the one thing that sits with them like an elephant on the beach: in less than twenty-four hours Layla's wedding was scheduled to take place.

Layla brings it up first. "The license is only good for forty days or something like that."

"Sixty," Toni says. Layla looks at her. "Just one of those pointless pieces of information I have in my head."

"Do you think we should just go to Vegas?"

"Do you want to go to Vegas?"

Layla thinks about it. She picks up a handful of pale sand, letting it slip through her fingers like water. "No. I want to get married on the beach."

"Okay. Remember you said you wanted me to make your wedding cake?"

"Yeah?"

Toni just smiles.

Chapter 94

Didi Flagstone sits by herself in the women's holding cell of the East Hampton Village police headquarters, a redbrick building on Cedar Street. A raucous party at Pink Elephant the night before had filled up the Southampton police station cells, so they had to bring her here.

The room is relatively spacious, with a barred door, pleasant blue walls, and a bench. Didi sits in her stocking feet, since her shoes had been taken—along with her alligator belt—when she was processed. She stares at the only other feature of the room, and what is probably the most disgusting thing she's ever seen in her life.

A toilet-sink.

It's made of a single piece of gleaming stainless steel. The toilet is lidless; the sink sits behind it where the tank should be. She can't imagine washing and relieving herself with the same piece of equipment.

They had actually put handcuffs on her when they took her from her home and led her to the police car. She was being charged with arson. She made several calls—the first to Henry at Shinnecock and the rest to an army of Madison Avenue lawyers at various other golf courses around the Hamptons—the Atlantic, the Maidstone, Hampton Hills.

They grilled her with questions:

No, it wasn't on purpose, Didi said. It was an accident.

What on earth were you burning in the middle of the night, Mrs. Flagstone?

She thought about it and finally answered. Garbage.

Yes. She'd swear to it under oath.

By the time she is staring at the stainless steel toilet-sink, the team of lawyers is almost certain the arson charges will be dropped. But she is still being held on the slightly less serious crime of burning refuse within town lines without a permit, until Henry and the lawyers can work out the details of her release.

Community service and a fine are likely.

Just outside the cell sits a white-haired woman flipping through a special edition of the *East Hampton Sun*. She's Didi's chaperone. The other three male holding cells are all equipped with closed-circuit cameras. But since it is considered rude to photograph female detainees in a jail cell in the Hamptons, a matron was called in to monitor the situation.

Margaret Latham was sixth on the list of possible volunteers who were called, and the first who was not busy with other long-weekend festivities. It's a red-letter day at the village police station. It was rare enough that a matron had to be hired to watch one detainee; it was even rarer someone would be called in to watch two.

Didi looks up to see a policeman unbolt the barred door. He unlocks Susan Schumacher's handcuffs and gives a gallant bow for her to enter the cell. Susan slumps inside, also in her sock feet. Didi is shocked to see she has company.

The officer turns to the white-haired woman with the newspaper. "Hi, Margaret."

"Hi, Griff," she says.

"Hot off the presses?" He motions to the paper.

"Still warm," she says. He leans over to read along with her.

The front page has two stories. Below the fold, Didi Flagstone in handcuffs being led from a cruiser.

FLAGSTONE FIASCO! is the headline. It's a an awful photo of the horsey left side of her face. The edition was printed before the whole story was out, so everybody who's anybody now thinks Deirdre Blackhart Flagstone is an arsonist.

And above the fold, Bill Mitchell's first big scoop of the year. He chose the headline very carefully, and was pleased with himself when inspiration struck:

PIPING HOT PLOVERS! it reads.

Susan Schumacher sits down next to Didi.

"How are you?"

"Hmmm. Fine. You?"

"Fine. I suppose."

Susan sighs heavily, staring at the toilet-sink. She knew she shouldn't have believed Bill Mitchell when he said he wanted to interview her about the signage. When she left him in the driveway she assumed he was going to go back to his car. If she had been monitoring one of her CCTVs in the back of the van, she would've known that he snuck past the house, hiding in bushes and gardens, down the property to her rare chicken coop. There were so many workers on the grounds, no one even noticed him. He climbed a stepladder, peeked inside a high window, and took several shots of her exotic chickens and the even more exotic piping plover nests. At that point in the season, Susan Schumacher had dozens of pairs of little plovers laying eggs in her coop. And had for many years.

She couldn't have known how happy Bill was to see the little birds. He remembered the sound of cackling and peeping when he was investigating the dried-up creek bed next to Susan's farm. As he snapped his photographs, lighting the dim straw-filled room with his flash, he heard the distinctive *pee-eep* of the piping plovers.

"Gotcha," he said.

After Susan was arrested and brought to the village jail, Jan Walters and Rick "Fish" Pyke from the Environmental Center were escorted by police onto Susan's property. An officer hacked the lock on the rare poultry coop, and Jan and Fish, in work boots and gas masks, went inside first. There was stomping. Banging. A few fat brown hens fluttered out.

More hacking and sawing and then a large pool of black and white flooded the ground as a scintillating flock of pale birds with stripes on their foreheads moved in a wave under the feet of the onlookers.

Pee-eep!

Pee-eep!

People had to lift their shoes to let the birds scurry past the No Trespassing signs to the beach. Susan was being charged under sections 11-0303 and 11-0321 of the Fish and Wildlife Law, since slaughtering an endangered species was considered "killing, harassing, or in any way disturbing" it—no matter how tasty said species could be.

The sensationalism of the two front-page stories meant that another story had been a relegated to the next page, in a little sidebar on the bottom right: a photo of Vic Fratelli standing in front of his restaurant under the headline THE PUMPKIN PROBLEM.

Susan's team of lawyers had convinced her to drop her complaint against Vic Fratelli's allegedly illegal advertising on the grounds that they'd all be busy with more important matters for the foreseeable future, crimes against the environment being viewed even more seriously in these parts than permit infractions.

Susan agreed and Vic was a free man.

The day's special edition of the *East Hampton Sun* cleared out faster than the weekend issue of *Hamptons*. As the summer colony read the secret ingredient of Susan Schumacher's famous "Belgian wren tartlets," a collective *ewwww* rang out across the Hamptons. White's Chemists reported that stomach remedies were cleared from their shelves before sundown.

When Toni heard the news, she winced. "I always knew those tarts tasted gamy," she said.

Sunday, September 6

The Wedding Day

Chapter 95

Sunday morning dawns bright and warm, feeling like the last official day of summer even though autumn is still three weeks away. The roads in the villages are busy with tourists picking up souvenirs and meeting friends for the last time. The beaches are crammed with bodies and beach towels. The lifeguards blow their whistles double-time.

When Toni, Layla, and Hudson made the decision to go ahead with the wedding only twenty-four hours later than the invitations had announced, Toni went into Now-What? Mode. She banded together everyone from the restaurant and even hired two servers from LDV who found themselves out of a job after Susan's bookings were canceled.

The florists who took the Flagstone wedding off their schedule a few days earlier now crowd the grounds with their trucks. The new hedges to fill the gap in the privet along Gin Lane are temporarily leaning against the side of the pool house so that no one will see the charred walls. The single tent that survived the fire holds ten tables of ten, each set with white linen and vintage china from Didi's cabinets, mismatched pieces from Toni's collection, and, for the evening, hurricane lamps from the Hope Garage filled with sand and seashells.

On the wide straight beach out front, a five-thousand-foot hose runs down the dune grasses, and a young man with sun-bleached hair—the winner of that year's sand castle–building contest—soaks the sand at his feet, crouching down to carve a wedding "altar" in the shape of a large swirling seashell.

Three rows of white chairs form a semicircle in front, enough for nearly a hundred guests who were able to attend the wedding. Iridescent shells and the starfish Layla brought for Spring Dinner are scattered in the sand.

Layla lies off to the side on her beach blanket, getting a few last minutes of sun. A rolled-up towel under her neck keeps her from crushing a head full of rollers. Her iPod is on and she swings her foot to some faint beat as Toni walks over holding a clipboard and a walkie-talkie.

"T-minus three hours. Time to get ready."

Layla shades her eyes and looks up. "God. I almost fell asleep."

"You're the only bride who could fall asleep on her wedding day." The radio crackles. "Base Station Alpha. Over."

"Alpha, this is Beta Two. The cake just came! Over."

"Oh, goodie! I gotta go!" She heads toward the stairs.

Layla calls after her. "Tone!"

Toni turns around, walking backward. "What?"

"Is there anything I can do to help?"

"Yeah—go get ready."

She hurries up the stairs to the house.

Layla looks out at the ocean. It's a perfect sunny day on Gin Lane, a fine mist obscuring the edges of the world. She stands, picking up her blanket and baby oil. The sand is flat where she was lying down. She smoothes it a bit with her hands and feet, feeling the warmth of the sun on her back. Her foot kicks something and it bounces ahead of her. She had asked Jorge not to rake the sand before the wedding—she wanted to keep it looking natural—but that was too heavy for a seashell. It must be a rock or sea glass. She picks it up to inspect it. It glints blue and gold in her hand.

On the pool deck, Toni oversees Vic and Jerome loading the cake onto a long table covered with a white cloth and a garland of flowers. "A little to the left," Toni says. "Half an inch to the right. Split the difference...."

The cake is more than three feet high, in the shape of a tall sandcastle, with opalescent pale frosting, a layer of crushed graham cracker crumbs at the base for sand, and covered in tiny candy seashells. Toni motions her thumb back and forth—left, right—until her dad and Jerome have it centered.

"Perfect," she says. She makes a little check on her clipboard. "Dad, you brought your tie?"

"Yep."

"Tie—check."

Around the pool, long tables are set up for champagne, minted and cherry lemonade, mixed drinks, and wine. The fourth is the dessert table, with three kinds of chocolate fondue, fruit chunks and pound cake for dipping, dishes of candy seashells, and, of course, the cake.

She hurries back into the house. "Where's the champagne? We need the . . ."

In the hallway, she bumps straight into someone carrying a box of glassware. He gives her a weak smile. "Backup team reporting for duty," Chris says.

Toni had been in the middle of making the frosting for the cake when the last of the RSVPs were coming in. Almost a hundred people would be attending—more than she expected—so she had to resort to her stack of résumés. When she got to Chris Ohm's name, she hesitated. Started dialing his number, then stopped, then started again.

For the first time that summer, he actually answered his cell.

Toni knew he was coming, but it's still a shock to see him there. They're staring at each other when Yuri swings past them with a case of beer on his head.

"Where do you want these, Johnson?"

Toni just motions to the pool deck. Lincoln and Frank are behind him with more boxes. They all look freshly shaved and scrubbed, wearing white polo shirts and beige bermuda shorts.

Frank holds a box from the Monogram Shop. She pulls back the flaps and sees dozens of pale blue cloth bags that were originally ordered as part of the favors.

"They're for people's shoes when they get here. Can you please take them down to the beach?" To Chris she says, "The bride insists we go barefoot."

"She gets her way, doesn't she?" Chris asks.

"Eventually."

Frank takes the box outside and Toni and Chris both start talking at the same time. "Thanks for coming," she says. He says, "Thanks for inviting me."

Then they stop and just smile at each other again.

"Everything looks great, Toni," he says.

"Thanks . . ." She feels that draw to him again, like the slow pull of the tide when she was a kid. "I . . . I hope you're not going to get in trouble or anything. For working this summer."

"Three months are up," Yuri says, coming up behind her. "We're free men again. Come on, Johnson, don't gaggy-lawl."

"I'll see you later?" Chris says, walking backward, as if not wanting to take his eyes off her.

She nods.

Lincoln sidles by. "For the record, it drove him crazy he couldn't tell you."

She watches them head out the door. Chris bumps into the door frame staring back at her. After he's gone, she feels an instant of dizziness, the chandelier swooping down the wall.

But she knows it's not her blood sugar this time. It's seeing him again.

In the Rose Room, Didi stands in front of her mirror. Her Oscar de la Renta gown is strapless, pale pink, with a chiffon overlay. She has a hat, which would've been fine for the garden wedding, but the beach would be too windy for it. Estella helps her on with her pearls and then hands her a pair of pink satin sandals.

"Apparently, we're going barefoot," Didi says.

She checks her reflection one last time, grabs something from her jewelry box, and heads into the hall.

She hesitates as she walks toward the Lily Room, now taken over by the bride—white décor being appropriate for a wedding day and the room being large enough for all the women to get ready. She knocks.

"Come in?"

Didi opens the door to see Layla trying to do up the back of her dress. She looks slightly flustered. "Can you help me?"

"Of course." Didi comes over, doing up the buttons on the back. She doesn't say anything about the tattoo that still shows. She remembers tying this girl's bikini strings only three months ago, but it feels like a lifetime away. "There," she says, stepping back and smoothing the train. "You look lovely, Layla."

Layla? Finally.

"Thanks. . . . So do you."

"Will you sit down with me?"

Layla frowns as Didi leads her to the bed.

"According to tradition, the bride is supposed to wear 'something old' on her wedding day. You probably know that."

"I have something already," Layla says. She motions to her beads and bangles.

"I have something for you too. My mother tried to give it to me on my wedding day, but I never actually wore it. I know your mother isn't here to do that for you, so maybe you'd accept this from me."

She hands Layla a worn Van Cleef & Arpels box. Layla's hands tremble slightly as she opens it and sees the multicolored bracelet. She knows there's something appropriate she should say right now, but she's so shocked all she can manage is, "Oh my God."

"It's a family heirloom," Didi says as she fastens the bracelet on Layla's wrist. "I haven't got around to adding yours and Hudson's birthstones yet. But we'll do that as soon as you're back from the honeymoon."

Layla jumbles all the bracelets together. "I love it," she says. "Thank you." But then she frowns. Her wrist looks like buried treasure washed up with seaweed. "Maybe we should take some of these off," she says. "Not these ones. Toni made them for me at summer camp. But these strings—and maybe this old shoelace?"

Didi's eyes widen. "I'll get the scissors!"

On her way out, she's nearly bowled over by a stampede of bridesmaids carrying garment bags. They skid to a stop when they see Layla, squealing in unison about how beautiful she looks.

"Did you get them?" she asks.

"He stayed open just for us," Tabitha says. They unzip the bags and pull out their new bridesmaid dresses.

After the wedding was canceled, the "seabreeze" gowns from New York ended up stuck on a UPS truck in Levittown. The girls called Steven Stolman's shop in Southampton, and they all went in yesterday and picked out a baby blue pique sleeveless cocktail dress that matched the men's ties.

Size six, Toni thinks as Tabitha zips her up. Nothing like a little heartache to drop a few pounds.

Ruth Fratelli, in a floor-length celadon green gown, has her camera around her neck and scoots the women into position in front of the window, Layla in the center, the bridesmaids around her, and her very pregnant sister, Leslie, half hiding behind her. Around each of their necks is a tiny diamond starfish pendant Layla gave them as bridesmaid gifts.

Ruth takes a couple of shots. "Toni, I can see your clipboard."

"Oh, sorry." Toni tosses it aside.

After a few more shots, Tabitha announces she needs more wine.

Toni turns to Layla. "T-minus ten minutes. Ready for your close-up?"

"Almost," she says. "One more thing." She takes Toni's hand and leads her down the hall to the Violet Room. She knocks on the door, and Bea tells them to come in.

Bea wears a royal blue dress and pearls. When she sees Toni, she beams. "Did you give it to her?"

"Not yet."

"Give me what?"

"You better sit down for this." They both watch as Toni steps back to sit on the bed. "Hold out your hand."

Toni does so and Layla places something in her palm. Toni is surprised to look down and see the big blue sapphire staring back at her.

"I found it on the beach today," Layla says. "I want you to have it."

"But I . . . are you crazy? No . . . no way."

Bea says, "A woman needs a little nest egg when she's opening a business on her own. We've talked about it, and we all want you to have it. Hudson too."

Toni stares at the ring. She stutters a few times and tries to give it back.

Layla says, "Toni, remember I told you that sometimes really bad things happen in life and you just have to deal?"

Toni nods and sniffles.

"Sometimes really good things happen—and you have to deal with those too."

Toni looks over at Bea, who smiles. "My mother always said it was for the *right girl,* Toni. And you are undoubtedly the right girl."

———

Down on the beach, Chris makes his way through the crowd, serving champagne with the other waiters. A string quartet plays classical music as Rhonda and Jerome finish lighting the six hundred votive candles Toni bought for the canceled Henderson party earlier in the season. As the sun clears the roof of Concordia, the beach is cast in the rose-pink light of "magic hour"—nowhere more magic than on Gin Lane.

Ruth Fratelli hurries down to take her place beside Vic in the front row. Didi sits next to Bea, the chair on the other side waiting for Henry. Hudson stands with the minister in front of the seashell altar and smiles at his mother, whose bare feet play unselfconsciously in the sand.

The string quartet plays through the entrance of the bridesmaids and groomsmen down the stairs from the house and across the sand. The groomsmen, like Hudson, are in navy blazers, pale gabardines, white shirts, and pale blue ties. Their pant cuffs are rolled up and their feet are bare.

When the bride appears at the top of the stairs, everyone stands. The string quartet plays a medley of Eric Clapton and "Here Comes the Bride" as Layla and Henry walk across the sand to the altar. With the sun going down and the waves crashing, Layla and Hudson become husband and wife.

Chapter 96

The sunset shifts in swaths of red and orange and gold. The staff corral the guests back up the stairs to the pool for hors d'oeuvres. By the time they head to the tent for the sit-down dinner, music and laughter roll out over the grounds of Concordia.

The courses are all local ingredients: fluke tartar, angel hair pasta with cherry tomatoes, snapper bouillabaisse. Toni watches everyone savor and enjoy.

Hudson and Layla say a word of thanks to the guests for making it on such short notice, and Layla lingers behind at the microphone. She toasts her new in-laws, her sister, her bridesmaids, and Bea. She even thanks Jorge and Estella for all their help. Then she turns to face Toni, a big smile on her face.

"If there's anything this summer has shown me, it's that there's nothing more important than family. And for me, Toni has always been my family. She's the best friend a girl could ever hope for. The most loyal person I've ever met. The greatest maid of honor in the history of the world. And this is a real bonus—she can pull a fantastic wedding off in two days flat."

Everyone laughs and raises a glass to Toni, who gets up and hugs the bride.

"I love you," Layla says.

"I love you too . . ."

Toni sits down, wiping her eyes.

"Just one more mention. My parents couldn't be here tonight, but I know they're watching us and—hopefully—giving us their blessings." She looks upward, wincing a bit. "Maybe it's for the best I can't actually hear what they're saying. If they knew I wasn't marrying a local, they'd never let me live it down."

The tent resounds with laughter.

The drinks flow even more freely as the deejay starts the dance on the tennis court. Bill and the other photographers work their way through the crowd. Texts, calls, and e-mails start going out across the Hamptons as the gates of Concordia open to casual friends. Toni runs out of business cards from so many requests and has to jot her name on scraps of paper or people's hands as they rave about the food.

Just before midnight, she starts to realize that her cheeks are aching from smiling so much and her feet are sore. Layla comes up behind her wearing white jeans and a white cashmere V-neck.

"Well, my friend, you did it. It was absolutely perfect." She plants a big kiss on Toni's cheek and hugs her hard. "I could never thank you enough."

Toni remembers the blue ring. "I think you did already." She sees Layla's Volkswagen Bug parked by the fountain, the top down, the hood and fenders decorated with white streamers and paper wedding bells.

"Time to go?"

"I'm exhausted. Besides"—she makes a growling sound—"I want to go home and have wild wedding-night sex! I'm sick and tired of having to cover my mouth whenever I—"

"Okay," Toni says, laughing. "I get the point."

Leslie goes to the microphone and announces that the bride and groom are ready to leave. Guests pour off the dance floor as the newlyweds get hugs and kisses before climbing into the car. Layla gets in behind the wheel and inches down the long driveway, the crowd following in a wave, everyone clapping and cheering. Toni is at the front of the pack, trying not to cry.

At the gate, Layla stops the car. She grabs something from the seat, turns around, and gets up on her knees.

"Toni, catch!" She swings her arm back.

Toni reaches for the object flying at her as naturally as if they were playing catch in Herrick Park. But it's not a Frisbee. She looks down to see she's holding the bouquet of daisies and white roses in her hands. As the car pulls onto Gin Lane, Layla honks twice and gives the peace sign.

Chapter 97

She hears someone come up behind her and turns to see Chris. He holds a small gift bag. "Hey . . ."

"Hey," she says. "Thank you so much for your help. You guys were amazing."

"Really, it was my pleasure." He looks around. "I didn't happen to see . . . your date tonight."

"He went back to the city—for good," she says.

"I tried that," Chris says. "It didn't work for me this time."

A whoop of laughter from behind him as Lincoln and Yuri load a very intoxicated Frank Broward into the passenger seat of the Mustang. Even from a distance, Frank looks green. But once he's buckled in, it's clear Yuri's in worse shape, stumbling around and singing George Michael songs at the top of his lungs.

"Some of the bartenders did a little too much taste-testing," he says. "Hope you don't hold it against them."

"I'm a three-strikes kind of employer," she says. "And really, don't worry about it. You guys saved the day."

"No, *you* saved the day," he says. "It was a beautiful wedding, Toni." He motions to the car. "I'm sorry we have to go so early. I've got to do the designated-driver thing. And we have to be out of the house at the crack of dawn tomorrow."

A hollow opens up in the bottom of Toni's heart. The end of the rental agreements signaled the absolute end of summer.

"It makes me feel like Cinderella. But it's the house that turns into a pumpkin, not the carriage."

Toni laughs. "Don't mention pumpkins in front of my dad." He seems confused, and she says, "Never mind."

He shifts his weight a bit. "Toni, I was . . . I don't . . ."

What was he supposed to say? It was the best summer ever?

Toni looks down at the bouquet. She feels as if she's saying good-bye to every lifeguard, camp counselor, and summer fling she's ever had.

"I—I got you something," he says. "Just a little something I found in the city." He hands her the gift bag. "I hope you like it."

Frank leans on the horn of the Mustang. Chris starts backing toward the car.

"You have my résumé, right? In case you need me for anything?"

She just smiles and nods.

Don't cry. Don't cry.

He doesn't take his eyes off her as he climbs in the front seat. He waves again and Toni watches until the car disappears behind the hedgerow.

"What are you doing?" asks Tabitha, coming up behind her. She smells like too many cocktails and is unsteady in bare feet. "You love that man." She points in the general direction of the Mustang. "And I can tell he loves you."

"You can?"

She sighs and hiccups at the same time, a semiviolent contortion that nearly knocks her off her feet.

"Yeah. Arturo never looks at me like that. Stupid cad." She turns around and points to him dancing with Poppy on the tennis court. "I think he's more interested in my sister." She holds up her wine to Toni. "Here's a toast for you: men suck."

Toni just laughs.

Tabitha drapes her forearms on Toni's shoulders and looks her in the eye in the very intense way specific to only very drunk people. "You did a *fab*"—she hiccups again—"fabulous job on the wedding, Toni. Layla's right. You're a genius." She plants a wet perfumey kiss on Toni's cheek, the first time she's not delivered an air kiss, and heads off to the tennis court to pry her little sister and Arturo apart.

Toni walks past the people lingering over dessert and drinks in the tent. She stops at the dance floor and surveys the crowd; her father and mother are actually discoing beneath the lights. Their divorce had been so messy and full of anger, she never imagined a day would come when she would see them having so much fun together.

In the house, she finds the kitchen spotless, the chandeliers turned down to half power. Members of her staff hurry by with drink or snack trays, smiling at her. It makes her feel a jolt of pride.

On the front patio, Henry and Uncle William laugh and clap each other's backs, their faces red from too much whisky.

She makes her way down the stairs toward the beach. The sand is cool and yielding beneath her feet. With every step she takes, the music and laughter of the party are dulled by the rush of waves. The last of the votive candles flicker softly, and rows of white chairs face the empty darkness of the sea.

But there is one chair set apart near the surf. A single woman sits facing the water, holding a pink shawl around her shoulders.

"Mrs. Flagstone?"

Didi turns around. "Toni, when are you going to start calling me Didi? You're practically family now. Pull up a chair. Join me."

Toni does so, sitting next to her, surprised by how relaxed she seems. "I didn't expect to see you out here."

"I don't come down here nearly enough anymore. I've become so fussy in my—" She stops and smiles. "Lately," she says.

Toni notices she holds a dried starfish in one hand, fitting her fingers between the five points as if she's linking hands with an old friend.

"You did a wonderful job, my dear. Everyone was raving about it. Saying it was the wedding of the year. I have a feeling you're going to be just fine with your business. I'm going to tell *all* my friends about you."

"Thanks, Didi . . ."

She notices the gift bag in Toni's lap and intuits she needs some time alone.

"I'm going to try to find my husband and see if we can't get another dance in before the night is over." She looks out at the ocean one last time, then walks barefoot across the sand toward the house.

Toni looks at her watch. It's after midnight. She takes a deep breath of air. It even smells like Labor Day. Salty, heavy, and a little bit sad.

She holds the gift bag on her lap, nervous about opening it. It feels like a perfect moment, as if everything would still be possible if she didn't do another thing in her whole life. She unties the ribbon, pulling out something rather heavy and flat. When she unwraps the tissue, a gasp catches in her throat. It's a heart-shaped Archibald Kenrick trivet. It looks exactly the same as the one she lost. Her heart pounds quickly as she reads the card.

Dear Toni,

They say you always find what you're looking for. I know I did. I hope you do too.

Love,
Chris xo

Labor Day

Chapter 98

Toni wakes up before her alarm. The sun coming through the window is at an angle she associates—and will always associate—with the first day of school. She half expects to see a new package of pencil crayons on her desk.

She gets up and strips her bed, piling the Beauty and the Beast sheets into the hamper. She unplugs the ballerina lamp and sets it in a box marked GIVE-AWAYS.

She sits on the edge of the bed and adds NEW LAMP/SHEETS to the bottom of a very dense To Do List. She sets the trivet and the iron on the end table where the lamp used to be. She tried it the second she got home last night and it fit perfectly. She wouldn't be surprised if it was the actual stand she lost in her move out of Dash and that somehow it found its way back to her.

Her father is up making breakfast when she gets downstairs. Without him noticing, she leaves a check on the dining room table in his pending file.

"You feel like breakfast?" He's cracking eggs into an old bowl.

"I'm picking up a wrap from Joni's."

"Are you doing it again?"

"Of course I'm doing it again."

She loads an old burlap bag with cleaning supplies, shoving in her white telescope last.

"I can't believe it's already Labor Day," Vic says. "That's it. Christmas is almost over."

"I really wish you wouldn't say things like that." She kisses his cheek. "Come on, Tuck."

"Stay on the main roads, bella," he says, but she's already out the door.

She drives with the windows down. The gardens once full of tulips and daffodils are now yellow and orange with turtleheads, sunflowers, and mums. The traffic heading west is at a near standstill, vans and cars filled to the roofline with suitcases.

But going east it's clear and free.

She drives down Old Montauk Highway, feeling the hills make her stomach flip. She goes to Joni's for an egg wrap. Then back to Round Swamp for Charlie's Arugula, Lisa's Ultimate Cookies, and Shelly's Sun Tea. She packs them all into a cooler.

She drives to Amagansett Square and buys an iced coffee from Sylvester & Co. She sees the clover-filled lawn in the shade of the trees and remembers their picnic. When she thinks about him, the pain ebbs and flows. Like the summer itself, she knows she has to try to let him go.

She drives past the dense cornfields, the highest stalks starting to wilt. She smells the musky bitterness of potato fields. Sees signs pointing the way to apple-picking orchards and cornfield mazes, roadside stands selling pumpkins and sweet corn.

She takes Tucker to Main Beach and sits on the sand for a while, holding his leash for the very last time that summer. The beach is half empty; only a few die-hard families are spread out here and there. Some of the lifeguards pack up the bathhouses and their lockers, hugging each other good-bye. She watches the cusp of blue ocean on blue sky for a long time. Every year she did all of her favorite summer things on Labor Day. It didn't matter how busy she was, or how long it took her, she had to soak up every last drop of summer.

She goes to Hook Pond to watch the swans, the cygnets almost as tall as their parents, strong and preening on the grass. She looks up to see trees already dotted with yellow leaves.

Chapter 99

At Concordia, every window and every door is open; furniture is being polished and rugs vacuumed. Jorge comes down the curving staircase carrying Didi's Vuitton suitcases.

"Are you ready, miss?" Estella asks.

Didi looks around the foyer one last time. "Yes, but I think we should stay later next year, don't you?" As Jorge carries her bags out to the car, she says: "Or maybe we can even come for Thanksgiving. I haven't been out for Thanksgiving since I was . . ."

The LIE heading west is one long stream of glass and steel. Boats, trailers, SUVs, buses, luxury cars.

In his gold Mustang, Chris listens to the others on their headsets. His Black-Berry, with the chip still in the corner, is on the dash in front of him.

"I can't believe this," Lincoln says. "It's worse than it was coming out."

"It always is," Frank says. "But it's subjective. They say coming down Mount Everest is just as dangerous."

"I'm sad, Johnson," Yuri says, sighing. "The fun part is over."

"Not forever, Yuri. There's always next year."

"Ohmster," says Lincoln. "You okay? You're quiet as a deer tick."

Chris says, "Mmm? I'm fine. No worries." He looks at the signs as they pass. LONG ISLAND EXPRESSWAY.

LIE.

"We need something to do," Lincoln says. "To make the drive go faster."

"A bet," says Yuri.

"I got it," says Lincoln. "Last one home picks up the dinner tab."

"Deal!" say Yuri and Frank.

Yuri pulls into the HOV lane and screeches ahead. Everyone around starts honking at him. *It sounds like a wedding,* Chris thinks.

Chapter 100

"Thanks for inviting me, Toni," says Georgia Randall. "It was the wedding of the ye-ah."

Toni stands on the threshold of Georgia's neat white clapboard office on Main Street. She blushes, says thank you, and hands Georgia some more cards as requested.

"Thanks. And this is for you." Georgia holds up a key ring with a tag attached. "You just take your time. No presh-ah from me."

Toni smiles and takes the key.

She gets back into the van and heads through the village, the pace already seeming slower and more relaxed. Tucker sits in the passenger seat, his head out the window as they pass the big windmill.

On Springs Fireplace Road, she sees two girls—one fair, one dark—walking along the shoulder, kicking at the gravel, and lost in conversation.

Local kids getting back their town, she thinks.

She passes a knot of cars along the shoulder of the road. A weathered farmhouse, half shaded by trees, stands on a patch of worn grass. A white sign out front announces the hours of operation.

She drives about a hundred yards past the house and starts to ride the brake. She looks at her watch, then at the farmhouse receding in her rearview mirror. She's struck by a desire to do something most tourists do during their first visit to the Hamptons. She decides to visit Pollock-Krasner House.

She leaves Tucker in the car and heads up the driveway, where a relaxed group of tourists gathers pamphlets and mills about. The old shingles are gray-brown with age, the enclosed white porch looks worn and unassuming.

She doesn't see anyone she knows.

She pays the nominal admission fee and decides against a guided tour, choosing to walk through herself. The house is like a time capsule of the fifties. The kitchen stove and refrigerator are ancient. The knobs and burners make her heart sting with memories she's never even known. The house is sparsely decorated with sculptures sitting in the middle of empty rooms. Up a narrow staircase, the bedrooms are untouched, night clothes laid out on beds. Downstairs a group of children sits quietly on the floor, transfixed by a black-and-white documentary about the life of Jackson Pollock as if it were a Disney cartoon.

In the backyard, she sees a light mist hovering above the pond. On the flattened yellow-green grass another group of children kneel beside craft paper canvases using sticks and turkey basters to create their own masterpieces. She walks to the barn where Pollock's studio was and gets the little protective booties she's heard so much about. The barn is a priceless mural of dripped paint underfoot.

His paintbrushes and paint cans are laid out on a ledge, protected by a layer of Plexiglas. Pure white light coming in through high windows shines on the floor. She remembers the poster in Dr. Weinberg's office, the explosion of black-and-gray drips. It seems so long ago that she sat there staring at it, worrying that her father would keep her up nights. Thinking that a drive down the expressway would mean stepping back in her life. Such pointless worry. Especially here.

She always felt the beauty and pain of the artist's story whenever she drove past the old farmhouse. The doomed genius whose life would end one night in a drunken car accident. Is that why she's never come here before? Because the Hamptons are such a terrible place to be when you're sad?

Yet there was no avoiding it. The story of Jackson Pollock's life was like a grain of salt that would never dissolve in a recipe. As much as the Hamptons were about glamour and money, they were also about the sadness of this one man.

On her way out the door, she's surprised to see an old woman standing staring at the floor. There's a small smile on the woman's face. Toni touches her arm, and Bea Flagstone reacts as if she expected to be meeting Toni all along.

"Just reminiscing," the old woman says.

"I do the same thing on Labor Day."

They walk arm in arm to the Phantom. Toni sees Phillip holding the door, the cats mewling in the backseat. The autumnal light comes dappling through the leaves.

"I can't thank you enough, Bea. Really, I—"

"Shhhh. Not another word. Just let the good things happen. Remember?"

At the car, Bea looks around. "I've always found it ironic that they would call the one day of the year we're not supposed to work Labor Day."

Toni smiles. "I've always wondered that too."

Toni kisses her cheek and she gets into her car. As the Phantom pulls away through the trees, she gives a little wave like the Queen Mother. Toni hears her say: "How exciting, my darlings! We're going home."

Chapter 101

Gardiner's Island off the coast of East Hampton is 3,500 acres of some of the oldest untouched forest in the country. It was originally purchased in 1639 from the Montaukett Indians by Lion Gardiner for little more than some gunpowder, a black dog, and a few blankets. For almost four hundred years, it has been privately owned by the Gardiner family. Once home to treasure buried by Captain Kidd, the island seems to stand as a permanent tribute to both the man-made history and natural beauty of the Hamptons themselves. It seems incongruous that in a part of the world where some real estate transactions are worth a hundred million dollars or more, the oldest wood-frame structure in New York State still stands there—a carpenter's shed built in 1639.

—*The Guru's Guide to the Hamptons*

The narrow road is empty, flanked on both sides by water and pink boulders that sparkle like shells in the late afternoon sun. She takes the S-shaped curve in her van, seeing the layered mauve stripes of the hills in the distance.

The driveways of the lean-to cottages sit empty, a single bright flag flapping on a pole the only indication anyone had been there in fifty years. She pulls in behind the old saltbox.

Row, row, row your boat
Gently down the . . .

Tucker jumps out across her lap the moment she gets the door open. He dashes onto the rocky beach to chase the big black-and-white seagulls. She takes out her cooler and burlap bag and shoves the white telescope under her arm. She climbs the wooden steps and takes the key out of her pocket. She opens the brass padlock, pushes the door, and steps inside.

She and her mother play sing-along at the picnic table.
She holds her father's hand as they look for shells on the beach.

She sets down her bag of cleaners and begins brushing the picnic table on the deck. As she works, her mind runs through a To Do List that has never seemed so long:

The money.

The mortgage.

The building permits.

But after a while, the air and the light and the water lapping beneath the pilings dissolve her worries. She no longer sees the cobwebs or the broken windows. Just the potential of the place.

Georgia told her the electricity wasn't hooked up, so she lights three hurricane lamps from the wedding, setting them on the railing. Across the bay, Gardiner's Island is a strip of black-green against the blue facets of the water. The sky begins its show of peach and pink for sunset. She unloads her picnic, setting it on the table. All her favorite things from the summer, and fresh gingerbread for the fall.

In the first-class lounge at JFK Airport, a god and goddess sit sipping champagne. Their luggage is checked for a month-long honeymoon abroad.

"Hey," Layla says. "I just wanted to say bye before we left."

Toni sits down at the table, slightly winded from her work.

"Did you check it out?"

Toni looks around. "I'm here right now."

"And?"

"And—I have to think about it, but it's a definite possible . . . maybe."

Layla covers her ear. "Toni? I can't hear you."

"Sweetie?" Toni moves the phone around. "When are they going to get better reception out here?" she asks Tucker.

"I'll call you when I get there!" Layla says, her voice crackling. "I love you, baby! I'll write every day!"

"No, you won't!" she laughs.

"Toni? Baby, I'll miss you! I love you so much!"

Layla waits a few seconds, listening to the static. She feels a tug of melancholy, like the year Toni left for camp.

"I love you too," Toni says.

She smiles and hangs up.

She goes back to her old telescope, polishing off the years of dust. She remembers needing to use a chair when she was younger. Now she has to bend over to see in the lens. She focuses it on the island across the bay, searching out the old lighthouse.

It's still there.

She shifts the telescope east and sees a fishing boat, then farther, toward the S-curved road and the pink boulders along the shoulder. A single boy walking in the opposite direction kicks at a few stones. Toni watches him, training her focus. In the lens, the electric sunset makes the world seem like something dissolving in a glass. Around the bend of the road, the glint of bumper as a car approaches.

She refocuses. As it gets closer, she sees a gold Mustang with a yellow surfboard angled out of the trunk. She looks up from the scope and the car seems so much farther away. She peers back in the lens, following him as he gets closer.

Chris stopped at the restaurant to find her. He saw her dad out front rolling pumpkins around the walk and stepping back to admire them. Vic Fratelli didn't look surprised to see the car pull up out front.

"What the hell," he said.

And he told Chris where she was.

On the drive, he practiced everything he was going to tell her.

"Toni, I didn't like who I was becoming in New York . . . I didn't like the person I was . . . I've been thinking, what if I didn't go back to the city? What if I stayed here? In the Hamptons? Maybe tried to help out places like O'Gorman's? Because I want to be with you, Toni. I like how I feel when I'm with you. I like the person I am. That's who I used to be . . . and I want to try to find him again. But I can't do it without you . . . I don't *want* to do it without you."

He talks to himself all the way across the LIE and Route 27, down Main Street and Three Mile Harbor Road, practicing what he'll say again and again. But as he pulls up behind the old van, all the words become a single refrain.

Toni, I love you.

She stands by the fire pit, smiling at him as he approaches; his footsteps crunch on the shells. Tucker runs over to greet him and gives his hand a happy lick, then goes back to chasing the seagulls.

They stare at each other for a moment. She feels the warmth of summertime fill her heart. "I was going to build a fire," she says. "Do you like s'mores?"

"Are those the ones with the marshmallows and chocolate?"

"And graham crackers."

"I used to have them when I was a kid."

"You haven't had a *real* s'more until you've had one of mine," she says.

"I bet not . . ."

"The real secret is a little salt."

As they build the fire, the sky turns from pink to red above them.

The seatbelt light in first class goes off with a *bing*.

Hudson leans back to watch the news on his screen. Layla undoes her seatbelt as the flight attendant pours champagne. She stares out the window at the white lights of the city disappearing below. They head east toward the Atlantic. She doesn't realize they're flying over her hometown until she sees the first flash of pink, opening like a flower beneath her. She touches Hudson's arm. "The fireworks," she says. They both lean toward the window, looking down.

Toni and Chris sit on a blanket, roasting marshmallows and laughing. The sky is violet-black above them and the stars are out.

Toni hears the first bang in the distance and it makes her jump. On the west stretch of the island several red dots explode in the air.

Then blue.

Then white.

Higher and wider and louder.

She feels each dull thud as if in her chest.

"I forgot," she says. "The Fourth of July fireworks are tonight."

She sees the flares, hears the pumps and whistling. He puts his arm around her, warm and rough-soft like an old beach blanket. She's so preoccupied her marshmallow catches fire and she has to shake it off the stick.

"Just listen," he says.

As she feels the tension drain from her, she smells the trees and the air, the saltwater, the smoke and burnt sugar. Another percussive shock in the distance. He kisses her then. She feels the softening of her heart. Another explosion, another kiss, another flash, another kiss.

Another kiss.

He lays her down on the blanket. He kisses her until she can't hear the fireworks anymore—at least not the ones outside her head. She hugs him hard as high above a plane flies by and around her the Independence Day fireworks light up the September night.

The drive back from the Hamptons is the saddest trip of the season. The traffic seems worse than ever and you can't believe the summer went by so fast. You take back a few postcards, some photographs, too many memories to hold at once. You try not to be sad. You try to tell yourself that the Hamptons are too crowded. Too expensive. Getting more overdeveloped every year. You try to tell yourself you didn't love it as much as you did. But somewhere around the Long Island Expressway, the complaining stops and the car gets very quiet. You stare out the window smiling to yourself. Because you know in your heart you can't wait—you just can't wait—to do it all again next year.

—*The Guru's Guide to the Hamptons*